Every Third House

ALSO BY DONALD FREED

PLAYS
Secret Honor
The Quartered Man
The Death of Ivan Ilych
Inquest: The United States vs. Julius and Ethel Rosenberg
Devil's Advocate (to be produced in England in the fall of 2005)
Alfred and Victoria (A Life)
Circe & Bravo
Veteran's Day
How Shall We Be Saved?

FICTION
Executive Action (book and film with Dalton Trumbo and Mark Lane)
The Spymaster
China Card
The Killing of RFK

NONFICTION
Killing Time
Death in Washington (The Murder of Orlando Letelier)
The Glass House Tapes
Freud and Stanislavsky: New Directions in the Performing Arts
The Secret Life of Ronald Reagan
Another America (editor)
Big Brother and the Holding Company (editor)
The Existentialism of Alberto Moravia (with Joan Ross)
Agony in New Haven

FILMS
Secret Honor
Executive Action
The King of Love
Of Love and Shadows (based on the novel by Isabel Allende)

Every Third House

Donald Freed

Penmarin Books
Roseville, California

Copyright © 2006 by Donald Freed.

All rights reserved. No part of this book may be reproduced or transmitted in any form or by any means, electronic or mechanical, including photocopying, recording, or by any information storage or retrieval system, without written permission from the publisher.

Editorial Offices:
Penmarin Books
1044 Magnolia Way
Roseville, CA 95661
(916) 771-5869

Sales and Customer Service Offices:
Midpoint Trade Books
27 W. 20th Street, Suite 1102
New York, NY 10011
(212) 727-0190

Penmarin Books are available at special discounts for bulk purchases for premiums, sales promotions, or education. For details, contact the publisher. On your letterhead, include information concerning the intended use of the books and how many you wish to purchase.

Jacket design by Jeff Potter, Potter Publishing.
Author photograph by Adrienne P. Nater.

Visit our Web site at **www.penmarin.com** for more information about this and other exciting titles.

Printed in the United States of America
1 2 3 4 5 6 7 8 9 10   09 08 07 06 05

ISBN 1-883955-37-8

Library of Congress Control Number: 2005904198

Dear Comrade,

Am playing the Strauss <u>Electra</u> at a good volume so as to drown out Mother—

"*Vivian!*" Cat-like, cutting through the music: "*Vivian!*"
"Mother—wait—I am trying to write a letter!"
"*Vivian!*"

—to drown out Mother (she's screaming for her Gilbert & Sullivan!) so that I can write this last letter to you. But she cannot be drowned out, not by any ordinary mortal, anyway, because she intends to be heard. As she always did, but you must prepare yourself for a shocking change in her from the woman you knew. Or thought we knew, when was it, a century ago? ...

"*Vivian!*"
"Ah, mother," she thought, "Who knows thee as I know thee?" Vivian sank back from the writing table into the music, turning her head slowly to follow the rain angling down on the New Haven Green. With her left hand she slowly massaged her right shoulder, clung to her own shoulder, then tightened her arm across her breast like a protective plate or a shield, debating whether or not to write him anything about May Day or *Glasnost*. No, she thought, just finish this letter and stay cool.

... *This last letter I will ever write to you, there, and instead of a poem of thanksgiving I can hardly produce prose, and I cannot blame it on the <u>Electra</u> (the music helps, sometimes) or on Clytemnestra (mother) either. Ha.*

"Vivian!"

TWO HOURS LATER—2 P.M.

I have fed her and she is catnapping now, or pretending to, it comes to the same thing. Still raining. Mail came, nothing from you. You asked about your letters: I have, in storage, some one thousand from you. They are in the attic, here, under lock and key, together with all the trial transcripts as well as the journalism and books dealing with the case, at least in part. I still think that Cornell or Wisconsin should have your papers unless, as you say, everything will be "subsumed" in the new book. But that leaves the letters and they are a cry—lucid and passionate—not heard since the day of George Jackson, or long ago, when I was a girl, Ethel Rosenberg (mother beat me with Oliver's [my dog] leash when I was detained by the New Haven constabulary for stopping traffic on the day the Rosenbergs were executed:

"They are innocent!"
"They are communists!"—smack.
"They are victims!"
"They are aliens!"—slap.
"They are Americans!"
"They are Jews!"—swat.)

ONE HOUR LATER—3:30 P.M.

This is a very bad class of day. Mother's awake, again, singing along with <u>The Mikado</u>. The <u>Electra</u> was driving me to drink. Christ! Her own mother testified against her—Ethel Rosenberg's—and mine was ready to do the same to me—"Ah, Mother, who knows thee as I know thee?" I lost my political virginity that day. "I've got a little list, I've got a little list."

I can't seem to wind this up, my dear. The rain and the Rosenbergs've got me down and my hand is shaking so that I'm afraid that my writing will remind you of the shaking scrawl of those early alcoholic outbursts (thank god that none of my letters remain, except in the FBI files). "They'll none of them be missed."

Allen wrote that "television was a baby crawling" toward the Rosenberg death chamber. He sends you love. Will you want to see him, or anyone? There are calls every day. <u>Time</u>, <u>Newsweek</u>, <u>Times</u>, etc. "They'll none of them be missed."

"Vivian!"

I feel like running out onto the Green in the rain and screaming. Actually, I feel like a drink as big as the Ritz. But not to worry. I have remained dry—a "dry drunk," to use your phrase—these eighteen years. I am "dry," as opposed to you who are "sober." I know the difference. But I will be sober as soon as you're here. Not that it's your problem or your responsibility. When you walk out, you walk out free. My hand is shaking uncontrollably now, as you can plainly see—"<u>Das ich ein kind war/ Nichte wusste.</u>" How's your German these days?

I want to mail this today in case they play a last minute trick and move you around before the release. Your room is ready and waiting, simple "as a cell," as you request. I agree: take a taxi directly here; avoid the media sure to be waiting at David's office along with your legion of liberal well-wishers and various toughs of the tender Left—forgive my pettiness and possessiveness, blame it on the '50s—I mean, Christ! Her own mother—

> This bitter burning brow,
> These dead shorn locks,
> My cheeks bleed silently,
> Remembering thee and
> They bloody sleep,
> Be rent! O hair of mine head.

3

"Vivian!"

I feel calmer now, cooler. I'll walk out in the rain and mail this, except I can see the little man from the <u>Register</u> watching the house from the Green. In the words of Richard Nixon, "Fuck 'em!"
Until the 17th, comrade,

Venceremos,

V.

Rose came at four o'clock to clean and prepare food and put Mrs. Battle back to bed.
"Rose."
"Hi, Miss Battle. Drizzling all day."
"Of course. How's *your* mother, today?"
"The same. How's *yours*?"
They had their daily laugh, the housekeeper and the poet, who had nothing in common for going on twenty years except their crazed and dying mothers and an earned respect for each other.

Vivian walked out across the soaked Green toward the post office. The rain had just passed, the sky clearing fast, the churches on the Green resuming their usual dimension. She took deep breaths; her eyes out of focus, like a gyroscope, scanned the Green, saw it all as a living picture in a stereopticon—saw herself, the blade of her body cutting across the green wet Green, her angular figure against the ground of the three churches, "Against the world," she thought, enjoying the electricity of the heavy weather working up to rain, again.

"Miss Battle! Ms. Battle. Angelo Castellano, the *Register*. Can I speak to you? Ms. Battle?"

Vivian stretched out her long stride. "Ms. Battle, will Mr. Howard come directly from prison to New Haven, to your house—is he going to live with—"

The round raincoat and rain hat bobbed along at her side. Was the man lame? The reporter lunged off the walk, trying to get in front of her to catch her eye, and slipped in the mud and went down, breaking his fall with his notebook, ruining it.

"They'll none of them be missed ... " Vivian sang to herself as she strode without turning her head past the courthouse—where once on May Day thousands had gathered on this Green to chant "Long Live Masai ... Long Live Vivian"—and posted her last letter to Masai in time for the five o'clock pickup.

She walked back home slowly, eyes down, not singing. Not in any particular pain, just preparing herself for what was coming. Don't try to control your thoughts, she lectured herself, turning up her walkway, her lips compressed, feeling the home-again feeling and would mother have died in the interim or Rose Gustini have murdered her, and this obligatory idea cheered Vivian up, after her fashion, so that she waved to Rose, who was quietly cleaning up in the kitchen, and climbed the stairs to the third floor.

The house was silent, as the old woman slept. The third floor was called the attic, but in life it had been a large combination study/library for her father. There was still an oversized photograph of General Eisenhower standing with Henry Wilson Battle III on a golf course, somewhere, in front of a gabled nineteenth-century clubhouse. Gangling black caddies, in the background, split their faces with hoping grins.

Leon will work here, she thought, and I will remove these memoirs and monuments from the Cold War and the death and times of the Battles and the Boyces and the Walkers and the Nortons and all the mighty Yale dead of the "American Century." Vivian pulled open a drape and looked down on a graduate and his family strolling below, pausing for a moment in front to point out the "Battle Mansion" to the proud parents.

No, she said to herself, don't touch a single artifact until Masai gets here, keep cool, fool, keep cool. You wrote your first poem up here, you made love to Carl Close and, ah, any number of other people up here and you never felt the need to redecorate.

She found the book she wanted and stood there in the failing light paging through the Rosenberg prison letters like layers of time, layers of flesh.

> ... after a listless game of handball (played solo, of course), a shower, dinner and an evening of enchanting music, during which you made passionate love to me, I finally succumbed to the homesick tears ... Oh, darling, how greedy I am for life and living.
>
> Always, Ethel

She put the book down and paced and turned back and picked up one of Leon's letters from prison and then threw that down, too, paced on and picked up the letter again and started to scan it as the door chimer sounded ...

1971

. . . so simple here in what Huey used to call the "Soul Breaker." Did I ever tell you about the first time I ever met Huey P. Newton in Oakland? Bobby Seale told me how he and Huey had been talking about a giant bank robbery to get money to start up the Black Panther Party for Self-Defense (as it was to be called then), and how Huey jumped up and whispered in that soft voice of his, "Forget the banks! Let's arm the black community and then we can walk up to the White House and tell them, 'Stick 'em up, you racist dog, we come for what's ours!'" Just like that. No profanity, no murder mouthing. Just his own poetry. Or was it? Huey P. Newton. The Black Panther on two legs. The die was cast . . .

May 1990

"Vivian!"

"Mother, wait!"

"Vivian!"

"Mother, wait, there's someone at the door—oh, my God—Oh! ... Hello."

"Vivian!"

"Hello. Just a moment, I was expecting—"

A girl, a young woman, a blonde braided young woman stepped forward. Vivian stood in the doorway squinting out, over the blonde braid, toward the street and the Green beyond. There was a tan unmarked car, parked, and four reporters. She assumed they were reporters because the round oily man from the *Register* was there sneering her way.

The girl moved into her face: pale blue eyes, the braid, old-fashioned wire-rim glasses, jeans, blue work shirt; talking in a bright breaking voice that made Vivian want to laugh; and the student, or whoever she was, her breath was sweet like a child's, as she moved her face closer. "My name is—"

"I'm sorry, I'm expecting—"

The girl lifted up a small red-white-and-blue briefcase, printed on it was UNITED STATES CENSUS '90. She held it up like a shield.

"Hello, my name is Kelly Bailey. I'm a Yale graduate st-student assigned to do follow-up census interviews in a four-block area—

interviewing the residents of, uh, every third house—pursuant to a st-study for the Department of Sociology-—ap-part of a study—to be published by the Yale University Press—here's my identification—the working title of which is, 'The Census: A Study in Bureaucratic Truth'—which is, according to Professor Erikson, a world-class oxymoron."

"Vivian!"

The stuttering face, the chubby pink lips, the small upper tooth brace—Vivian had to give out one yelp of hysterical laughter over the screaming of the Verdi and her mother; had to look up at the blue seamless sky and shake her head, causing the knot of reporters to turn and look out to the Green to see if she was signaling to someone. But the census taker bounced up like a blonde ball to make a gurgling chuckling sound just under Vivian's high nasal snort.

"Vivian!"

"My mother—not well. Come in for a minute. I only have a minute, I'm expecting someone—just let me turn down the music—will you have a cold drink?"

"Just a glass of water, please. It's, uh, quite warm ..." Left alone, she put her red-white-and-blue case down on the seventeenth-century chess table, then set it on the floor, kicking it out of the way, and looked around the large ground floor drawing–dining room. My father should see this, she thought, to understand what real taste is: the Queen Anne and Georgian drop fronts, the twin desks and tables, the wing chairs and a linen press that you would grovel for, hypocrite.

Suddenly, the opera music stopped and a door slammed in a further room. Footsteps. The girl glanced out the leaded front window. No one there except the peering reporters perched like crows on the corner.

Vivian reentered, without the glass of water, talking in her contained clipped old New England way, looking out the window, then turning to the pink-skinned young census taker. "Ms. ah ..."

"Bailey. Kelly Bailey. A-ha."

"Ms. Bailey. I studied statistics under Professor Shaw, I say 'under,' and I failed." Again, she needed to expel a tense cry of laughter, and, in counterpoint, the girl bobbed and bubbled as if they had been laughing in tandem like that since childhood even though Vivian was thinking—I'm old enough to be her mother, who is she, do I know her? "Failed, Ms. Bailey … 'Every third house'—with a story behind every door?"

Both of them, again as if by habit, glanced quickly out the window and then down at the red-white-and blue official census case. The girl's glasses had clouded up and her voice was tense. Vivian took this in, as well as the shape of the girl which was soft and somehow blonde but, Vivian knew, would be sensuous even classic after the long adolescence.

"Um, Ms. Battle, of course your answers will be totally confidential, Title XIII of the Federal Code guarantees—"

"Do you know who I am?"

"Um, you mean your reputation as a poet?"

"I mean, do you know who I am?"

"You mean—uh, well, the Battle Library—"

"That was my father."

"And the, uh, the—"

"Norton Theatre was—"

"Was your uncle, I know, because my father went to school with your cousin—"

And they laughed again in shared absurdity, both openly looking out the window at the sight of the reporters—"Crows!" called Vivian, "Exactly," the girl chimed in—causing a second round of sniffing and bobbing.

"Now, Ms. Bailey, you know I can't speak for my extended family."

"Oh, no, the census is occupied with the facts not the truth, ha-ha—"

Kelly opened up her census kit with what seemed to Vivian to be an expert touch and produced a form. "List everyone who lives at this address."

"Vivian!"

… "Leonora Walker Norton Battle."

"Is that all?"

"… You're not affiliated with the media, are you, Ms. Bailey?"

"No, ma'am."

"Or any law enforcement agency?"

'No, ma'am." As if on cue, they both snapped their heads toward the window and then back … Vivian stared at the girl.

"Uh, Ms. Battle, is, uh, MRS. Battle related, uh, how is MRS. Battle related—"

"Vivian!"

"My mother."

"Thank you. And does MRS. Battle consider herself to be: 'Caucasian, Black or Negro; Indian American; Eskimo' or—"

"Do you have a category above 'White?'"

Why aren't we laughing again, Vivian wondered. "No ma'am," Kelly said carefully, blue eyes big behind the wire rims.

"Well, then, 'White' will have to do." Turning her back, staring out the window—Where is he, where is he? "And, ah, there is another person who is coming to live here, ah, temporarily."

"Is he—"

"And he is more or less black." Vivian could feel her moving closer, her pressure. Outside the window, the reporters were glowering directly at her. Another unmarked car, pale blue, cruised slowly past.

"And is he a: 'Roomer. Boarder, or Foster Child; Housemate or Roommate; Unmarried Partner; Other Non-relative?'"

A siren rose in the distance. Nothing on the Green. The student's glasses slipped down her stubby freckled nose. She's sweating, the poet observed to herself, but I'm cool. She smiled at the girl, "He was, he is my co-conspirator." Kelly tried to wrinkle the glasses back up onto the bridge of her nose. Another siren sounded closer. "Ms. Bailey, you know who he is, don't you? You read the papers. You know the 'story' behind this door, don't you?"

"… Yes, ma'am."

"Is that why you're here—because you were told that 'Masai' aka Leon Hurley Howard was coming here today from prison?"

"I swear to you, Ms. B-Battle, that we're supposed to c-call at every third house on our list. I was never—"

The closer siren peaked and diminished and both women turned their heads to the window. The reporters had turned, too, and were venturing out into the Green. They had seen something. The pale blue unmarked police car cruised by again.

The girl, Kelly, peeked at Vivian's face. Beautiful, she thought, noble: drawn, pale, no make-up, brave big gray eyes; watched the poet's brave eyes leading her to the window, gray eyes riveting deep into the Green, focusing like an archer who draws a long bow—a twenty-year-long bow—and unleashes an arrow of longing for another shore.

Kelly watched the poet move, with a balletic angularity, to the window, then to the door, to open it; her body reaching out, the gray eyes locked onto the black cipher on the middle Green, just crossing past the church, a hundred and fifty yards away; a mere black blur, to the girl, like an insect crawling under an upturned blue tabletop of sky.

Closer, and she watched Vivian seem to grow taller, lean and electric, and the blur, the insect, the man a football field away now, crossing past the courthouse where for six months in 1970 they had brought him each day in chains—hobbled, limping, shuffling, sheriffs with shotguns, clanking past the press, and I wasn't even born yet, and she, Vivian Norton Battle, walked free alongside him, pregnant, they said, with that terrorist's hellspawn, and I wasn't even born yet.

The reporters were running, now, to meet him as he passed the courthouse with its sculptured big-breasted goddess of Justice; the man was no longer a black insect in the middle distance, to the watchers, but an animal, bear-like, just fifty yards away, and closing on the house.

JANUARY 1970

THE STATE OF CONNECTICUT

v.

LEON HURLEY HOWARD

Marvin Merle, State's Attorney for the County of
New Haven, accuses Leon H. Howard of:
(1) Conspiracy to commit kidnapping;
(2) Conspiracy to commit murder.

DEFENSE QUESTION FROM MR. GARRY: If you were in that place instead of Mr. Howard, and you were a black man, would you feel satisfied that there were twelve jurors sitting in judgment on your case ... Your life is at stake.
ANSWER: I think I'm a fair man.
QUESTION: Because the defendant, Mr. Howard, has been indicted by a grand jury, do you feel there is some element of guilt?
ANSWER: Yes.
QUESTION: I think we have to challenge for cause, your honor.
THE COURT: No.

QUESTION:	In your own mind do you associate the Black Panther Party with violence?
ANSWER:	Yes ... What I read in the papers.
QUESTION:	Do you believe there is such a thing as white racism?
THE STATE:	Objection.
THE COURT:	Denied. Racism has nothing to do with it.

1971

. . . nothing to say against a luxury de-tox center (that's all it is) but the root of this thing for you or anyone else including me is that the whole process of decolonization is disorder and madness because we are breaking up a sick relationship and a dependency, an <u>addiction</u> that was started and bonded by violence in the first place. But no English doctor is going to know what any of this means so my prescription is for you to get to the British Museum and sit at Karl Marx's desk (or Lenin's) and read you some Frantz Fanon or J. P. Sartre or any of these other big niggers!

The noise level just went out of the range of hearing so that means it's suppertime, and you know what--I'm hungry and I'll eat it, just like any other pig. Who was it said, "We are all monsters who've been called Human Beings too soon"? Nietzsche or Kazantzakis? Can you get me <u>The Last Temptation of Christ</u>?

                                  All Power to the Monsters,

                                  L.

May 1990

Masai, aka Leon Hurley Howard, barged past and through the reporters. Vivian slammed the door. The girl backed away from the window, her eyes snapping frames in time as fast as the photojournalists crowding up against the windowpane.

The girl shooting with her eyes: the poet, Vivian, closing the drapes; the man, the prisoner, putting down a large suitcase; the voice of the media rising in the street; the black man, the terrorist, straightening his dark cheap suit, prison issue but it clung to his rangy hard-muscled frame; another siren starting in the distance; "Vivian!" the old woman crying out from the depths of the house …

Kelly watched herself watching them move stiffly together, watched Vivian reach up and touch the gray hair of his sideburns, heard her say, so softly, "Hello, comrade—long time passing …" Watching: Who did he look like—Malcolm X? The glasses, the wide brow, but, no, this one was much blacker and over six feet at least two and a half inches and shoulders like an Olympian, and the woman touching him came to his chin; they were both tall, taller than life, and she loved and hated them at that moment as if the rest of her life depended on it.

"Vivian!"

The poet flinched, focused, "Mother, God—Oh, ah, this is Ms., ah … mm, mm, she's making a census study, she says, of some kind. Every third house—they stop at every third house."

Kelly hung back like a thief in the shadow of the window while the two tall ones observed her gravely. Then the man gave a low rumbling chuckle and Vivian breathed out a throaty melody of absurd delight and so, involuntarily, the young census taker bounced out a glottal shock of a laugh herself. "Please excuse me," she said, but the old mother's scream, "Vivian," cut their laugh off.

"I'm coming ... And there's a story behind every door ... Leon, let me go and put her music on."

Alone, both of them stood still. "I'll just collect all my, uh, junk." She moved one foot and then froze again. He looks a little like the photographs of Patrice Lemumba, she thought, staring up at him. The music blossomed from the old woman's quarters, *Madama Butterfly.* "I'm not-I don't-I'm not a-I don't work for the *New York Times.*"

"Good." His voice was low and musical, Paul Robeson's, she thought, was that his name? Somebody like that. She said, "I'm nobody."

"Is that right?"

"Absolutely."

"You're shaking. Do you want to use the facility?"

His diction was standard, perfect, better than Dan Rather's; breathe, she told herself, keep your eyes up, look at his cheap dark tie. "No," she stuttered, "No thank you, sir."

"Are you afraid?" She could only nod, swallow and nod slowly. "You know who I am? I'm reading your lips ... Are you here just by coincidence, do you really go to every third house?—You do? ... So you're really nobody—You're not a deception or a provocation or an instrument of the *New York Times?*—Yes, no? You're nodding and shaking both. Take it easy ... No, or the *New Haven Register,* or the *Bombay Times,* or *Der Sturmer?* ... But you do read the papers? Especially the old ones in the Research Library. Is that where you read about me?"

The Puccini was louder now. Where was Ms. Battle? He was playing with her, torturing her, she was wet with perspiration, it was breaking out all over her body, why couldn't she look him in the eye, her back was going weak, her knees, don't let me fall, she prayed, don't let me fall at his feet! "What?" she stuttered, "Oh, ah, *Race and Class in America.*"

"Mm-hm. And then you went and looked us up in the library morgue?—Say what?"

"Yes, sir."

"The morgue ... You're shaking again. Did you want to use the accommodations? ... So you looked us up—in the headlines. 'TWO HELD ON CAPITAL CHARGE IN NEW HAVEN.' You read that one ... You remember the sub-head? 'Activist Aristocrat and Black Panther Leader Indicted'—something like that, wasn't it?"

She felt her face burning, he was shaming her; she jerked her eyes up to his face—his eyes deep, watching—she swayed, "I—please—I—may I—I have to—"

"Go. You have to go?"

"Home. To my, uh, I'm, uh ..." Please, Ms. Battle—save me, my body's coming out in a rash, he is torturing me!

"What else do you remember?"

"Nothing." Thank God! Here she is in a wave of music.

"I'm sorry, I just can't leave her alone. Leon, I—" and stopped to look at the man looking at the girl and listen to his voice so resonant that the words thudded like jabs flicking against the census taker's red, wet face.

"Police Chief Anthony Donato charged today that Vivian Norton Battle, scion of a Yale University trustee, was being held on a charge of conspiracy to kidnap Secretary of State Henry Kissinger and Governor Nelson Rockefeller of New York. Mr. Donato stated that Miss Battle was a 'pillar of the community' and may have been drugged or in some other way brainwashed by Mr. Masai Howard, the Black Panther Party leader.' And like that ... Does it come back to you now?"

"I wasn't born until August 1970."

"That's no excuse."

"I mean, you're a myth."

"Hmm, and you're a sociologist—what's the party line these days?"

He's torturing her, Vivian thought, or is he? But the blonde imp dared to ignore her: "Oh, ah, the, uh, end of, uh, Ideology and History and Politics and Psychology—except for Behavior Modification—ha, uh, you know ..."

"Yes," Vivian took a step toward them.

"And Revolution?" Masai squinted at the girl.

"Oh, yes, completely."

"So—and the future, the millennium?"

"Uh, 'Crisis Management'—'The Age of the Individual.'"

"Leon—" Vivian tried to laugh. He cut her off.

"Crisis Management. 'Low-Intensity Warfare'?"

"Beg pardon?"

"What's your I.Q.?"

"Too high to measure."

At last, he looked at Vivian and signaled with a chuckle that she could exist again. "Leon, you're going to be upstairs—"

"Vivian!"

"Christ!" The poet's voice was fierce, the girl jumped, Vivian's eyes glared, Masai nodded and closed his eyes, remembering the backlash of her outrage two decades ago. "I can't leave her alone," Vivian mumbled, "Wait a moment." Stalking out and back, thrusting the wheelchair into the room, "Ms. ... ah, will you watch her for just a moment, please; come on, Leon, Christ!"

The girl and the old woman watched each other in silence. The girl knew that the old woman was around one hundred, everyone in New Haven knew that and who she had been. Here she was bundled up on a warm day in a light linen coverlet of some kind, thin blue lines on ivory, bald almost, a rat nose, and the usual smell ...

A reporter banged on the door, a siren rose in the distance; the old woman muttered at Kelly, "... do to you in the barn—grandfather told Florence—I'm going to Rochester ..." The girl pretended not to hear, turned away, fingered open Masai's briefcase. The old lady screamed for her daughter, Kelly jumped again.

"Coming, Mother," Vivian and Masai returned, "My jailer," Vivian tried to smile at Kelly. Masai saw that the girl had peeked into his briefcase. He came to her and opened the case and showed her a page. "Shit-Storm Coming," he said softly.

"I was, uh, I was just—" He cut her off, "That's the title." Vivian joined them in a tight triangle, "But nobody knows that—" Kelly looked up at their faces, "You wrote a—"

"A jailhouse Manifesto," Masai whispered, "Shit-Storm Coming."

"Vivian!"

Someone banged on the street door, again, Vivian's voice was a sword, "Get out or I shoot! Jesus!" Silence ... "I'm right here, mother. Christ!" A half whisper: "I'll put her music on. Excuse me, goodbye Ms., uh ..." stalking out leaving the old woman.

The girl whispered to the man, "A new book—how exciting!" as if the old lady would overhear.

"What's the caption for the review?" He maintained a tone of mock conspiracy, under the Gilbert and Sullivan sounds from the mother's quarters.

"What?"

"Make up the caption for the book review," and snapped his fingers once, and she jumped again.

"Former '60s Militant Returns to Christ in Prison."

What Vivian saw as she reentered was the two of them laughing silently and her mother watching. Then they all looked at her.

"I've edited two books," Kelly stuttered. In the silence, the siren whined out and the Gilbert and Sullivan fell, "Please don't lock me in here," the old mother pleaded in a hoarse whisper. They all turned to look at her, now, but another siren cut in loud and high coming closer; the man was at the window in two strides, Vivian after him.

"Well, I better go," the girl started to whisper, but Vivian's voice was bitter and in the clear as she and Masai watched through a crack in the drapes. "World War III," she said, then, as the siren screamed past, her voice rose like a battle cry over it—"The gangs. The black war gangs!" Kelly stood rooted, wondering, is she talking to me?

"In Projectville," the man's bass rumbled under. "I'm going to tell," the old lady hissed. Vivian turned away from the window to stare at Kelly, "Be careful—when you go out."

The student leaned forward slightly but her feet stood still, "I know, it's frightening, you can't, uh, walk the streets." The man turned back to look at her. They both looked at her before Vivian responded, "No ... Can't leave the house ..."

They looked at the girl and she looked at them as the sirens faded and the Gilbert and Sullivan played up and out, and she felt again as if she were watching them from an inferior position at the base of a statue or an inverted triangle. Finally, the man, Masai, asked her, "Do you want to help me with the research for the last section of this book?"

"Me?"

"The title of the last part is 'The Future.'"

"Leon—" Vivian started.

"I'll pay you something. Vivian will."

The girl felt her face go red again, "Oh, no, I wouldn't—" Vivian broke the tableau by collecting the census forms, handing them to Kelly, then picking up Masai's briefcase, "These are yours—and these are ours," and turned toward the front door but Masai kept on, "Call me, here."

"If it's alright," Kelly said.

"How old are you?" Masai asked, "What's your name?"

"Twenty—I'm going to be twenty. Uh, Kelly Bailey." Vivian waited, her eyes half closed, then opened the front door—then jerked her mother's wheelchair around and pushed it out of the room. Masai turned back to the window. The student tiptoed toward the open door, "Thank you, goodbye, I'll call, thank you," and closed it after her.

Vivian came back in and looked at Masai. He stared out the window, his back thick, tense, turned to her. Another siren rose in the distance. "That'll be the 'ambulance,'" Vivian said. "Turn that music back up," he growled.

"What?"

"Drown 'em out."

"They're not coming for us."

"Naw."

The siren retreated. He looked at her and through her. "Hello, comrade," she said softly. His eyes shifted into focus, he made a face and moved slowly to embrace her in a heavy hug that was, she felt, somehow ghostly, his arms around her powerful but abstract.

Upstairs in her father's old quarters he unpacked his manuscript and the linen from his suitcase. Vivian opened a closet door, "I picked up some things for you": in the closet hung sweaters and slacks, corduroy and khaki; on the floor moccasins, slippers, tennis shoes; in the old steamer trunk were shirts, shorts, socks, no pajamas—"You wrote you were still the same size—you look even bigger to me. Hmm. How do *I* look to *you*?"

"Taller."

"Seriously. I'm fifty years old."

"You look hot to me."

"Stop it. Don't tease me like you did that student. We call that 'harassment' now," she tried to make her tone playful.

"You reckon she might turn me in?"

..."No. Hardly ... Are you hungry?"

He took her in his arms, again, looking at her this time. "You look fine. Fit. Lean and clean. I like your hair like that." He touched her breasts tentatively, she covered his hand on her left breast. "You still miss it?" he asked. "It's been more than fifteen years," she said. "But yet and still," he said. "No," she shook her head, "not until today." He took off his coat and tie and rolled his shirtsleeves up high. "I'm making some chops," she said. The muscles of his upper arms rippled.

"You go ahead and 'burn,'" he said, "I want to lay out this manuscript, it's a mess ... Over here? What's all this? The court transcripts ... You hold onto everything, don't you, girl?"

"Oh, yes," she said, "'deed I do."

EBRUARY 1971

EXAMINATION OF THE HIGH SHERIFF BY THE DEFENSE CONCERNING THE NEW GRAND JURY SYSTEM:

QUESTION: MR. GARRY: How do you go about selecting these Grand Jurors? Such as in this case against Mr. Howard?

ANSWER: I go to the various towns, the twenty-six towns of my county.

QUESTION: And you pick out people that you know to serve?

ANSWER: Not exactly. I pick them from all classes and color-wise. I never ask their religion. And so forth. I find out if they are electors and decent people.

QUESTION: What standard do you follow to see whether a person is "decent" or not.

ANSWER: The same standard we have on all juries.

QUESTION: By the way, are you an Elk?

ANSWER: Yes.

QUESTION: It is true, is it not, sir, that the Elks Club excludes by its own constitution any member who is of the black race?

ANSWER: It's under consideration.

QUESTION: I see. Let's talk about Mrs. Abbie Creem. How did you get a hold of her?

ANSWER: I know her. I knew her husband before he died. I know who she is.
QUESTION: What ethnic group does she belong to?
ANSWER: I don't know what church she goes to.
QUESTION: I am not interested in their church. Religion is immaterial. I am interested in the color of their skin.
ANSWER: She is white.
QUESTION: Now, Mrs. Creem is a person whom you have had personal relationships with, and I am not implying anything improper now, Sheriff.
ANSWER: The only experiences I have had is having her on the Grand Jury. I am not going to have anyone on that you can tear apart on their respectability.
QUESTION: What do you mean "their respectability?"
ANSWER: A person that is considered a nice decent person.
QUESTION: By whose standards, yours?
ANSWER: It is my standard because I am picking the Grand Jury.
QUESTION: In other words, you decide who is decent and who isn't?
ANSWER: Right.
QUESTION: Let's talk about Mr. Joseph Phelen. Would you say he is over seventy?
ANSWER: Over sixty-five.
QUESTION: White?
ANSWER: I don't recall.
QUESTION: You don't know whether he is a white man or not?
ANSWER: He is white. I thought you said "wife." Excuse me.

 1990

5/20/90

To: DIRECTOR, FBI

From: SAC, NEW HAVEN

Subject: COUNTERINTELLIGENCE PROGRAM
NATIONAL SECURITY
TERRORISM

RE: New Haven Airtel 5/13/90 concerning LEON HURLEY HOWARD a.k.a. "Masai," former Black Panther Party "Minister of Education" and VIVIAN NORTON BATTLE. HOWARD is a male Negro born 2/11/41, Baton Rouge, LA. BATTLE is a Caucasian female born 5/5/39, Paris, France.

It is to be noted that Howard intends to return to New Haven to stay for an undetermined period of time at the home of V. N. Battle. BATTLE is heiress to the banking fortune estimated at over four hundred and fifty million dollars of the late HENRY WILSON BATTLE III, a personal friend of the, then, Director Hoover. Battle lives with her mother who is a victim of Alzheimer's disease.

HOWARD completed his prison sentence on 5/16/90. He went directly to the Battle mansion on 5/17/90, and has not left the house since then. No one has visited the Battle house since 5/17/90 except for KELLY M. BAILEY, a Caucasian female born 8/4/70, and presently a graduate student at Yale University.

According to a confidential informant, BAILEY has arranged with the Department of Sociology at Yale to remove research material to be used by HOWARD for a manuscript of some kind in preparation.

Permission is requested by this office to determine by surreptitious methods

1. the nature of HOWARD's manuscript;

2. the nature of HOWARD's relationship with BATTLE (an unindicted co-conspirator of HOWARD's in 1970 on Criminal Conspiracy to Kidnap), and the Yale student, BAILEY.

BUY U. S. SAVINGS BONDS ON THE PAYROLL SAVINGS PLAN

May 1990

"Dr. Irving, oh hello, I'm sorry I'm late, but I was having a fi-fight, a big fight with Daddy about whether or not I am allowed to work on the book with Masai and Ms. Battle, and of course he agrees with you that I'm 'asking for trouble,' but, I mean, you are both wrong, in my opinion, because Vivian Battle is not a n-nut, she is a well-known poet, and he, *he* is not a terrorist, *not*—he is simply a Cinqué of 1990 ... I *knew* you wouldn't know who Cinqué was, I mean don't look at me as if I was Patricia Hearst or some '60s simp, I'm talking about the *original* Cinqué! Right here in New Haven, right here! The Amistad ship rebellion in 1835—a slave ship, a slave rebellion—nobody knows anything about this fucking country—and Cinqué was, uh, a huge specimen who led the rebellion, and they captured him and locked him up right out there on the New Haven Green—on the *Green!* And it was like a fair: the men in black, the women all bound up, the oxcarts and the oyster booths ... And a linguist from Yale came there every day until he was able to establish communication with him, Cinqué, create a language between them! So that he could prove that Cinqué was a fugitive slave—who was being held illegally—and after twelve years, *twelve years*, John Quincy Adams won Cinque's freedom—his *freedom!*—hand me a Kleenex, please ... Thank you ... And you're *smiling*, and thinking that that's my—*Yes!* Yes, I could have been that linguist! *Yes!* I could have, because Masai and I have more in common than you and my father put together. We speak the same language and that's—and there is *nothing sexual* at all, number one, this is purely political—plus which, I am being *paid*, for the first time in my life! I'm doing something besides reading, to use Daddy's standard complaint, although you and I both know that Daddy is not down on reading, he's down on masturbation, and is he ever down on 'Big Black Books in Ms. Vivian's Room—oompah, oompah, oompah, oohmm!'—Daddy's down on big black books—'Control yourself, Kelly, control your thoughts, dear'—but I can't, no one can—but I *can* work on the big black book, because I *believe* in it—what?—a shitstorm coming to tear this cultural concentration camp into a million pieces. Those sirens screaming out there—he says those are the birth pangs—and I am in on it, I am part of it—what?—the *truth* of it, for God's sake! The truth about Yale and the Yale Corporation—and this hospital—and the names that we are going to name: Bundy and Vance and John Hay Whitney and Haskins and Watson and Blair and Dilworth and, uh, uh, Mosley and Miller and Skull and Bones and Buckley and Bloomingdale and all the other war criminals that have held us here in slavery for the last five hundred years! ... And we are going to spare no one—*no one!* Including my father, including you, because your religion or past suffering is no excuse and will not protect you—no one!—because I agree with Masai a hundred percent that the chips are going down and that we are going to 'cut the issue,' Dr. Irving, and that *there-is-a-shit-storm-coming!*"

JUNE 1990

Climbing the stairs, carrying the iced tea, "Ice tea time ... Leon—sorry to interrupt—iced tea and a ham sandwich."

"Thanks. I'll take the tea."

"Well, I'll take the sandwich, in that case, ha!, always hungry—it's sweltering."

"Eat."

"Mm ... Is Kelly—is the girl, the 'Kelly Girl,' coming today?"

"Not on Sunday.

"Never on Sunday?"

"Eat."

"Mm ... Why am I starving, why do I look like an elongated version of my mother as Katherine Hepburn as Mary Queen of Scots when all I do the whole day through is eat for two?—'Starving, ass-aching Puritan lady desires to meet black revolutionary sex symbol—no smoke, no drink—send mug-shot.'"

"*New York Review of Books* please copy." He rattled his ice and mopped his neck, watching her devour the sandwich.

"I don't read it anymore," she said, finishing up the crumbs, "not since the good old days when they published instructions for how to construct a do-it-yourself Molotov cocktail on the cover. Ha."

"No."

"No ... 'Please send hair sample and list of hobbies' ..."

She knelt, her face down flat on his knee, just resting. Her head

29

was hot, he could feel it through his khakis. Her hair was cut so short that he could see how red with heat her neck was and he remembered how her breasts and her body turned red, then, when he touched her, when he used to touch her.

"Comrade," he breathed, not touching her. He looked over her head out the large wall dormer window, out toward the water. Where are they? He listened, where're the sirens? Just a motorboat drone from somewhere out on the sound.

She spoke into his thigh, "Do you want me to make love to you?" ... He closed his eyes against the summer glare from the window and started to sing softly.

"I needs money, gives it to you honey, poppa's got them one and two blues ..."

"Should I," she said, "Should I suck you?"

Without opening his eyes he reached his right hand down under to touch her breasts, stopping on her left side.

"The left one," she said, "there's nothing left of the Left."

He let his hand stay there ..." 'Small change I can't use' ..." He closed his eyes again. Her voice was small, "I mean we *have* made love, once or twice, in our time."

"Oh my, yes," his voice was just a breath.

"Mississippi," she smiled up at him, her cheek damp and flushed from the contact with his leg, knowing that he would hum a phrase of "Mississippi Goddam," joining him in the melody. "Beverly Hills," she moved, trying to make him open his eyes, "with Genet tongue-lashing them out at the swimming pool," she stroked his thigh with her forehead.

His voice melted into hers like a fugue, "... Tongue-lashing, 'struggle'—say it in French." Rubbing him with her head, her voice resonant in her throat—"*Debout, vous gauchistes ratés, vous tendres gauchistes ...*" Then it came back to him, her translation, and he mumbled along with her: "Stand up all you failed liberals, you soon-to-be-jailed liberals, stand up for once and call out for the victory of the Vietnamese people and the black bloods on the block, over the death-squad Democracy you call America!"

And opened his eyes and took off his glasses. "Right on!" his voice sank down again … "So let it never be said that we did not make love," she said looking up into the blood-shot eyes of his remembering. "Nooo," he said. "New York City," she cued him.

"Manhattan."

"The Theresa Hotel," she prodded.

"For instance."

"Fidel Castro's suite."

"The struggle against the Yankee beast continues. 'La Lucha Continua.'" … He touched her breast again. "Gone," he murmured.

"You remember it?" She smiled a sad smile.

"Deed ah do," he touched her hair. "Prison," he said.

"Making love in prison?" She rubbed her head under his fingers. "I remember that," he said. "Me, too," she said, "deed ah do … Under the table in the library like, ah … Let me."

He closed his red eyes, again, and let his arms drop. Singing the blues, again, softer still—"Small change I can't use, Poppa's got them one and two blues …"

FEBRUARY 1970

THE DEFENSE: Let's talk about John Pakacimas. How did you get ahold of him?
THE HIGH SHERIFF: He was recommended to me by my deputy.
QUESTION: Which one?
ANSWER: Deputy Demapolis.
QUESTION: Who?
ANSWER: A sheriff named Demapolis in Waterbury.
QUESTION: I see you went back to Waterbury for this man, again?
ANSWER: No. He is a Lithuanian.
QUESTION: You mean he is a Lithuanian?
ANSWER: Yes.
QUESTION: It sounds like Greek to me.
ANSWER: No. He is a "Lith."
QUESTION: What did you want a Lithuanian for?
ANSWER: I wanted to mix it up.
QUESTION: Did you think Mr. Howard of the Black Panther Party was a Lithuanian?

June 1990

Date: 6/29/90

To: DIRECTOR, FBI

From: SAC, NEW HAVEN

Subject: NATIONAL SECURITY, TERRORISM

RE: New Haven 6/22/90: New Haven is unable to develop Confidential Informant beyond living quarters of LEONORA NORTON BATTLE, mother of subject VIVIAN BATTLE.

The following is overheard conversation of L. N. BATTLE: 6/20/90:

> The barn's warm. Bossy's warm. (unclear) Lady's scratching, she knows. Grandfather showed Lady, too. (unclear) Me and Bossy and Lady. Lady and Bossy and me. (unclear) I'll tell her the black man did it. (unclear)

BUY U.S. SAVINGS BONDS REGULARLY ON THE PAYROLL SAVINGS PLAN

July 1990

Vivian sat at her writing table. She looked at a piece of blank white paper, then she looked out the window at a black dog on the Green, its tongue lolling in the heat. She listened for her mother to awaken, but the idea of opera music in this weather was painful, very. She wrote on the paper, "Love is not love that pity—," then she crossed it out and cocked her ear up toward Masai's area—she could hear him and the girl laughing. She wrote, "Love and pity are two daughters—?" then she crossed that out.

Upstairs, Masai watched Kelly stack Xerox copies. The girl moved about, between the tables heavy with books and manuscript, with a naïve sureness and even an awkward grace. White T-shirt, long blue shorts, white tennis shoes. The fan raked across them ruffling loose papers and her blonde bangs.

"Ms. Battle was such a—*is*, ha, such a fine poet," Kelly said when she saw that Masai was following her with his eyes. It caught her breathing short. "Uh, we're, uh, we've got everything that, uh, we need to start on the conclusion, the 'Future,'—so if she's—I could come here every day, if you wanted me to, to work on it with you, if she—you wouldn't have to pay me any more because—"

"Sit down," he said.

She sat, legs apart, flat footed, heavy braided, weighing ten pounds less than that first day; coming into her own, her father and doctor and everyone thought, meaning, she knew, womanhood, nubility, fertility, property, danger. Masai took a deep breath. She wrinkled her wire-rim glasses higher up on the snub of her nose. He took off his glasses and rubbed his eyes. The first siren of the day broke the quiet.

Below, Vivian wrote and scratched out: "In the dark backyard and prison of time—"

"*Vivian!*"

Upstairs, they could hear the overture of *The Desert King*, from the mother's floor. "Did you know Mrs. Battle, ah, senior, before she—"

"She was always crazy."

"She was?!"

"You better read some of your research. The ruling class is by definition removed from reality, and Mrs. Senior is a blue-ribbon member of the ruling class."

"… I have to use the facility," she said, with a half suppressed smirk. The sunlight bounced off his glasses, as he lifted them, to cover his eyes. He watched her go out of the alcove, her tennis shoes. He lifted his T-shirt to feel the fan. The commode flushed. Kelly came back in, her face was flushed. "Should I come tomorrow?"

"I don't need any more research right now," he said. "I know," she said, "but I have all those statistical tables of correlation between c-class and the university, the trustees," her upper brace flashed, forcing him to look at the pink patterns of her lips. "Government, finance, business: William McChesney Martin, Spencer Dumaresq Mosley—"

"No," he said, "everybody knows that, except maybe your old man—stand in front of that fan and cool your face off, girl—no, I have to write—"

"I could—you could dictate to me, I could take your dictation, I can type a hundred and—"

"No, I don't work like that, I have to write it first by hand, in the dark on toilet paper—" Her eyes bulged out behind her wire-rim glasses and he had to laugh low, unbend and stand up like he would

35

to quiet a child, "No, no, I'm talking about when I first went in, stay cool, I'm just playing with you, don't pay any mind. Revolutionaries in prison are crazy, too, crazy as trustees—the difference is they know it—sometimes ... I appreciate your help, little comrade."

Tears turned to blue pools behind her wire rims, "M-Mr. Masai, what about my census stats—it's raw, it's real, your book could—"

"You'd be my spy?"

"Well, well, n-not the names, but all the—"

"All the confidential, privileged, private, protected information that you collected from 'every third house.' You'd be my spy. You'd pass me the information that belongs to the government of the United States, the raw data, and I'd base my predictions in the last section—of a shit-storm coming—on you."

"On me?"

"Like Lenin did."

"Like Lenin?"

"But I'd hold back your name."

... "Is she—is her name—are you dedicating the book to her?"

"The book is dedicated to Stagolee."

"Who's Stagolee?"

Vivian put another record on without even marking whether it was one of her mother's collection of long-dead operettas or one of her own German albums. No one plays records on a phonograph anymore or uses a dial telephone for "goodness sake!" her attorney had pointed out, remonstrating with her, to no avail, to install a stereo cassette-VCR-cable-answering machine and Xerox and FAX. But now she would have to get the Xerox because Masai needed it, to duplicate, she thought, to multiply, to be fruitful and multiply. And what about a shredder to more quickly and efficiently destroy these bum poems that now litter the floor and, while we're at it, one of those beepers, a pocket beeper for Ms. Kelly Bailey so that we can communicate from floor to floor regarding any type of food or room service that might be required, day or night, upstairs at Revolutionary Research Central—

"Vivian!"

No one could hear her singing shout into the teeth of the machine and the sirens.

> Let me remember. I am she,
> Agamemnon's child, and the mother of me
> Clytemnestra, the evil Queen,
> Helen's sister. And folk, I ween,
> That pass in the street call yet my name
> Electra ... God protect my shame!

July 1990

Date: 7/2/90

To: DIRECTOR, FBI

From: SAC, NEW HAVEN

Subject: NATIONAL SECURITY TERRORISM

The below material is derived from a CONFIDENTIAL SOURCE and must be maintained only in Headquarters cities and SEAT OF GOVERNMENT and is not to be transmitted to Resident Agencies.

Subjects identified as LEON HURLEY HOWARD a.k.a. "Masai," a male Negro born 2/11/41 Baton Rouge, LA. Howard is a former member of the BLACK PANTHER PARTY and VIVIAN NORTON BATTLE, Howard's unindicted co-conspirator in the 1970 instant case: *#C371458: United States v. The Black Panther Party.*

HOWARD and BATTLE do not leave the premises. KELLY BAILEY, a Yale University student, and housekeeper ROSE GUSTINI come daily.

Information excerpted below was received on date indicated from a CONFIDENTIAL SOURCE.

This informant provides information which must be paraphrased to protect identity and classified for national security purposes when disseminated outside the Bureau.

#1 12:26 P.M.

Mrs. L. Battle: "(unclear) Daddy said, go ahead and rub his skin and see if the coal dust comes off (unclear) and Grandfather said don't touch him (Unclear) Mother said-said-said-she said-Mother (unclear)"

BUY U. S. SAVINGS REGULARLY ON THE PAYROLL SAVINGS PLAN

August 1900

"Eleanor, Eleanor! Do not touch this lamp again, you will burn your fingers. Go to the garden, my dear, but stay away from the barn unless an adult is with you. Do you know what an 'adult' is? Oh, you precious thing, we're all going to eat you up ... Daddy is that you? What? Yes, she loves the Red House, and so do I! What? Yes, go out, it's a golden day. Careful the lake. Go with Granddaddy, darling ..."

July 1990

"I wanted to ask you how come—"

Masai cut her off, "I haven't got time to fool with you this morning." Sometimes, she thought, his voice has a tense regional, southern call and cadence. But he was smiling at her, "I need you to type up this excerpt from the interrogation of Nat Turner. Put in a profile of Thomas Gray, you know who he is? and set the scene, et cetera."

"Where will you be? Of course I know who Thomas Gray is."

"Downstairs, girl. I know you know."

She sat in silence at the word processor that she was teaching him to use; laughing loud when he always claimed, "It won't number the pages!" She listened to hear something from below. Nothing.

> "It is best to begin by noting that Nat Turner was not the author of *The Confessions of Nat Turner*—at least not in the conventional sense of 'author.' ... He did not write the words which appeared on the printed page, and he did not give overall structure to the document. The *Confessions* was a joint production—with many of the major decisions in the hands of local lawyer and slaveowner Thomas R. Gray ..."

Masai, may I suggest the following excerpt?

> 'I here proceeded to make some inquiries of him, after assuring him of the certain death that awaited him, and that concealment would only bring destruction on the innocent as well as guilty, of his own

color, if he knew of any extensive or concerted plan. His answer was, I do not ... It has been said he was ignorant and cowardly, and that his object was to murder and rob for the purpose of obtaining money to make his escape. It is notorious that he was never known to have a dollar in his life, to swear an oath, or drink a drop of spirits. As to his ignorance, he certainly never had the advantages of education, but he can read and write (it was taught him by his parents), and for natural intelligence and quickness of apprehension, is surpassed by few men I have ever seen ... He is a complete fanatic, or plays his part most admirably. On other subjects he possesses an uncommon share of intelligence, and a mind capable of attaining any thing; but warped and perverted by the influence of early impressions. He is below the ordinary stature, though strong and active, having the true negro face, every feature of which is strongly marked. I shall not attempt to describe the effect of his narrative, as told and commented on by himself, in the condemned hole of the prison. The calm, deliberate composure with which he spoke of his late deeds and intentions, the expression of his fiend-like face when excited by enthusiasm, still bearing the stains of the blood of helpless innocence about him; clothed with rags and covered with chains; yet daring to raise his manacled hands to heaven, with a spirit soaring above the attributes of man; I looked on him and my blood curdled in my veins.'

Note: Then cut to page 5 of the *Confessions*. I don't think he was crazy at all. Do you?

K.

1972

. . . but it is also the fact that, as George Jackson wrote from San Quentin, "the monster—the monster they've engendered in me--will return to torment its maker from the grave, the pit, the profoundest pit." The violence that is being bred and nurtured and taught in these soul-breakers is in direct ratio to the institutional violence of the Mother Country. It is coming but the question is will this violence be revolutionary or reactionary--on the part of niggers, I mean, not the Army or the FBI or the local pigs--I'm talking about the bloods on the block. They are the ones who are going to give their lives one way or another. These young black men are not going to change their names to Ibn Saud, and they sure can't change their skin, they are not going to Yale in dashikis and beauty parlor afros to take a PhD in Pan-Africanism. They are going to kill your mamma and she is going to kill them. That's one way. But what Huey said is what I see--black youth is going to kill itself (reactionary suicide) unless we get some kind of historical break--or make it.

In ten or twenty years only a fraction of the working class, black or white, will be needed to run the industrial base, which by that time will have been mainly moved overseas (you see it in London and Paris, and give my love to Genet when you see him).

The war against the Panthers is the start of a much larger war. If the Panthers are exterminated then the political phase of the struggle will give way to a social and criminal control siege of attrition. Starve them out. Pit the niggers against the new black bourgeoisie then, finally, the niggers against themselves: slow-motion genocide.

When are you coming back to Amerikkka? Talk to the lawyers about visiting. Come back soon. London is full of Third World trash woofin' all that native "Negritude" madness. Better come on home. I'm sorry I can't agree with you about McGovern. He won't fight.

                    Power,

                    L.

July 1990

In Vivian's dream, Masai and Kelly were naked. Kelly was on top. Vivian watched. Church bells rang ...

Vivian opened her eyes. The church bells on the Green were striking. Vivian kicked the summer coverlet off, trying to breathe. Moonlight. Silence. The dream covered her with nightsweat, the dream was the nightsweat itself, she knew that, more than just the usual hot flashes of her ten-year menopause, "moonopause" she had written in a much-debated poem in 1985.

She heard Masai's soft step on the stair, descending. She sat up. She could sense his presence outside her open door. "Leon."

He stepped in, one leg picked out by the moonlight. "That robe is a sight." He was bulging out of an old ivory-colored terrycloth robe of her father's. "Too hot to sleep."

"To work," he said, and sat in the window seat so that the moon framed his head with a silver halo while his face disappeared in shadow.

"We could go out to the lake," she said, "You could work there. There might be a breeze." "No," his voice was a murmur. "I mean in August," she said, "through Labor Day ... Kelly could come out—if you needed her."

"I don't need Kelly," a low half laugh.

"What *do* you need?"

"A second wind."

"Lie down here, comrade, by me."

"All that time in the joint I had so much energy I had to do push-ups—six sets a day. I was the man of steel. I was ready to vault over the walls to your house in one leap and lift you up in one long last leap of love ..." After a full moment, she asked, "Whatever happened?" Silence. Church chimes.

"I don't know. Just got the blues," he said.

"Leon, you're up there with that child fifteen hours a day, you're working her to a frazzle, yourself, too, you're up in that heat trying to start a revolution out of your own head. That's all ... Can't you rest, can't you give some other organ beside your brain a chance? Can't we, for pity's sake, get out of this mausoleum for a few weeks—go out to the cottage and write? You've done enough research for ten books—so have I—we both have, a lifetime of it!"

"Was all that 'research?'"

"Deed it was. Blues is research. Let's go up to Maine, to the Red House."

"... I didn't plan it this way, Vivian."

"What way?"

"I figured I could wind up the book in three or four months."

"And now?"

"I don't know ..."

"And after you've finished it?"

"I don't know."

"You and me," her smile, to him, was like a famous photograph.

"Mm-mm."

"... I needs money-y-y ..."

Both laughing softly, standing, Vivian's hip cracking, standing in the window with the Green spread naked and moondrenched before them as far as they could see. Masai watching her gaze out on the scene of their triumph and defeat. His voice touching her.

"Ghosts?"

"Mm."

"Ghosts on the Green."

"Mm ... the dogs."

May Day, 1970, and 20,000 demonstrators shut up when I mount the speakers' stand. Frisbees, balloons, dogs, children, media, police, National Guard in one gigantic gene pool on the Green, but when they call my name there is a great hush and a stillness except for the dogs who race after each other in endless circles; the playing dogs will make a poem of all this, I think, and so I decide to begin with that image to the throng on the Green:

"Brothers and Sisters, Comrades, I bring you greetings of revolutionary solidarity from the Minister of Education of the Black Panther Party, Leon Masai Howard ... You have speakers here from all over the country, famous people, great artists, so I want to be brief and, anyway, I'm over thirty years old and a poet to boot and there's a limit to what you people can be asked to believe ... You see those dogs—those sets of dogs—they are playing, they are joyful, they are the good news from the nervous system, they are the gene pool, the life force—they are us!"

A questioning silence and then the laughter, building into a roar of affirmation, some of the students embracing, dancing, the roar continuing as the dogs wheeled in their mad ellipses.

"This trial is not, finally, about Panthers or pigs, it is about those dogs, that life force: the new, the unborn, the future. The New York Times ran a shameful headline this morning: 'Guns on Way From Boston'—the only guns here today belong to the organized-cannon-fodder-and-violence-of-the-State! Yes! Yes! Right on! ... The dogs're our sign of life and love and continuity— our sign—and I want to leave you, here in front of Center Church, with the words of the German pastor, Martin Niemoeller:

> *In Germany, they first came for the Communists and I didn't speak up because I wasn't a Communist.*
>
> *Then they came for the Jews*
> *And I didn't speak up because I wasn't a Jew.*
>
> *Then they came for the trade unionists*
> *And I didn't speak up because I wasn't a trade unionist.*
>
> *Then they came for the Catholics*
> *And I didn't speak up because I was a Protestant.*
>
> *Then they came for me–and by that time*
> *No one was left to speak up.*

July 1990

Date: 7/30/90

To: DIRECTOR, FBI

From: SAC, NEW HAVEN

Subject: NATIONAL SECURITY
TERRORISM

The below material is derived from a CONFIDENTIAL SOURCE and must be maintained only in Headquarters cities and SEAT OF GOVERNMENT and is not to be transmitted to Resident Agencies.

Subjects identified as LEON HURLEY HOWARD a.k.a. "Masai," a male Negro born 2/11/41, Baton Rouge, LA. and VIVIAN NORTON BATTLE of New Haven, Conn. Howard is a former high-ranking member of the Black Panther Party,
Information below is based on a new CONFIDENTAIL SOURCE. The informant provides information which must be paraphrased for national security purposes when disseminated outside the Bureau.
Subject HOWARD is believed to reside in third floor study. Subject refuses all telephone or personal communication. New Haven will continue to attempt to obtain copy of book in progress. It is unknown whether subject or V. N. BATTLE may be armed. Subject K. BAILEY is at the Battle residence approximately fifteen hours per day,

seven days per week, and has terminated all outside relationships. Subject's father will cooperate with the Bureau concerning subject's manuscript and future plans of subjects.

C.I. REPORT

BATTLE:	(unclear) do you want to try?
HOWARD:	Do you?
BATTLE:	I don't think (unclear) without a drink (unclear)
HOWARD:	You can't drink.
BATTLE:	Never (unclear)
HOWARD:	No (unclear) . . . were celibate. Took the vow.
BATTLE:	And it got out.
HOWARD:	(unclear) . . . census spy (unclear) (laughter)
BATTLE:	The scandal.
HOWARD:	(unclear) the end of the Cold War.
BATTLE:	What (unclear) (laughter)
HOWARD:	Big black buck and his (unclear) not coming.
BATTLE:	(unclear) like the Soviets—not coming.
HOWARD:	Not coming. No one coming. (unclear) without us they'll fall on their face. (laughter)
BATTLE:	(unclear) hair will turn nappy overnight.
HOWARD:	(unclear) have to start without us. (laughter)
BATTLE:	Because we're not coming—we're going—we're going ̄because there's a shit-storm coming. Have I got it right?
HOWARD:	You've cracked the code. (unclear)
BATTLE:	We're going. (unclear) I understand. . .But where are we going?

END OF C.I. REPORT

BUY U.S. SAVINGS BONDS REGULARLY ON THE PAYROLL SAVINGS PLAN

March 1970

THE DEFENSE:	Do you think the races should be kept separate, Mrs. Maher?
ANSWER:	Well, that's the way they were meant to be.
QUESTION:	Do you think black people are different?
ANSWER:	Not really.
QUESTION:	Will this defendant have to prove himself innocent to you?
ANSWER:	If he hadn't done something, he wouldn't be here.
THE DEFENSE:	Challenged.
THE COURT:	Denied. Why don't you put the questions on the positive side?
QUESTION:	Now, Mrs. Maher, have you ever heard of the ghetto culture?
THE STATE:	Object. That is not at issue here.
THE COURT:	Sustained.
QUESTION:	Now, we may have a language problem here—
THE STATE:	Object. There is no language problem.
THE COURT:	Sustained.
QUESTION:	Mr. Rubino, would you believe a police officer or an FBI man sooner than you would Mr. Howard?
ANSWER:	Who?
QUESTION:	My client, right here.

ANSWER:	What?
QUESTION:	Are you hard of hearing, sir?
THE STATE:	Are you nervous, sir?
QUESTION:	Challenge, your honor.
THE COURT:	Excused. |//

QUESTION:	Mrs. Carr, do you have any preconceived opinions in your own mind about my client or this case?
ANSWER:	They're a different color—him and Vivian Battle—they're a different creed. That's what happens when you mix them together.
THE COURT:	Excused.
THE WITNESS:	Yes, I know too much. Am I to get paid for today?
THE COURT:	You will.
THE WITNESS:	I know too much, so I'm out because I told the truth ... Drug addicts!

AUGUST 1990

"... It's almost time ... Dr. Irving? ... I'll call you when school starts, around October, September ... I'll be alright ... I'm moving into Vivian's, I've told my father. He cried. It was disgusting. I felt sorry for him, his face was so red, he thinks the police'll raid Vivian's house and shoot it out and I'll be caught in the cross-fire like, uh, what's-her-name ... two minutes ... Anyway, thanks for, uh ... I'm not, I haven't been, uh—When I c-come back, if I come back I want to be, uh, I want to be treated with, uh, like an equal! They, Vivian and Masai, they treat me with—they—like—they treat me as an—with respect—like a—not someone's daughter, someone's patient, a student, a virgin—there's your next patient coming in, ding-dong, or is it your wife! I'm sorry, your late wife—hah!—Oh, God, I'm so weary of it, my neurosis, my virginity—I know, I know, it's not the same thing, but it's part of it ... I have to go now, I know that, you've, you've, you've, you've been very decent, really ... It's a question of fear, that's to say courage, a question of courage. My father will not give me 'permission to be' and what's worse, much worse, is that I will not give myself permission to be, I haven't, but I will now, I'm going to live with them and finish the book with Masai and—what?—of course it's a 'project'—it's not a baby, I'm not having his baby, it's not a *ménage à trois*, I don't know what they do together and I don't care, I don't ... Alright, goodbye, I'll see you after the, uh—goodbye ... Oh, God, goodbye—"

1973

. . . the nigger discovers that his life, his breath, his beating heart are worth as much as the white master. It is from this fact that he is re-invented. Because if my life is worth as much as a cop's life--never mind J. Edgar Hoover--then it follows that I have as much right to kill him as he does to kill me--or, if you insist on non-violence, then I have as little right to harm him as he does me.

It is a horrible indictment of this country that it has reverted to assassination in the last period: Malcolm, Medgar Evers, M.L. King, Fred Hampton and the B.P.P. et al. This roots back to the planned murder of slave "rebels," the killing of Sitting Bull by U.S. agents after his victory over Custer. Why are they so afraid? Why does a president, a commander-in-chief with his arsenal of weapons and nuclear bombs go berserk when a nigger--and it doesn't matter whether he's violent or non-violent--when he stands up and demands an accounting? This is why I say to you, again, be careful, because when you use your position as a writer, etc., to speak out, you become no better than a nigger to the little gray men who swore out our death warrant the first time we ever--but that's another story, comrade . . .

                              L.

September 1990

"Are you writing?" Kelly came down the stairs, barefoot, into the front parlor. Vivian sat hunched over a blank sheet of paper, gazing out the window at the Green. "Neither of you use a word processor and he won't let me put it in mine, the book, even though it'd be safer in the computer than stacked around like it is—my God, but it's hot!"

"Indian summer," Vivian said. "Have some iced tea."

"You want some?" Kelly tried to stretch her shorts so that they wouldn't hug her in the heat. "It's so close upstairs. I think my room is the coolest in the house ... Should it be 'Indian summer' or, uh, 'Native American summer?'"

"*Vivian!*"

"Should I go put your mother's music on?"

"No. Let her swelter. Air conditioning's another of her taboos."

"I've read almost all of the trial records. Incredible. How did you stand it?"

"I didn't ... We should be up in Maine."

"I mean it was like the Dreyfus case or something."

"The Rosenberg case."

"But they were guilty—or weren't they?"

Vivian finally looked at her, looked her over—"No ... No, they were innocent. Young and innocent. Like you."

55

The girl blew down into her tank top. "They were? Am I innocent? What should I read, I don't really know anything about them."

Vivian looked at the girl's bare feet on the dark carpet, itching to slip off her own sandals. "I'll find you something."

"*Vivian!*"

"Ignore her. I don't want any more music today ... No word processor, no air conditioning ... Could you and Leon work out at the cottage? It's a good ten degrees cooler there, at all times, and there's a breeze ... Never mind, I'll talk to him ... You and I could go if he didn't, ah ... The trial, hmm ... You *have* studied the Dreyfus case?"

Kelly slid down on a loveseat, out of the sunlight, swung her legs up and over the armrest, "I wrote a term paper on 'The Origins of Modern Propaganda': 'There began to be a discernible distaste for life, an incapacity for effort, a renunciation of ideals. It was a period of decline and fatigue—of 'mysticism and, uh, uh, sensuality in literature and the arts. The heroic ages were past and ...' uh ..."

"No," Vivian said, "Leon's case was different." She slid off her sandals and wriggled her toes, looked at them, then up at the girl, then away again, out the window at the Green. "There were twenty thousand people out there. There were rumors that gun-toting radicals from Boston were on their way to confront hecatombs of Minutemen hidden on campus; that there was a machine gun posted on the tower of Calhoun College; that the CIA had occupied the Skull and Bones building to protect the secrets. Hah!"

Vivian stood and laughed, then she sank down on the carpet next to the loveseat. Kelly's freckles glowed in the shadows. "Genet talked about Dreyfus."

"Genet was there?"

"And how."

"Tell me."

"'As for Masai Howard, I repeat, there must not be another Dreyfus Affair ... The life of Masai Howard, the existence of the Black Panther Party, comes first, ahead of your diplomas ...'"

"My God, Genet! I wasn't born, but I was there!"

"'The life of Masai Howard depends on you,' he said, 'your real life depends on him and on the Black Panther Party!'"

"Jesus Christ," Kelly breathed and pulled at her shorts where they had hitched up.

"Genet and twenty thousand people!" Vivian leaned back on both arms, "My dear, they did the dog right here in Babylon—that's the way Leon used to rap."

"He did? You never wrote about it? Why not?" The telephone rang inside the house. "Leave it," Vivian said. "That damned fly."

"Kill it," Kelly said, "I will ... missed ... 'The fly buzzed.'"

"Dostoyevsky," Vivian mouthed it with a Russian accent. She took hold of the student's foot, tickled it, the girl squirmed and gasped. Vivian held on to the foot, lightly ... "And all the time the speakers were speaking, the dogs chased each other around and around ..." She closed her eyes and stroked the foot for a moment ...

"What dogs?"

"The dogs of peace. They never stopped. Peace and Love."

"Was that their names?"

"No. No one knew their names. No, they *were* Peace and Love. I mean we stood on the stage speaking to the 'Masses' about Peace and Love, but down there on the grass—at 'a lower order of abstraction'—the dogs turned and turned in their mad circles. And then the Panther singers sang, 'Take it from the greedy/give it to the needy' ..."

The student arched her foot to make her toes touch Vivian's fingers. "You've got to write a poem about it. Ken Lyman told us, in Post-Modern Lit, that you were, 'arguably,' the best poet in America. You have to write about it."

"The best woman poet. Ken would've said 'Woman Poet.'" Vivian opened her eyes and smiled at the girl, then she turned the foot in her hand and inspected the bottom.

"Read my palm," Kelly chuckled like a first-grader.

"Your soul."

"Huh?"

"Soul."

"My soul, yes my sole. Ha! Read my soul."

"Let's see … Hmm … Keep still … This foot, these feet, where will they carry you, what path, what by-path—over what path, what pavement—to trample on what grass, with what dogs—"

The girl wiggled her foot, "I want to go down to, what's that street? Where it all—where you met Masai."

"Before you were born," Vivian looked up into her face.

"Before I was born," the girl said.

"I'll get in touch with L'il Joe—if you really want to go,"

"I do. I d-do. We could, you know, start it all over again!"

The poet was up on her knees, pressing a long kiss on the dirty summer foot, laughing, looking ten years younger. "Keerist, you make me want to write a poem!"

*S*EPTEMBER 1990

"Watch your step." Vivian guided Kelly by the elbow across the six-inch cracks in the sidewalk.

'"I shouldn't have worn these sandals," Kelly said, "and this dress is just sticking to me." She could sense the men in the liquor store doorway looking at her. "I'm feeling a little dizzy."

"Stop a minute," Vivian held her arm. "Stop. Catch your breath. It's hot as hell—Julio! Hello, comrade."

"Hello, comrade." The men in front of Hocus-Pocus the House of Spirits stepped and shuffled out of their square of shade onto the steaming sidewalk to greet Vivian. Julio was a yellow-eyed man somewhere between forty and sixty, ash-gray skinned in a sleeveless jersey. "How you been, Vivian? All right! How's Masai doing? You remember Franco? And Elrod—he's shorter than he used to be." Laughter.

"I do. Good to see you. Who's that in the doorway?"

"That's Robert from Hartford. Come on out here, brother, and pay your respects." Laughter.

Vivian shook all their hands. "This is Ms. Bailey. She's helping me on research." The men nodded.

Kelly sucked in hot air. "H-h-h-h-how d'ya ..."

Julio reached out toward a fit-looking young man. "This is Huey, my sister's boy, in the Marines."

"Well, Huey," Vivian smiled.

59

"I reckon you know who he's named after," Julio smiled back and the other men chuckled.

"Gentlemen," Vivian wiped her forehead, "let's get out of this weather." They all chuckled again with approval. "Kelly and I have a date—with L'il Joe and Big Man. Everybody's welcome. We're going to discuss whether to start up the black history group again." She turned to the young Marine, "Huey, you'd be welcome. Ask your uncle, he'll tell you how it all started." Julio nodded and murmured, the others smiling and nodding.

Kelly's face was hot and red. Vivian handed her a handkerchief. The men watched her. She could see the spark of pride and affection in their eyes when they looked at Vivian.

"Where's it going to be? Bootstrap? Mm-hm." Julio looked down. "Masai coming?" Franco lit up another Kool.

"Not today," Vivian held on to her smile.

"Well," Julio spoke as he and the men stepped back into the shade, "You all go ahead and tell L'il Joe to let me know what y'all decide."

Vivian looked into his red-rimmed yellow eyes and smiled with her eyes. "Gentlemen," she tipped her head and started Kelly moving. The men all nodded and there was a chorus of "All right" and "Right on."

They walked slowly, past a half block of burnt out blasted storefronts. Vivian paused in front of one, "This was the first Panther office," she said, more to herself, and then walked again, to the corner, where Operation Bootstrap had once flourished. It was cooler inside and full of shadows. Kelly jumped when a voice spoke out of the gloom. "Vivian."

"Hello, Joe," Vivian laughed, "Hello, Big Man."

Kelly jumped again when she saw what had appeared to be a piece of office furniture tilt down to the floor. "Right on," said the broad big young man who was called 'Big Man' in honor of two long gone Panthers of similar size who had been called, for identification's sake, Big Man East and Big Man West. "Right on," Big Man said.

"This is Kelly Bailey, who's working with Masai on his book, doing a lot of research, and on her own as well.

"Right on," said both young men.

The poet guided Kelly to a dilapidated desk and eased her down. L'il Joe studied Kelly, guessing that the girl was about his age, maybe younger. Her skin was mottled and slick in the soft light. He looked down at her sandaled feet. Vivian took in L'il Joe's gaze and Kelly's hollow breathing, then she walked to Joe and took his hand. "How are you doing, Joe?"

He looked up at her. "Thanks for the check. I gave it to Miss Gwen. Big Man and me're both staying there."

"She give you grits, Big Man?" Vivian asked.

"All he can eat," Joe said in a tone that made them all laugh.

"Right on," chuckled Big Man, lighting up a Kool. Kelly coughed.

"Mr. Jefferson," Vivian said to Kelly, "is the possessor of a deadpan, ah, delivery, as you will find out, that can be devastating." They all sat smiling and silent for a minute. The street, outside, was shining in the heat, but there was almost no sound except for occasional traffic.

"Say, Vivian, you think I could get a job, part time, at Yale?"

Vivian looked closely at L'il Joe. He was not quite as tall as Leon or as dark; his features were a bit finer, the hair was the same, the timbre of the voice was lighter—she tried to remember Leon's voice when she had first met him—the diction was good, perfect standard, like Leon's: he's his son; why question the fact; use your eyes, use your head. "At Yale?" She looked away.

Joe knew what she had to be thinking. He had been close to this woman since she first started coming to visit, and to bring him gifts, when he was a little bitty thing living with Father James and his family, when he was called L'il Joe and everybody said that he was so quick and so smart that it was no question that he would go to Yale on a scholarship someday. He had loved her, then, dreaming that she was his beautiful white mother. Loved her then and later, but after grade school in love with her, too, until high school in her black history seminar, that she taught with Father James. All he could think of then was her and Masai making love back before he was born. Sometimes he would stay away from the class to free himself from the rush of imagery of the two of them together. And he knew that she knew and would know about his dreams awake and at night, and see in her mind's eye the striations of his lean adolescent arrow of a body ... "Part time."

"You mean work part time *and* take classes?" Kelly coughed, "That's what *I'm* going to do."

They all turned to look at the new girl. "I m-m-mean ..."

The poet rescued her: "Yes. Sociology. That's Joe's line of country, too—or at least I used to think it would be." Joe and the girl were looking at each other. Big Man had closed his eyes. Vivian said, "You could easily get a scholarship, if you decide you want to go to Yale. His grades at the community college were—"

"I dropped out last semester."

"Right on," Big Man rejoined them.

"What happened?"

Joe stood and walked to the window that looked out on a dark alley and leaned against the wall, half of his face and one shoulder in light. "I'm not going to school anymore. We came today because it was you."

"I know."

"That's why I want to get a little job. I want to do my own reading and writing. You started me, but I want to go on now myself." He turned further away and they could see his shoulders bunch. "I've studied the movement with you, been all through it from Cinqué and Nat Turner down to Huey and Bobby and Masai—and I see a new 'Reconstruction' coming. A bunch of these Ivy League cats are publishing shit about how slave resistance led directly—they don't say how—to today's Negro—call him what you want—and his shiftless, lying, shirking trickery, laziness, and sociopathy. The slaves ran away, again and again, they don't deny that, but here's the big news: all those runaway slaves—always came running back home to

Massa—except for the few crazy niggers who're still running." He turned back to face them, the light from the window gathered around the close-cropped hair and the high cheekbones of his taut face.

"K-K-Kardiner. He—" Kelly could not contain herself. L'il Joe had touched a nerve. "Abraham Kardiner," Joe almost jumped away from the window, right into Big Man's wide-open face—"She knows about Kardiner's study in the '40s about how the male Negro was by *definition* insane!" Silence, and then, unaccountably, they all burst out into full-throated, eye-tearing laughter, and it went on, off and on, for a good ninety seconds.

Finally, Vivian, still wiping her eyes said, "I met Abe Kardiner as an old man and he told me that his study had a major flaw, and that was his neglect of that small sampling error of politicized African-Americans, male or female, whose insanity or historical consciousness, or whatever you want to call it, is, ah, mediated by their intelligence, discipline, revolutionary strategy ... He admitted he was wrong."

Joe looked down at Vivian, his voice was almost hushed. "He was wrong because he didn't see Malcolm X or Martin Luther King coming," he made eye contact with Kelly, whose face was red-hot again, then back to Vivian's cool eyes and pale skin. "But he wasn't so wrong about your average brother. But all these new books proving that slavery wasn't really a holocaust and that slaves gained enough control by day-to-day sabotage, and crop poison and animal torture, they call this 'Resistance'—and, then, the few outright crazy slaves who get away to the swamps, terrorize all the slaves who didn't rebel and run openly, terrorize the good darkies so bad that these sane slaves have to appeal to Massa and Missus for protection!" Joe was angry, now, though his voice never rose, his eyes flashed first down at Vivian and then across the room at the girl. "This is the line at Yale, now—'Slavery Light!'"

"So you've read enough books?" Vivian grinned, and, then, they all laughed low, just for a moment.

..."No, I read 'em all. From Right to Left. And the Left's worse than the Right."

"It is?" Vivian frowned.

"As bad as. The Right swears by the old Bell Curve: niggers aren't crazy, they're stupid. But that's a whole lot better than the revisionists of the Left, whose game is: niggers aren't stupid, they're crazy." No one laughed. But they breathed in because it was apparent that L'il Joe Jefferson was becoming a full-grown black man.

Big Man smoked, Kelly coughed again, Vivian just rested her eyes on this youth to whom she would have given any amount of money; more, she would and did give him all the love she had, but the question that pulsed inside her and inside the dim gutted office, over and over again, was—*what can I actually do?* "Joe, do you think that you might want to work with Kelly—for money—on the research for the book, Masai's book?"

"Did he ask for me?"

"He doesn't, ah, know that you—"

"No, that's alright."

"How about your own writing? Book, film, a docu—"

He was pacing again. "You see the Spike Lee film?"

Kelly had to speak. "I thought it was b-brilliant."

Joe drove on, "And the August Wilson plays over at the Yale Rep?"

"Every one," said Kelly.

"Wait," Vivian said, "What's your point?"

"In the film, the 'Mayor' is a drunk! The guy who hangs around peddling pictures of Malcolm X and Martin Luther King, he's crazy! Crazy. And Wilson's plays—all the men who relate to the dialectic of slavery and racism are *crazy*. The cat's a stone poet, but the story's always the same: Politics equals madness. And I'm talking about the cream of the crop—it's a giant step backward even from something like *Raisin in the Sun*. These cats—"

"I—," Kelly tried to join in, again, but Vivian spoke over everybody.

"Big Man, what do you want to do?"

The action stopped. Joe slumped down in the sprung desk chair.

Two children ran past the outside door laughing. Big Man lit up a Kool: "Me and Joe're tight."

Vivian's eyes canvassed him, his sheer bulk, then shifted to Joe hanging off the broken chair. She heard Kelly's gasp of fear, she swung around to face a streetman standing in the doorway.

The man had wild hair and a huge overcoat despite the heat. He filled up the doorway, the room. The sight and stink of him had the younger woman climbing up the back of her chair. Vivian breathed in through her mouth. L'il Joe and Big Man looked at the monster. A full minute passed before Big Man spoke. "Say, brother, what it is?" And that broke the spell.

"Is he Masai's son?"

Vivian wouldn't say a single word on the hot walk home. When the girl asked her question, the poet didn't even blink.

1974

Dear Comrade,

Let's talk about today being "Bloomsday," and the exit of Richard Nixon from the political scene, <u>again</u>, and hence I am saving instead of sending this and all the other letters—they may read your letters but they will never read mine! We can talk about whatever we choose except that what I want to say to you I cannot express, not even in poetry, though I am trying, because everything to do with what we have done together is still too painful for me to express. In words. If you were here in person—in the flesh!—then, comrade, we could kiss each other's wounds. <u>Jesus!</u>

(An hour later)

Now—Nixon: did you know that Mother knew Dick Nixon in the early '50s and that I met him in San Diego when I was around twelve? I thought he was funny and his wife was mean, but now I know that they were really characters out of the collective imagination of this crazed culture as made manifest through Sinclair Lewis, Sherwood Anderson, Dos Passos, even first cousin to Babbitt, Faulkner's Snopes: they predicted Nixon, his rise and fall, and they <u>understood</u> and, finally, pitied them. But can you tell <u>me</u> why none of the Cold War historians—political scientists—sociologists never really understood the Nixonian "Silent Majority," much less Tricky Dick himself? But our novelists did, starting with Melville and Twain, and,

I think, some of the poets like Sandburg, and certainly Frost, but never any of the experts or weighty thinkers. They write about Nixon as if he were elected on another planet and came to earth to betray the American Dream. For God's sake, can't they see that he is the American Dream—the third-string high school lineman, sly and shy who lost every battle and won the war? Because, like Joe McCarthy (who Mother rather liked), like Joe McCarthy, Nixon was the butt of all the jokes, that everyone kicked around until it came time to do it. Only in America. Nixon was "HOMO AMERIKANUS—LATE IN THE AGE OF ATOMS—NOW EXTINCT."

But Mother claims that I, as usual, do not understand "people like Mr. Nixon" who, in any case, "should be locked up in St. Elizabeth's," while "the wife," as she refers to Mrs. N., should be "sent to a health farm to dry out." She insists the two daughters "are tramps" and always refers to Tricia as "Trixie."

She is a monster, Mother, still a monster, still capable at any moment to drive me into hysterics of laughter and tears. It is now clear that my entire literary-political-sexual career has never had the slightest effect on her supreme self-confidence as the Doyen of the Yale Corp. and Center Church, or the merry widow who I happen to know has been fucking her lawyer (D.E.G., remember the Silver Fox?) since, at least, Daddy's death in 1950.

I never fazed her, so isn't it lucky that I have never done anything simply to enrage her? You laugh? So do I, my love. But it is true that after I was with you, she never fazed me either, and whatever I did I did for myself, which is to say I did for myself, with you, and in the revolution. Have you gotten around to Euripides' Electra yet? I want to do a new translation. After she murders her mother she covers the corpse:

Robe upon robe I cast
On her that I hated sore,
Robe upon robe I cast
On her that I loved of yore.

DONALD FREED

If there ever had been a chance for another revolution here, the question is not whether or not I could have killed my mother, for the archclassenemy (one word) that she is, but whether or not I could have killed anybody—Nixon, Mother, Kissinger, Hitler, <u>anybody</u>. We have to talk about this.

(Tuesday)
I may as well go on since this cannot be mailed ... Back to <u>Electra</u>, I'm making some trial sketches, I'm sending you the Gilbert Murray translation—I think it's right on your studying a Greek, an ancient Greek book in that place and yet where better could you comprehend Prometheus or Philoctetes or Electra? Have you come across <u>Aidos</u>? I mean why does Electra trap her mother with the lie that she's just had a baby by a peasant untouchable? And Clytemnestra falls for it and gets hacked to death when she comes, against her better judgement, to try to help Electra: "She bent her knees to the earth/the knees that bent in my birth/and I—O her hair, her hair!"

Is it the fact that my desire for a child with you is shaping my thinking to the effect that only world-wide-spread intercourse and multi-racial offspring, together with revolution—and, indeed, as a function of revolution and rebellion—can curb the murder of the Stranger or the "outsider" by the "group?" This is what J. Edgar Hoover knows and why he hunts down miscegenation as the root cause of revolution and chaos. And I think that Mr. Hoover is right. Hoover knows that incest, never mind miscegenation, is the <u>general</u> condition of the one human race, and that, just because it is general, incest must be taboo in the particular case, <u>and</u> our love, you and me, is only the sign of our <u>lust</u>, and it is our lust that spells out the great anti-myth of not only race but class and condition, all three, and even gender because the iron law of reality requires both genders to "make" babies and, so, sets at naught any final <u>existential</u> difference between the combined sexes—doesn't it?

This is how Freud went wrong in this matter of "penis envy" (don't you prefer the Greek "phallus" to "penis" or do I hear you say you "hold with prick?"). True, I crave to have a phallus—in this case a black one (yours)—but not detached from your long, lean, lucid (I can't help myself now) long, lean, lucid body ... I simply refuse to interrupt this long, lean, "lucid" letter to masturbate, again—until I have made my point: quickly, then, what I want is your black cock (let's agree on "cock," or your old term, "Johnson," which is always my second choice and always good for a laugh) want your cock (and is it any more "black" than any other part of you, filled as you are with all those "white" and "Indian"—and, therefore, Asian or "yellow"— genotypes, any more than my vagina is "pink" [this is getting out of "hand"] want your cock in me where it's dark inside, where there is no color in the dark (Jesus!) your cock inside my darkness, like the fish in its cave at night.

(written and filed—not sent)

August 1990

Date: 9/12/90

To: DIRECTOR, FBI

From: SAC, NEW HAVEN

Subject: NATIONAL SECURITY TERRORISM

The below material is derived from a CONFIDENTIAL SOURCE and must be maintained only in Headquarters cities and SEAT OF GOVERNMENT and is not to be transmitted to Resident Agencies.

Subjects identified as LEON HURLEY HOWARD a.k.a. "Masai," a male Negro born 2/4/41, Baton Rouge, LA. and KELLY M. BAILEY, a student at the Yale University. Howard is a former member of the BLACK PANTHER PARTY,

C.I. REPORT

HOWARD:	Cut that light off.
BAILEY:	(unclear)
HOWARD:	What?
BAILEY:	It's my turn (unclear).
HOWARD:	(unclear)
BAILEY:	Did you ever want to be white?
HOWARD:	Did you?

BAILEY:	(Laughter-unclear)
HOWARD:	(Laughter-unclear)
BAILEY:	Your turn.
HOWARD:	(unclear)
BAILEY:	My turn again, then. Who is (unclear)?
HOWARD:	(Laughter-unclear)
BAILEY:	How do you pronounce it, then? "Stagger Lee?"
HOWARD:	(unclear) not Stagger Lee. "Stagolee."
BAILEY:	Who is he?
HOWARD:	(unclear)
BAILEY:	Please.
HOWARD:	"Drylongso."
BAILEY:	Who is he?
HOWARD:	(unclear)
BAILEY:	(unclear) who they are?
HOWARD:	(unclear) I'm sorry (unclear) sleep here, tonight?
BAILEY:	(unclear) to you (unclear) want me to do. I feel I (unclear) part of this (unclear) intend to put my name somewhere in the credits of (unclear)
HOWARD:	(unclear)
BAILEY:	(unclear) the credits of your book.
HOWARD:	(unclear) "Research Consultant?"
BAILEY:	Fine. That or "Slave." (Laughter-unclear)
HOWARD:	(Laughter-unclear)
BAILEY:	Your turn.
HOWARD:	That's alright.
BAILEY:	No, go ahead. Ask me anything (unclear) intimate, private, anything.
HOWARD:	Do you work for the police?

END C.I. REPORT

BUY U.S. SAVINGS BONDS REGULARLY ON THE PAYROLL SAVINGS PLAN

August 1990

"Vivian?"

"In here!"

"*Vivian!*"

"Just a minute, please, Mother, I was just there!"

"Vivian?"

"In here, Kelly!"

"*Vivian!*"

"Shut up!"

"Vivian—oh, I'm sorry, I couldn't hear you over the music."

"Bloody Victor Herbert—'Extraordinary how potent cheap music is'—what's up?"

"I want to ask you something."

"Follow me," Vivian waltzing through the music into the kitchen, swung open the old-fashioned ice box door, took out a pitcher of iced tea and poured out glasses for Kelly and herself, "You look all pink and freckled and hot and bothered, as usual. Drink up."

"May I close the door?" Kelly closed the door, then she washed her hands at the sink and dried them and saw that the poet was holding the cold glass of tea against her neck and studying her.

"Is your mother, is Mrs. Battle alright?" Kelly sat down and touched her cheek with her glass. "That call that came this morning?"

"Yes?"

"Was it, uh, an, uh, you know—"

"It was Mr. Maggiori. From the *New Haven Register*."

"Was it, uh, you know, a very personal, uh …" She made herself look directly at the poet.

Vivian raised an eyebrow, "What's the matter?"

"I don't know. You came up and said that somebody had just called to say that, uh, somebody had, uh …"

"Died. George Sams."

"George Sams … had, uh …"

"Died. Been killed. Shot in a dope deal … What about it?"

"Well, after you came up and told him, after you left, Leon, uh, we went on working for about five minutes and then he went over to the window and started staring out the window and he wouldn't— I went on by myself for a while and he just kept … I mean, who was George Sams?"

May 1970

THE DEFENSE: Mr. Sams, is it true that you told Mr. Carmichael that you had every intention of destroying Mr. Howard and the Black Panther Party?

GEORGE SAMS: No, sir.

QUESTION: You did not say that?

ANSWER: No, sir, Mr. Garry.

QUESTION: So if it's in this tape recording of yours, that's an incorrect transcription, is it?

ANSWER: Could I have some water?

QUESTION: Are you taking Thorazine, Mr. Sams?

ANSWER: I don't know, I just go in the Medic Room and tell the, you know, describe to the doctor that I can't sleep, I'm suffering from some migraine headaches. And the doctor, he prescribes something for me, I don't go into asking him what he's giving me. And if he give me any drugs, and it's too powerful—I have it for the records to the institution that I don't want any drugs. So the doctor just give me something to sleep. They don't work.

QUESTION: Alright. Now, sir, after you joined the Black Panther Party in 1968 did you—how were you referred to? Did you have a nickname?

ANSWER: I have nicknames, like Crazy George, Madman,

EVERY THIRD HOUSE

	Detroit George—different names—I had the name Dingee Swahoo, which was an African name.
QUESTION:	Dingee what?
ANSWER:	Dingee Swahoo.
THE COURT:	Alright. S-w-a-h-o-o.
ANSWER:	It's an African name, and Minister Masai—
QUESTION:	"Masai"—you mean Leon Howard?
ANSWER:	Masai, he gave the name, he gave me the name "Madman No. 1," which was in San Francisco. Him and Chairman Bobby.
QUESTION:	What other names have you been known by?
ANSWER:	That's about all. No, lately I have been called "Number 1 Agent." I have been called "Rats," "Snitch"—a lot of times, you know, basically, it's— Rats, Snitch, Agent—lots of times, you know, these is—to me these names are just that people be misled by, because they don't know no other thing. Somebody push the rhetoric and they follow it. It means not that much to me.
QUESTION:	You have also been accused, for many, many months prior to you being arrested, as being a "pig" have you not?
ANSWER:	Yes.
THE PROSECUTION:	Object.

August 1990

"More iced tea?"

"I remember, now, who he was," Kelly said, sucking on a cube of ice. "He was one of the main witnesses to testify against Leon. Why did he—didn't he tell some girl and she told the police, or something like—"

"The girl told her father. She was a student at Yale. White."

"She was?"

"And she had fallen under George Sams', ah, spell, and he had bragged to her about how he knew that Leon was involved in a conspiracy to kidnap or kill Henry Kissinger and Governor Rockefeller, and a good deal more about the coming 'campaign of terror'! And Ms. Gill, her name was, swallowed George Sams' story, and then one day, he beat her up and she went running home to daddy."

Kelly swallowed the ice and shivered. Vivian was watching her, again, as she shivered in the heat. "What did Leon—was George Sams an FBI agent?"

May 1970

THE DEFENSE: You talked to a Miss Susan Petty many times in July and August of 1969, didn't you, about Mr. Howard? Petty, P-E-T-T-Y.

GEORGE SAMS: Mr. Garry, I just don't think that I should continue, you know, in this case, which you are trying to use people as they are and paint them, that I should continue to use young ladies' names in this testifying case. You know it's not my—I haven't said nothing about Vivian Battle or none of them. And you notice in my testimony I try to protect the Panther sisters in the case anyway, because the only thing they was doing was the same thing I was doing, and that is following orders, but it seemed though you want to pretend everybody had they own price in the crime, and everybody was following orders, and that's just what I was doing— Chairman Bobby and Minister Masai give the orders, and we follow them. Because the real responsibility lie in the leadership, and I'm a Party member, and that's why I'm accepting the truth here, today.

THE COURT: Order.

THE DEFENSE: You say that Masai, Mr. Howard, drinks "Cutty Sauce."

August 1990

"Thank God." Vivian's mother's music played out and the poet braced herself for the old woman to scream her name. But the house was suddenly silent.

"Was he crazy?"

"Who?"

"Uh, George Sams?"

"Look ... Why don't you go and read the trial transcript."

"Well, I did, when I first—when he asked me to help him with the book."

"Mm. Well—why don't you go and read it again."

"I know, but I just thought—"

"Read the record."

They looked away from each other in the silence, in the heat. A minute later, the girl stood up and went to the sink to rinse her glass. Her cheeks were flushed, again, as she walked slowly out of the kitchen.

Vivian sat alone, and heaved in some air, as she always did when the need to inhale a cigarette came over her. "Come back," she called out, her voice searching for the girl, "Come back, I'll tell you about George Sams." Kelly reappeared in the doorway. Vivian looked across and down at the girl's bare feet, and half smiled. "You want to know who was crazy?"

The poet stared into her empty glass and told the story of Crazy

George Sams. Some of the story. But it didn't add up for the younger woman. "It doesn't make sense to you, does it?"

"No."

"I know. You see, to understand Sams you'd have to know about Tackwood."

"Who's Tackwood?"

"... I'm going to let you read my trial journal, covering George Sams. And my interviews with Louis Tackwood—"

"Who is—"

"If you swear to me that you will read the material in my room, make no copy, and never talk about it to Leon."

Low thunder and the sky turned a shade darker. Vivian could see that the student looked pale in the rainy light, her armless blouse rising and falling faster, now. "I don't understand," Kelly said softly. Vivian poured two fingers of tea into her glass. "Because Sams and Tackwood were government agents. They're dead men."

"They're dead?"

"I wouldn't know. But anybody they hurt at that time—starting with Leon—might kill them, if they're still alive, or might take a dim view of anyone who seemed to be taking too deep an interest in old or new plots to destroy the Panthers ... So, make up your mind." Vivian drained her glass and walked to the doorway to stand close to the girl.

"'There will be rain tonight,'" Vivian said, her eyes shifting for an instant toward the purple sky.

"*Macbeth*," answered Kelly, but didn't smile.

"'Then let it come down!'" Vivian finished the quote. "Think it over. I'll be in my room."

May 1970

V. N. BATTLE TRIAL JOURNAL:
The Thirteenth Day (January 23, 1970)

Sams!

George Sams, Jr. The name is a savage joke. "Jr." Nothing, son of Nothing; Nothing, Jr. There are millions like him in the ghettos of the Third World; they do not exist until through an act of violence they materialize for a split second before sinking again beneath the level of history.

"'But I have never got outside that circle. I have never broken out of the ring of what I have already done and cannot ever undo,' he thinks quietly, sitting on the seat, with planted on the dashboard before him the shoes, the black shoes smelling of Negro: that mark on his ankles that gauge definite and ineradicable of the black tide creeping up his legs, moving from his feet upward as death moves." This was even more true for Sams than for Faulkner's Joe Christmas.

Sams was like Richard Wright's Bigger Thomas—"Confidence could only come again now through action so violent that it would make him forget."

THE COURT:	Cutty Sark?
THE WITNESS:	He constantly—"Cutty Sauce," liquor, he drinks all the time. This man tell the members not to drink, and he

> drinks all the time, he does the same thing, and if you do it, he gives—he's on the stage at the rally hollering about members smoking weeds, and he's drinking "Cutty Sauce," the liquor in the bottle, and I don't think that's fair, Mr. Garry, and I can expose all of it.

QUESTION: *Why don't you go ahead and do it?*

ANSWER: *Well, the Black Panther Party—and see that you are on the Central Committee. You know, I expect—you sit there and tell these lies and you try to incriminate people. You can't do it with me.*

QUESTION: *I'm on the Central Committee of the Black Panther Party?*

ANSWER: *Yes, you are the lawyer of the Central Committee of the Black Panther Party and you got on the David Frost Show and said the police killed the Panthers. You know the Panthers killed some of the Panthers ...*

From the bowels of the courthouse a group of prisoners is being led in singing hymns. The rough chorale drifts dimly up into the courtroom, where the man whose mother had said he was "fit for the garbage can" is led hulking in, after a merciful recess, for another session. The pitiful bravado that he had displayed when trying to spar with lawyer Garry is gone. He walks like the "field nigger" that he had used to boast of being back in the days when Eldridge Cleaver deified the madmen and the bad niggers.

Since the terrible ten-minute eruption, Sams had sunk into himself, he sat sideways facing the window, the hand with the handkerchief in it shielding his face.

Garry works carefully, lugging up the contradictory transcripts from old hearings and statements to confront George Sams, Jr., with himself. But Sams is impeaching himself now almost from sentence to sentence. He is not lying. He simply is no more responsible for his words than he was for his actions.

He had begun in an institution, he was in one now, he would end in *an institution. He would be brought out, from time to time, to eat raw meat like a geek in a carnival. The state would get a few more days' work out of him.*

The nigger from Alabama (he is very black and looks like a "Scottsboro Boy") is stamped "competent" by the psychiatrists, the judges and State Attorneys, the police and the F.B.I. But unlike Prospero—who said, finally, of Caliban, "This thing of darkness I acknowledge mine"—the State takes no responsibility for him. The whole instant case turns on whether or not the Panthers used Sams, but there is no doubt about the State's use of him. George Sams and Leon Howard are interchangeable pieces of black meat in the chain of logic that the Panthers call "The New Haven Railroad."

Garry's hand trembles turning the pages of the wild old testimony; this is the kind of broken monster that he could defend and explain: Sams' complete deracination, the long torturehouse of racism. But the State has no shame over the use of this man—who looks like a nineteenth-century African, somehow an "older" body image than the "modern" Panthers sitting in the front row of the court gallery.

Mr. Merle, the State's Attorney, has had an extra chair installed for the convenience of his long-haired son, who is here on his school spring holiday, watching the coon show.

Sams is punchy; he mumbles his answers at random. The motes of late light are on Garry's white hair and George Sams' natural, which covers some old bullet slugs (he said he had "an iron plate in his head," but X-rays showed only the slugs, and then he said he thought he had an iron plate in his head).

Now Garry is finishing, and Sams will be handed over to Katie Roraback for more. It is a judgment on everyone, this ruined non-entity. No one had been prepared for the pity and terror of him.

After six months and two million dollars, all the raids and arrests, the State had finally unveiled its evidence. Sitting there, sweating through the cheap jacket that they had bought for him, he is evidence of some other unspeakable crime of which he is both the victim and the witness.

Almost every answer has to be read back. The pale court reporter with the New England accent produces an almost psychedelic version of Sams' run-on street rhetoric and heavy accent, something out of Joyce or Beckett signaling the death of language.

He did not "keep up with the day," he said, and here he sat on his birthday, which he did remember along with his garbage mother, and he had told some girl that he had raped somewhere that if he ever saw his mother he "would cut her throat." It was his birthday, and the collar of his stiff new shirt stuck up over his coat.

Masai watches him. Here is the Stagolee that the Black Panther Party was formed to save. There is a part of George Sams in every Panther, there must be—without a renaissance in these damned creatures there can never be a revolution and that is why the Panthers for so long could not give up their bloody rhetoric. Well, we have paid for it now. The sheriffs laugh openly at his spectacle.

Once he calls Masai Fred Hampton, the dead Chicago Panther hero. He closes his eyes. That is the truth. Dead. The singing of the Gospel hymns down in the basement had stopped. Not just Fred Hampton and all the others, but God himself is dead here in New Haven, where He started in the New World.

The judge adjourns early. No one, not even Mr. Merle, wants to ask any more questions of this unreconstructed Stagolee who sits brushing mindlessly at his pants.

NOTE: Elaine, I'm publishing these courtroom notes in the L.A. Free Press (you remember Art Kunkin), unless you want them for the B.P.— but I've written them and the other pieces, basically, for white readers. See you next week.

V.

August 1971

ORAL HISTORY OF LOUIS ELBERT TACKWOOD
taken by V. N. Battle
June–August, 1971

I was a premature baby, you know. My mother and her brother got in a fight and he hit her in the back with a skillet, so for a long time—I'm gonna tell you how I got so smart—for a long time when I was about six years old, I couldn't play with other kids—couldn't even go out of the house. All I could do was read. And they found out early in life that I didn't like to read little books. I used to like heavy books, you know, so they started giving me the more books, the more books, the more books, so by the time I was six I was pretty well up on things.

I went to Riis too. Jacob A. Riis, it's a school for all boys. You know, incorrigible boys. I wasn't even incorrigible when I went there, really. I was when I left though ... After reading *The Prince* and Napoleon's thing and a few other books and, basically, I read the complete history of Hitler, really. What was very interesting was, I always fantasized about myself—I knew I had the brains to do it—I was digging organizations. And I said, one day I'm gonna get me an organization together ...

Only three men in history impressed me: Heinrich Himmler, the Nazi mastermind; Machiavelli, the Italian aristocrat; and Adolf Hitler.

I tell you one cat who impressed me, Bertrand Russell. Yeah, I dug Bertrand, Bertrand Russell. Yeah, Bertrand Russell was a hell of an influence on me, cause I dug his concepts on a lot of things. People called him communistic and radical and a lot of things, but the cat was righteously heavy. Oh, I tell you a cat I dug ... I dug, pardon me, the fuck out of and I dug his concept of doing things. I'm gonna tell you, man, like he was brilliant. One of the most brilliant cats that ever lived and I just thought about it, too, but this cat here was all those people wrapped into one. And I'm gonna tell you, like I idolized the cat really in a hell of a little old way, Mahatma Gandhi. His concept of the nonviolent thing was so beautiful ... yet he wasn't opposed to violence. See my point?

... I wish I'd been younger—lived younger to hear speak—I read up on—he was a lawyer—Clarence Darrow. The famous monkey trial. I would have been able to dig him. Like Kerouac was the real thing. I dug existentialism for a while ...

The federal government created the ghetto, welfare checks ... The whole black system ... the whole system ... is pimping. It's more than petty capitalism. It's capitalism in its truest form ... raw capitalism ... a pound of flesh.

Yeah, ask some of those women, getting out of buses every morning, where are they going? "To work." "What's your old man doing?" "Ohh, he working ... but he been laid off." Black women can go get a job faster than a black man. And if she can't get a job, well, then have more babies.

I know, people look at me sometime and say, "Where you goin', man? You just don't know where you're goin'." I know where I'm goin'. You've got to go with the tide. The overall plan.

I'm looking to ... how will I put it? ... to be a black Ralph Nader, but not for everybody. I'm not going to be a consumer advocate ... I'm advocating one thing ....

NOTE: Elaine, I'm sending copy to C. G. and other lawyers. Be careful of Tackwood. Tell friends that if he contacts them to direct him back to me. Remember, this man is a legendary double-agent. I think he could have been a literally fabulous story teller writer. *Could* have been. But watch out now.

                        Love,

                        V.

August 1990

11:15 P.M.

"This is fantastic," Kelly kept her voice low, "It's pathetic." Vivian laid down her book. Kelly coaxed the file pages back into the folder, "Was he—he was different than Sams, I mean Sams was a pathetic creep, but Tackwood was a great character."

"He was named after Louis Armstrong." Vivian looked out across the dark Green, then back at the flushed face.

"I know," Kelly said, "but you know that he would never fit into any Yale psych or sociology class, they could not explain him ... Where are they now, I mean uh—whatever happened to them?" Vivian smiled a little. "I mean are they—w-were they—"

"I don't know," Vivian said. "If they're dead, they're in heaven as 'God's spies,' because they worked for this 'Nation Under God.'" This made the student sniff with literary amusement and that encouraged Vivian to go on, "Lucifer was a renegade and a double-agent and 'the brightest fell.'"

"*King Lear* and, uh ..."

"*Macbeth*," said the poet, "'Angels are in heaven, but the brightest fell,' shall we talk about Shakespeare—Tackwood as Iago, Sams as the cutthroat whose face Richard III fancied?" The half smile was still there, but the eyes closed in on Kelly, cool, not cold, but calculating.

"What is it?"

"You're doing enough work on this book with Leon to give you a doctorate in American something or other, but you've never talked to any hard-core ghetto person—except for L'il Joe—and you don't really get anything about Sams or Tackwood from the record ... Don't cry now, young lady, at least you're trying—up on a high, high order of abstraction—but at least you're working with the man who knows and who, if he would only go down into the ghetto, could make a difference to these, ah, young black men. Then you could go with him and have your eyes opened. Then you'd see who these 'gangbangers' are, their slow-motion suicide that Leon and Huey P. Newton called 'Reactionary Suicide,' the thousands of A.I.D.S. orphans left behind now, and growing. If you could get him to go down there to talk to Joe and the others—and you go, too, and save yourself, and maybe save *him*."

Kelly stood up, her back popped. "Can I sleep in here—on the floor? I'm nervous."

"On the floor?—Listen, you've read about this 'truce' now between the gangs, but you don't know that a truce is interpreted by the FBI and the police as a mortal threat, and so they're, even now, sending in the *epigoni* of George Sams and Louis Tackwood to provoke a violent new round of gang war—and Leon is the only one who could go down there and warn them, the gangs, what is being done to them ... You want to sleep in here on the floor?"

"Please."

"Like a dog?"

"Yes."

The poet held out her hand, the girl took it, they looked at each other, Vivian holding on: "Kelly, your book, none of the books about American slavery and its ramifications can encompass the reality. Don't you feel that?" The girl squeezed the other's hand as if to signal, "Tell me."

Vivian bared her teeth, her breath short, staring deep down. "Close the books and open your eyes. What do you see?" The girl held on. The poet spoke into the depths—"You see people. People with dark skins—stay with me now walking the fields and the streets of North America—you have it in mind, you see it? ... I see it. I see them. You see <u>them</u>? Alright. Tell me how they got here?"

The younger woman's arm started to cramp up, "You m-mean the middle—"

Vivian's face swung up, "We can't hide behind terms like 'The Middle Passage' or statistics, twenty million or fifty million, I'm asking you what are these *Africans doing* here?

"*Africans! Why?*"

The girl had to wrench her sweating hand away from that paralyzing grip, "You m-mean—" The older woman rose up and laid her hands on the other's shoulders, her voice a whisper: "Don't even try. There is no answer. There're books and words and stats, but there's no answer. They shouldn't be here. I'm shocking you. They know it and we know it. It's impossible. We can't go back, can never undo it, can't escape it. Living corpses: Our lives were ruined before we were born. I'm talking about *ours*, let alone theirs. I will not, you must not dare to talk or write about *theirs*. Not a word." Then, into the girl's ear, the whispered pants. "Ruined ... nothing left but suicide ... or rebellion ... not George Sams, not Leon, Leon's name is Legion—not all of them—*you*—you and *me* ... now—you still want to sleep with me, here, on this bed of rusty nails?"

2:45 A.M.

"Mmm" ... Masai moaned. In the dream his grandmother—Addie Mae Gatewood *née* Perry—was jerking up corners of the carpet looking for dollar bills that Elsa claimed she had hidden there in discharge of her debt to Addie Mae. Addie stooped, swooped, snapped like a whip, a fierce and furious rush and concentration of energy while huge Elsa leaned in the doorway, blocking out the sun. Addie, lean as a knife, galvanic, electric, snorting in a vain attempt to clear her sinuses, rotating on the sharp and African angle of her hips to glare back at Elsa lolling in the doorway with her crazy grin in place.

Then, in his dream, the two women in the shadows of the sunlight were Vivian and Kelly and they, too, were glaring. Their eyes were actually almost walleyed with passion, goggle-eyed and gleaming with rage or lust, in the sunlit shadows of the hot closeness of the Louisiana day. In the dream, the two women were four women were two women.

"*Bite!*" Elsa was calling out for Addie, calling her "Bite," for unknown reasons, striding up the red dirt of Turner Avenue carrying a great mound of pecans wrapped in an old table cloth on her head.

"Bite!"

"*Vivian!*" Another cry—Leonora's, Vivian's mother—hoarse and sobbing, fighting for space with the cry in the dream:

"*Bite!*" "*Vivian!*" the combination, of the two struggling inside and outside of his dream for articulation, made Masai moan.

3:02 A.M.

Leonora dreamed she was in the barn, again. Hot hay. Cowsweat and haybugs; straw filtering through the yellow dustheavy spills of sunlight. Sweatwater running down her body and her bowels trembling, her pulse pounding—deaf and blind until someone blocked the light, filled the door, shut the door, cleared his throat—"Oh, dear God, *Vivian!*"

3:03 A.M.

"*Vivian!*"

Mother, Vivian thought, I should go and sponge her, and myself, too, this beastly heat, this bloody change of life, she thought, and kicked off the sheet. There was some moonlight, but the girl asleep on the floor was lost in shadows. She waited for Leonora to call out again, thinking the girl, Mother, Masai, they're all scared to death of me.

Nothing, and nothing outside on the Green, no sirens or dogs or drunken students or black kids high on the latest junk. She spread her legs and arms so as to pick up any currents of air. Dead calm and not a sound: her mind's ear and its eye moved out across the Green and the three churches, through the courtyards past the Law School and on to the silent graveyard under the arch ("THE DEAD SHALL RISE"), pausing there to breathe in the sullen marble-reflected avenues of gravestones (Buckley and Bush and Blake and Angleton and all the mighty Yale dead; her grandfather and her mother's grandfather, then a turn and the black marble of her father in the sour moonlight, HENRY WILSON BATTLE III B. 1893 – D. 1950; LOVING HUSBAND OF LEONORA AND FATHER OF VIVIAN).

Dear drunk daddy, she thought, "Horseman, pass by," and brought her mind's eye and ear home to the sweltering and silent house, waiting for her mother to cry out into the night again, wanting her to break the suffocating silence. Then, against her will, her feverish body was transported and spread naked on the black nightcool marble, shivering, her buttocks and breasts hard—"Horseman, pass by."

Vivian sat up and put her feet on the floor; she was of two minds. The empty Green. The Church of the Regicides tolled the quarter hour, then the others a fraction later as always, then the silence again. The "gangbangers," she thought (searching for another word as she always did, settling for "youth") the black youth from Projectville on the television talk show telling the moderator that the New Haven Bloods made it a practice to pick out their own coffins. Then, in the night, the word came back to her—"Niggers."

3:03 A.M.

Kelly woke when the old woman called out for Vivian. "Heat rises," echoed through her head. She rubbed her cheek against the Irish quilt on the floor, and grasped in the darkness for the remnants of her dream about her psychotherapist, Dr. Irving: his office, brown and dark, and she lying on the couch asleep; powerless, unable to wake up and knowing that even if she could wake she would be incapable of sitting up.

The bedsprings creaked above her. She opened her eyes again as Vivian sat up and put her feet down on the floor. Was she getting out of bed to go to the lavatory? If she does I'll follow her and urinate, Kelly thought.

The pale feet on the floor did not move. Is she checking up on me? Is she sneaking up to be with Masai? Go on, I'm not stopping you. My sole and exclusive interest in helping with the research for this book is my belief in the fact that we should all contribute what we can of our time, money and skills for worthwhile social projects such as a serious history book of modern African-American history. And you are at liberty to conduct your own relationship with Masai, day or night, with or without me, personal or professional. I am not your jailer, Ms. Battle, not your judge, anymore than I am your slave, or my father's, or Dr. Irving's, or, for that matter, Masai's! I am no one's slave and no one is my slave! "As I would not be a slave so I would not be a slaveholder." Full stop. I am not interested at all in anything but complete equality. I do not desire to be over anyone or under anyone. What other people do is their business, and I do not stick my nose in other people's business, nor do I want theirs in mine. I believe in the fundamental, constitutional right of privacy. I am not an object. My body belongs to me. Her body belongs to her. His body belongs to him. You can't scare me, you can't make me run away. So go, go on, go ahead, go to him, go, go, go!

The bedsprings made contact again, in the silence, and the moon-colored feet swung up out of sight.

$\mathcal{S}$EPTEMBER 1990

Date: 9/9/90

To: DIRECTOR, FBI

From: SAC, NEW HAVEN

Subject: NATIONAL SECURITY
TERRORISM

The below material is derived from a CONFIDENTIAL SOURCE and must be maintained only in Headquarters cities and SEAT OF GOVERNMENT and is not to be transmitted to Resident Agencies.

Subjects identified as LEON HURLEY HOWARD a.k.a. "Masai," a male Negro born 2/11/41, Baton Rouge, LA. and VIVIAN NORTON BATTLE. Howard is a former member of the BLACK PANTHER PARTY. Battle is Howard's unindicted co-conspirator in the 1970 instant case: *#C 371458: United States v. The Black Panther Party.*

C.I. REPORT

HOWARD: (unclear) changes. I need to use a (unclear) of the parlor for all the first draft (unclear) by the end of the year (unclear) she can move in to the (unclear) and sleep up there.

BATTLE: She can sleep in a guest room (unclear) the point is what her father will say.

HOWARD:	Can you talk to him?
BATTLE:	What would I say to him?
HOWARD:	You asking me?
BATTLE:	(unclear) an unpaid research project (unclear) shit storm coming (unclear) school.
HOWARD:	She's going back to school.
BATTLE:	When?
HOWARD:	When I finish.
BATTLE:	Leon, let me help you.
HOWARD:	Alright. Call him.
BATTLE:	Alright (unclear) can't we go to Maine to cool off?
HOWARD:	I can't work anywhere but here, for now, you go up there.
BATTLE:	I'll work with you here. Allen Ginsberg's in town to read poetry at Yale.
HOWARD:	(unclear)
BATTLE:	He called. He would like to see you. Should I have him over for dinner or just—
HOWARD:	Just say no.

BUY U.S. SAVINGS BONDS REGULARLY ON THE PAYROLL SAVINGS PLAN

1974

Comrade,

   Thanks for the books. The trial sections are sharp and the bio on Charles Garry—"When the Fix Is Equal, Justice Prevails." Right on.
   Relating to your last visit and our discussion puts me in mind of what my grandmother (Addie Mae Gatewood/Perry) used to tell me about how "it used to be," and how she would catch the bus on Lee Street to go to work and how they would have to stand even though there were plenty of empty seats in the white section. With their feet and backs hurting after work riding home. So one day when the driver cursed her she gave him the sharp side of her tongue and this cracker pulled his gun on her (they all carried guns) and ordered her back into the nigger section of the bus "or else." Granny told how she told the driver "Go ahead and shoot me then" and sat in front until they came and carried her off to jail. After that she moved "up north" to Flagstaff, Arizona for a few years, until the climate got the

better of her, but there _is_ a point here relating to our conversation.

Thinkers today would call the bus driver and his gun "Violent," and they would say that Addie Mae was "Non-violent" because she simply claimed her rights and waited peacefully for the bulls to come and arrest her. You would say that Addie Mae was ready to die for a principle but not to _kill_ for it and was therefore non-violent.

First thing, there wasn't any "principle" in it. Addie was rebelling in the most concrete way possible. She was so _violently_ mad that she was ready to kill that cracker--if she could have--even if she had to _die_ for it. She simply lacked a weapon or I should say the _idea_ of a weapon or of systematic, planned violence. No, she was thrown back on her magnificent instincts and her cosmic rage. Now if it happened ten or twelve years later and there had been a gang of ministers there ready to pray and sing over that act of rebellion and claim Addie for the cause of Christian non-violence, then she would have become a famous "freedom fighter" of the Church and the State, instead of which that burst of murderous anger settled in her hip and she stalked off "up North" to Flagstaff, Ariz. She walked out of Louisiana singing loud--"The Sign of the Fire by Night"!

Elsa--I never did know her last name in all the years she used to come to the house, when Granny was working for the Oppenheimers—used to come along Turner Avenue with a big bundle of pecans wrapped up in a cloth on her head. Elsa was big and strong (maybe six feet and two-fifty) and she stuck up strong against the empty field, stepping along and singing out "<u>Bite</u>!" For some reason Elsa always referred to Addie as "Bite." So, Elsa would come around and pick up all the pecans in the yard, then she'd come in the house near dinner time so that Addie would have to feed her. They would eat standing up in the servants' kitchen, and I'd be there on my school dinner break sitting at that old linoleum table while the two of them yelled and fought over me.

The dialectic of their fight was whether or not "colored folk is treated better in Chicago," as Elsa claimed her daughter could prove, or, as Addie swore, "Leon, you listen to me, son. I've <u>lived</u> in the North, I've lived in Flagstaff, Arizona--huh-uh, girl, don't cut me off, now--I've lived in the North and they treat you the same all over--let me talk--that's how come I came back to this little old town, because it's no different in Chicago or—I said, don't cut me off, girl--Leon, they will do you the same way in Chicago as they will right here. If you try to stand up they will put you <u>under</u> the jail, boy, or carry you off to Pineville and <u>chain</u> you up--wait a minute, I'm talking now--don't come round here trying to tell this boy what your daughter said, and don't come round here right around dinner time cause I got my work to do--here, stand over here so I can clear this table--let this boy eat his dinner, now, he's got to get back to school to get his education, that's the only chance he's got to lift himself up because going to Chicago don't mean nothin, you got to take care of yourself! Huh-uh, don't say a word, child, that's why when my foot hits the street I don't wear no tennis shoes, nooo, child, I dresses up even if I'm only going to church and I've got some <u>change</u> in my pocket, honey, and I wear some high heel shoes!"

Then she and Elsa would hang onto each other and laugh till they cried. But you get the point. In all her stories and songs Addie was really only trying to teach me that I was going to have to fight my way out, <u>outside</u> of the system, and that's why she carried me to the wrestling matches at Mike Mule's Arena (but that's a story for another time).

I've been thinking about what you said about my writing a book about Addie Mae and those days, but I have to deal with the here and now if I write anything, and bury my history into the history of the masses. I don't want to look back unless it's to pick up a fact (like you would an axe) to chop your way forward.

AFTER SUPPER

I have my multi dictionary here (thanks) and it tells me that the original Greek <u>Agon</u> or "trial of strength" is the common ancestor of our "trial" system of law along with the "sport" of wrestling, boxing etc. where the antagonists struggled for victory (because "Victory" is the aim of the struggle or the trial, and <u>not "Justice"</u>). In any political trial the State must claim victory and it always does except where the "fix is equal." The Power of the State is irresistible except for the power of the people. The way you "fix" the legal process is by introducing popular power ("judicious indignation") into the courtroom, the jury room, the media, etc. This process is vulgar as hell and to get your hands on the dynamics of what happened in all those political trials we won and the few, like mine, that we lost you need to have gone to Mike Mule's Arena on Wednesday nights with Addie Mae Gatewood.

You start off walking right after supper, first dark, up Lee Street through what we used to call the "Quarter." Poor as it was, dingy and shadowy and cheap as it was, Lee Street was full of life. Full of life. Walk on past the shine stands and the barber shops and the beauty parlors and notions shops (can anybody tell me why the American Black is the cleanest and most compulsively groomed and shined and shaved pauper in the world? And especially in the South where Addie made sixty dollars a month in those days of the late '40s).

Through the rough R & B from the juke joints bouncing off the street, Granny greeting old acquaintances as she stalked along with me trotting behind until we reached the snow cone stand and stopped to buy a paper dish filled with strawberry-colored crushed ice. Sweet and cold. Then we were there, Mike Mule's Arena! Lord have mercy.

Mike Mule's Arena was a sprawling ramshackle

old firetrap, covered in front with thirty years of wrestling posters, with separate entrances for Colored and White (like every other facility of that time), and Mike Mule, himself, stood right in front on the sidewalk in his suspenders and panama hat with a stump of a stogie clamped in his iron jaws, heavyset in his 60s (that was old then), nodding his head in a set smile (I looked up to him then, now I see he could have been Adolf Eichmann standing smiling the way they did, at the entrance to a concentration camp, smiling and nodding and barking out "Right--Left--Right").

Anyway, we'd go into the hollow echo and peanut smell and sweat of the hall and climb up to the Nigger Section. The excitement. Old and young were as high as for a Super Bowl today, and down below the white people, too, just as high, and most all of them working class or lower. Then, clang!, the old fire bell rang and Ben Levy (a fireman, himself) shuffled into the ring and the light in the hall went down and the limelight covered the ring and five hundred true believers leaned forward in an act of faith.

"Ladies and Gentlemen, the first match of the evening, with a 30-minute time limit, from Norman, Oklahoma, weighing 203 pounds--Chief Little Beaver! And from Brooklyn, New York, weighing 211 pounds, Angelo Cistoli!"

Before we get carried away here trying to be Ernest Hemingway, let me make the point about the fix being equal in the courtroom and how that fix allowed for some alternative to

EVERY THIRD HOUSE

violence. Alright--you know that all the matches at Mike Mule's were fixed, as they are everywhere up to this minute, and everyone in the audience knew then, as they do now, that the matches were fixed, that those big burly men wrestled in a different town every night of the week and then after all the grunting and groaning they would be seen at the best Bar and Grill in town eating big steaks together. But here is the point: we knew but we suspended our disbelief exactly as you would watching <u>Hamlet</u>, we knew and we didn't know; to the wrestling audience this is not a Sport it is Theater, it is Drama and secretly it is life and death politics.

When Leroy "Jack" McGurk (who had been a college champion and was not fat and could actually wrestle in the Greek style, and could have been a great champion if it had been a sport), when he triumphed over that greaseball of evil incarnate, Juan Humberto (from Mexico City, Mexico, at a sleek 220 pounds of rippling muscle and grease with slick black hair and a scarred face, looking like Anthony Quinn), we, up in the nigger section were in heaven because the clean white hard-muscled gladiator Jack McGurk had vanquished the dark and dirty Mexican--for us!

Jack McGurk the All-American Boy was our white hope, our champion in the morality play of good and evil. These things have to be fixed so that Good can win, <u>every time</u>. There is no place for chance in art or a lumpenproletariat art form like modern American wrestling, because there has to always be a place, one place (now on TV), where there is *justice*; where the man who has been savaging the hero (biting and gouging and strangling and cutting and garlic and tape and, once, the Green Mask pulled out a bottle of knockout drops and Addie Mae had to be held back), destroying our hero--while the blind Ben Levy, the referee, saw nothing and never heard our howls of pity and outrage--where this monster would at the last moment of moral and physical anguish be, himself, overthrown and quickly counted out.

The Educated Class--Left or Right--watches this spectacle in the arena, shakes its head and pronounces the fixed and obviously faked events as the extreme of mass False Consciousness in America. But I can show you why that judgement misses the point. The Proletariat and the lumpenproletariat want something that is a combination of Justice and Revenge. They want an election, they want a trial, they want a wrestling match, and in a Democracy the underdog must always seem to win; the hero is not a Caesarean lion devouring a helpless Christian, the hero is an abused and battered victim of villainous dirty tricks who pulls himself up off the mat, and with the transported and invincible crowd climbing out of their seats with their eyes and mouths torn open in one unbroken and terrific roar of anguish and triumph our ruined champion brushes aside the suddenly vigilant referee and confronts Evil! Evil begging, pleading for mercy from the Avenger, from us, the crowd, but no, this is not a Greek tragedy, there's no pity here because this <u>is</u> an American tragedy, and when the moment of truth comes there can be no pity, no thought of pity, but our champion, just to be sure, turns to the audience open handed, while Evil grovels, and we (We, not Caesar), we cry out Evil's doom, and Good turns on the sub-human monster at his feet and drags the thing up on its legs and Good smashes Evil to the canvas (pretends to, no man could live through such a beating one night much less <u>every </u>night) over and over and over again, then Falls on him for the count. The bell clangs, the winner's arm is raised, the hall lights come back on, the big wrestlers in their shiny silk robes wave and chat as they walk back to their dank dressing rooms--and we, we the judge and jury, the life blood of the winner, we are spent, exhausted, revenged, and saved. We can go home now.

You say that the Ruling Class uses precisely such "two party" spectacles and rituals as a counter-revolutionary hypnosis so as to keep the Masses in a permanent and passive trance. That is only partly true and must, also, be placed in context. The problem is that the "we" who watch and weep in this arena, we know, too, that it is a fake! Yes! The Masses know it as well as the Ruling Class, and what's more, in the same repressed way we know that Mike Mule's Arena is a house of illusion, we also know that the White House and the Supreme Court and the Pentagon are too! You don't know that, but we do. But we know that only in <u>our</u> house of dreams is the violence <u>faked</u>. Because there the fix is in for <u>us</u>. But in all the official arenas of the State the violence is <u>real</u> and we are the unrisen underdog and canon fodder without end. But the Educated Class can't see the absolute hoax of the State, the Academy, the Party, the Church, etc. as they can so exactly see through Mike Mule and the wrestling ritual. Only the Ruling Class and the Masses know that it's all fake, from top to bottom. But the retribution and violence for challenging this official hoax is real and terrible--so the Masses strike a silent bargain with the State: the two extremes on the social scale conspire not to reveal to the middle and educated classes the absolute lies on which their happy lives are all based.

You know only too well what happens when the zombie wakes up. In our arrest and trial it was not black man and white woman sex that brought on the legal circus, not even the spectacle of Kissinger and Rockefeller "at risk," and not just your money and name alone. It was the <u>combination</u> of the Ivy League Debutante and the Nigger, in bed together <u>politically</u>! That was too much. Too much for the State and too much for the jurors, White and Black, whose counterparts had been pardoning Black Panthers who <u>had</u> broken the "Law" across the country. If we had been in the courtroom chained together we would have won, no question about it, but with you an "unindicted co-conspirator" and media victim, we never had a chance. You understand, don't you, that if we <u>had</u> been guilty, <u>had</u> kidnapped Kissinger, and <u>had</u> been tried together in chains then we <u>would</u> have had a real chance, an overwhelming probability of a hung jury (not that they would ever have let us go)!

Shall I take pity on the poor pig who has to read all this and wind it up? We who sit in the Nigger Section and the prisoner's dock--not in the jury box--we know all about the invisible violence behind the black robes and the flag and the documents and all the emblems of State and Church, and out of this fear that dogs us night and day we invent a new identity that can survive with what we hope is a shred of dignity to cover our naked terror and so we hide out in Mike Mule's Arena a.k.a. City Hall and cover our ass with the flag. So the fake violence inside the Arena is a cover for the down-on-one-knee plea for mercy that we, <u>the villain</u>, beg for; & this spectacle inside the arena in conjunction with the scenario outside--Law and Order--completely mistakes the relationship of forces between the "individual" and the State and scrambles the brains of the spectators (did I ever tell you about how the police when they used to stop us to frisk us up against a police car they would jab you with a pin so that you'd jump and swing out and then the pigs would close in and beat you silly, but remember in the wrestling matches the Bad Guy always rubbed tape or garlic in the Good Guy's eyes until blinded and mad with pain the sleeping giant of virtue awoke to his full powers and showed the villain no mercy, so if you turn the arena and the street on their head then the two spectacles for Good and Evil and Law and Order equal each other and everybody lives and dies in one long RIP of false consciousness in which the idea of Violence and Non-violence are control codes to keep the band playing until the party's over).

Where does all this leave the Black Panther Party? Nowhere because we haven't even <u>begun</u> that discussion, we've just been talking about the <u>context</u> for the discussion, the Idea not the Act much less the <u>Idea</u> of the Act, and I don't believe I could go too much further without boiling all these metaphors down to a scientific historical base & I question whether I have any of the requirements (except the time!) to do that. Maybe you could boil it all <u>up</u>--because you're the poet--when we write our book together?

I think of you. You know what that means. You are the poet.

All Power to the People,

L.

September 1990

Date: 9/30/90

To: DIRECTOR, FBI

From: SAC, NEW HAVEN

Subject: NATIONAL SECURITY, TERRORISM

Information excerpted below was received on date indicated from SOURCE, on activity, Number 8 Chapel Street, New Haven, Connecticut.

LEON HURLEY HOWARD is a convicted Black Panther Party Terrorist.

This airtel must be maintained only in headquarters offices and SEAT OF GOVERNMENT and is not to be transmitted to Resident Agencies.

#2 12:14 pm

A book by Howard will be completed by Christmas. The book (Untitled) will be a manifesto for revolution and terrorism. Howard's secretary KELLY BAILEY has taken up residence at the above address in order to work at night according to Source. Bailey's father, RANDOLPH K. BAILEY, ESQ. 1100 Commonwealth Avenue, Boston, Massachusetts, is in contact with the SAC in the Boston area. Mr. Bailey is very concerned about his daughter and wants the Bureau to approach VIVIAN N. BATTLE to urge Bailey's daughter to return home for the summer holiday. Bailey is also concerned that his daughter may be sexually involved with Howard or Battle or both. According to Source in London, Battle had a homosexual affair in England sometime in the 1970s.

BUY U.S. SAVINGS BONDS REGULARLY ON THE PAYROLL SAVINGS PLAN.

1972

Leon,

Here, through David, is some rough draft of the <u>Faust</u> play. I need your help and criticism, obviously, and doubt whether I should even pursue it. Right now, it's therapy, and I could work on it in London, if we go. Or I could go back and talk to J.W. about real therapy, whatever that is, I don't know, I've gone a little mad here.

THE CHARACTER OF DR. SOOKERMAN YOU WILL RECOGNIZE AS A CRUDE COMPOSITE OF ERIK AND DR. COHN, WHO HELPED SET UP THE PANTHER FREE CLINIC HERE. I LOVED THAT OLD RED. HE DIED LAST MONTH, UP IN HIS EIGHTIES. HE GOT REDDER AS HE GOT OLDER. LIKE ERIK SAYS, "PERSISTENCE OF STYLE," HE HAD IT. I HOPE I DO. When I went off the deep end last year after you were gone, Dr. Cohn looked me right in the eye and told me, "People who belong together—need not be glued together." That helped for a while.

        ARISE YE PRISONERS OF
        STARVATION,

          V.

September 1990

TO KELLY BITCH BAILEY--

  LISTEN BITCH KEEP YOUR WHITE HOOKS OFF OF BLACK MEN! IF WE CATCH YOU EVEN NEAR A FINE BLACK STUD LIKE MASAI HOWARD WE IS GONNA CUT YOU UP SOMETHIN TURRIBLE!

                            POWER TO THE PEOPLE,

                            A SOUL SISTER

October 1990

The first of the steeple clocks in the church on the Green tolled three. The sound of the bells and the clear sunlight poured over the bowed heads of Masai, Vivian and Kelly as they searched and read through mounds of documents piled right across the three tables that now stretched the length of the nineteenth-century formal parlor. The old woman sleeping in the corner snored softly.

"Here's something for the oral history section," Kelly said. Masai and Vivian looked up. Everybody felt relief after the long summer heat. Vivian turned to gaze out the window, "It's a beautiful day." Sirens registered in the distance, rising. The girl stepped over two boxes of Xerox to look. Vivian and Masai watched her frame herself in the yellow parallelogram of the sun window. "They're not coming for you, Baby Face Kelly," the poet's voice was not unkind.

"Help!" They all turned their heads to stare at Leonora for a moment. She stared back, then her eyes closed again and her head sank.

"What?" Kelly asked. "They're not coming for us," Vivian repeated. "I know," Kelly looked at Masai. The sirens passed. Kelly turned back toward her work. "No one is concerned about us," Vivian said softly, and the three bowed their heads again.

"Please don't lock me in here!" The old woman's voice was pitched to the level of the diminishing sirens. "My jailer," Vivian took off her glasses and rubbed her eyes and forehead. Masai rose and moved around the edge of the room to Leonora's chair. She did not look up at him. He guided her chair around the periphery to the window. His voice was kind. Like a father, like a mother. "Alright. You're safe." Kelly and Vivian were watching him when he looked over at them. "They're going to Projectville."

"The gangs?" Kelly met his eyes. Vivian broke in, "You mean Masai's children?" They both looked at her now. "No, they're not afraid of your big black book." Masai looked out the window, the old woman stared down at his feet. Vivian waited until the girl looked at her, then she said, "White people know that black people know that white people know."

"I know," the student's eyes clouded, "b-but I never turned in his, n-never turned in your name to the government, to the, uh, Census …"

They studied her pink-and-white confusion. Masai chuckled. "I don't exist?"

Kelly shook her head. Vivian snorted, "You're a sampling error," she turned to the student with a shrug, but still not unkindly, "So you broke a law." Then she sang a resonant phrase from Brecht, "First do something wrong and you'll survive!"

Kelly tried a smile, "I don't know why I didn't turn in your form— I mean, they know where you are. I mean …" She shook her head and put one hand on her breast as if making a sign of remorse. They watched her. The old woman was looking out the window again, toward the Green.

Masai leaned forward and spoke in a low tone: "You still go in there to the office every week?"

"The Census Office? … I still have to check the printout from my team's, uh, you know, from all the, uh …"

"Alright. Next time you go in there, check out something for me on the seventh floor."

"Sure. Sure."

"Seventh floor is the Department of Justice section for New Haven. Go in there and get me a copy of a program called 'Weed and Seed.'"

"W-weed and Seed? W-will the they let me, uh ..."

"Tell them that you're what you are, a Yale student working on an urban study ... tell them anything you want to. I need it for the last chapter. It's not a classified document."

"Why don't we all march down there and get a copy"—Vivian's voice began to crackle with the gallows humor that made Kelly want to laugh and cry at the same time— "We're taxpayers, in theory, some of us are on the Census rolls, sorry, wait a minute, we could take mother with us—alright, alright, what is 'Weed and Seed?'"

"It's the White House crime plan for the cities."

"Ahhh—counterinsurgency, COINTELPRO redux."

Masai nodded, then they both nodded and turned back to the student. They watched her. She looked down at her hands on the table, "I'll try." Vivian hummed something more from Brecht, "But the one who gets screwed will be you," but her smile was wide and warm and that made Kelly smile and that left Masai looking at their big smiles. He sniffed and jerked his head at Kelly's pile of documents, "Next."

"Umm, *The United States* v. *Leon Hurley Howard a.k.a. 'Masai.'*"

"No," said Leon, "Next."

"Wait," said Vivian, still smiling, "Our case has to go into this Marxist detective story of yours." He shook his head slowly. "Why not?" Vivian's voice flicked out.

"Nothing personal."

"Nothing personal?!" She gave a rare whoop of joyous laughter, Kelly topped that, dissolving with the shared happiness as Masai shook with silent mirth. They laughed, recovered, broke again, until Masai's voice laid down the law, "That's enough. Next."

Vivian's eyes still shone, "Slave driver," she said. He grinned. "Next." Kelly picked up the document next in order. "It's an old newspaper clipping," she scanned it quickly. The old woman spoke softly, "Vivian." Kelly's mouth was open. They watched her face drain, leaving her freckles stranded in midair. She stood up and walked out slowly. Vivian followed her. "Vivian," her mother moaned.

113

DONALD FREED

"She'll be back," Masai tried to pitch his voice for the old woman's sake, "Right back." He glanced down at the document that had driven Kelly out of the parlor.

"Please don't hurt me," Vivian's mother whispered from her corner by the window. Masai looked at her. She was a black dot against the bright window. He went over to her. "Hurt you?" he said, and sat down on the window seat, next to her, and touched her shawl as if to adjust it.

Leonora suddenly clutched his big hand and raised it to her lips to kiss. He felt his legs turn to water and his mouth hung open. She kept kissing his hand, then she stopped and looked up at him, then she let go and his hand just stayed there poised in midair, until he regained volition and moved the hand up to touch her thin white hair. The pale blue eyes looked up at him. Helpless.

"No one's going to hurt you," he whispered. Then, as if with perfect logic, he began to read to her from the document in his other hand, in the way he might have read a bedtime story or a fable to a child. Stroked her hair and read.

NEGRO J. H. BURNT BY CROWD AT ELLISTOWN

This evening at 7:40 P.M., J.H. was tortured with a red-hot iron bar, then burnt ... a crowd of more than 2,000 people ... many women and children were present at the incineration ... after the Negro had been bound and a fire was kindled. A little further away another fire was kindled in which an iron bar was placed. When it was red hot, a man took it and applied it to the Black's body. The latter, terrified, seized the iron with his hands, and the air was immediately filled with the smell of burning flesh ...

"*Vivian.*" Masai looked up, Leonora was staring at Vivian and Kelly standing in the archway listening. Masai looked at them. "Mother, you listen," Vivian said and looked into Masai's eyes.

The red hot iron having been applied to several parts of his body, his shouts and groans were heard as far away as in the town. After several minutes of torture, masked men poured petrol on him and set fire to the stake. The flames rose and enveloped the Negro who implored to be finished off with a shot. His supplications provoked shouts of derision. ... *Chattanooga Times*, February 12, 1918

Masai put the paper down. He stared out at the Green. The church bells chimed and Leonora screamed for Vivian. Everyone moved at once. Kelly came into the room, Vivian wheeled Leonora out, Masai turned back to the table.

"Masai, I'm sorry, I—"

"I don't think you should work on this book anymore."

"Please, I want to, it's the most—"

"I don't think you can stand it."

"Please, I'm a trained social scientist."

Vivian stood in the archway again. *Madama Butterfly* played again from Leonora's room. Masai looked back at the student, "You've been trained?"

"Yes."

"By experts?"

"Oh, yes."

"Leon," Vivian said.

"But yet and still." He kept looking at Kelly.

"Beg pardon?"

"Yet and still—you have become a traitor to your trainers, right?"

"Leon, let the girl go if she—"

"I want her to go."

Kelly began to hop around the table between the two of them, like a child, "Please, please, no! This book, the two of you, the three of us—"

"*Vivian!*" Leonora screamed from inside the house. Vivian whooped again, "And a cast of millions!" Kelly laughed and cried at the same time, "I love the two of you and this book so much!" She pulled a Kleenex out of her cords and started to mop up her face. In the silence they watched her. Masai kept his voice soft.

"You see a therapist?"

"... Off and on."

"Now and then." He smiled a little. "Yet and still ... Alright, I'm going to give you one more chance." He dug through a pile until he found a document and handed it to her, and sat down. "Sit down," he spoke to Vivian without looking at her. Vivian sat. Kelly tried to read the document.

> 15,000 people, men, women and children, applauded when petrol was poured over the Negro and the fire lit. They struggled, shouted, and pushed one another to get nearer the Black ... Two of them cut off his ears while the fire began to roast him. Another tried to cut off his heels ... The crowd surged and changed places so that every one could see the Negro burn. When the flesh was entirely burnt, the bones laid bare and what had been a human being was but a smoking and deformed rag curling up in the flames, everyone was still there to look. *Memphis Press*, May 22, 1917

Silence. Not looking. "She didn't vomit," Masai said. "You may stay." "Thank you," Kelly said, still shaking.

"Don't cry now," Masai looked at her, "you'll get used to it. Then, like Norman Mailer said—you'll get bored."

"No."

"She's outraged," Vivian said, "*En*raged."

"Yes!"

"You want Justice?"

"Yes."

"She wants Justice.—Teach her. She's ready, Leon."

"I'm not your slave. You do your own dirty work, Miss Ann." Masai turned back to his documents. The poet walked to the window, stared out at the Green. Kelly waited. Vivian talked, still looking out at the Green, "... The white trash—that lynched that unnamed black man in Memphis in 1915 or whenever it was—"

"1917."

"Those red neck, wool hat cowards, that whole lynch mob ..." Vivian stopped. She stared out, then she slowly turned to look at the student. Kelly's eyes were red and big again. "What?" she breathed.

"They're all, ah, 'Gone with the Wind' ... you understand?"

"Gone, uh, w-with the—"

"So you cannot save that black man. So you vomit. Because you cannot now, in abstentia or in effigy, kill—I said kill—make dead that whole 1917 Memphis mob.—Yes or no?"

"No." Kelly winced, Vivian's voice was drawing blood.

"No. Because they are already dead—and rotten." Masai looked up, the tail end of the whip of her voice had grazed his face. "Dead and rotten," she hissed; "and gone to judgement," he muttered over her whisper.

"Do you understand a word of this?" Vivian sat and faced her. "No. Yes. I don't know," Kelly looked only at Vivian.

"Yes. She's nodding yes. I am talking about why people make a revolution. Make it or go mad. Understand? ... The revolution begins when you assassinate Henry Kissinger or Governor Rockefeller or President Bush. True?—Yes or no!"

"No."

"Why not?" Masai's voice was like a hot breath on her cheek, but she only looked at Vivian. "Because." "It's just vengeance?" the poet half whispered to the student.

"Yes," Kelly mouthed the word.

"Just murder?" Masai said.

"Yes."

The poet leaned in close to Kelly's face, only their lips moved: "Madness!"

"Yes."

Masai watched them, their heads almost touching, kissing—Vivian's voice soft now, "That's why we didn't do it. Because you have to be mad to hope for justice in this world." She touched the girl's hair and brow, "Go out now, in the air, out of here. Breathe. Both of you—go out."

"B-but the book—no, wait, in the book, Masai, you say that you wrote that the, uh, the—I'm paraphrasing—the Negroes that were lynched, South and North, were, very often, not really suspected rapists, etc., uh, but, uh—the brightest and the best, the natural leaders who would, some day …" Winded like a sprinter, "The book …" She tried to start again.

"The 'book.' Leon, tell this child what Chairman Mao said about the 'book.'" She angled her head to look at Masai. They locked eyes. Masai spat out the words to Vivian instead of Kelly. "Chairman Mao said that a revolution is not writing a book, or painting a picture … A revolution is an insurrection, an act of violence …"

Kelly watched the two of them. Why were their eyes sad? Kelly sighed. "Then wh-who-who-who should we kill?"

They looked at her. Masai snorted, then they began to laugh hard. Kelly's eyes opened, Vivian doubled over whooping, hanging onto the girl's shoulder, Masai staggered over booming and leaned on her other shoulder so that he and Vivian stood over her embracing her as if she were their child and she looked up at them and laughed with joy. They laughed a long time, then they subsided, but no one moved away from the embrace or spoke until the student reached out and picked up a handful of old leaflets. "All these leaflets …"

Masai and Vivian looked down at the table and picked up some of the leaflets, too. The poet let the leaflets fall like leaves from her hand, down into a box on the floor, as if into an open grave, "Mm—all these buttons; 'Free Huey,' 'Free Bobby,' 'Free Masai' …" letting the buttons and badges drop into the box like stones. A church on the Green began to intone five o'clock.

Masai dropped a badge. "Power to the People."

"Malcolm Lives."

"What happened?" Kelly spoke as the badges fell.

"We Shall Overcome."

"Power comes out of the barrel—"

Kelly reached out and held their hands. "But what happened?" They looked down at her. She held onto their hands—one black, one white—and her body, herself, the medium connecting the two.

Vivian's long fingers played across her lips and chin, "Happened to America? To us? ... There was an informer. An *agent provocateur*. She looked just like you."

The student's jaw dropped, again. She looked over at Masai. He nodded. "A green-eyed monster..." Kelly's head drooped. "My God!" she whispered. Vivian nodded, "Mm. Never trust anyone under thirty." The room was filling up with the golden light of late afternoon. "This book—" Kelly started. "Is another book," Vivian finished.

"No," the girl said. She let go of their hands. Masai stepped to the window. "Oh," Vivian said, "You mean someone is waiting for this book?"

"Yes."

"Who?"

Kelly's color was high again, "The, uh, the, uh, the students, uh, the progressives—"

"The niggers." Masai's voice bounced off the window. "Oh," said Vivian, "the niggers over in Projectville?" Masai turned into the room, "The 'niggers under the mud.'"

Vivian started for the door, talking. "The niggers under the mud—to use the ancient idiom—not the niggers in Projectville who can't read—metaphysical niggers in your Big Black Book—"

The student stood up, "Vivian—"

"They've been waiting, along with the FBI, everybody waiting for—"

"W-waiting for Masai!" Kelly stood, trembling slightly, between Vivian and Masai.

"Why?" Vivian breathed the question.

Kelly backed away, closer to Masai. Frightened, brave. "Because Mao was wrong. A book—c-can be a revolutionary act."

Vivian looked at them. "Can it?"

Masai put his hand on the student's shoulder. His voice was formal sounding, again, "That's why they torture poets."

"Is it?" Vivian surveyed the room, its volumes and boxes of documents, the table covered with the abstractions of time gone. Her eyes were liquid. "Well," she sighed, "all power to the imagination." They looked at her. She took in the remains on the table, smiled, turned away, walked out singing—"Where have all the flowers gone/long time passing/where have all the flowers gone/long time ago ..."

July 1970

QUESTION: THE STATE: Now, Mr. Howard, you heard the testimony of George Sams?

ANSWER: Yes.

QUESTION: Did Mr. Sams, in fact, come to the home of Vivian Battle on the night of August 11, 1969, as he testified?

ANSWER: He was there.

QUESTION: Yes he was. He was there as your security guard, was he not?

ANSWER: No.

QUESTION: Well, then, in what capacity was he there?

ANSWER: As an agent of the FBI.

THE COURT: No outburst. You've heard the order.

QUESTION: At what time did George Sams arrive at the—by the way, were you living in the Battle home at that time?

ANSWER: No.

QUESTION: Alright, at what time did Sams, Mr. Sams, arrive at the Battle home?

ANSWER: Late.

QUESTION: Ten o'clock at night, eleven, midnight?

ANSWER: Near midnight.

QUESTION: Alright. Now, who was present when Mr. Sams arrived?

ANSWER:	Myself and Vivian Battle, Dr. Ahmeen, Ali, and Susan Petty, if that was her name.
QUESTION:	Was Dr. Ali teaching at Yale at that time?
ANSWER:	Right.
QUESTION:	And who was Susan Petty?
ANSWER:	An agent-provocateur for the FBI.
THE COURT:	Bailiff, maintain order. Order.
QUESTION:	Isn't it a fact that both you and Dr. Ali were having intimate relations with Miss Petty?
THE DEFENSE:	Objection, your Honor, Susan Petty is going to be a witness for the prosecution and at that time we intend to expose her as acting under orders of the Federal Bureau of Investigation.
THE STATE:	Your Honor, Mr. Garry knows that Susan Petty has been missing since February of this year and that she may have been murdered to prevent her from testifying here in this case.
THE DEFENSE:	Mistrial! I ask for a mistrial. Your Honor, this is outrageous—
THE COURT:	Bailiff, clear the courtroom. Adjourned until 2:30. I will see counsel in chambers.

May 1973

London is rain, rain is London. But Dublin is worse. I went over with Mother to sell or trade a townhouse there, I don't know which, as I took a wee drink to keep the chill of the rain out and the next thing I remember is Mother pushing me into a cab at Heathrow. But I have taken my final revenge on the old witch: I have joined Alcoholics Anonymous U.K. I will never ever take a drink again in this life, thus returning the role of the "Madwoman of New Haven" to its rightful owner: Mother.

A.A. and its "steps" is a fascinating phenomenon, and I was right not to consider psychoanalysis (though that, too, would have been a mortal blow against Mother). Underneath the A.A. rhetoric of God and Guilt there is, actually, an authentic existential credo of choice, responsibility, and finitude ("I suffer from Alcoholism: a progressive, fatal disease"). And the other A.A. people (we meet at the Shaw Library, near Kings Cross) are the very ones that the Left has claimed to speak for, and who were <u>not</u> at any of the New Haven "cells" I tried to set up, or biracial coffee hours, or "Church on the Green Alliance for Justice," etc. I wish I could send this to you and tell you my thoughts on intoxication, sobriety, and revolution.

So, let me change the subject. My condition of permanent hangover should suit my kind of poetry (especially the <u>Electra</u> translation and the <u>Faust in Harlem</u> opera or whatever it is) so I'm going to find a place and give it a fresh try. My problem is whether or not to come back to the States to visit you first, or take a house in Surrey when Mother returns in March. She states that she can now return because she agrees with Mr. Ford that "the long national nightmare" of Nixon and Watergate is over. Incidentally, she says of Ford that he will do, temporarily, because he "studied law at Yale as a poor boy."

Some important people have talked with me about your case, cruel and unusual punishment, etc., and intend to write a letter to the <u>New York Times</u>. This was all started by Harold Pinter, who had read one of your letters from prison published in the <u>Guardian</u>. Mr. Pinter is a rare gentleman. These plays—that people pretend both to understand and not to understand at the same time—are, in my opinion, very great epic poems written in a demotic vocabulary just as Euripides, Luther, and Cervantes, in some degree, revolutionized meaning by changing the idiom of expression from the Ideal to the Real. In this sense, Harold Pinter is far and away the most political and revolutionary poet in the world. But when you get to know him a bit, you discover that he is also political in the ordinary sense, albeit with profound radical sensibilities regarding the "victim and the executioner" and the present-day American Empire. Introduced him to Mother at the opening of a revival of <u>The Caretaker</u> and he read her like a book:

ME:	Mother, may I present the author, Harold Pinter.
H.P.:	How do you do?
MOTHER:	Vivian insisted I come along.
H.P.:	Well.
MOTHER:	Of course, the change has been extraordinary.
ME:	Harold, congratulations on a powerful production.
H.P. (TO MOTHER):	Change?
MOTHER:	What?
ME:	Your direction is impeccable and—
H.P.:	"The change"—you referred to the change.
MOTHER:	Ah, you mean years ago.
H.P.:	Exactly! ... (to me) Excuse me. (exit)

You had to be there. Mother knew that he had her <u>Ancien Régime</u> number. Anyway, he and others want to try to involve some part of the continental literary community to protest your trial and sentence. I think I will wire you this news, by itself, for the authorities to ponder. Yes.

Jimmy Baldwin was here for a PEN meeting and he also was very articulate about your identity as a writer and political prisoner, as is Irish and French PEN in general. Pinter laid on supper after the meeting and Jimmy got off into stories about Satchel Paige, who he claims was Faulkner's equal, at the demotic level, and maybe Shakespeare's, to wit: "You win a few, you lose a few. Some get rained out. But you got to dress for all of them." I have always felt that Mr. Paige translated Homer the best of all with, "Never look back, something may be gaining on you."

(Later)

There is no point in going on with this except that it helps me to pretend I'm communicating with you. A.A. is not enough. What I feel like doing is walking out across Hampstead Heath.

In the '40s, Father was living in Washington working for the war effort as one of Roosevelt's "Dollar-a-year men." I was around five years old and had stayed back in New Haven with Mother. We had a maid named Christina from Sweden. She was much younger than Mother and she cared for me in a way that Mother did not and, I realize now, could not. I helped Christina clean the house and always wanted to take my meals in the kitchen with her, and go to church on Sundays with her. I had terrible nightmares then, and Christina would try to comfort me. And one time my screams had disturbed Mother and she came in and found Christina rocking me in her arms and I was sucking her breast, like a child, which goddamittohell I was! And Mother discharged her on the spot. And I really went berserk then and I only stopped a week later when Mother told me that Christina was dead.

Something in me died with that lie because I knew as a five-year-old that this woman in the fawn robe who was lying to me was quite capable of making Christina dead, making me dead, and that is when I began to bide my time—even as you are doing your time, and my "biding" is not unlike your "doing."

And now, here I am in the rain country. High and dry, an A.A., and still looking for the truth that I found in Christina's rosy breasts. One tit for Poetry you might say, and one for Revolution. But you know what I mean. You, of all people, know what I mean even when I don't know what it is I mean.

Enough! I have to come back to see you. We have decisions to make. With the end of the war and Hoover dead and a Democrat in '76 and Pinter in London and Sartre in Paris ... Listen, my love, I will suck you and you will suck me until the mothersmilk of revolution baptizes us and we are born again!

I love you,

V.

Not, not, <u>not sent</u>: London 5/2/73

July 1970

QUESTION: THE STATE: Now, sir, it's true, isn't it, that you told Special Agent Dumar that George Sams was your bodyguard on the night of August 11, 1969?

ANSWER: LEON H. HOWARD: No.

QUESTION: Have you seen the transcript of your—

ANSWER: I've seen it. It's incomplete. I told them that George Sams came into town on the 10th, the day before, and claimed that he had been ordered by California to provide security to me and Miss Battle because there was supposed to be some kind of death threat.

QUESTION: Against you?

ANSWER: Against both of us.

QUESTION: Death threat from who?

ANSWER: I don't know, he was confused.

QUESTION: But you told him he could stay, didn't you?

ANSWER: I tried to call Oakland, but I couldn't get through to the Central Office.

QUESTION: So you let Mr. Sams provide you with security?

ANSWER: No, I told him to wait until I could talk to Oakland. That was on the 11th, then that night the raid went down.

QUESTION: You were arrested?

ANSWER:	Right.
QUESTION:	Along with Miss Battle, and Dr. Ali, and Miss Petty—
ANSWER:	Right.
QUESTION:	And Mr. Sams. And you never saw George Sams again until he testified in this courtroom?
ANSWER:	Right.
QUESTION:	And why was that?
THE DEFENSE:	Objection! Objection!
ANSWER:	He was segregated because he was a pig!
THE COURT:	Overruled. Order!
THE DEFENSE:	Mistrial, Your Honor! In my thirty years—
THE COURT:	Bailiff, clear this court!

OCTOBER 1990

The Green looked at Leonora. The Green looked in at her through the window. It has been watching me for twenty years, she thought. Behind her, the others moved around the table working. On the Green, the leaves skipped up to the window to peek in at her. In back of her Vivian whispered something to the black man. "Put it in," he said. Put it in, Leonora thought. Then she thought of Ernest Tree.

"Drive out to the Fair Haven house, please, Ernest." Ernest. He was as black and shiny as the new 1925 Packard and there was nothing servile, in the Southern sense, about him and he spoke a clear Northern near-grammatical speech. She felt the tickle in her throat again. Tickle in her throat, tickle in her bladder.

"Ernest?"
"Ma'am."
"Did Mr. Battle say what time he was, ah, returning?"
"Said Thursday."
"Thursday?"
"Yes'm."

Tickle in her throat. Father used to go up to Boston. Grandfather, too. Look at the cows.

"Be careful of the cows."
"Yes ma'am."

"They're a menace. Be careful."
"Yes'm."
"I'm going to report this. Whose are they?"
"Could be Mr. Guinn."
"Guinn. I know that man."
"Yes'm, friend of your grandfather."
"Stop!"
Cowflesh flowing by. Ernest's big black neck. Thick. Cowsmell-passing.
"We're going to be late, Ernest."
"We can go now."
"Mother's waiting."
"Yes ma'am."
"Drive on, now."
Tickle in her bladder.
"Ernest."
"Ma'am?"
"Never mind."

Behind her at the table, Vivian asked the black man, "What about this speech by William Lloyd Garrison?"
"Put it in."

October 1990

Date: 10/3/90

To: DIRECTOR, FBI

From: SAC, NEW HAVEN

Subject: NATIONAL SECURITY, TERRORISM

Information excerpted below was received on date indicated from a CONFIDENTIAL SOURCE. Source reports on KELLY BAILEY, VIVIAN BATTLE, AND LEON HURLEY HOWARD a.k.a. "Masai," of the Black Panther Party.

The BPP is a violence-prone black militant organization formally headquartered in Oakland, California, with chapters located throughout the United States. In the opinion of New Haven the BPP underground chapters are waiting for a signal from Leon Howard to mobilize and launch urban Terror Campaigns.

Information below indicates that BPP covert operation is in process and is indication than the BPP is again organizing.

Subject BAILEY was followed from the Battle residence to the New Haven Federal Building and observed to enter at 11:13 A.M. on 10-1-90. Subject went to the Census Bureau for approximately 30 minutes, then she went to the Department of Justice Division, the same floor as this office.

Subject filled out an application for research material and was provided with a copy of the enclosed document. Subject then entered the lavatory. Subject then returned to the Battle residence.

SAC, Boston reports that subject's father, RANDOLPH BAILEY, wants kidnapping charges filed against Howard and Battle. Mr. Bailey has retained private investigators and intends to turn over to the Bureau their findings. Which he states contain evidence of illegal use of drugs, firearms, explosive devices, and conspiracy to overthrow the government of the United States by force and violence. Mr. Bailey has gathered evidence of "brainwashing" and also claims that his daughter has been turned into a sexual slave to both Howard and Battle. Mr. Bailey was a close associate of the Director FBI until Mr. Hoover's death in 1973.

BUY U.S. SAVINGS BONDS REGULARLY ON THE PAYROLL SAVINGS PLAN.

October 1990

Date: 10/3/90

To: DIRECTOR, FBI

From: SAC, NEW HAVEN

Subject: NATIONAL SECURITY, TERRORISM

WEED AND SEED INITIATIVE
Table of Contents

Introduction	1
Strategies	5
Six-step Implementation Plan	7
Department of Justice Pilot Demonstration Programs	9
President's 1990 Initiative	12
Program Possibilities	14

October 1990

In Masai's dream, the boy hurried along at Addie Mae's side. Each carried a box of groceries.

"Happy Christmas," she said, "Leon's carrying y'all a bird." Mrs. Watson stood in the door, two hundred pounds, the children at her knees. "God bless Miss Perry," she repeated, "Leon, go right in, son," wheeling clockwise with the children in tow so that the boy could edge in sidewise with the box of staples and the goose. Inside was dark and cold.

In the dream, the frost on the vacant lots sparkled in the winter light—shone like tears. His grandmother's high heels picked through the red ruts. He could not get ahead of her, he tried to keep up by walking in her footsteps.

Then they were inside church. The singing braced him, he felt the force around him on all sides. "I am weak, but thou art strong ..." Then the minister led them in a deep-voiced "Sign of the Fire by Night," then the big-necked man was gone.

Then a dog chased him across the lot where, before, he had played baseball with the white boy. He had to stop because the dog made his knees shake so violently that it was impossible for him to move.

Then Addie Mae's high heels came into the corner of his seeing and the dog was gone and he, Leon, was running after her erect striding, her high buttocks, her black purse swinging, through the glinting frost, homeward bound.

October 1990

Someone upstairs flushed the commode. The churches on the Green began to toll midnight. Where her left breast had been, there was an ache. They are defined by their sex, she thought, Leon and Kelly will not, cannot sleep together because that is, finally, all they have in common: their ravenous hunger for each other's body and their Taboo. All they have is their symbolic male child, their big black book; and they know that if they have sex it will be the end of the book, the end of all of us; it will be suicide. Death, she thought of it again. I'm not writing any poetry. I thought when he came out of prison I could start work on the epic, on *Amerika*. He'd work on his big book and I'd work on my big poem. We would be the most renowned couple in the world, the new Sartre/de Beauvoir; the frenzy of fame, Antony and Cleopatra—"Be it known, that we, the greatest, are misthought/for things that others do: and, when we fall/We answer other's merits in our name/Are therefore to be pitied ..." She put on Antony's sword—but she was black and he was white, "Whilst I wore his sword Philippan"—too much muscles from prison now, thin then, thick then, through thick and thin, "Thou, Antony ..." Now I lay me down to sleep ... *le style indirect libre* ... *La force des choses*, the force of circumstance "has brought me to Paris today with M. Howard, of whom Jean Genet ..." Bonnie and Clyde, like the old days, "Someday they'll go down together; and they'll bury them side by side; to few it'll be grief—to the law a relief—But it's death for

Bonnie and Clyde ..." I'm not going to sleep again, she thought, listening for Kelly and Leon upstairs, listening for mother, waiting for the quarter hour to toll from the Green: The poetry and doggerel and music running through her poor head. Stop! Darkness. Silence. Then on the blank silent screen of her mind she began to play tricks again. First the music from her mother's favorite Gilbert & Sullivan bounding across the screen, then the absurd new lyric:

> *Vivian:* I am a major minor poetess though they say I've made my life a mess—
> *Vivian & Leon:* Life a mess—
> *Leon:* Unless—
> *Vivian:* Unless?
> *Leon:* I confess.
> *Vivian:* You confess, I'll undress.
> *Leon:* Your lost breast.
> *Vivian:* Metastasis. Less and less—what a mess.
> *Vivian & Leon:* Life a mess!

She made a small chuckle sound in her throat. They would have written their epic works, toured the West as film stars of Rebellion, adopted children, toured the East as the Post-Socialist Adam and Eve, more children, toured the Third World as the patron saints of Revolution—then what? The portrait was bleeding into parody. Can't control it, can't control your thoughts, Erikson said to Huey and Leon at the Yale Press, deepest idea ever discovered by Freud, by anybody, control your thoughts, control *their* thoughts, secret of fascism ... Back to the Grand Tour—Mandela, Havel, the Pinters; the United Nations; the year 2000 and the Century with a Human Face! Breathe, relax your arms, breathe, "I am a major minor ..." Breathe. He has to finish the book. He can't do that if he fucks her. And he can't finish the book unless he goes down into Projectville and talks to the gangbangers. Otherwise he can never finish. I'll make him go. Then, after he goes and finishes his book, I'll finish my poem. Good. That's a good plan. Good plan. Sleep now. Night. Dark night. Black night.

12:30 A.M.
Kelly walked through the house—in her dream—searching. Mother. The little room that wasn't there. Mother? The cold empty house—who's there? Hello. Hello? Who's there? ... I know you're there. Walk. Hello? Who? Please ... Wait ... Please—wait—stop—please—no ...

Masai watched her jerk in her sleep. The half hour chimed on the Green. She muttered in her sleep, "No," and he watched. The moonlight angled across her. He crossed his pushed-up prison arms across his chest and hugged himself.

Kelly licked the ink off the Xerox pages—in her dream—and it tasted like strawberry jam. "I'm happy," she told herself, "because today is a red letter day, and when I am good I am very very good, and when I am bad I am horrid." She ate the pages, then she stacked the paper into perfect black stacks. Perfect. Then she ate some more. "Eaney meaney miney moe, catch a gypsy by the toe, if he hollers make him pay, twenty dollars every day, my mother told me to pick this one ..."

Masai watched her kick off the quilt. They don't just want me to kill myself, he thought, they want me to kill all of them, the old lady, all of them. "Ummm," the girl moaned in her sleep. They want mass murder. Mm-hm. Right here in the mansion. Mm-hm, sure do. Strangle them. That or cut their throats. "FORMER PANTHER SLAYS THREE." The girl rubbed her crotch and murmured. Mound of Venus, he thought, and snapped his middle finger sharply against the head of his phallus to force bring-down. If I kill them all with a gun, then it's over; if I go down to Projectville, then they make it look like the gangs—no, what they care about is the book ... He watched her. Girl, he thought, girl, your nature. Have mercy.

He rose and went toward her. He covered her with the old quilt from Vivian's nursery, and glared straight back through the window into the face of old Man in the Moon.

1:01 A.M.
In her dream, Vivian watched Leon and Kelly stand together in a

pool of moonlight. Like ghosts, slow dancing, the girl stroked him with her whole body, body kiss, body music, the beast with two backs—ripe bodies, rotten, filling up the world— kiss him, kiss him, kiss his face, kiss his body, kiss him—but in the dream it was Vivian's voice that crooned over the naked ghosts dancing in the moonlight—
"... someone cut off his ears, another removed his sexual organs ... dragged the corpse through the streets of Waco ... the body was covered with wounds from head to foot. A shout of joy from thousands of throats, when the fire was kindled ... a storm of applause—"
"Vivian!"

1:09 A.M.
"Vivian?"
"I'm coming."
"Vivian."
"Mother—you have to die."
"You and that man—Mother said never say nigger."
"You are over ninety years old— "
" —And the girl, the child— "
" —and you have to die."
" —and I'm going to tell Daddy on you— "
" —one of us has to die."
"... The black man. Let the black man die."

July 1970

QUESTION: THE STATE: You say you arrived at the Battle mansion at around 9:30 P.M. on the night of August 11, 1969?
ANSWER: LEON H. HOWARD: Correct.
QUESTION: And Miss Battle, Miss Petty, and Dr. Ali were there when you arrived?
ANSWER: Correct.
QUESTION: And where was George Sams at this time?
ANSWER: With me.
QUESTION: He was your security?
ANSWER: No.
DEFENSE: Objection. Repetitive. Asked and answered.
THE COURT: Sustained.
QUESTION: Mr. Sams was with you. He entered the house, the mansion with you. He sat in the room with you and the other three. Is that correct?
ANSWER: Correct.
QUESTION: And you began to talk?
ANSWER: What?
QUESTION: The five of you began to talk?
ANSWER: We talked.
QUESTION: You began to talk about a certain plan, didn't you?
ANSWER: No.
QUESTION: A certain plan. Mr. Sams quoted you as saying that,

quotes, "A colossal revolutionary act would force Nixon to overreact," close quotes, and quotes, "declare a state of national emergency," close quotes. And then you went over the plan again. You heard Mr. Sams so testify, didn't you, Mr. Howard? ... Mr. Howard?

THE COURT: You may answer, Mr. Howard.

ANSWER: Judge, you saw George Sams sitting right here. You could see he was insane.

THE COURT: Order! Mr. Howard, this is cross-examination, and you must answer. Continue, Mr. Merle.

QUESTION: You heard Mr. Sams testify under oath that you assigned each one there a task in the plan to kidnap Henry Kissinger? ... Let the record show that the defendant is nodding his head in the affirmative.

THE COURT: Please answer verbally.

ANSWER: He testified.

QUESTION: And Dr. Kissinger was scheduled to speak at Yale on September 21st, a little more than one month later? Isn't that correct?

ANSWER: Correct.

QUESTION: And on the evening of August 11, 1969, you so informed those present at the Battle mansion, correct?

ANSWER: That's incorrect.

QUESTION: Well, we'll see: Mr. Sams testified under oath that you said to Dr. Ali that the time had come to hold a war crimes tribunal, is that correct?

ANSWER: I have stated many times that the government of the United States is a criminal conspiracy against the people of Vietnam and the—

QUESTION: Your Honor, may the defendant be instructed—

THE DEFENSE: Let him answer!

ANSWER:	—against people of color in Southeast Asia and here in our own cities.
QUESTION:	We are focusing on the events of August 11, 1969. Did you on August 11, 1969, say to Dr. Ali—
ANSWER:	I talked about the war, I talked about—
QUESTION:	If you will let me finish my—
THE DEFENSE:	Let him answer!
QUESTION:	Let me ask!
THE COURT:	Gentlemen ... Mr. Howard.
ANSWER:	I stated and I have stated that Henry Kissinger was a war criminal, among others, and that Dr. Ali and some of the professors at Yale should confront him with his crimes when he came to speak in September, as had been done at Ann Arbor.
QUESTION:	I see. And did you then instruct Dr. Ali and Miss Battle to arrange for a tea party—
ANSWER:	No.
QUESTION:	—a tea party at the Battle mansion for Dr. Kissinger and several Nobel laureates critical of the war in Vietnam—let me finish, please—after which, after which Dr. Ali and Miss Battle would detain Mr. Kissinger, Dr. Kissinger, on a pretext and—let me finish my question—and hold him hostage and—wait!—and demand a confrontation on national television—wait—
THE DEFENSE:	I ask for a mistrial—
THE COURT:	Order! Finish, Mr. Merle.
QUESTION:	A confrontation on national television between Dr. Kissinger and yourself, Mr. Howard—
THE DEFENSE:	Your Honor!
THE COURT:	The defendant may answer.
ANSWER:	No.
QUESTION:	And didn't Mr. Sams further testify under oath that Dr. Ali and Miss Battle would represent that you

	and the Black Panther Party had nothing to do with the hostage taking but were only cooperating so that violence could be avoided?
ANSWER:	… Is that a question?
THE COURT:	Can you rephrase it?
QUESTION:	They would take him hostage—
THE DEFENSE:	Objection. Vague.
THE COURT:	Sustained.
QUESTION:	Miss Battle and Dr. Ali would take Dr. Kissinger hostage. Two, they would demand national television coverage. Three, they would demand that you be allowed into the house to confront Mr. Kissinger as if he were on trial for "crimes against humanity."
ANSWER:	… No.
QUESTION:	You did not hear Mr. Sams so testify?
ANSWER:	I heard him.
QUESTION:	Under oath. Let the record reflect that the witness is laughing … Alright, and George Sams' role was to accompany you as a bodyguard because of the Secret Service and all of the potential violence that might break loose after the kidnapping—strike that—In other words, Miss Battle and Dr. Ali would be holding Henry Kissinger at gun point and they would order the authorities to produce you to accuse and confront Mr. Kissinger on T.V., and you would be seen as an innocent Black Panther official who was simply bowing to the demands of a couple of Yale terrorists—wait—and Mr. Sams was to be your bodyguard. Now you may answer.
ANSWER:	… Didn't you leave out Susan Petty?
QUESTION:	What?
ANSWER:	Miss Susan Petty.

QUESTION:	What about her?
ANSWER:	She was there, too.
QUESTION:	Yes?
ANSWER:	But Sams never testified as to what I had ordered her to do—
QUESTION:	Mr. Howard—
ANSWER:	—because you don't want Susan Petty's name mentioned here, because your case is over—
QUESTION:	Your Honor—
THE COURT:	Mr.—
ANSWER:	Your case would be over and your career would be over, Mr. Merle, because Susan Petty's real name was Jane Marie Flanigan—now you let me finish—and she worked for the New Haven P.D. and after you ran this frame-up she threatened to expose your ass and you killed her!
THE COURT:	Order! Order! Order! Order! Sheriff!
ANSWER:	Where is she—where is Jane Marie Flanigan?
THE COURT:	Remove the prisoner!
ANSWER:	Where is she?!
THE COURT:	Sheriff, remove the prisoner!
ANSWER:	Where is she?!

1974

Vivian,

Thanks for the books. I need some more: Sartre, Fanon, Marcuse, Adorno, Spengler, Hegel, Nietzsche, Freud, Erikson (on Gandhi), Camus, Dostoyevsky, Marx (The German Ideology).

You know generally what I have by these guys, so pick out others. I spend as much time looking at their style as I do the contents, sometimes, especially Nietzsche. That cat could write--"I love the great despisers for they are the great adorers, and arrows of longing for another shore!" He's better than old man Freud on the subject of guilt, but Freud beats all of them on the subject of violence, "The State forbids any act of violence to the individual so as to monopolize it for itself." That is heavy.

Well, I got the reds today, as compared to the blues, thinking about everything, sitting here like a boy trying to mumble some German. Huey used to say that Marx was a racist, too, but he didn't take it personally. Huey's people were from Louisiana, like mine, so we

EVERY THIRD HOUSE

always understood each other like homeboys. You know that Huey P. Newton was named after Huey P. Long, didn't you? Huey's father Mr. Newton used to tell us how old Huey Long would rant and rave about how he wouldn't allow white nurses to touch niggers layin up in the hospital. Mr. Newton said that when the black people heard that they knew that was old Huey's way of getting money to build some new hospital for <u>them</u>. Harvard and Yale said that Huey Long was a mad dictator, but Mr. Newton named his special son after him, and not because "slavery is endless" but just the opposite.

Mr. Newton was like Steve Gatewood. Steve Gatewood married Granny when I was living with her at the Nelsons (I showed you the house when we drove down to New Orleans). Addie didn't love Steve in a romantic way, I don't believe, but she respected him and so I did too, the way I later respected Mr. Newton, and the way we respect ourselves, when we can, and that is possible, more possible because of the Steve Gatewoods of this world, or of <u>that</u> world!

Addie would stamp up and down her room and the back porch that gave off it and lay down the line 'bout how "Steve Gatewood is a hardworking colored man and he don't ever come calling without he bring something, even if it's only a one dollar box of candy. Um-hm, working three jobs, child, don't say a word!"

The three jobs were at the sawmill, preaching & selling suits by catalogue. He would come up the drive after supper, bathed and dressed in a dark suit that looked like it was cut out of steel sheets and a tie and hat and shined shoes, all this after working like an animal all day in a sawmill right out of slavery times that was, I'm telling you, ten times worse than what I have here. Except he had Addie and his self-respect.

He would clomp up the steps into the light and remove his hat. His body was planed and angled from a life of heroic work in the fields and mills so that he looked and walked like he had been carved out of iron or steel, too, like Addie herself, who moved always with a bruising speed that was her sign and signature in the way that Steve's deliberate iron-clad body and voice was his. "Alright." And he was announced and opening the screen door and putting a heavy deliberate shined shoe up on the porch. "How you this evening?" And Addie a blur of energy in the kitchen doorway, snorting to clear her sinus, "Leon, set that chair up for Steve by the door. Let me bring you a cup of coffee."

He would bend and sit, "Alright," and take the coffee, "Alright," and wait for Addie to clean up the Nelson supper and then join him on the porch in the twilight.

They would only exchange a few words about church, they would never stoop to gossip, and there was nothing about their work that anyone would dare to talk about, and they could not have been able to stay awake much past 8:30 at night after that work in that heat, but they sat there in the almost dark in proud exhaustion hardly able to even see each other or me on the steps and what they had between them was respect & I knew then and I know now that respect is not love minus something, it is love plus something and that there is no more precious human thing in this life. I loved Steve Gatewood and I respected him and he stayed with me over the years and he's with me here tonight--along with you, the three of us, no four with Addie--when I should be studying my Marx in German, but this nigger got the reds <u>and</u> the blues tonight.

Steve died by the time he was fifty. Worn out, worn down. Addie buried him and quit the Nelsons, "I'm going back to Blackmans Laundry. Steve's gone now, boy."

The point, Vivian, is that there were black men like that who, as you say, not only survived but they prevailed. In their way. Mr. Newton, he lived on to move to Oakland to work in the shipyards during the war. He paid all his bills in cash every month, and Huey and his brother Melvin used to have to go around in person and pay off the utilities and merchants, etc., because Mr. Newton never owed anybody anything. So when the academics write their post mortem now for the Panthers and look for sources in Fidel Castro or Chairman Mao, forget it. The Panthers are descended from every slave that was ever kidnapped (let alone the Indians and slave Masters and itinerant Honkies and assorted White Trash--Huey used to claim that he had a Jewish great-grandfather!), but in modern times no one knew it but those slow-walking deep-talking men in their hats and ties--Steve and Mr. Newton--they were the forerunners of the Panthers: Huey P. Newton was his father's son--and, in a way, so was I Steve Gatewood's.

The slave or exslave can have pride, dignity, respect. They are not the same thing. Pride and dignity and even power are not the same thing as respect. "The black man." The Black Man. Malcolm always talked about the Black Man. They all do. We all do. The black woman does especially. "What we gonna do 'bout the black man?" That's why a lot of black women had to hate you. The Black Man, in capital letters, is still just old you-know-who: a nigger. When you heard Elaine Brown and them say "Nigger, what you doing?" you always winced, but, child, they were just discussing the "Problem of the Black Man" from another point of view. Listen to Bessie or any good blues, who you think it is "makin his four-day creep?" The Black Man the B.M.--the bowel movement--the BLACK MAN in capitals. Huey tried to change the equation. He tried to introduce respect into the vacuum between slavery and violence. But very few understood, starting with white radicals and including hip observers of the scene like Eldridge Cleaver. He never understood.

Eldridge talked jive. He said that "Malcolm talked shit" and that talking shit was the iron in a young nigger's blood. That's why he turned against Huey because Huey did not plan to exterminate White America. Eldridge thought he was John the Baptist to Huey, but he was just Judas Iscariot. They, none of them, wanted to see the law books in our <u>other</u> hands. The FBI wasn't afraid of a few niggers with guns (they loved it). What terrified them was law books, hot breakfast programs, free clinics, co-ops, Sickle Cell Anemia Programs, and, if necessary, yes, guns. Huey like Malcolm knew that "Black" Revolution was a suicide love letter to J. Edgar Hoover. Eldridge and Edgar--they got to be a hot item, didn't they? (LET ME KNOW THROUGH MY LAWYER IF <u>ANY</u> OF THIS IS CENSORED OUT BY THE GREAT MINDS HERE THAT SPEND THEIR WAKING HOURS LOOKING FOR A NEEDLE OF REVOLT IN THIS HAYSTACK OF TIME. AND TELL DAVID OR KATHERINE THAT THEY'RE HOLDING BACK SOME OF THE BOOKS THEY SENT, PRETENDING THEY COULD READ THEM--AND TO GET ANOTHER COURT ORDER IF THEY HAVE TO TO MAKE THEM LET HENRY POPKIN FROM C.U. COME IN HERE FOR MY GERMAN AND HISTORY TUTORING.)

Time to do some sit-ups.

We know how you can provoke black men into killing each other. There's always a Tackwood or a George Sams who you can say to, "Say, brother, the nigger sold us out, it's time for that nigger to die." Killed by a friend. Addie Gatewood used to love to read the back page of the <u>Town Talk</u> on Monday. She'd cough and laugh through her cigarette smoke, "Have mercy--'Merilee Grady stabbed by a friend!'" She'd hop around with the outrageous wonder of it, then another, "'Archie Lamarr Thomas shot by a friend!'" Laughing convulsions, me too, dancing around, crying, farting--<u>understanding</u>!

Comprehending how come slaves always kill each other--on Lee Street on Saturday Night, or Algeria, or Angola, or New Haven! How all it takes is a wink or a nod from the Man and instead of killing him, the Man, we kill a nigger or at best an occasional police slob who's more scared than the nigger--it doesn't even take a wink or a nod for the slave to lunge at himself in the mirror <u>because he can't live without respect!</u>

Huey Newton wasn't Malcolm X's son, he was Walter Newton's son and Steve Gatewood's and the rest of them. Stagolee can't be Malcolm or Martin King or Willie Mays--He's got to be Steve Gatewood. Everybody in prison builds their body constantly--George Jackson did a million push-ups, they say--we got nothing but bodies beautiful in this joint, but self-respect? Only here and there. That's what's on my mind tonight. "Preachin' 'bout it tonight. Let the church say Amen."

Like Addie said, my own father could've been one of two sailors passing through New Orleans in 1940. They would have been serving in the officers' mess. They could have been friends or rivals or both. My mother was just twenty, working at that time cleaning in a hotel--not a whorehouse because Addie came down from Rapides Parish every few weeks to make sure that her big beautiful daughter was still working at the Roosevelt Hotel under the sharp eye of Calvin Henderson, Addie's old friend, and taking her classes in stenography. Addie told me my life story only two or three times, short and

bitter, and it always ended, "You came here to live with me when you were eight months old and your mama went back to school. That's when she got sick and passed. Mm-hmm. Sure did. You going to be alright. You going to college."
"How did she die, Granny?" -- "Your mama passed on November 4th, 1941. I got to do my work now."

I just realized that was thirty-three years ago today, or rather yesterday. I don't believe in ghosts. But here I am in lock-up max. You can't hear much and at night it's like a tomb. My mother died thirty-three years ago. How did she die? Was Granny telling the truth?

"How did she die?"
"Epidemic flu."
"Why?"
"Get on, now, they be wanting their supper, directly."

I'd go outside & ask their dog why. Spot. Why? Addie was sharp as a razor blade. I never saw her cry. Laugh, lord yes, but cry never. She'd slice like a knife through that house with a fury and a momentum that left me (and death too) in her wake for years after she should have been dead.

What happened to my beautiful mother down in New Orleans? It's cold in here, like time is frozen, and I don't believe in ghosts, but I can still see Addie turning on a dime, her eyes red and yellow, taking off with her joints popping like a .22 pistol--and never another detail, let alone which of the two sailors it might have been and what might have transpired between those two Navy men and Addie.

That's it. You always thought there was an opus of biography that I was holding out on you, but that's all there is, you could write it on an index card: "Nigger. Killed by a friend."

I can't keep my eyes open. But I don't sleep until after last rounds. If they want to kill me it will have to be between two and five in the a.m. That's why I keep writing and writing. I don't believe that I will ever get out of here. One way or another I will die here. That's what I believe--on nights like this. Then I wake up in the morning feeling like Hercules and start talking German to the guards and pretty soon you can hear the laughter of all the work crews bouncing off the metal walls, rising like angels from hell, over the walls, over the rotting and ruined mill towns across the valley, all the way to New Haven. You hear it too, girl, don't you-- you're the poet!

      Power to the People,

      L.

1970

QUESTION: THE STATE: So, you told Mr. Sams that the plan was that Dr. Ali and Miss Battle would testify that the Black Panther Party was in no way connected to the kidnapping of Dr. Kissinger and that you and Mr. Sams were innocent pawns in, ah, what was meant to look like an act of terror by rich white radicals?
THE DEFENSE: Objection. Compound and leading.
THE COURT: Mr. Howard, did you understand the question?
ANSWER: More or less.
THE COURT: Go ahead, then. Overruled.
ANSWER: You say something about rich white radicals?
QUESTION: I beg your pardon?
ANSWER: Dr. Ali's brown, isn't he, from Pakistan?
QUESTION: Miss Battle's white, isn't she, Mr. Howard?
ANSWER: But Dr. Ali's brown, and he's not rich.
QUESTION: But Miss Battle is.
ANSWER: Her family.
QUESTION: In her own right, isn't she?
ANSWER: Can't say.
QUESTION: You can't?
ANSWER: Cannot.
QUESTION: Why not, sir?
ANSWER: I don't know anything about her personal life.

QUESTION:	You don't? Mr. Howard, isn't it a fact that you had a sexual relationship with Vivian Battle for more than a year?
THE DEFENSE:	Objection.
THE COURT:	Overruled. The witness opened the door. You may answer.
ANSWER:	My relationship with her was political.
QUESTION:	Political?
ANSWER:	Political.
QUESTION:	Did you have sexual intercourse with Miss Battle, or did you not, sir?
ANSWER:	We had a political relationship.
QUESTION:	Political *and* sexual?
ANSWER:	All politics is sexual.
QUESTION:	It is?
ANSWER:	Right. And all sex is political.
QUESTION:	Your Honor?
THE COURT:	Quiet. Mr. Merle, I think you ought to try another line of questioning. Order. Quiet.
QUESTION:	Very well. I do not think any of this is funny. Mr. Howard, did you order George Sams to contact the FBI after the kidnapping—strike that—was it your plan that if Mr. Kissinger was successfully held, at the Battle mansion by Miss Battle and Dr. Ali, that you would stay in contact with the FBI and the authorities through George Sams in order to create an alibi for your involvement with the abduction of Dr. Kissinger? ... Let the record show that the defendant is shaking his head and laughing to himself.
ANSWER:	I'm laughing out loud, Mr. Merle.
THE COURT:	Order.
QUESTION:	Mr. Sams made it all up?
ANSWER:	Right.

QUESTION:	You never discussed the so-called Kissinger Plan on the night of August 11, 1969?
ANSWER:	Look, you know what happened. Henry Kissinger was a personal friend of Vivian Battle's family, and whenever he came to Yale to lecture, et cetera, he would drop in at the Battle place for a visit. Vivian knew him, and she said that Kissinger liked to debate young people and pretend that he was against the war and the status quo, et cetera, so we talked about Vivian and Dr. Ali engaging Kissinger in a discussion of the war and then casually mention that she had invited me over to, uh, "say hello."
QUESTION:	What does that mean, "say hello"?
ANSWER:	To join the issue.
QUESTION:	What does that mean?
ANSWER:	To go in there and jam him on the war and U.S. imperialism and racism, et cetera.
QUESTION:	"Et cetera?"
ANSWER:	War crimes, crimes against humanity, genocide, torture, crimes against the Vietnamese people, crimes against the American people, treason, mass murder, crimes against children, subversion, et cetera!
THE COURT:	Order! Order! Proceed, Mr. Merle. Order! Proceed. This time you opened the door. Order!
QUESTION:	You were going to "jam" him?
ANSWER:	Confront him.
QUESTION:	You and Mr. Sams?
ANSWER:	Sams? Sams couldn't carry on a conversation except with a lunatic.
QUESTION:	He was very articulate in his testimony here on Tuesday.
ANSWER:	He was programmed. He was brainwashed.

THE DEFENSE:	Your Honor—
THE COURT:	Order. Quiet ... Mr. Merle, let's not get detoured again.
QUESTION:	You say your intention was to merely "confront" Dr. Kissinger?
ANSWER:	Right.
QUESTION:	And what does the term "confront" mean to you, sir?
ANSWER:	To face the truth.
QUESTION:	The truth? And what is the truth?
ANSWER:	Pontius Pilate.
QUESTION:	What?
ANSWER:	Pilate.
THE COURT:	The witness is referring to the Bible, Mr. Merle.
QUESTION:	The Bible?
THE COURT:	Yes, sir, Pontius Pilate, the Roman governor asked Jesus, "What is the truth?"
QUESTION:	I see ... Now, sir, you planned to confront Dr. Kissinger on September 21st, 1969?
ANSWER:	Right.
QUESTION:	While Mr. Sams and the others held him against his will.
ANSWER:	Not at all.
QUESTION:	Mr. Howard, do you expect this jury to believe that Henry Kissinger would have willingly met and talked with you?
ANSWER:	If I were invited by Miss Battle to her home. That was the plan.
QUESTION:	And all of you were going to "confront" Dr. Kissinger, is that right?
ANSWER:	Right.
QUESTION:	And you expect this court to believe that Dr. Kissinger was going to sit still while you attacked him?

ANSWER:	Well, he's a coward, but he's so arrogant that he might have stayed to take us on and win a big propaganda victory in the media.
QUESTION:	I see, but it wasn't your intent or your plan to hand this man, that you've called a "war criminal," a big propaganda victory, was it?
ANSWER:	No, we knew his arrogance might make him stay and our plan was to start out easy and let him talk and let his aides open the door so that the Secret Service agents and the media could hear and see that Kissinger was having a fine time putting the parlor pinks and me, an autodidact coon show, in their place.
THE COURT:	Quiet.
QUESTION:	Then what, what was the next part of your plan?
ANSWER:	Well, we were going to let him talk his jive, and Miss Battle was going to keep refreshing everybody's wine glass and Miss Petty, she was going to laugh and pretend to be hypnotized by his genius and to kind of, you know, come on to him.
QUESTION:	And why was all this deception necessary?
ANSWER:	To keep the man there.
QUESTION:	So you could do what!
ANSWER:	Confront him.
QUESTION:	You mean kill him, don't you?

November 1990

Date: 11/2/90

To: DIRECTOR, FBI

From: SAC, NEW HAVEN

Subject: NATIONAL SECURITY, TERRORISM

Information excerpted below was received on date indicated from a confidential SOURCE. Source reports on activities regarding the Black Panther Party and its organizational activities since the release from prison of former BPP leader LEON HURLEY HOWARD a.k.a. MASAI.

The BPP is a violence-prone black militant organization believed to now be headquartered in New Haven, Connecticut, at the home of VIVIAN NORTON BATTLE.

On 10/31/90 Vivian Battle met at the Blue Buck Bed and Breakfast Inn, near Fair Haven, Conn., with former BPP leader MICHAEL ZINZUN.

Zinzun has been active on the West Coast in politicizing gangs and working with other former BPP members to build an underground revolutionary army, according to reliable sources.

Zinzun met with gang leaders in the New Haven area before leaving for New York City on 11/1/90. According to source, Zinzun instructed gang members to stop their killing of each other and to unite against the common enemy. Source states that Vivian Battle is funding Zinzun's activity on the East Coast.

Source obtained a copy of BPP plan for urban organizing. Source states that the new BPP will have both an above ground and underground wing. Source states that Zinzun did not meet with Leon Howard while in New Haven in order to maintain strict separation between overt and covert cells of the BPP. It is believed that Vivian Battle will act as liaison between the legal and illegal branches of the BPP, as she did in 1968 and 1969.

Attached is working draft of New Haven document to be modeled on the Los Angeles document that was circulated after recent violence following the shooting of Julius Coover a black honors student by an off-duty Los Angeles Sheriff's Deputy on 4/11/90 in Los Angeles.

BUY U.S. SAVINGS BONDS REGULARLY ON THE PAYROLL SAVINGS PLAN.

ATTENTION!!

BLOODS, CRIPS MEMBERS CLAIM POLICE ARE SABOTAGING TRUCE EFFORTS

THE COALITION AGAINST POLICE ABUSE URGES EVERYONE TO SUPPORT OUR YOUTH AND THE TRUCE.

—JOIN TOGETHER— DEMAND JUSTICE NOW!

ALL POWER TO THE PEOPLE

FOR MORE INFORMATION
CALL MICHAEL ZINZUN AT (214) 733-2107

November 1990

2:00 P.M.

Kelly listened as Vivian mounted the steps to the top floor. Masai stood in the window drinking a cup of tea. Kelly tried to get a bill of lading, selling slaves, dated 1823, into her new computer. Vivian stood in the doorway.

"Leon, Michael Zinzun's in town ... Shall I have him over here? Kelly, you have to meet Michael. Two hundred fifty pounds of brain and brawn, a black patch over the eye the police used as a target, a street sociologist of such genius that he was able to organize a 'Coalition Against Police Abuse' that forced the ACLU to sue the Los Angeles Police and win a multi-million-dollar settlement based on police spying—"

"Could I meet—"

"—And now he's working on gang truces all over the country ... Leon, should we—"

"I can't do it."

"You can't?"

"Not now."

"When?"

"When the book's done."

"You have to finish first?"

"Right."

"But, look, Michael's been in the streets for twenty years—while you were inside—and he's watched this whole generation grow up and begin to commit suicide through gang warfare, and finally now he's getting—he and some of the old comrades and former gang members are getting somewhere and they've got these truces starting that are so fragile—"

"—That the 'Weed and Seed' program is going to destroy?"

"Exactly. So, Leon, I thought you'd want to meet with him and feature his work in the conclusion of the book."

"Masai, if you—"

"Why don't you go to the library now. I need to talk to Vivian."

"Alright. Goodbye."

The student's face was flushed. She shut down her word processor deliberately as if she were performing the act before hundreds of eyes. Leon stared out at the Green, his blue denim shirt was tight across his shoulders. Vivian watched Kelly descend the stairs, then she closed the door, not so much for privacy as to ward off her mother's inevitable scream for help.

"Michael Zinzun wants to see you... This is the man you need for the book. He is the link to the gangs."

"Tell him hello."

"Will you talk to him?"

"No."

"Leon—you trust him, don't you?"

"Zinzun is the last Panther."

"What do you mean?"

"He survived Ronald Reagan in California, he survived Reagan in the White House, he survived the LAPD and the FBI—the brother is the last Panther and I would trust him with my life."

"But you—"

"I won't see the man, no, because there's no reason to, he doesn't need me, he doesn't need any more trouble."

"But you need *him*. You have to breathe some life into this book. If you won't go out to the world, you've got to bring the world in here. That girl is not enough, she's nothing, she's your pencil, a paper clip—you need Zinzun in here—when you and the Panthers started out you talked to people, went door to door, didn't you? Talked to the brothers on the block, the people in church, the barber shop, everyone, and you came up with your 'Ten Point Program'—You were street sociologists—could you look at me, Leon, when I'm talking—geniuses, like Zinzun is now, because you went from 'practice' to 'theory,' from the street to the program, and this was something unseen, like the lawbook and the shotgun, a new dialectic, a new Marxist *gemeinschaft* that included the *lumpenproletariat* from the get-go!"

She picked up a Xerox copy, then let it fall. "History. Records. Xerox. Copies of copies. Tombstones. Talk to him, then talk to the Crips, all of them, while they're still alive. At least, for God's sake, introduce him to L'il Joe. You have to do that much."

He walked out of the cynosure of the window alcove over to her. They stood close together. Their eyes touched, then flinched away to map the other's body. He unbuttoned her vest, then her shirt and pushed aside the prosthetic brassiere that masked the scar of the missing breast. She waited, looking over his left shoulder at a bright corner of the window.

His eyes encompassed the concave scar tissue. He breathed, then he looked at her full right breast.

"Erectile tissue," she said.

"Poetry," he said.

"You go see Zinzun," she said.

"No."

"He's the last Panther."

"No."

"A living Panther is better than a dead lion. Do it for L'il Joe. Please!"

"I'm not a Panther anymore."

"Please."

"I'm a book."

2:45 P.M.

Leonora watches her daughter sit at a desk and cross out something on a writing pad. She waits for the bells. The black man and the girl are upstairs. Vivian looks over, Leonora pretends to sleep, remembers:

> Early morning, March 12, 1936, she pretended to be asleep, when Henry slipped into his bed. He had not come to her bed in over a month. Was that good or bad? He said he wanted a son, but did he want her? Do I want him? Do I want a child? Her husband snored lightly. She felt like a cat moving in the dawn light across the room, into the dressing room, and pulled open the top drawer of her husband's bureau, and counted the French prophylactics under the big handkerchiefs: there were eight left, two weeks ago there had been two dozen. She touched the silver foil. I could kill him, she thought. I could become a communist, I could have a child with someone else. With Ernest; a colored child.
>
> The handkerchiefs smelled of pepper, as always, why? She closed the drawer silently. It was too early to go downstairs, she dared not return to the bedroom. She sat at the dressing table and thought of poison. Then she felt the presence, felt rather than thought, of the men in her life—her grandfather, her father, her husband. They were there inside her, utterly intimate and peculiar like the ambience of pepper and expensive linen in the drawer, like horse manure and hay in the barn, and her father's bay rum body and gin-reeking mouth: the men. Men. Their roots hanging down. She studied her hand, a freckle or an age spot there, she stared at her wedding ring; she remembered Dr. Grayson, she could go to him for advice. "And I should have," she told herself later, "I would have if it weren't for the little fact of his root."

Vivian closed her tablet and stood up, "Mother, I have to go out, Jan is here if you need anything, and Rose is coming.—Jan, hi, I'll be right there.—Goodbye, I'll be back by five or so."

She walked into the foyer and watched Kelly help Jan off with her leather jacket, as if in a dream. They looked at Vivian. "Hi. Mother's in there. I'll be back by six." They stared. "I have to, ah ..." Jan went in to the old woman. Kelly tried to help Vivian on with her long English coat. "Go back to work," Vivian said. "Don't worry, I'll be home before supper. Tell Leon it's pork chops for a change."

3:32 P.M.

Vivian sat on a bench on the Green—directly in front of the Church of the Regicides watching the dark and bright leaves fall and blow—with her eyes out of focus, remembering old Novembers and other Vivians. Trying to keep all the colored leaves, dogs, and children and nannies and homeless wanderers in a single unfocused perspective, one unbroken vision to be stared at like a painting, like a theory of life and not an overwhelming wave of broken light crashing in on her carrying everything before it—the dogs and children and homeless, the red leaves and the stone churches—in one terrific surge of light and belltolling sound washing her out and back and away.

Her breathing shortened at the effort to hold the entire vista in place, to control the rush of dizziness, to keep the level Green from tipping over and running down over her. The tolling subsided at last and her eyes locked back into focus. An ageless homeless black man stood in front of her looking into her face. Behind him the shadows on the Green were lengthening into their winter perspectives. The homeless man's gray and yellow face worked, his blue lips moved soundlessly in a prayer or a curse until she withdrew five dollars from her wallet and handed it to him and he trudged away in the direction of the courthouse, her eyes following him into the shadow of the building until the stone steps and columns interdicted the forward progress of her gaze.

Qui Transtulit Sustinent, the same flag stirred in the combined shadows of the Roman columns. Her mind's eye broke through the stone pile to the vaulted echoing corridor inside the municipal labyrinth, and into the narrow courtroom—and there the hushed and frightened voices of the jurors two decades ago broke their silence ...

QUESTION: Do any black people come to your home?
ANSWER: A Puerto Rican was over once.
QUESTION: Are there any black people in your church?

DONALD FREED

ANSWER: No.
QUESTION: Were you here May Day?
ANSWER: I left town.
ANSWER: Some of my better friends are colored.

... then sank again into the stone and marble. Shadows pouring from the courthouse across the Green directly towards her. She pressed her knees together and closed her eyes:

THE COURT: Overruled. You may answer.
THE WITNESS: VIVIAN N. BATTLE: As I remember we were waiting for Mr. Howard and Susan Petty began to say that Henry Kissinger should be executed when he came to Yale.
THE DEFENSE: Excuse me, Miss Battle, was Susan Petty serious, was she sober at this time?
ANSWER: I don't know.
QUESTION: You say you waited from 6:30 until 8:30 for Mr. Howard, and during that time was there drinking?
ANSWER: Dr. Ali, Susan Petty, and I drank beer with our supper.
QUESTION: Did Susan Petty smoke a marijuana cigarette before Mr. Howard arrived?
ANSWER: Yes.
QUESTION: Did you smoke marijuana?
ANSWER: No.
QUESTION: And why is that?
ANSWER: Well—it was illegal.
THE COURT: Quiet.
THE STATE: This is not a joke.
ANSWER: Because it was illegal, any of us who considered ourselves senior, um, political cadres could, if we were arrested, jeopardize a number of people and

create a public image of, ah, decadence that could then be used to turn the working class against us.
QUESTION: Did Dr. Ali smoke that evening?
ANSWER: No.
QUESTION: Did you ask Miss Petty not to smoke an illegal substance?
ANSWER: Yes.
QUESTION: Tell the jury what you said to her and what she said to you.
ANSWER: I said to her, "Not here. Masai's coming."
QUESTION: She put it out?
ANSWER: Yes.
QUESTION: Did she then continue talking about Mr. Kissinger?
ANSWER: Yes.
QUESTION: What did you hear her say, specifically?
ANSWER: That he should be "offed."
QUESTION: What did that mean?
ANSWER: She was using a ghetto idiom. To wit: to "off" is to kill.
QUESTION: Go on, please. Why did she say that Mr. Kissinger should be "offed?"
ANSWER: Because he was Henry Kissinger—and he—
THE COURT: Quiet. Continue.
THE STATE: This is not a show.
ANSWER: —And he, Kissinger, was a mass murderer, she called him Dr. Strangelove and she claimed that he had tried to rape her at Harvard.
THE STATE: Objection!
THE COURT: Will counsel approach the bench. (Out of the hearing of the jury, at the bench): Mr. Garry, where is this going?
GARRY: Judge, this testimony is crucial to show that my client, when he arrived, Susan Petty had already

MERLE: been talking about taking revenge on Henry Kissinger, this was her obsession—

MERLE: Your Honor, this is more of Mr. Garry's melodrama, it's hearsay that he drops in here to give the jury a side show and completely—

GARRY: If it's hearsay, Judge, why don't they produce Susan Petty who—

MERLE: —Because you—

GARRY: —Who was their agent!

THE COURT: Keep your voices down. I've already instructed you that the fact that Miss Petty is missing is not to be discussed in front of the jury. I want that very clear. Now, Mr. Garry, I will let you pursue this on the condition that you tie it in as fast as you can. Then I think we can take the luncheon recess. Alright.

QUESTION: Miss Battle, could you just sum up in your own words Miss Petty's personal feelings for Mr. Kissinger as she expressed them to you on the night of August 11, 1969, in your home?

ANSWER: Well—she said that she had audited a seminar that he, Kissinger, was teaching in 1965, I think, and that he had asked her out. And his wife was out of town, so he brought her back to his house and they smoked "grass," she said, and then he stripped down to his underwear and began to strut around and pose and model—

THE COURT: I will clear the courtroom if there is another outburst. Conclude now, Miss Battle.

ANSWER: Yes. She said that she laughed at him and he screamed at her in German and tried to rape her.

QUESTION: Alright. So she hated him?

ANSWER: She said so.

QUESTION: Did she say she wanted revenge?

THE STATE: Objection.

THE COURT:	Sustained.
QUESTION:	Alright. Now, how long did this discussion of Kissinger go on before Mr. Howard arrived?
ANSWER:	Well, the discussion shifted to a comparison of Henry Kissinger and Adolf Eichmann and—
THE STATE:	Objection!
QUESTION:	Let her answer! Just tell us what you said.
THE COURT:	I'll allow it, for the moment.
ANSWER:	I said that in the case of a war criminal like Adolf Eichmann, or Henry Kissinger, that it makes no sense to execute them, because it removes responsibility from the culture that produced them, it buries the truth and the everlasting repercussions of their crimes, so I stated that these bureaucratic monsters be put on trial, public trial, on television and then turned loose into the world—to be shielded or destroyed as the case may be, but not by the State, any State—and whatever fate awaits them.
THE COURT:	… You may go on. You are against capital punishment?
ANSWER:	Isn't it the State, your Honor, that produces the man who follows its orders? I mean if Nazi Germany had won the war, there would have been statues of Eichmann right across Europe. The war criminal is a creature of the criminal State, and that State has no legitimacy whatsoever to take another life. Justice and the State are a contradiction in terms. So if, your Honor, the good citizens of this valley wish to tear Henry Kissinger to bloody pieces out there on that Green—after a trial on television—so be it, they are the injured party, they are history!
THE COURT:	… Miss Battle … You're a writer, a well-known

	author. On the night of August 11, 1969, were you speaking "poetically" or "politically"?
ANSWER:	... Your Honor, I appreciate the question, the distinction. ... I'm an anarchist, Judge Bryan. Mr. Howard was, as you know, a member of the Black Panther Party. Dr. Ali has been identified in his writings as an "independent socialist." As an anarchist I can certainly entertain the concept of putting a major official or State criminal on trial as both a symbol or, to use your word, a poetic act as well as a political act. Both. So, on that evening I was debating the efficacy of such an act with Susan Petty on both a symbolic and an existential or political level. Does that make sense? ... I should say that Susan Petty also was not an anarchist. In fact, at that time, even that night, I believed that there was a very good chance that she was some sort of police agent, and so did Mr. Howard. My point being that under no circumstances would Mr. Howard or I have entered into a plan of any kind with Susan Petty to as much as smoke a "controlled substance" much less kidnap Mr. Nixon's vicar, Dr. Henry Kissinger.
THE COURT:	Thank you, Miss Battle. Counsel.
QUESTION:	When you say that you're an "anarchist"—will you tell the jury what you mean by that?
THE STATE:	Objection.
THE COURT:	Overruled.
ANSWER:	By "anarchy" I mean the opposite of "chaos." The exact opposite. Anarchy means, really, without "archy," without a ruler of some kind over you. What is "over" you is your conscience, not the State or the government's law or "superego" but your own conscience. I happen to be a nonviolent

anarchist. I am responsible for my actions. I hold myself to a far higher standard of conduct than any State. Anarchists tend to believe in something called "mutual aid." Mutual aid means combining with others to function in a human culture: to pick up the garbage; to maintain police and fire services; to form an army if necessary; to decide on taxes; to rebuild a ghettoized city; to stop a war: Provisional, functional combinations acting under provisional and temporary leadership to a given end, an end that is the product and result of its own means to the most exact degree.

QUESTION: ... You are nonviolent?

ANSWER: Personally, yes.

QUESTION: Do you believe in the government of the United States of America?

ANSWER: Ah, I "believe" in the "Spirit of '76." In the "Common Sense" of Tom Paine—in the anarchic thrust of our original revolution. Lincoln had an anarchic tendency, I think, and so did his vision of the Civil War. Lincoln was the only major politician of the time to understand the meaning of John Brown. You see, John Brown was a true Christian anarchist because he worked with the slaves themselves to overthrow the—

THE STATE: Objection, your Honor, the witness is—

THE COURT: Alright ... Miss Battle, on the night of August 11, 1969, or at any other time, did you ever discuss with Leon Hurley Howard an actual plan to kidnap or harm in any way Dr. Henry Kissinger?

ANSWER: Never.

QUESTION: Thank you. Your witness, Mr. Merle.

THE STATE: Miss Battle, you've testified and you've written at length about your belief in "nonviolence" and

	"mutual aid" and "peace" and "radical Christianity" and "civil rights." So let me ask you, were Leon Hurley Howard and the Black Panther Party nonviolent advocates of radical Christianity?
ANSWER:	I think that's a non sequitur.
QUESTION:	Was Leon Hurley Howard a nonviolent Christian?
ANSWER:	Ask him.
QUESTION:	I'm asking you.
ANSWER:	I can't answer for him.
QUESTION:	You can't? You knew him, didn't you, very, very well, knew him intimately, didn't you, knew him as well as it's possible to know someone, didn't you?
ANSWER:	I knew him.
QUESTION:	You certainly did. You were sexually intimate with him, weren't you, on many occasions, you—
THE DEFENSE:	Objection!
THE STATE:	Cross-examination, your Honor.
THE COURT:	Objection overruled.
QUESTION:	You had sexual relations with him?
ANSWER:	Yes.
QUESTION:	Many times?
ANSWER:	Well.
QUESTION:	So you knew him!?
ANSWER:	I loved him, sir. I love him.
QUESTION:	You love him, you know him!
ANSWER:	They are not the same thing, Mr. Merle.

4:10 P.M.

Vivian's bench was swallowed up in shadow. No wind now, but chill; the bank clock clicked "4:10 P.M. – 52°." She stood; the children on the Green, the nursemaids, were gone. Turned and took a few steps toward her house, then stopped still and turned in the other direction, south, and took a few stiff steps. The homeless man, or another homeless man, was a black blur in the middle distance ahead of her, moving away, leading her down.

It was dark down in Projectville. Deceptive as ever, Vivian thought, the houses looking solid and the same as when the Irish and Italians lived there, when they were the townies of the fierce pitched battles between Town and Gown, in her mother's day. The "Model City" she thought, stoking up contempt to keep her going deeper into the dark. "City of the Covenant," her lips twisted, breathing cold air in through her mouth, "City of Churches," straight ahead under the gauntlet, under the gallows of broken streetlamps.

Orchard Street was the same except for the old Panther headquarters: boarded up, graffiti covered, weedgrown. Vivian stopped, breathing, hunching her shoulders. She was angry—"He should be here. Leon should be here with me"—using her anger with him as a shield—as he, if he were there physically, would have been her shield. Then the knowledge of her fear punctured her anger so that all she wanted was to go home and talk to Leon and kiss his wounds. She turned to go and there were the four shadows of the black adolescents, standing staring.

"Hello."

"… Who you?"

"I, ah, used to work here."

"Where?"

"Right there."

"… Work?"

"Yes. That was the New Haven office of the Black Panther Party."

"… You black?"

"No."

"… Who you?"

"It didn't matter then."

"What?"

"Race."

"It do now."

"I know … did you ever hear of Masai?"

"Who that?"
"He, ah, was the leader, here, of the Black Panthers."
"Masai?"
"Leon Masai Howard."
"... Yeah, I think I heard of the dude."
"Mm-hm, me too—he dead?"
"No."
"He's not?"
"No. He's alive. He went to prison. He's out now."
"... Where he at?"
"He's staying at my house. Working on a book."
"... He gonna come back down here?"
"Panthers startin' up again?"
"... I don't know."
"... You got some money?"
"A little."
"... Say, man, let the bitch go."

1970

Vivian shuddered. The attorneys' room at the Bridgeport facility was all metal, gray and cold. David Rosen leaned toward her, she bent forward without removing her hands from the parka's deep pockets. He whispered, "They're under a court order here not to eavesdrop on attorneys, but watch out, they think Leon's Che Guevara." He leaned back, she stayed hunched over, her gaze coming into focus on David Rosen's long slim fingers, his Harvard class ring, the frayed cuff of the Harris tweed and his battered watch.

A good soul, she thought, he is a true David, a sensitive scholar who never smiles, pale and luminous as the young Disraeli. She inched her hand forward to cover his, he flinched involuntarily, she squeezed and looked up at him, "Thanks for arranging this, David, I know how difficult it was." He looked at her, his big brown eyes were as wide open as a boy's.

The guard brought Masai in, chained hand and foot. "He needs the use of his hands to go through these documents," David said. Masai clanked down into a chair across from Vivian, their eyes went directly for each other. The guard shook his red head, "I can't do it."

David Rosen picked up his misshapen briefcase, "Let's go see the warden," moving out the door, forcing the guard to follow. The attorney held the heavy door open for the much larger but confused guard, further pressuring him to leave the room. "We'll be right back," David made eye contact with Vivian. "The warden'll settle this. Five minutes," and he was out, with the guard hurrying after the slim imperious advocate.

Masai leaned forward, "That was slick—y'all planned that?" She pursed her lips and nodded. "Shh," he smiled, "how you doing? You going to London? Don't go to Algeria, don't talk to Eldridge, don't go to Cuba. Shh. For now, stick with white people—be careful."

"David says that he can't bring me in to see you once you're assigned out of here upstate."

"This is it. At least until after the appeal. Be careful what you write, too."

"They read everything?"

Masai nodded. There was a piece of lint stuck in his big Afro. The blue prison uniform hung loose, his eyes were red with fatigue.

"Then I won't write at all," she said and stood up. "Sit down," he said softly and brought his manacled wrists up to rest on the table. "They'll be back in a minute. Open your blouse."

The tears started out of her eyes. She pulled her coat open first, then she unbuttoned her wool shirt. He held her eyes, he saw her tears. Then he looked down at her breasts for a long time, almost twenty seconds, until the drops poured out from his eyes, too. Each saw the other's tears. At the same instant they closed their burning eyes tight. Blackness.

November 1980

11/12/80

Dear Leon,

Are you sitting down? I'm actually mailing this to you instead of filing it, under "epic poetry," because certain things have happened.

For ten years I wrote the letters and did not send them, filed them, as a protest against what was done to you. Now, with the Election of Ronald Reagan both David and Katherine feel that your parole hearings will continue to be negative, especially since Reagan's first act is going to be to pardon all the convicted FBI agents indicted for civil rights violations against the peace movement, the Panthers, etc. You were correct: Reagan is in and, to quote further, there appears to be a "shit-storm" coming. So, for the next ten years, if need be, I will allow the Department of Corrections censors to touch my epistolary offerings.

"When sorrows come, they come not single spies, but in battalions": On the day I received your letter that your grandmother, Addie Mae Howard Perry Gatewood, had died in Gary, Indiana—my mother Leonora Walker Norton Battle was diagnosed as suffering from Alzheimer's disease. She is now officially nuts and cannot leave the house, etc. I want to say something about your grandmother, but first I have to complete this catalogue of woe that only begins with the arrival on the scene of Ronald Wilson Reagan, the rejection of your hearing, your grandmother's passing in her 10th decade, my mother's mad entrance into her ninth decade. This is only the short list and it ends with this entry: *I am going into the hospital tomorrow to have my left breast removed. I have very little to say about this event, I am running on hydromatic and I do not wish to dwell on the details until the end of this letter, if then, so let's talk about something else.*

Addie Mae. Of course, I only met her that one time and she was ill and old and nearly blind by then and, at any rate, I think, took a dim view of me. But over the years she somehow became one of my good mothers and I always thought of her through your eyes, as she once was in her prime, and I imagined her, before you knew her, in her youth, lanky as she must have been, a demon dancer driven by the Canal Street funeral marches of that day into the ambulatory frenzy that I've only seen photographs of. Anyway, she was alive for me and a part of my love for you and when I received your note saying that she had passed, I took it harder, much harder than when Bert Roberts called to confirm that Mother was now legally crazy. But, then, you see, I had "known" Addie Mae, and I had never, really, known my mother. Now that she's gone round the bend and begun to babble in a kind of Joycean stream of consciousness I may get to know her too well and wish she was again the haughty, distant, ice-cold bearer of the secrets that held sway here in this mausoleum for all these years.

—THERE'S THE TELEPHONE—BE RIGHT BACK—

It was the man who's doing the operation tomorrow, a Dr. Sebring, he wants me to sign something, they're all afraid of lawsuits. I'll sign, I've had a second and third opinion. I've lived without you and I can live without a breast. I will be more angry, that's all. Most people don't think I could be any more angry or hateful than I have always been so, like the missing breast, no one will notice. That's all I have to say about it right now.

Addie Mae: I had a dream in which an old black woman was here in this house walking through the empty rooms, with the majesty that I associate with your grandmother. And I was expected to follow her. So I did. I did.

Cancer! I almost told David to file a suit. This Cancer

EVERY THIRD HOUSE

Establishment is the medical equivalent of the Pentagon killing its own people. So I took refuge in Nietzsche:

> *Does not nature keep secret things, even about this body, e.g., the convolutions of the intestines, the quick flow of the blood currents, the intricate vibrations of the fibres, so as to banish and lock us up in proud, delusive knowledge? Nature threw away the key; and woe to the fateful curiosity which might be able for a moment to look out and down through a crevice in the chamber of consciousness, and discover that man, indifferent to his own ignorance, is resting on the pitiless, the greedy, the insatiable, the murderous, and, as it were, hanging in dreams on the back of a tiger ...*

Jesus ... The churches on the Green are tolling 3 a.m. "ding-a-ling-a-ling for you but not for me ..." Shite. "A dying animal," Yeats and Freud using the same phrase, but a "Death Wish," I don't know. I do know that if mother were competent she would definitely wish to die instantly. She had no virtues, as far as I'm concerned, except <u>virtue</u> in the Latin masculine sense, and she would never consciously have put herself in my hands. Now I will inherit and she never wanted that. She planned to give everything away to Yale and then live on like Queen Lear on my kind nursery, anyway she would want to die if she could see her Katherine Hepburn image being smashed to pieces, but I am not in the dying vein. Just the opposite. That is why I do not want to even go into the hospital. The one thing that Addie Mae did say to me was that, "They killed my mother in the white folks hospital over in Pineville. Child, don't say a word, they killed her!" I wrote it down, I used it in a poem, I remember it and I am thinking about it tonight!

Addie Mae. How did she die in Gary, Indiana, do you know? Why Gary, etc? Addie Mae was "fighting mad" she said, and took on the doctor at the "white hospital" and raised such unshirted hell they dragged her off to the asylum in Pineville—I am hearing those words and thinking about Addie tonight. Who do I fight? I've already threatened to seek disbarment, or whatever the hell it is, against the anesthetist if he gives me too much, "Do not plan to reduce me to a vegetable," I smiled icily, "as I have left strict instructions with my solicitors to act against you," all in a high British accent cleverly modeled on Lady Antonia who, herself, is modeled on the Queen of the Amazons, so that the anesthetist, a Dr. Pink, almost lost consciousness himself. Ha!

Well ... I had better say goodnight now. I will try to sleep, but I will think about you. We will think about you, my breasts and I, and the extreme left one will wink "so long" to you. I've just had a bright thought! They put you in prison and subtract your time one day at a time. I have been "free" all these years, but now I must forfeit a piece of myself, a pound of flesh, all at one stroke—twenty years for you, twenty minutes for me; time for you, flesh and blood for me; if you still have your body, I still have my "freedom." You have your body, but since you cannot use it you do not have it in any actual sense—so what I'm driving at is that this surgery has one bright secondary gain—It brings us closer together, that's why this breast of mine on her last night on earth is winking at you at this moment, because somehow part of me is leaving this world and entering the Kingdom of Time where you rule supreme—I think there's a poem in all this, anyway I feel much better. Much.

I'll let you go now, thanks for staying up with me all night. It was quite cozy, really, you and me and Addie Mae.

My love,

Vivian

P.S. In the case of Murphy's Law or Catch 22, I've left instructions with the lawyers. There is a document from me to you that xxxxx let's just say that I have made arrangements as any wife would do for her husband whom she loved more than death itself.

V.

November 1990

Kelly trudged through Trumbell thinking, "Fake!" glaring at the *faux* stone antiquity of the walls and buildings, "Complete fakes!", almost all of Yale having been reconstructed by the government worker programs of the 1930s, "W.P.A. fakes" to look like "Oxbridge clones" she screamed silently at a passing teaching assistant who smiled at her coldly. She scuffed by, thinking, "He knows, too."

Her boots scraped the cold stones. There was a raw wind blowing off the sound, there was a factor of windchill, but she was hot with the remembered humiliation of that night with Adam Phillips. She put it out of her mind, and turned toward the Federal Building, but it would not stay out. She tried to trick her mind with a "This snow I know" sequence of poetry, but her body remembered.

"This snow I know and so I go ..."
"Hot cider after class, my family's away?"
"This snow I know ..."
"Your paper on the 'Mill Girls Movement' was champion."
"This snow."
"Shall we take a shower together, and then I'll rub your body with oil? No more. I promise. You came into this house a virgin, you will leave it a virgin ..."
"This snow ... and so I go ..."

And she smelled the talcum powder again, and she swallowed hard as her body remembered.

Her father's limousine almost ran her over as she crossed Maple, head down.

"Kelly!"

He opened the door, "Get in, sweetheart." She stared. "Get in, we're blocking traffic." She stared. "Kelly, get in!" He clicked the door closed and they swung east heading for the highway. "Daddy."

"Surprised?"

"I am."

"Good, I have a surprise for you. Where do you think we're going right now?"

"... I don't know. I'm working today."

"No, you're not ... You're having Thanksgiving dinner with your *pater*. Fasten your seat belt."

"What?"

"A feast at the King's Tavern, in the enchanted forest. You remember?"

"... Now? Thanksgiving's tomorrow."

"I know and you said you couldn't come home. So I came down here to surprise you.—Well?"

"Daddy."

"Take the next exit, John—K-K-Kelly, beautiful Kelly, you're the only g-g-girl that I—"

"Daddy, shut up!"

"... adore."

"Shut up. It's only four o'clock."

"A feast ... You remember you used to think there were Indians lurking over there, you pronounced it 'lurching.' —What a character you were. —Still are ... How's your book coming along?"

"Fine."

"Good. When will you be finished?"

"Soon."

"Very good. You're signed up for next semester, you know?"

"I know."

"I talked to your chairman, Adam Phillips."

"... What did you say to Dr. Phillips?"

"Nothing. Just that you would be back after the holidays."

"... What did he say?"

"Phillips? Good, he said, good. Said he wanted you for T.A., teaching assistant, as soon as you finish your orals."

"... What? Say that again."

"What?"

"T.A. ... He said T.A.?"

"T.A. ... Yes."

"As in tits and ass? After my 'orals'? What are you talking about?"

" 'Teaching assistant,' T.A. ..."

"Why did you call him, Daddy? I'm going to have him arrested—don't call him, if I go back I'm going to work with Kai Erikson, if I go back, which is very doubtful, we may need at least another year for editing, et cetera, so please!"

"... Why are you yelling? ... Hungry? ... You remember the King's Tavern? ... Kelly? ... Ahh, what about Dr. Irving?"

"... What about him?"

"... You're not thinking of making a citizen's arrest of Maurice Irving also, are you?"

"A 'citizen's arrest'? Is that supposed to be a euphemism for 'kidnapping'?"

"Kidnapping?"

"Kidnapping, Kissingernapping—maybe you should go and see the great Dr. Irving."

"Would you want to go to, you know, go together to see him?"

"Ugh."

"... Turn right up there, John ... You haven't seen him—Irving?"

"Did you call him, too?"

"No."

"No. I haven't seen him. ... Don't call him, please."

"... How are you fixed for money?"

"Fine."

"Your allowance starts again as soon as you go back to school and, uh, back to—"

"—Back to Dr. Irving. Money's not the question."

"No, but you have to have money."

"I have money."

"From whom?"

"I'm working, Daddy."

"You're being—"

"I'm working. I get a weekly salary—"

"But you're not—"

"Plus room and board."

"… I'm still paying the rent on your Chapel Street place."

"I know, I told you to stop."

"No, it's there when you need it."

"You're wasting your money."

"Am I?"

"And your time."

"Time and money. Time is money."

"Clever, Daddy."

"Not wasting my life."

"That's good, Daddy—I said that's good."

"… Here we are. Hungry?"

"Is John coming in?"

"What?"

"John, are you going to eat?"

"Kelly—"

"No ma'am, I've got a big dinner tomorrow."

"Okay, good."

"Kelly—can we go in? John, I'll see you at around six."

Randolph Bailey and Kelly were the first guests of the evening. Chuck Taylor watched them walk in.

"Chuck."

"Randy."

"Who's this?"

"Kelly, do you remember Chuck Taylor?"

"Kelly, I knew you when you were this big. Isn't she a beauty? I love the 'cords' they wear, and the boots. You don't remember me, do you?"

"How do you do ... Where's the washroom, please?"

"The ladies room is through the bar and to the right."

"Thanks."

"... Randy, I've set you up over here by the fireplace."

"Chuck, there's a Mr. Ledoux that's going to join us."

"Not Frenchie Ledoux?"

"Yes. You know him?"

"For years. Hell of a man. I'll set up another—"

"No, Chuck, wait till he actually comes—it's a surprise for my daughter."

"Right. Here she is. —Kelly, how would you like a champagne cocktail?"

"No thanks. May I have a Diet Pepsi?"

"Randy, the wine, everything's ordered, so no menu today. Enjoy yourselves, wonderful to see you, Kelly."

Sam D'Amico, the waiter, served smoothly. Chuck Taylor leaned on the mahogany, sipping his old-fashioned, watching father and daughter in the glow from the real log fire. Turkey and nut stuffing, cranberries *français*, mixed potato *soufflé*, vegetables *anglais*, all in heavy lead plates, with wine goblets for both red and white, and brewed decaffeinated coffee with mince, pumpkin, berry pies for dessert: Kelly picked out only a few forkfuls of food. Her father ate a respectable portion. They talked very little.

"I'm spending tomorrow with the extended cousins. I told them to serve me ham ... Everyone sends you love. Maybe you'll be home for Christmas. Do you want to go to St. Kit?"

"I have to work."

"Christmas and New Years?"

"More wine, Mr. Bailey? Miss Bailey?"

"Thank you."
"Not for me."
"... You don't work on holidays."
"I'm working seven days a week."
"Three hundred and sixty-five days a year?"
"Yes."
"Is it necessary?"
"Of course."
"... This book?"
"Mm."
"You're not eating."
"It's early."
"What?"
"I'm not hungry."
"You look thin."
"Mm, anorexia nervosa ..."
"What's so funny?"
"Nothing."

At 5:47, a tall, well-set-up man in his early fifties walked into the restaurant. He took off his plastic raincoat, nodded at Chuck Taylor and walked over to the Bailey table. Bailey stood up.

"Hello."
"Kelly, this is Leo Ledoux, 'Frenchie.'"
"How do you do, Ms. Bailey? I'm actually half Irish."
"Hello."
"Sit down, Frenchie, and have Thanksgiving dinner."
"Just some pie and coffee."

A few people now stood at the bar, the Thanksgiving weekend was beginning. The proprietor, Taylor, shook hands with expensively dressed guests and, to start off the sullen festivities, ordered complimentary champagne cocktails for all.

"Kelly, Mr. Ledoux is a Special Agent with the FBI ... I asked him to join us for a—Kelly, sit down."
"I don't believe you did this!"

EVERY THIRD HOUSE

"Sit down."

"Ms. Bailey—I want you to understand that I am not, not, here officially. I am here as a friend of your father's. Period."

"Kelly, please—sit down for a moment, then we'll go ... Thank you ... Frenchie and I are friends. He used to work in Boston. We're friends. We talk every few months on a social basis. I'm very grateful to—"

"Could you get to the point?"

"You know you're a real bitch!"

"Randy!—Ms. Bailey, Kelly—this was my idea. I want to tell you something and then I have to get home, we're going skating. You like winter sports?"

"I beg your pardon?"

"Kelly, there've been nine bank robberies in this area in the past six months. All of them by masked men, most of them black. All of them linked to known black gangs."

"Coffee?"

"Just a drop, thanks ... They're building up a war chest. Waiting for Masai."

"... What? ... Waiting for Masai?"

"Right. He stays clean, never leaves the house, uses the Battle woman as his courier, uses you as his research cover—then when the book's ready he comes out and announces the formation of a new Black Panther Party. Goes public. Organizes nationwide. The war begins."

"War?"

"War. You're caught in a crossfire ... I came here today because you're in danger and I want to help you. War. Not like the '60s. We know that there are 300,000 gang members nationwide, 1,000 in New Haven alone."

"Mr. uh—"

"Frenchie."

"I know something about New Haven."

"She worked for the Census."

187

"We know."

"... There are about 1,000 male blacks in New Haven between the ages of 15 and 21—"

"—Kelly—"

"—so you're saying that all 1,000 are gang members?"

"... 300,000 nationwide."

"... Mr. Ledoux, the FBI records of the period show that there were never more than 5,000 Panthers—nationwide."

"That's the point. This is different. This is a war."

"... Kelly, Frenchie wants to help, honey."

"How?"

"Ms. Bailey—I have to tell you something, off the record. Masai Howard is considered the most dangerous, uh, militant in the country—but personally, and this is off the record, I think the man is being used."

"... What do you mean?"

"The man was in prison for almost twenty years. Hard time. He's in there reading, studying, working on his book. Outside, certain people are waiting, making plans and waiting. Twenty years pass and the bank robberies start. Someone's building up a war chest. Masai comes out. He goes to the Battle mansion. He locks himself in. The bank robberies increase. Old Panthers begin to show up around the country. You know Michael Zinzun?"

"... No."

"You've heard of him?"

"I don't know."

"Vivian Battle's in contact with him. Zinzun crisscrosses the country and then he reports to Battle. Or is it the other way around?"

"... What?"

"Who wears the pants? Does Masai give the orders to Vivian and then Vivian gives them to Michael Zinzun—or does Vivian give 'em both orders—and does she get her orders from London?"

"London?"

"You want a chocolate sundae, Kelly?"

"She goes to London every year—or does Zinzun give the orders—you see, I don't think Masai's the big man, I think he's a figurehead, and they're just using him. I feel sorry for the man. I do."

"You mean, because, uh …"

"I think he's being set up."

"… You do?"

"That's strictly off the record."

"… wh-who, uh-who do you …"

"I don't know. But unless I can find out, there's no way I can stop the man from being a target, when in fact he may be no more than a pawn for Moamar Kadaffi—who uses British intellectuals to control Vivian Battle to set up a Masai as a cover for terrorism and who knows what else is coming … So, because of your father I decided to take the chance and sit down with you and see if there wasn't some way we could get out of this mess and maybe Masai, too."

"I am grateful to you, Frenchie, for what you're doing for me and for my daughter."

"I just don't want to see the wrong people get hurt when this goes down … Kelly, can you help me on this? Go to London with Vivian Battle, work with Michael Zinzun, find out who's running the gangs and the bank robberies, et cetera. Then I could contact you through your dad and we can talk, and figure out a way, maybe, to get you and Masai out of this, before the war starts."

The agent leaned in close. "L'il Joe Jefferson," he said. "Who's that?" Mr. Bailey leaned forward, too. "What about him?" Kelly's voice dropped. Their heads huddled together. "Dangerous," the agent whispered, "stay away from him. He's a dead man."

Kelly's father stood up and walked to the bar to pay the check. Kelly stared at the fork marks on the linen. Ledoux's long hand moved toward her. "Never call me. Contact your father. He'll invite you for a dinner, et cetera, you accept. That's all."

A log popped in the fireplace. She gave a jerk. There was another report. The FBI man nodded slowly. His eyes were as black as his hair, his skin was olive. Frenchie, she thought, he's half Corsican probably, probably African way back, two hundred years, ancestor, does he know it?

His lips angled sideways and he mouthed something. "What?" Then he breathed the words over to her—Masai's words—"I said there's a shit-storm coming."

They drove back to New Haven. It was dark. Kelly said not one word to her father. She watched the road. She twisted her lips tight together. She peered out into the dark forest flashing past.

Indians lurching, drunken Indians, the correct category is "Native American," the white race is finished, my father is a criminal, he taught me to laugh at Indians lurking in the forest. Mother laughed. Mother went to her art class to draw charcoal sketches of a black model. The time she took me, the girl disrobed, amazing.

"Take me again, please, Mother!"

"No."

"Mother, —you want some water, —with a straw?"

"Dahh—"

"What?"

"Don't drink—my glass."

"... Grandma Bailey's here."

"Ahh?"

"Grandma Bailey's here to see you."

"Naah-ha."

"... Alright. I'm going now, Mother ... It's graduation night ... Goodbye."

"Aahhh-ha."

The white race is kaput ... Me and Frenchie save Masai. Frenchie dark, "swarthy," phenotype, genotype, full of sperm, we hide out in a hidden estate in Rhode Island, The Battle Foundation Estate. Masai lives there, what do we do? We work. Frenchie guards the estate; Frenchie is naked, he has a machine gun and he guards us. Masai and me we read, we write, we eat, we walk in the gardens, the Indians lunch in the woods, but they don't dare challenge Frenchie. Frenchie and Masai. Frenchie and Masai and me. Me and Masai. Me and Frenchie.

"C'mon, Kelly, let's sing you-know-what."

"No."
"Aw, please."
"Daddy, no!"
"Come on, once a year:

> '... When the men of Eli break through the line
> What is the song we hail?
> Bulldog, Bulldog, Bow-Wow-Wow
> Eli Yale!' "

"Stop the car!"
"What?"
"Stop the car! I have to vomit!"

8:13 P.M.

Leonora heard Kelly slip into the house. Vivian and the black man didn't hear, they kept arguing upstairs. Mother and Daddy kept arguing upstairs. Mother and Daddy kept arguing upstairs. Leonora could hear the voices through the wood:

> "... Trumbell. Then they went ... alone!"
> "... I won't hear ... Leonora is ... you're ..."
> "—your voice to me you stupid cow ... my word ... that pansy father, don't open your ... stupid ... to ... you cunt you dumb stupid cunt and you're ... into a cunt just like you ... cold cunt like you only she's not stupid like you she ... to marry a fruit like ... a hundred million dollars but ... a cold cunt like ... marry a fruit like your father so you wouldn't have to sleep with ... a real man, you can't stand real men ... drove me to other women because you're a cold calculating cunt like your daughter who froze me out ... some nerve to dare to mention drinking to me ... crazy as your mother, crazy Walker women all of you ... three generations of scheming murderous cunts ... me, you'd like to kill me, cut my throat, wouldn't you? Go ahead you ... Go ahead! Stand up! Stand up you ... you cunt you whore you bitch you cow you sow you!"

Flesh. The sound of it. Slap, slick, slip, slop, slide, sluice, slime, swallow. Leonora lay rigid, listening to the silence. Her heart pumped. She licked her lips. She remembered the barn.

The hay. "Jingle bells, jingle bells" ... bundled up on the sleigh. Cold cheeks, rosy, not clammy—cold, clean, clear, Daddy dear, Mommy dear. If I die here in the hay ... "On bob-tail high ..." Drooling into the hay. Swallow. "... take it while you can ..." Mother. Stand up. Oh, dear. The black man and Vivian stopped yelling, upstairs, and started laughing. They know, Leonora thought, they know, too.

"*Vivian!*"

1983

Comrade,

   Vincent Costansa is assistant to the Warden here. He's a human being whose job it is to read segregated prisoners' mail. He has always treated me decently, but after he read your letter to me of April 3, he came down and handed me the letter in person and said, "Howard, marry this woman, no matter how you have to do it, this woman is the tops." Then he turned around and walked away, tears in his eyes. Then I read the letter.
   Your "Meditation on Fat Man" should be published just as it is as a poem, or whatever, because it blows you away. I showed it to Paul Allen. Paul's an old-time bank robber who knows more about Tolstoy and Dostoyevsky probably than anyone in the world. He's in the kitchen now and the food is much improved, and when he read it he teared up too, and wants to set it up in type here and distribute it through the system in the prison newsletter and tear sheets. Alright? When you can get guards and cons both bawling over a vision of nuclear

winter then maybe you've proved something about non-violence, anarchy, Christian love, etc.

Paul Allen sits up all night smoking Kools and telling me that I'm misunderstanding Tolstoy. Now, Paul was a bank robber and he has a feel for "evil" that everybody in the joint has to respect. Paul was featured in <u>Life</u> magazine in a big white hat in the '40s as the new Dillinger and Pretty Boy Floyd etc. He would like to meet you, if you can ever stand to visit again, as he says that you all have a lot in common. The guard, Vincent Costansa, likewise would like an autographed book of your poetry. The fact is these men are half way in love with you and after "Meditation on Fat Man" goes out on the grapevine, cons and screws all through the system are going to go to sleep beating their meat to the tune of "Mutual Aid."

Seriously now, you've plunged your life into the sociology of poverty, but can anyone outside it ever really "know" the poverty of the wretched of the earth? Take Addie Mae when she was coming up in Bunkie, LA, picking close to a bale of cotton a day!

Addie told me that from "can't see to can't see" you worked in the cotton fields, you were a child, but they "was workin' the women just like they do the men." She'd start into to sing about "19 and 10" and the "Captain" and the dogs. Don't ever believe that somehow U.S.A. oppression is less than these other dictatorships--it's not less in quality or in <u>quantity</u>. You hear what I'm saying? And Addie would go into her war dance singing, "Should've been on the River, 19 and 10--they was driving the womennnnn, just like they do the men." Your hair stood up.

SATURDAY

It got too late, I lost my train of thought. What I was trying to say is that non-violent Anarchy needs peace and stability, at a minimum level at least, to have a chance. What the damned of the earth have is endless war. What we have now is not peace. Not for black or white. Paul Allen the old bank robber can run down that poor white Bonnie and Clyde story for you until you think you haven't even visited America. It's not just a bunch of old photographs in some books from the 1930s (by the way, thank you for sending the Walker Evans/Agee book), the white race in this country has been swindled so bad it's turned an Episcopalian like you into a Marxist—non-violent—Anarchist poet that everyone here has fallen in love with. Paul Allen and his gang knew how to wear duds good as a nigger, I mean white hats, gold key chain and all, and they had their music, too, and their religion and their own war, but they had not been slaves, quite, here, so in a way that was worse for some of them. This is heavy stuff and I need a lot more from Paul before I can even work up a good footnote on it.

You say you're still trying to get a focus on Addie. She was just a skinny kid down in Bunkie fighting that cotton when her mother took ill. Of course there weren't any colored hospitals in a little place like Bunkie, none any closer than Pineville, outside of Alexandria (built before the days of Huey P. Long) so they took her in there and she died, or rather they killed her, as you know from your oral history, Dr. Battle. Can't mail this today, so I'll try to wind it up tomorrow.

MONDAY

Feeling good today. John Cheever came in last night to teach a writing class and he and I and Paul Allen had a good talk about how the Red-hunts of the 1950s killed the novel in America and everything else. I like him even though he's shaky on his history of America before 1900. Had a talk about <u>Othello</u> and how Iago is a punk. Paul said the joint's full of Iagos.

So here's the Leon Howard—Paul Allen Theory of the Wealth of Nations. Modern (Post Renaissance) capitalism is founded on crime. It is all power and nothing else, and the problem is that the under-industrial or Third World or Revolutionary states cannot capitalize enough to overcome the colonial powers of NATO, etc., because they cannot sell slaves or opium or other people's oil and gold, etc. as cash crops and so they go Stalinist or they "democratize" and fall apart under the force of the "Free" markets. So what is to be done? "Rob banks!" quoth Brother Allen, the White Panther.

But you ask, alright, so there's a new flag etc., but what happens after, if we win (far out as that idea is), how do we keep from becoming beggars on horseback? Because there's no capital to build socialism or fight off capitalist subversion, so are we suggesting God? No. Well, then, what crime is it that we are contemplating that is vast enough to fund the Revolution of the 21st century?

"What crime?" you ask.

I am working on it.

Blood to the Horse's Brow,

L.

November 1990

Vivian cooked the Thanksgiving feast. She put the sweet potatoes and the scalloped oysters in the second oven at 350° and thought about drinking wine and smoking and cooking. She took the cranberries out of the mold, calling back the Thanksgiving at Charles Garry's house in San Francisco, in the kitchen "burning" with Bobby Seale while Huey Newton lectured Garry and Masai, in the living room, about the meaning of the film *Sweet Sweetback's Badass Song* and how Karl Marx's unconscious racism kept him from understanding the revolutionary role of the *lumpenproletariat*, but all Garry would say was "Eldridge Cleaver's a con and he always will be."

She remembered and exhaled a silent laugh and stared out at the snow clouds, then checked the turkey, basted it (thirteen pounds, small, she thought, pitiful), and walked into the big parlor. "Two hours," she called. Masai looked at her, "Go ahead," he said to Kelly, "read it out loud."

The girl cleared her throat, "Counterintelligence program, Black Nationalist–Hate Groups, Racial Intelligence. Black Panther Party (BPP). Re NK at 9/18/69. Authority is granted New Haven to mail the cartoon submitted in referenced letter. When mailing this cartoon, care and strict security is to be maintained. New Haven should advise if any results received from this mailing."

"Dinner's in two hours," Vivian turned to leave.

"What is this?" Kelly sought out Vivian's eyes, Masai looked at her, too. Vivian turned back into the room and took one Xerox out of Kelly's hand.

"This cartoon of a pig, designed and mailed anonymously by the FBI, under the title, 'VIVIAN BATTLES A PIG,' was produced to frighten merchants who might otherwise have contributed to the Panthers' Hot Breakfast for Children Program, and, at the same time, it was intended to sow suspicion in the Panthers about white support." She handed it back.

"But the pig—"

"Is me." Vivian looked at Masai, but he was at the window watching the Green turn white.

"Oh," Kelly said, "these are classics of American sociology."

"Indeed they are. Note the pseudo-ghetto spelling and writing style here. Last month Pig Battle spoke at a rally for Huey Newton and kept shouting, 'We are all Panthers, we are all Panthers,' and urged the crowd to protect the Panthers—'with our lives if necessary.'

BUT WHO WAS IT TALKING TO PIG BATTLE JUST TEN MINUTES AFTER THIS RALLY??? IT WAS THE N.H.P.D.

<u>All power to the People.</u>"

Vivian handed it back again, "So if anything happened to me the Panthers'd be blamed—two birds with one stone." Masai cut in— "Put all the FBI documents in the Appendix I folder."

"Right. After the list of murdered Panthers."

"Mark it, 'The War at Home.' "

Vivian touched Kelly's elbow, "Would you go and—"

"She can't help you cook now."

"No," Vivian said, "what I need for her to do is to go and turn on Mother's music before she wakes up." Masai nodded once, Kelly put down the paper and started out, "What was J. Edgar Hoover's problem, exactly?" she asked *en passant*.

"He liked black men," Vivian shut the door after the student and walked over to the alcove and stood next to Masai, talking to him in a low warning tone before the girl came back. "You going to stop for dinner? ... Her father called me. Threatening deep trouble—if you don't let his daughter leave here and go back to school ... I think he has a point. The manuscript looks to me like it's running to about three volumes."

Masai pulled the heavy drapes across the windows.

"What's the matter?" Vivian moved a step deeper into the new shadows and pulled the drapes back open.

"Someone's coming," he whispered.

"Here?" she asked. "No ... When does it end?" her question trailed away.

"The book? We haven't even started on Volume Four. —That's the one on sex. You want that one, don't you?"

"What I want is for you to take the responsibility for this manuscript that young people are supposed to read and bleed and die for ... I want you to consider going away—Please leave the drapes open."

"—Volume Four tells all about how the Panthers raped the Daughters of the American Revolution—"

"—to South Africa with me."

"... And produced a race of super swine ... South Africa?"

The music spread through the house from Leonora's quarters. *Madama Butterfly*, yet again, Vivian winced, "Christ!" under her breath, then, "South Africa. Why not? We might have a chance there. We don't here." Closer to him, making him look at her instead of the white Green and the stupid Christmas decorations in front of the courthouse—"You don't understand what's happened here while you were gone. In theory, yes, but not —Leon, this is not the same country—you are under house arrest!—if you—"

Kelly leaned her head through the door; "She's awake, I think she wants—"

"Kelly, could you just give us a few minutes, please?" Vivian and Masai looked at her, her pink flushed face, the gray sweat suit loose now because her baby fat had been burned off up there in that attic with him. Vivian thought, Potiphar's wife with her breast and haunch everywhere you look. "Certainly," the girl said, backing out. *"Vivian!"* Leonora screeched from within.

"Leon, you've got to come with me, into the projects, and put these boys into your book, before it's too late."

"You think I'm afraid to go out there?"

"Then go. You've served your time, every day of it. The cell door's open."

"... When I get ready to go out there, I won't come back. I'll go out there with the book, and I'll stay." He reached for the drapes.

"Don't threaten me, Leon. If you went out there and tried to give your book to these gangbangers they'd laugh in your face, they'd call you crazy—they'd kill you, comrade." She tried to laugh, it came out like a yelp, she tried to pull the drapes open, he held her wrist.

They're going to 'Weed and Seed' them out before you ever get there," she said, I'm losing them, they're dropping out of the Center Church program because the police won't let them live and they're—the kids—ready to kill cops and some of them think that I'm keeping them under wraps, away from you, and they've been waiting *six months* to see you—six months is a lifetime to these kids, four of them are dead since you came out, that you'll never meet, and the pre-teens, six out of ten have lead poisoning, dying of—"

"What?" He pulled her by the wrist a half step closer. The music pushed in from Leonora's quarters. She looked into his eyes, they held eyes, their eyes were naked, they blinked, their heads were pounding, "It's in the papers, you're the great researcher, don't you read the papers? The poor children of this country are being retarded and, ah, handicapped and killed by the lead poisoning in these tenements and projects, it's not on the front page like the drive-by shootings and the gang shoot-outs but it's known, it's out there, it's not Auschwitz, it's not hidden—seven in ten!" Her breath was short, under the music, her voice in his face, her head was splitting. "Now," she whispered.

"Everyone's ready. Michael Zinzun and his ironmen, the youth, some of the Rainbow Coalition."

"What they ready for?"

"Close down Projectville. This is the 'Model City,' isn't it? This is

Reagan's 'City on a Hill'." Close down Projectville—a siege, galvanize the whole country."

"Who?" He mouthed the word.

"You. Me. Whoever. We issue a call."

" 'Come to New Haven!' "

"Exactly. I've thought it through."

"Go ahead."

Kelly was back in the doorway watching because they didn't see her this time; they were so close together in the shadows that they looked like one body to the girl. The music washed past her, she strained to hear Vivian.

"I have maps. You've been upstairs, I've been down, you took the high order of abstraction, I took the low, you want to see my maps?"

"You crazy?"

"'History will decide who's crazy!' Ha!—Leon, comrade, here's the plan. Alright. Mmm ... We organize rent strikes—listen—one unit at a time in Projectville demanding an urban 'Marshall Plan'—when the confrontation comes we burn down that unit and the families retreat deeper into the project and move in to share living space with the next unit and so on until the, ah, the—"

"We burn our way all the way back to the campus on live T.V."

"Don't patronize me, big man, I'm talking about a giant metabolism of intersecting and fundamental needs and passions—all these, *now*, waiting for the nonviolent plan of action that will take a year to organize *if*, and only if, you take the leadership. Because there's enough money for a model action like New Haven, and there's a student base to come in as a teacher-corps when the rent strikes close the schools—and none of this takes away from your bloody book because, just the opposite, it will *make* your book because it'll be the *record* of what we *do* here!"

"The New Haven Commune? —You the roughest white woman goin'."

Kelly couldn't hear what Masai said to Vivian, but she could see her stiffen and try to pull her arm free. Then the music stopped, like a wave of sound retreating it left her uncovered in the doorway so that Masai saw her out of the corner of his eye but Vivian was riveted on Masai's face, pulling back with her whole weight against the strength of one of his arms, her heels dug in, fixed in struggle, panting but otherwise fixed.

"The faces," panting, "all their faces, all the faces that you will never see," gasping, "L'il Joe Jefferson, you have to meet him, he's *you* at twenty, he's a leader, he's like Huey, he's like you, he's like your son!"

As if to fill a sensory vacuum, the odor of the Thanksgiving feast cooking in the kitchen seemed to infiltrate where the music had been. Kelly smelled it, it made her dizzy with hunger. Leonora would smell the food now, and scream out, and they would turn and see her, except Masai already sensed that she was there as if he could smell her, her fear and hunger, above the aroma of the cooking bird, but Vivian was blind and deaf and without any sense except the pull and weight of her body against the flexed arm, until her voice broke out of the silence,

"Do you hate me—because I didn't go to prison?"

"Everybody does their own time ... Go baste your bird."

"Those are your sons out there, Leon, some of them, and all you 'iron men' who sprayed your seed around here before—"

Kelly could tell from where she stood that he had tightened his grip on Vivian's wrist just enough to cut off her breath. Vivian was up on her toes seeking leverage. She spat it out, *"You seeded them and they're weeding them. You been crying wolf all these years and now it's here—genocide—it's happening, weed and bloody seed, your bloody seed—ah!"* He tightened and she went right up on her toes and her voice moved up high into the nasal register where screams visit. "You blame me—because for twenty years, almost, I said that your book would be our baby!"

"Help!" Leonora shrieked and Vivian fell forward against his chest. He had to hold her up. She hung against his chest, rested there with her eyes closed, they were one physical mass again, merged into the heavy folds of the drapes. He tilted his head toward Kelly, red-eyed, then Vivian opened her eyes and little by little she focused on the girl, too. Silence, and then from her quarter Leonora cried out again. No one moved.

"Sh-she's laughing," Kelly said. "She's not crying, she's laughing." They all waited. Vivian spoke to Masai but she never took her eyes off the girl. Her voice was broken.

"Our baby ... But it was just a metaphor. Just a lie. Just another face that we will never see."

Masai held her up. They both kept looking at Kelly. "She's gone crazy," he said almost tenderly, as if to make her their judge. Then it was Vivian's turn again, "No, I'm sane. You can test me. This is 1990, the year of the census. This is now—the year of the census—and that was *then*—the year of the Pig."

They looked at her, waiting, resting their case. Kelly swayed in the archway. Then Masai took Vivian's throat lightly in his right hand and held her that way, looking at her, but Vivian's gaze never left Kelly's face.

"...'Now, how dost thou look now? O ill-starred wench! ... Cold, cold, my girl! Even like thy chastity'..."

He looked back at Kelly and stretched out his left arm and she moved toward the two of them as if the scene had been rehearsed forever, until she could go no further and settled against his chest next to Vivian so that they were both within the ambit of his arms, all together in the alcove of dark and heavy drapes, one mass, together. Silence and the aroma of the bird until he slowly kissed them both on their mouths. Vivian, first, then the girl, then Vivian again.

Leonora smelled the food. Then she died. As she started to die she said to herself, "I don't care." Then she saw stars and said, "Oh, dear." Then her bowels and her memory gave way and what was past, now and then, washed out of her:

Leonora sat at the children's table kicking Bettina softly but steadily. Each cousin's face was Christmas clear: Bettina, John L., John III, Walker, Madeline, Pauline, Cooper. She watched their mouths. Mouthing, she thought, mincing, munching, mucking. The hot vomit rose in her throat, her stomach turned over, because the turkey trussed up in the middle of the table on the old silver platter was her—they were going to eat her. Like in the barn. She staggered off the porch into the house and up the stairs, past the arch and the grownups' feast. Out of the eating and the laughter, voices chased her. "Who's that?" and Grandfather Norton's settled baritone answering, "That's little Leonora."

At High Hill, after Miss Randolph's Academy, she told Doctor Whitehouse about the time she thought she was the turkey on the Christmas platter and how it made her sick and how she still couldn't eat much of anything and that was why she was so thin and anemic and nervous. But she didn't tell the doctor anything about the Sundays after Father Gruber's sermon and "Jingle Bells" at Christmas.

That spring they were taken to Chattanooga, where Mary Garden sang "Pale Hands I Love" and Leonora informed Doctor Whitehouse that she felt ready to go and resume her schooling.

"You feel more at ease?"

"Yes, sir, I do."

"And the thoughts?"

"It's better."

"The arguments, your cousins, mm, the turkey?"

"Yes, sir, it's better."

"You feel you can eat and go back to school and concentrate on your education?"

"Yes, sir."

"Then what? Marriage, a family—how do you see it?"

"I'm interested in medicine."

"... I see. Your mother mentioned a tour of the continent. Would you profit from that, do you think?"

"Well, I think it would do my mother some good."

"—I see. Why do you say that?"

"You don't know my family, do you?"

"I know of them, of course, but I've only actually met your mother."

"You are lucky, Doctor Whitehouse."

"Why do you say that, Leonora?"
"What?"
"I say, why do you say that?"
"Why do I say what?"
"You said, 'I was lucky because I don't know your family personally.'"
"—I never said that."
"You just said it."
"I didn't say it, you said it."
"... I said it?"
"Yes, you did. You surely did ... but I won't tell anyone, Doctor Whitehouse ... Goodbye."

After that, in the barn, she took her revenge. She urinated on the place just to the left of the ladder if you faced the west wall just even with the cobweb window. Then she defecated at the other place, behind the wagon bed where it was never light. She tried to vomit, tried to faint, but she couldn't, so she went back to the house and drew a quart of kerosene and three matches and came back out and set the dry bales by the door on fire, and turned, walking, back toward the house without looking back so that when her mother asked her, later, her answer was the literal truth.

"Leonora—we had a fire in the barn."
"We did?"
"Didn't you see the smoke?"
"No."
"Well, luckily I did. Minnie made these noodles especially for you."
"I'm eating them."
"Your appetite is better."
"Yes."
"... I rang the bell when I saw the smoke."
"You did?"
"Everyone heard it. Ernest ran down, and Annie, and Minnie and they saved it, part of it, well, anyway, kept it from spreading ... Where were you, when I rang the big bell, I mean?"
"Where was I? I don't know."
"You must've been in the house, dear."
"Hm ... I must've been asleep."
"Asleep?"
"Yes."
"I see ... Yes, well, you know, Minnie cooked these especially for you."

Leonora was smelling the food and remembering and dying. "I don't care," she repeated, "they can all go to hell, I'm going to Maine, Grandmother Walker's. I don't care." Then she called out her husband's name—"Henry"—but there was no one there to hear. Then, "Mother"—then to herself again, "I did no harm." She hung on to that idea—no harm—hung on like a hand in need, to Ernest Tree's black hand.

> "Miss Leonora, put your foot on this one, that's right, don't be scared, I catch you—now give me both hands—now put your hands on my shoulders, there we are, now jump. There we are!"
> "Oh!"
> "Don't let your mother catch you in that tree."
> "'Tree'? Your name's Tree."
> "Sure is."
> "Where did you get that name?"
> "Mm-mm-well. They say that my granddaddy worked for a man, in Georgia, named Tremont. That's the story."
> "Tremont?"
> "And when he came up North they used to call him 'Tree,' you know, for short, and that's how come I came by having it."
> "Tree."
> "Honey, let me brush you off, then go in the house and wash yourself before your mother sees you."
> "Tree, I didn't do nothing bad."
> "Not a thing in the world."

Now she died with her hands and legs full of memory—clinging to the worn black hand then her legs were pumping running toward the cottage Grandmother Walker's Maine cottage the Red House racing—"Ernest take care of me—Ernest take care of Vivian—Ernest take care of us—"

207

NOVEMBER 1990

NEW HAVEN REGISTER		Saturday, November 27, 1990

LEONORA NORTON BATTLE; SCION OF TWO NOTED FAMILIES, YALE TRUSTEE
By Richard Medico

Leonora Norton Battle, scion of two of America's most prominent families, of natural causes at 95. Mrs. Battle, the widow of Henry Wilson Battle III, was related to two American presidents through the Norton and Walker families (her maternal uncle) and to President Woodrow Wilson through her husband, Henry Wilson Battle III, the late comptroller of the House of Morgan in the 1930s and early 1940s.

Mrs. Battle died in her New Haven townhouse, considered a priceless state trust house, on New Haven Green on Thanksgiving Day according to her attorney, Barrington L. Foster II of the Manhattan firm of Cromwell and Sullivan.

When her parents died in the 1920s, Mrs. Battle is said to have inherited fifty million dollars to add to her husband's fortune. Mr. Battle with his cousin, Jock Hay Whitney, helped finance the new radio communication corporations of those days.

Mrs. Battle succeeded her husband as a Yale University trustee on his death, at which time she resigned as Republican National Committeewoman, in which role she had campaigned for General Eisenhower, once leading a delegation of well-known business leaders to call on General Eisenhower at Columbia University in

1949, where he was then president, in a bid to encourage Mr. Eisenhower to become the GOP nominee for president.

Later, after Mr. Eisenhower did run for and became president, Mrs. Battle was chosen to represent the United States in Paris at the Bi-Cultural Congress that took place there in the years 1954–1958. When the Congress was exposed as a front for the Central Intelligence Agency, Mrs. Battle resigned and returned to the Yale Board of Trustees.

Mrs. Battle is survived by her daughter, Vivian Norton Battle, a prize-winning poet whose first book, published in 1965, *The Dead Shall Rise*, won a number of poetry prizes, including the Rockefeller Award.

In 1969, Mrs. Battle's daughter was arrested in a notorious New Haven conspiracy case involving white antiwar dissidents like Miss Vivian Battle, Yale students, and the Black Panther Party for conspiring to kidnap then National Security Adviser Henry A. Kissinger, during a speaking engagement at the Yale Law School.

Mrs. Battle came to her daughter's defense and, with the help of Dr. Kissinger, persuaded the court that Miss Battle had been manipulated by the so-called Minister of Education of the Black Panther Party, Leon H. Howard, who was convicted of conspiracy to kidnap Dr. Kissinger, and served his full sentence of twenty years in …

December 1990

"Come in." Vivian sat in her window bay washed in cold moonlight. "Come in, Kelly, what time is it?"

"You're up? After two."

"Naturally. My mother ruined my sleep while she was alive, why should her ghost have pity on me now?—Sit down. It's cold, let's go down and have a hot drink."

They went down to the butler's pantry and heated cocoa. "You may have a marshmallow." They sat at the wood table Leonora had brought from Ireland in the '20s, in the soft light of the French bottle lamp that she had sent back from Paris in the '30s.

"I never knew your mother, uh, before, but I know that she must've once been a powerful woman and that this must be a bad t-time for you."

"Thank you. And for all the help this week ... Yes, she was a, they were all characters ... Do you know Gertrude Stein?"

"No."

"She said that who you are depends on what sky you were raised under, I'm paraphrasing, but Leonora, her crowd, was raised, grew up, underneath this New England sky. Out there, on that Green, that was their stage, Center Church and the Church of the Regicides and before that, in the day of her grandfather's father, when the churches were meeting houses, and if—you've probably studied all this, I'll let you go to bed, I'm—"

"No, go on, I'm not—I'm interested."

"You're a good soul."

"I am, I'm interested—in your mother, in you and her. The whole thing."

"... Well ... The life of the town was in the churches. If you had money, power, they called you 'Mister' and you sat in the front pews. Next came the small merchant class and they were called 'Brothers and Sisters,' last was the craftsmen, 'Goodman and Goody'—there were no seats for the servants and slaves, or, of course for the Indians from whom it had all been stolen in the first place—anyway, this was the 'Fair Haven' she grew up in, that's the old name, and the sky over her head was the same sky that hung over the original 'Fundamental Agreement' down below the Green."

"The Fundamental Agreement, that's funny."

"The Fundamental Agreement was that cunning mix of theocracy and mercantilism that made the family fortune, and the New Haven First Church of Christ the ruling circle around here and a few families the 'chosen people' until C. W. Norton, my great-grandfather, spread the Word through the Valley and extended the mixed blessing of the Fundamental Agreement to Branford and Milford and Guilford and Stanford, who, in turn, cloned their own ruling circle and more or less enslaved the new Irish and Italian immigrants whose epigoni and pony-tailed heirs now wait for the end in the ruined mill towns of the Naugatuck Valley, at St. Anne's and Holy Name of the Virgin, while we crouch at Christ's Church and Trinity and United and ..."

Kelly watched Vivian's lips shape and cut out the words in long swooping parentheticals, the hands smoothing the way for the words and all the time brushing the air aside, or as if arranging and rearranging phantom drinks and cigarettes. She stared at Vivian's faded bathrobe, cheap even when it was new, and touched her own soft cashmere sleeve, smiled to signify that she was listening, and licked up some marshmallow. Vivian's cocoa will be cold if she doesn't stop long enough to drink it, she thought, so I better take her marshmallow ...

"... Mother said her grandfather beat his wife, I know he beat his servants, they all did, father to son, husband to wife in the long retaliation since Genesis.... You have to go there—Derby, Ansonia, Shelton, ah, Seymour, Thomaston—the Catholic masses, this was Leon's jury, not my mother, her class does not serve jury duty anymore than they ..."

Kelly watched the moving hands, the shaping lips; it was cold, Vivian hunched up in her thin robe. Kelly wanted to hug her, keep her warm. Where was Masai, why didn't he take care of her, why didn't he sleep with her? The United clock sounded 2:30. Kelly licked her cup and tuned in again.

"... 'the witches do say that they form themselves much after the manner of Congregational Churches'—Ha! These people were corrupted root and branch by these witch-hunts. The children, my mother's childhood because of it, it wasn't just communists under the bed, or, later, Black Panthers—they traded away their personal lives including their sexual lives, these compulsive traders, traded away their private lives for their political lives and their political lives *were* their paranoid private lives, that's why I knew that I was adopted because it was perfectly clear to me that my forty-four-year-old mother had never slept with my father and that I, therefore, was some Italian or Irish waif from the Valley that they had adopted for their own inscrutable reasons, and that every year when Mother made me go in the touring car—with old Ernest Tree at the wheel, to distribute Christmas presents to destitute white children over in the Valley—I always believed that those white and wasted children were my natural siblings, and that one of these times Mother would slam the limousine door shut and order Ernest to drive off and leave me there—Christ! You never bargained for this, did you? Ha!"

The girl smiled and shook her head. "You're a good soul," Vivian said again. "I'm not tired, really," Kelly said, "it's getting really cold, should I make a fire in the fireplace in your room?"

"No, thanks. You have to get up early, so do I, I have to go over to my attorney's. I just want to talk to you a minute about the, ah ...

your father called me. He's concerned about you. I tried to reassure him, but I don't know, but I said I'd talk to you, so—will you forgive my impertinence?"

"My father's a liar."

"I know, but still ... He has a point, for the wrong reasons, but still a point, but I have a new option for you now. My mother's will's going to be read tomorrow. I'm going to have a lot of money in a few months. Enough to leave this country with Leon so that he can meet people in Europe, who've supported him over the years, and talk to them about the future, and then come back here and turn the book in and then, mm, who knows? But I want to give you some money, a large sum, so that you're not stuck between staying here or going back to your father or his 'plan,' etcetera."

Kelly felt the full focus of Vivian's eyes and voice and hands on her. Her eyes flinched away for an instant to the front of the robe to the flat absent breast, to the full breast remaining—"the remains," she thought—"The b-book's up to Masai—"

"The b-book's up to Masai, exactly." Vivian's voice suddenly had the edge of Leonora's and they both heard it. "After the holidays you have to go back to school, that was the original understanding, but now if you like, you can go to some other school or just study or whatever you, ah... But I want you to go somewhere—so that I can, ah, so that Leon and I can get away for a while to make our plans."

"... Couldn't I go with you? Or stay here with Rose and take care of—"

"No." Vivian beckoned Kelly to her, spoke in a low tone, "I've had a word, a talk, with Rose, and with Jan—they won't be staying on." The girl shifted from foot to foot, "I thought your mother, that, uh ..." Vivian shook her head. The girl sighed. "I could stay and help with the, you know, the—"

Vivian put her hand on Kelly's shoulder, sensing her fear of separation and knowing that she had to make it worse: "Kelly—Rose and Jan couldn't work here anymore because the FBI was pressuring them to do all sorts of things, including installing listening devices,

213

and Jan's father is a policeman and they got to him, and it would be worse with anyone new. So—let's just close up the old place and 'light out for the territory,' like Huck Finn, shall we?"

Kelly put her hands over her face and turned away, Vivian kept her grip on the girl's shoulder. "It's a sad day. Rose was here for many years and she's very upset. But that's where we are. You said yourself that government comes to every third house, remember?"

Kelly wiped away the tears, tried to smile; Vivian took her hand and kissed it, "No more servants, we'll be poor—sweet child, I'm joking, 'kidding on the square,' we used to say—when we were very frightened, like you are now." She held the young woman in her arms.

"Where—"

"Go to bed. Or sleep here ... I'll say goodbye to Rose and Jan and the gardener for you. But what you have to do is make a plan for *yourself*—shh!—I know, I know," and her voice was softer than Kelly had ever heard it. "I don't know where we might go or when, that's the problem, and you must not determine or define yourself or your life by us, by Leon—"

"No, I—"

"—any more than by your father!" They stepped back from each other. Vivian looked at the curdled film covering her untouched cocoa, then back across at Kelly.

"Kelly, you're free ... I'm going to give you a 'grant' for your work—of a million dollars."

$\mathscr{D}$ECEMBER 1990

Date: 12/3/90

To: DIRECTOR, FBI

From: SAC, NEW HAVEN

Subject: NATIONAL SECURITY, TERRORISM

The below material is derived from a CONFIDENTIAL SOURCE and must be maintained at the SEAT OF GOVERNMENT and is not to be transmitted to resident agencies.

Subjects identified are LEON HURLEY HOWARD, a.k.a. "Masai" a male Negro born 2/11/41, Baton Rouge, La. Howard is a former member of the BLACK PANTHER PARTY. VIVIAN NORTON BATTLE, born 5/3/39, Paris, France, Howard's unindicted co-conspirator in the 1970 instant case: *#C371458: United States v. Black Panther Party.* And KELLY BAILEY, born 5/2/71, Medford, Mass., a student at Yale University who may be being held against her will by Howard and Battle.

BATTLE: (unclear) the Yale Corporation. Ten million to Center Church (unclear) assorted cousins and a mere pittance (unclear).

BAILEY: How (unclear).

BATTLE: (unclear) entanglements and talks (unclear) free and clear.

BAILEY: Good Lord.
BATTLE: (unclear) the first of the year. Leon?
HOWARD: (unclear) sell the house (unclear).
BATTLE: Give her a lump sum.
HOWARD: Give her a million dollars.
BATTLE: That's it exactly.
BAILEY: Wait.
HOWARD: She wants more.

This conversation was obscured by physical contact noises of some kind and what appears to be loud crying and laughter. The New Haven office has learned that the law firm of ROSEN AND WEST represents the interests of VIVIAN BATTLE with New York City law firm of SULLIVAN AND CROMWELL re: the probate of the will of LEONORA NORTON BATTLE who deceased on 11/27/90 at New Haven.

According to a source, Mrs. Battle's will stipulates bequests in excess of 100 million dollars in stocks and bonds and more than 300 million dollars in real and other property. Vivian Battle, daughter of the deceased, is to receive the family home on the New Haven Green, a property in Wells Beach, Me., and cash and stock worth 25 million dollars at the current market price.

New Haven hereby requests permission to effect entry to the BATTLE mansion and to develop confidential sources close to Battle's bank, law office, physician, family members. This request is being made to the SOG on an urgent basis because of the following grave developments:

#1. There is evidence that LEONORA NORTON BATTLE was murdered by a conspiracy including LEON HURLEY HOWARD, VIVIAN NORTON BATTLE, and a person or persons unknown but including JOSEPH H. JEFFERSON A.K.A. "L'il Joe," a known gang member and B.P.P. recruit, and other members of the B.P.P. Said murder planned and executed for the purpose of securing large funds through Vivian Norton Battle, for the purpose of:

#2. Securing funds to finance the revival of the BLACK PANTHER PARTY: to rent offices and party domiciles nationwide; to purchase business fronts; to purchase arms and ammunition in preparation for a campaign of terrorism; to finance travel and offices abroad in order to coordinate worldwide terrorism activities.

#3. There is evidence that KELLY BAILEY is also being held against her will and that her life may be in danger. New Haven is attempting to contact Bailey through her father, but requests that a search warrant be authorized by the SOG and kept in readiness at New Haven with the United States Attorney.

It now appears that the Howard book will not be ready before 1/1/91. The Manhattan office has been alerted to query sources and Friends of the Bureau at major publishing houses, publishing journals and at the *New York Times* to alert the Bureau as soon as the Howard manuscript is offered for publication.

BUY U.S. SAVINGS BONDS REGULARLY ON THE PAYROLL SAVINGS PLAN.

DECEMBER 1990

Vivian watched Masai drain his cup of tea and stack a spread of documents. He's happy, she thought, no, not happy, but somehow, ah, fated, um, fated to finish—what? the book, with me, with Kelly and me, his life? The hair stood up on her forearm, she rubbed it, then poured more tea, thinking—this girl is drawn down from her adolescent bulk, nubile, now she looks ten years older, her eye is twitching, too much research, she's under a strain, part of her wants to leave, to quit, she can't stand that guilt. I could help her, I should help her. "I'll check the mail," she said.

The letter was in a cheap white envelope, Vivian held it between two fingers and the envelope in the other hand in the same fashion, "Another letter from the reading public for your file." They looked at her, she was going to make them stop, "You do the honors, Ms. Bailey, please." Kelly sighed, read in monotone:

DEAR MISS BATTLE,

YOU SYPHILITIC NIGGER LOVING MOTHER FUCKER YOUR DAYS ARE NUMBERED, BASTARD YOU AND ALL YOUR COCKSUCKING BLACK RUGHEAD DOGS ARE GOING TO DIE VERY, VERY SLOWLY AT THE HANDS OF WHITE MEN, MAYBE IF YOUR YELLOW BALLS WERE CUT OFF AND PUT IN YOUR VILE JEW—

COMMIE—NIGGER SUCKING MOUTH—YOU MIGHT LEARN—
DEATH TO NIGGER DOGS AND WHITE PUSSYS LIKE YOU.
SIGNED,

                   A PATRIOT

Kelly closed her eyes and panted, pretending to be overcome. Masai and Vivian watched her closely. Masai stretched, "Tea—Is that the real thing or just a cheap FBI forgery? You all are the linguistic critics around here."

"I think it's genuine. Note the use of the term 'rughead,' something of an archaism, would you agree, Dr. Bailey?" The student allowed a sick smile and buried her face in her cup. They all sipped their tea. The old house creaked. Vivian made the choice to pursue her quarry, "There's another one in, ah, prose that spells out in exquisite detail how you must have raped and murdered my late mother."

The student stared open mouthed; Masai's face closed up, he watched Vivian but spoke to Kelly, "Did you find the Stalin for me?" She kept staring at Vivian, too, "'The Negro Nation in the South'—Yale doesn't have it." Vivian laughed at both of them, nasal, "'The Negro Nation in the South'—you'll find it in the stacks at Bellevue." The student breathed through her mouth and stared like a moron. Masai chuckled, "More and more like her mother everyday." Vivian snorted again, then a high whining echo, "Vivian—Let me out!"

"See?" Masai tried to distract the girl. Kelly wiped her lips, "Your mother, she—"

"Let her rest in peace ... my offer's on the table. Finish the rough draft, take the money, get away for awhile, think it all over, perspective, your options, your choices—" Vivian laughed her normal resonant report "—a breath of fresh air, a change of scene—'Take the waters, the mud, the salts,' as Mother used to say, ha!—"

"She's crazy," Masai touched the student's shoulder, she stirred. Vivian threw her head back and launched a last laugh up at the crossbeams, then she sat down silent.

Masai finished his tea, "Um-hm—that old lady knew the truth. We used to stalk each other, talk about a cold war ... But later—after she went crazy, I believe that she knew the truth."

"About what?" Kelly's face was recognizable again. Masai looked from one to the other.

"... About this prison, here."

Vivian lifted her cup, put it down, her eyes had turned inward and deep. The cold sun filled up the room. Kelly saw the marks of time on the poet's face, the planes and the depressions, the vanguard of wrinkles moving toward her eyes, the bony hands with their spreading brown freckles, and Kelly felt a stinging in her eyes. "She knew about this prison here," Masai repeated to himself.

"She knew about the barn," Vivian said in a clear voice without focusing her eyes.

"'Help!'" Masai articulated a miniature imitation, "she knew the truth."

"About wh-what?"

"The barn."

"The b-barn?"

"That she was locked into ... Into which she was locked—by your father." Vivian's eyes focused back into the room.

"My, m-my father?"

"Or was it *her* grandfather?" Her voice was dry, dominating as in that time when her sustained and savage irony had informed the poetry that she broadcast to hushed and angry crowds, "Yes, it must have been. Because they all look alike—don't they—all those great men in the barn together?"

"Oh, the b-barn, that's a b-brilliant metaphor, like Bohemian Grove—"

"No. A metaphor's a lie. This is the truth: that all the generations of child molesters, and whoremasters, and slavemasters in the long filthy floorshow since the congress of the Serpent and Eve in the Garden—down to Joseph Stalin and Henry Kissinger—are one and the same Great Man!... My mother understood very little, really, but she *did* understand *that*—from quite an early age, I suspect—and *that* is what drove her mad!" She rose, they stared, an audience of two to her bitter muse.

Masai's cup and saucer rattled when he finally put it down, a police siren raced back across their hearing, a church on the Green struck the quarter hour, then the room was hushed again. Masai shaped his words deliberately, "Is that what drove you mad, too?"

"Oh, no. Not me." She looked down at Kelly, "You."

"M-me?"

"Y-yes y-you—y-you're the one looking for Joseph Stalin, aren't you?" The girl's entire body turned red. "Yes."

"Stalin!" Vivian went nasal again, "Have you tried the Home at Niantic for the Criminally Insane!"

"'Vivian,'" Masai mimed her mother.

"You are both certifiable!" She knew she had to get out of the room. "Why?" Kelly's question slowed her down, Masai stood up to help Vivian's leaving, "Joseph Stalin was not a liberal," he said, touching the girl's shoulder.

"Maybe I'd better—" It was too late, Vivian stopped and turned back and cut her off. "Yes, unlike your father, he was not a liberal of the old school."

"M-my father—"

"He did not hold with integration and affirmative, ah, action, did he, comrade?" The girl tried to get up, but his hand on her shoulder kept her down, at Vivian's mercy, "No, he had an *idée fixe* quite at odds with our well-known *folie* of the melting pot—"

"Please—" the girl looked up at Masai.

"I'm leaving," Vivian said, "I'm going to leave you to your search for Stalin, and I'm sure that Leon will tell you what his plan for America was, and it's just as feasible and pragmatic today as it was sixty years ago, and so elegant was Uncle Joe's deduction that I am sure that your book will reach, inexorably, the same precise conclusion and that you will then set about ushering in the millennium of the 'Negro Nation of the South'—"

Masai took a step around the girl's chair toward Vivian. Vivian put her hand, spreadfingered, where her left breast had been: "It was a great battle cry—and a brilliant battle plan—you give every black man forty acres and a mule—"

Masai moved—but she kept on, "and then you exterminate the white population of Arkansas, Alabama, Georgia, Mississippi and, ah, I forget the other one—" Masai stood between Kelly and Vivian, closer to Vivian, on top of her.

"And you move twenty million black peasants in and ..."

Vivian couldn't look around Masai's bulk to see what Kelly was doing. She couldn't see Masai's face clearly, either—because he was staring over her head—until she took a step back, then she saw that his eyes were red. When she saw that his eyes were red and blind to her, she dropped her own head.

After some time Vivian drew a long slow breath and then she left the silent room.

1972

Vivian—

  This comes via D.R. instead of the mail. Send your answer back the same way. I have to write this fast as I can so D. can take it.

  I've been in the hole for a week. Something going down. Anything could go down here. You know Elaine Brown. Talk to her. She came here with David, we talked, she can run it down for you, especially who <u>not</u> to talk to & what jokes such as "escape" not to laugh about.

  The word is that there's a list: Fred Hampton, George Jackson, Huey, me, Elaine, etc. They got the first two, but Elaine will explain why we have to try to expose this new level of outright death squads here inside the Mother Country--or else they are going to pick us off one by one.

  First take the writ that David's going to draw up to get me out of the hole and do a rewrite and add in material that David will give you. You have got to take the line that there is a <u>secret</u> war going on and that Fred Hampton and George Jackson were government conspiracies, executions. And then put the spotlight on me and demand Amnesty International, U.N. observers, etc. Get it out through the <u>New York Review of Books,</u> etc., and circulate it through the whole underground press, with the address and phone of the Warden, Governor, U.S. Civil Rights Div., etc.

 Now, listen, comrade, if something does happen here, you've got to know that it was a contract--I don't care if they find me poisoned, shot, hung and with a suicide note in my own blood--it will be murder. Then go ahead & make a goddamn lamp shade out of my life and shine the struggle through it all over the world--retail my black ass in every ghetto in the world and say that these imperialist henchmen and their lackeys may win here & there but they will never win <u>over</u>! We may die but our vision will live while they are already corpses and zombies. This all sounds crazy and paranoid but you know that I know what the score is and that a paranoid is a cat who's got all the facts.

 They started in on me with a course in adult education and therapy and church privileges and I turned them down flat because I knew that they were trying to build a dependency relationship to get me into a trick bag but then they started acting crazy and telling me that the Panthers were out to kill me because "someone" had spread the word that I was "cooperating" and that they were going to have to segregate me for my own safety in a hospital or cooperating witnesses facility & I got David up here to put them on notice that we were going into Federal Court to stop this shit, & he crawled all over them. And they picked a fight, which I saw coming, but they put me in the hole anyway. That's fine, I'm safer here than I would be in the population and it gives a little time to get something out.

Alright, through the grapevine I got a lot on the murder of G.J. and David's talking to some lawyer in California for the Prison Project out there, and all the testimony's going to be turned over to you to use in your article (check with D. about the names you can use.)

What I think is the biggest threat is that they'll get me in the Behavior Mod Center and hook me up on some so-called "anti-psychotic" or "anti-violence" drug "therapy"--You've got to stress this brainwashing that's going on wherever Panthers are being held. Hook it up with the NPI at UCLA and Clockwork Orange Springfield, Mo. & Marion, Ill., etc. and the NIH "anti-terror" experiments at Vacaville, Ca, and Detox program in NYC--open up those horror chambers. Any research you need call M.K.

I'll try to stay in the hole as long as I can 'til you all get the story out--

DO NOT TRY TO GET ME OUT OF SOLITARY.

Remember if anyone comes to you talking about a jail break, say you'll think about it--then you go straight to David and then swear out a complaint with the U.S. Attorney--I mean anybody! IT WILL BE A SET-UP!!!

Do your best, but if something happens, don't blame yourself because it's like we always said, anybody who passes the civil service exam can kill us today and I have been here on borrowed time for a good while now and it's like my grandmother told the bus driver one day, you better just go ahead and shoot me down like a dog 'cause I ain't fixin' to turn around.

It doesn't matter any more whether I live or die because either way I'm cannon fodder for the future, I've had enough and I'm ready, so go ahead on & in case of an "incident" tell Father N. and E.B. to arrange the funeral & you read my message and let E. introduce you as my wife and the "mother of our children," and then you say that our children were all those little boys & girls that we fed in the Hot Breakfast Program and that we taught in the Liberation School, that held our hands and looked so shy-- God in heaven I want to die for them if I can't live for them or have to spend twenty years in this soul breaker watching my motherfucking back.

You remember how my Louisiana homeboy Huey used to quote Chairman Mao: "Death comes to everyone but it varies in significance. To die for the reactionaries is lighter than a feather. To die for the people is heavier than Mount Tai." When you're done writing think about going back to London, but whatever you do don't let anyone talk you into going underground, etc., the Party's stand is clear that no one goes underground until they _have_ to. That's what they want is for us to go underground because then we're fair game.

So, again, whatever happens, stay cool & scatter my ashes around New Orleans and drink a Jax for me in the Quarter and go back to that crib we stayed in on Burgundy and lie up on that high bed and watch that ceiling fan turn, watch it turn, baby, turn --

                                      Power to the People,

                                      L.

December 1990

"THE DEAD SHALL RISE." She half ran through the arch into the graveyard.

"Kelly—over here. Watch your step, those old stones'll get you right in the shin, half sunk in the ground—stand here, cut the wind, the, uh, what is it? 'Fisk family's' our shelter.—How are you?—We'll make this fast, it's cold. How'd you get away?" The FBI man was bundled up like a football fan.

"What?"

"They let you just walk out, this time of night?"

"Mr. Ledoux, I promised my father I'd see you once because he said that you would tell me if my, ah, friends were in danger."

"Are you afraid? Did they threaten you, Kelly?—You're shaking."

"I'm c-cold. Now, what is going on?"

"You tell me."

"Nothing."

"Book almost done?"

"Well, it's ..."

"Then what?"

"I don't know."

"... We know about the money."

"What?"

"The money she's come into now. They're looking to make a weapons buy."

"To buy weapons?"

"A huge buy."

"They are not, who told you—where'd you get that?"

"The word's out."

"Where?"

"On the street."

"That's insane."

"Why would they need so much, there's still an arsenal left over from the 1970s—you know about that?"

"No."

"I'll tell you what, one of these days I'll walk you through our computer and you can see for yourself the guns and ammunition the old Panther Party had stored around the country—not talking about 'self-defense,' we're talking armaments for a small army—Kelly, you're freezing—Look, you're going to need our help soon, as soon as the so-called book's finished these people are going to move. These people are on a timetable."

She danced from one foot to the other. The FBI man tried to wrap his muffler around her, she danced away, "I don't know what you're talking about."

"Did they kill the mother?" His voice was pure Boston.

"What?"

"We think they killed Mrs. Battle to get the money. You could help us with that, in a trial, but what we're concerned about is that right after the holidays they're going to make you an offer you can't refuse. They'll involve you in an illegal act of some kind and then force you into one of the underground cells. From then on, every APB in the country lists you as 'Armed and Dangerous.' You're a 'kill on sight.'"

"What underground cells?"

"They have an underground. Safe houses, arms, false IDs, explosives, an infrastructure and an order of battle and a *timetable*. All you have to do, Kelly, is tell me tonight that you'll 'cooperate,' that's all. You say the magic word and that goes in the big computer at the

S.O.G., the seat of government in D.C., and when we go after them, you live. You live to tell about it ..." Reaching toward her again.

"No."

"So, if you really don't know anything about the money or the guns or the plans or the old lady, fine, just keep on doing what you're doing and keep a record of whatever you can find out about any violent or criminal or terrorist activities. Look, it's like we told your father—who's a helluva man by the way—told him that through no fault of your own, you've stumbled into a criminal conspiracy, with the best of motives, a nationwide ongoing terrorist conspiracy, and now you're in deep jeopardy and you have to think of Kelly Bailey and Randolph Bailey and your whole future life—and you have to think of your country somewhere in all this. Because these people are not what they pretend to be—"

"No!"

"Let me just finish. You're a brilliant student, you look inside our computer, *objectively*, and you'll see who these people are, that's all I ask is that you look and decide for yourself, don't take my word for it. Got a daughter your age and I'm saying to you exactly what I'd say to her, 'Judge for yourself' and at least look at the facts before you burn your bridges because it's your life and once you step over the line then it's too late and I can't help you and your dad can't help you, only God'll help you because these people are digging their own graves and it would be a crime for you to go down with them because you're too darn good-hearted to look at the facts about who these people are because they've taken advantage of your decency and your ideals to insinuate themselves into your confidence and drag you down with them talking about Revolution and Love—No, don't answer me now, just promise me you'll think about what I'm telling you, that you'll look at all the evidence before it's too late. Will you promise me that? ... Jeez, you're freezing, poor kid. C'mere, jeez, mm ..."

1978

Dear Vivian,

I have your note, through Katherine. Forget about it. It doesn't matter how many niggers there are in the Carter White House, no president is going to pardon me or Geronimo or Leonard et al. So, later for all that.

John Cheever was here. Talked about you when you were the White Hope student, sends his love. Is there anything I should know? Anyway, he's a good guy. Talked me into working on one of these journal exercises. Said it would help loosen me up for the Book. I don't know if it would help. Between the German and the Book looks like I can't make much progress. Anyway, here's what I wrote:

> I can remember a white boy named Fred. We were both around nine or ten years old. This was in Bunkie, LA.
>
> Fred had a new ball <u>and</u> bat. It was a "Louisville Slugger." Fred said it was a major league bat. We used to play a two man baseball game in an old weed lot near Fred's

house. Fred called me by my nickname, which at the time was "Boo."

One day, in the summertime, he didn't come to the field. I waited, then I left. That's all, that's the end.

I remember my grandmother, Addie Mae Gatewood, and going to church with her on Sunday mornings and evenings.

The older people were the backbone of the church. In the hot Sunday morning or the cool evening, the salt of the earth marched starched and straight. The women, a lot of them, wore stiff white nurses' uniforms if they didn't have smart suits or dark dresses like my grandmother. And hats, hats, crowns!

Inside it was close. The fans in the hands fanned. The fans were donated by Kramer Bros. Funeral Home. Grandmother sang in the choir. My favorite was "The Sign of the Fire by Night." The church rocked. Then there would be a sermon. I fell asleep. One of the assistant ministers was a quiet man named Steve Gatewood. My grandmother later married him.

It seems a long time ago, now. Thirty years--"rolling on, just before, as they journeyed on their way."

I don't know, it reads to me like it makes me regress to try to go back like that, in the same way psychotherapy can have a reactionary effect, but it's like anything else, it depends on how it's used. But is a revolutionary psychologist possible? Alright, Franz Fanon, but who else? Whereas we know the CIA has as many psychologists as it wants, so that's why I stick to reading Fromm and Erikson et al.

   I'm going to wind this up. That journal gave me the blues. That white boy, with the Louisville Slugger, old Fred, why didn't he ever come back to that old weed lot to play again?

Power to the Writers,
Du must dein Leben Andern,
L.

P.S. The word just came in about the madness at Jonestown in Guyana. The line here is that it's all FBI/CIA. Paul Allen says no. Says that Jonestown is "Jonestown, U.S.A." He's right on. If you win you're Fidel Castro, if you lose you're Jim Jones. Jonestown was as American as cherry pie. A jungle is a jungle is a jungle. Jones is Johnson is Nixon is Carter. 1,200 people is chump change next to the thousands that these madmen and their gangsters have bombed and tortured to death.

   I had a cousin who went to Jonestown with her kids, so did Huey, after the B.P.P. went down. Everybody here had been murdered so they went to that jungle with a new "leader," to Jonestown, U.S.A. Shit.

L.

December 1990

When she heard the ragtime piano music dancing up to the attic, Kelly pricked up her ears like a dog. Masai said, "How'd she get that music sheet?" He put his pencil down and rested his chin on his fists at the arc of his arms.

"What is it?"

"It's sheet music from Reconstruction. Go down and get it." He closed his eyes, she rose to go. "Tell her—bring it up here. Later. Take a break. I'm—come back up in an hour. Make it two. Go ahead."

Vivian pounded out the old minstrel tune. Kelly walked through the rooms toward the poet's study. Vivian saw her coming and stopped. "Too loud?"

"He wants it, the sheet music. What is it?"

Softly, Vivian played a reprise, singing softly, "Although it's not my color, I'm feeling mighty blue ..."

"What is it?"

"It's a 'coon song'."

"Really? ... Is that how they sound?"

"Mm. Wonderful old vaudeville. Seductive as hell ... going back up?"

"No, I, um ... It's starting to snow."

"Mm. Shall we build a fire?"

"Alright."

"Cheer up. Hand me a log."

The fire was a red Rorschach among the stones. "Here, lie down, put your head in my lap, I'll massage your temples."

"No, you've been working, too."

"I know, but you have the headache. Come on, I have a poet's hands." That made them laugh so the girl stretched out with her head in the poet's lap, and the poet touched her temples and golden hair and eased her pain, while the snow fell silent and complete across the Green. Both of them closed their eyes, breathing, and slept for a few minutes. The fire was yellow now in the room of gray shadows that Kelly watched flicker and play across the ceiling.

"... He loves you."

"... He loves you."

They laughed together softly again. Kelly tilted her head back further to catch Vivian's eye, then looked at the ceiling again. "You love him." Vivian tweaked the girl's nose.

"And you love him, and I love you, and you like me, and my mother—hated—pretended to hate—everybody in the world, and he swears that I'm going to be just like her." They laughed a little. "Your head feel better?"

"Oh, yes, thanks."

"Good—no, stay. Ugh, I'm giving orders again. Sorry. He says I'm going to be just like her."

"And that I'm going to be you."

"Mm. And we'll go on forever. Take in a new Census girl every ten years." The girl did not laugh.

"No, seriously," Vivian said, "as they say, I think that one of us has to leave." The girl started to sit up, but the poet held her, "Wait. Your silence about the money I offered you tells me that you've made no plans and that you're just going on with the book and letting events make your decision for you. Wait ...

"But I mean, something has to give. If he won't go away with me, then you two go. I mean just go, go to South Africa, go to … I mean he … Kelly, he has to go somewhere. He has to do something—it's seven months and he has not left this house. Not once. So."

The girl let her head and shoulders sink down again. Logs popped, the fire had passed its apogee. "If we stayed here, I mean, if he stayed and, uh, you know, the book was a big, uh, I mean, why couldn't he be an American Mandela. I mean, he talks like him sometimes ... Sometimes like the old records of Malcolm X. Sometimes like a man from Mars."

"Like Paul Robeson—I saw his Othello, here in New Haven, when I was your age—he used to write from prison about Othello." The snow muffled the sounds of the sirens and the bells from the Green and beyond. "Like Nat the Prophet Turner who spoke Elizabethan Biblical English, according to the surviving eyewitness who played dead 'til the raid was over ..." She sighed, "No, child, Leon Howard is as American as cherry pie. He'd starve to death in Africa." She chuckled, "You should have heard him in the old days when he was the baddest, talkin' blood on the block ... I have to check the roast. Stay here, put another log on, I'll bring you a glass of sherry, shall I?"

"Mm, are you cooking yams and—"

"Pork roast, of course. You'll have to learn all that." She stopped in the doorway, "I mean, if you're the one who goes away with him you'll have to learn to 'burn' Southern style." They smiled. Kelly rose to build up the fire. She knelt. The house was silent. Outside the snow came down.

"You'll like this, it's English," Vivian said as she came up behind the girl, at the window, and handed her the sherry with a formal gesture.

"Thank you. Mm, thanks. Why does one of us have to go away? Couldn't we just go on, for a little while, like we are?" Vivian looked at her, then she closed the door. "Go on?"

"Yes—just for a little while."

"Until the book becomes an entire library, the Ministry of Truth for the once and future Revolution, assigned reading by every guru and guerilla with tenure to white women everywhere, from Yale on down." Vivian licked her lips, looking at the untouched glass of sherry. "Drink your sherry, for God's sake, I'm sorry ... I made up some tuna salad for you so you won't have to choke down any more pork. Ha!"

"Don't you have any hope for this country...at all?"

"All the hope in the world—but not for this country..."

The poet peered out at the snow piling up, shivered and moved over in front of the fireplace and lifted her skirt up a little in back so that the fire's warmth could play over her legs; she laughed again, "The sight of you struggling to swallow a steady diet of pork chops and rice and gravy instead of your nouvelle lean cuisine is..." Laughing softly, kindly even, "But it's filled you out—and at the same time you've lost weight—if you follow me." The student blushed and turned away to sip her drink, Vivian turned away, too, and stared into the flames for a long time. The bells sounded far away.

"Hope?... I have as much hope for this country as I do in the sure and certain hope of the resurrection of my lord and savior Jesus Christ." She turned back to face the girl. "And I don't say that with any particular glee.—He has to leave here, Kelly. With you or me or by himself if that's—"

"But he says that New Haven is the 'Finland Station' and that New York is St. Petersburg, 'the city that cannot be trusted'—I finally figured out all the references for that, and—"

"Dostoyevsky."

"Yes."

"Yes. And that 'without the Revolution, the people cannot live and will not die.'"

"Yes." And the girl burst into tears. "I can't drink at all," she sniffed. Vivian bit her lips hard, but she did not go to her. The girl looked for a Kleenex. "He's read every book in the..."

"In the prison library system and that includes the U. of C. Yes, he had twenty years. He tried to become a book. He's been poisoned by books. This house is his library and his prison, and he's making you into his jailer, because I won't do it." The girl flushed.

"... Um, he, um, he keeps saying that, uh, 'the wops and micks and Yale Jews along with the Bloods in Projectville in solidarity with

237

the, uh, the Just Assassins—I haven't worked that one out yet—in, uh, solidarity with the heroic Yale students, in the, uh, spirit of, uh, 1970'—which I take to mean the, uh—"

"The year you were born and he died." Vivian let go of her skirt and moved away from the fire into the colder zone of the window. "For one day there was rebellion and life and courage out on that Green. In front of those silent churches. A sight so heart-stoppingly beautiful that the hardened Italian restaurant owners of Woodin Street wept openly to see the children of the rich and the wretched of the earth dancing together that day and singing out 'Free Masai—Free Vivian—Free Vivian—Free Masai. All power to Masai—All power to Vivian—All power to love.'"

She turned and dropped her forehead against the cold glass of the window. Kelly tried to see the track of the poet's tears on the damp pane. "Love," the girl repeated softly, "he said the same thing, that without love the people—and, Vivian, he had tears in his eyes—that without love the people cannot live—"

"And will not die! Oh, God!" Then at last a sob tore out of her throat and Kelly ran to her. They held each other, each weeping down on the other's sweater.

Vivian found Kleenex for them, then they sat in the window seat and looked at the snow. Vivian touched Kelly's shoulder. "Don't you know that he's torturing himself and lying to you?" Her voice was so loving and sad it made Kelly try to remember her own mother. "No," she said, touching Vivian's hand.

"He is," Vivian nodded, "he asked me—on Thanksgiving Day when you were out of the room vomiting—he asked me if I wanted to commit suicide with him."

"No ..."

"Then you came back into the room, remember? and told me that there was something wrong with my mother. You remember."

The girl bit her upper lip. Her eyes fell, then they focused on where the poet's breast used to be. Vivian stared over the girl's head, her voice distant, "... Said we could strap ourselves with plastique and blow up Trump Tower."

The girl was trembling again, Vivian dropped her hand and slid back a few inches and crossed her arms across her breast. Kelly's voice came out husky, "He was joking, he's always talking about 'Revolutionary Suicide.' He says he's worried about you. He was joking."

"Was he? More sherry?"

"No thank you."

"No ... He was not guilty in 1970, you know. We were not." The last red of the fire and the ice blue of the window were now the only points of light in the room. "It was 1969 and the country was berserk. Hmm. So the few of us who were still sane began to talk about kidnapping Henry Kissinger or Nelson Rockefeller. Talk about it, half seriously, talk about it. It made perfect sense then, and in time it would have happened—so the secret police took all that talk and woofin', as we called it then, we white Negroes—took it and completed the 'conspiracy' and began to arrest what they called Radical Racial Rabble-Rousers, and nigger-lovers like me. Then came the 'show trial,' right over there." She pointed across the Green to the courthouse. They both looked, then watched the snow tumble down for a minute.

"And the New Haven 'railroad' carried your friend and mine straight to state prison, and then, naturally, given his particular brand of sanity, he was thrown into 'Isolation,' into a time-chamber, and stayed there, off and on, for two decades. You understand what I'm saying? Twenty years."

Kelly said, "I know," and shook her head, "I feel so, uh, you know, so helpless, I mean, that is why I cannot, you know, leave him, because I feel so, um ..." The girl hugged her knees and rocked with frustration. Vivian kept staring out through the white curtain, and talking with that poet's lyric resonance that made the student feel that she was being mesmerized.

"... When they first took him up to the prison a guard walked ahead, in front of him, calling out—'Dead man—Dead man—Dead man—*Dead man walking*'!" The girl listened to the voice ring out the warning, riveted, rocking no more.

"While I, the crazy communist millionaire, was under 'house arrest' to Mother, in 'eternal exile,' writing him letters I never sent, and reading his letters to me—and they were pathetic, terrifying and pathetic, at first. Later—but at first everyone believed that he would be murdered in prison—he would smuggle out desperate and contradictory demands and plans to me through the attorneys, written on toilet paper ..." She dragged her eyes away from the window and searched the girl's frightened face.

"And the 'Movement' in America died." Her head sank. "And, ah, Leon's guilt just grew and grew." The poet's lanky frame folded in on itself, her long graceful neck always held so high drooped, and now it was the girl who longed to reach out to hold and comfort, but she, too, held herself back.

"His 'guilt?'"

Vivian's voice drooped down like the rest of her. "Some people go to prison because they're guilty, legally—but if you're innocent and sane, the way Leon was, then you *become* guilty *because* you're in prison."

"Because ...?"

Vivian slowly lifted her head. Mechanically, she pushed herself off the window seat and stood at a right angle to the girl. Kelly watched the woman literally pull herself together and walk to her desk and pick up a large folder. "I'll be right back. We have to finish this. You have to—I have to make you understand what's going on here. Look at this, you can read it later." She handed Kelly the folder.

"What is it?"

"Stagolee," she whispered, and left the room.

In the bathroom, Vivian sat on the commode and stared at the framed holograph of a front page of the *New York World* dated September 14, 1873. The long-ago advertisements and news items were a blur in the gloom. Church bells sounded. She stared at a framed Panama Canal stock certificate until her eyes went out of focus.

Kelly held a fading page of type up to the window.

—NATE SHAW—

1923, them old boll weevils stayed in my cotton until they ruint it. I didn't make but six good heavy bales and it weren't bringing twenty cents. About twelve and a half and fifteen cents. And it got lower than that, fell to half of that, lower than any man believed it could fall in the years to come.

Just before I got ready to move away from Two Forks—I hope God will be with me—Mr. Stark tried to get me to destroy the house. He had it insured; told me, "Nate, your time is up on this place and you moving elsewhere. I want you to destroy this house when you leave."

He tried to put me up to burning the building down before I left. He had jumped and sold the place just about the time he found I was going to move. And he wanted me to burn down the dwelling house after he sold it. You see, he could collect on the insurance until the other man moved onto the place. It was sold all right, but he still had possession. And if I destroyed that house—I was put in a place that all the facts of my life come to me—in jail …

Kelly squinted and paged through the pile. Vivian came back in and stacked up the pages, "You can take these with you."

"Are these—w-who are they, a-are they—" Vivian leaned against another Irish table that she used for a desk. "The forerunners," she said. "To understand who Stagolee is you have to start with the forerunners."

"Who *is* Stagolee?"

Vivian moved to the fireplace and held out her hands. "While Leon was in those isolation holes reading every book ever written from Aristotle to Zilboorg, Stagolee was out there dying in the garbage can of history."

"Who is *Stagolee?*"

Vivian went to her big wooden file cabinet and began to look for something. "Stagolee is the man that Leon calls the 'Nigger Under the Mud.' You have to come to grips with that man, you have to face that man ... Leon was in there trying to read Karl Marx in the original German—and it seems he began to be consumed with what Marx called 'the only revolutionary emotion'—shame. You know the passage?"

"No."

"*The German Ideology*, I think, at any rate, the thrust of it is that 'shame' leads to action, that's why it's revolutionary. But if you're in chains, for any reason, this shame bleeds into existential guilt, so that Leon, the victim, is made guilty, not only by the State but by *himself*."

"I've never really understood Existentialism."

The poet laughed one short note; leaned on the edge of the table working her lips, then exhaled all her breath. "There was a war here." She glared out over Kelly's head at the swirling white flakes, then down at the girl. "A war ... We lost." Her eyes softened, the girl looked near tears, again. "Stagolee lost—again. Now Stagolee's children, Leon's sons—they're mowing each other down out there!"

"Why?"

"Goddammit, didn't you work for the g'damn U.S. Census?" Her voice was harsh, hissing at the girl, "Didn't you?"

"Yes."

"Well, what did it say?"

"What?"

"The census—the stats—the stats, the bloody stats!"

"Oh!—uh, one in four black men in their 20s is, uh—"

"In jail, and under 20 it's one in six and the life expectancy of a black male is less than that of a man in Bangladesh! And it goes on, doesn't it!"

"It, uh—"

"It goes on!"

"It goes on ... But—I'm sorry—but *why*?"

"Keep your voice down.—Because the Powers That Be disappeared

Leon, *desaparecido*. Disappeared Leon and every other black leader—every father, every model from Nate Shaw up to Martin King—You've read those obscene 'Prevent the rise of a black messiah' FBI COINTELPROS of J. Edgar Hoover's—every black father figure or role model has been removed from the scene. *Desaparecido*—just like Salvador. Girl, there was terror here."

Except for the fire the study was dark, the snowstorm had cut the day by one quarter. "A war ..." the girl repeated.

"A war."

The girl stood. "I have to go to the bathroom. I'll be right back."

Vivian straightened, talking, "When you lose a war you feel guilty. So you *use* people. Wait a minute, I used my mother—let's tell the truth—to keep me in this house or, as she would have put it, 'off the streets.' You're using Leon and me—you can go in a minute—Leon's using you and the book. Don't cry. The man was locked in a cage for as long as you've...*been alive!* Never mind the four hundred years before—in a cage—and now he's here with us, under *house arrest*. And out there in those metaphysical streets—where he refuses to go and you've never been, both of you refusing to leave this mausoleum—out there an entire generation of black youth is being driven to suicide, and I don't mean 'Revolutionary Suicide' ... Go to the bathroom. I'm sorry."

"'Metaphysical streets'—why don't you write poetry anymore?"

"Go to the lavatory, then I'll read you something."

Kelly sat on the toilet and studied the Panama Canal Zone Certificate as she did each time.

EXTRAIT DES STATUTS
De la
Societé Civile Pour L'Amortissement Des Obligations
A lots, Emission Du 26 Juin 1888

In the study, Vivian tried to look out the window, then she put on her desk lamp and sat down and opened a folder. Kelly came back in and found her in the pool of light. As soon as the girl reentered, the poet began to read with quick and quiet passion.

THE REBEL

My name—offense; my Christian name—humiliation; my status—a rebel; my age—the Stone Age.

THE MOTHER

My race—the human race. My religion—brotherhood ... And I had dreamed of a son to close his mother's eyes.

THE REBEL

But I chose to open my son's eyes upon another sun.

The poet pushed the folder away. The girl still stood near the door, the spill from the desk lamp caught one moccasin. "You wrote that?"

"I'm translating it," the poet said, "Aimé Césaire wrote it." She took off her glasses.

"Jesus."

"*Les Armes Miraculeuses*. The Miracle Weapons. *Et les chiens se laisaient.*"

"The dogs, uh ..."

"The dogs shut up."

"... I mean, it's powerful ... Does that m-mean that you're writing again?"

"I don't know. Why?"

"B-because you—"

"I might let you alone? Hm."

"No."

"Every therapy has to eventually end." Vivian turned off the lamp and the blue light through the window dominated again; the silhouette of the girl sank down on the couch. Kelly's voice seemed stronger, "Why does he call you Iago sometimes?"

"... I don't know ... Because he loves me ..."

A shadow sliced across the girl where she sat backlit in the blue window light—Vivian stood up. The girl half turned to see at what Vivian was staring. "Oh, dear," she said, "It's another, uh—"

"No it's not," Vivian said.

The women stood together and stared at the hulking homeless man staring at them; standing in the pouring snow, half covered, half obscured, staring back at them. The girl paddled in the air for Vivian's hand.

"Look closer," Vivian's voice had the start of a moan to it.

"What?"

"It's Leon."

"... Oh, dear."

"He's been watching us."

"Oh, dear," and she would have fallen forward onto the couch if Vivian had not held her. The girl's teeth were rattling, Vivian shook her. The man in the window watched, he was now almost invisible in the snow.

The poet held the girl, covered her face, and stared back at the man and sang, loud enough for him to hear, Desdemona's death song:

"... Her salt tears fell from her, and softened the stones. Sing willow, willow, willow. Sing all a green willow must be my garland.

"I called my love false love: but what said he then? Sing willow, willow, willow. If I court moe women, you'll couch with moe men ..."

The light failed, the snow came down, the women stood in their embrace. The man stood in the window, then he disappeared altogether. After a time, the church bells tolled five o'clock, and the women heard someone dancing and singing up in the attic.

Masai went into the attic bathroom and slowly, like a sleepwalker, stripped off all his clothes. His lips were moving as he went out into the office. He began to shuffle and mumble, still naked—then, with power, his body began to fill the room and his voice whipped out the lyrics of the terrifying old coon song:

Although it's not my color, I'm feeling mighty blue
I've got a lot of trouble. I'll tell it all to you;
I'm certainly clean disgusted
With life and that's a fact,
Because my hair is wooly and because my color's black.
My gal she took a notion against the colored race,
She said if I would win her I'd have to change my face:
She said if she would wed me that she'd regret it soon.
And now I'm shook, yes, good and hard,
Because I am a coon.

Coon! Coon! Coon!
I wish my color would fade;
Coon! Coon! Coon! I'd like a different shade.

Coon! Coon! Coon! Morning, night and noon,
I wish I was a white man 'stead of a Coon! Coon! Coon!

1989

Leon,

"Operation Just Cause"! They have bombed an open city, they have killed thousands and Noriega was <u>their</u> man! This unmatchable cowardice has set a precedent for anyone to do anything to anybody in this country. The 1992 campaign has begun.

It is now clear that my congenital idiot cousin, George Bush, must be stopped before he kills more. <u>New York Review of Books</u> is after me to write something.

I've made a few notes:

Look, if an American marine is killed—if they kill an American marine, that's real bad. And if they threaten the wife of an American citizen, sexually threatening the lieutenant's wife while kicking him in the groin over and over again, then please understand, Mr. Gorbachev, this president is going to do something. (12/21/89)

It is ending badly. According to spokesmen for D.C. Comics, Superman—the Man of Steel—will die next year, fighting to save Metropolis from the super lunatic "Doomsday," an escapee from a cosmic insane asylum.

It is ending badly—Superman and George Bush and the "American Century"—ending in madness. You see, George Bush was both Clark Kent and Superman, just as America was the Camp of Victory and the

Shining City on a Hill and the burning hell of the metropolitan ghettoes.

But the Bonesman, Superman, gave his all, a hero to the last. He jogged, he golfed, he played tennis and horseshoes, he boated, he fished, he hunted, he hiked, he whored, until he dropped.

At Yale, over the archway into the cemetery is inscribed "The Dead Shall Rise." That is where George Bush will lie and his epitaph will read: "HOMO AMERIKANUS—LATE IN THE AGE OF ATOMS—NOW EXTINCT."

What would you think about the two of us going away to write, for a year or so? Italy? The problem is Mother. What do I do with her if we go? There are two problems.

1. She could live in Debra Walker's Maine compound with old Mrs. Walker and the retarded girl. (This is the George Bush Walker family, a little less than kin and more than kind—I mean, not since the Jukes and the Kallikaks has one family so weighed down on the life of the nation.)
2. But if I shipped her up there there's no question that the Walkers and the Wrights and the Nortons would close ranks and I would never receive a penny after Mother's death, assuming that she precedes me (doubtful given the maniacal tenacity of her grip, not on sanity or life but on me!).

At some point we should discuss money. I know most of your feelings about Mother's money, *but* if "Time is money," isn't the reverse true, and her class owes you more time than could ever be computed? The point being that her money should be used! They made their money in New England trade, which grew out of shipping and, I have no doubt, originally, slavery. That's bound to be the great crime behind their great fortune, reduced though it is now by an epigoni of drunks and plungers. (I had an ancestor in Harding's cabinet who was caught renting out the Lincoln Bedroom to a Wall Street *arriviste*.—)

OH, CHRIST, I AM DRUNK WITH OUTRAGE AND I WANT YOU HERE NOW!

9:00 P.M.

It is evening now and I'm slightly recovered, and looking at the <u>Faust</u>. Strange, I started out to write a play about you, but now I see that it's only about me. Well, naturally, but who needs a verse drama about <u>me</u>?

I kind of like the character of Jonathan Faust, I suppose because he's part of the man in me. You know, comrade, there's nothing like a couple of decades of more or less celibacy to bring out the whole cast of characters waiting in the closet. When Freud talked about every intercourse "involving four people" he was, as usual, being very conservative!

Oh, I'm feeling better. Even bad writing can work wonders, though you may not agree, if you ever have time to put aside your manifesto to read these ravings, but I do love you so much my darling man, but I am scared to put it all down—in black and white—because though D.R. will deliver this to you without reading it—no question about that—there's always a chance that someone will get a hold of it before you can swallow it and if I am going to permit strangers to watch me making love to you they are going to have to be the right sort of people!

All Power to <u>Lust</u>,

V.

P.S. Word just came in: Huey P. Newton's been murdered. A dope deal gone wrong, the news says. Can we agree never to discuss it? Please, for pity's sake.

V.

December 1990

Vivian scrawled in her journal, "I do not want it to happen!" as soon as she saw, from her window, Kelly leave the house at eleven in the evening of the first day of the Christmas holiday recess. It was not simply the sight of the girl—in her green stocking cap and fur-lined boots, her rare and expensive Swedish military shortcoat lined in real lambskin—skipping away from the house in the bright moonlight along the still white street that brought the skin on the poet's arms and back up in ridges, as she wrote: "Because, in theory, there's no reason why she shouldn't go out at any time for any reason, in fact I want her to go out, to get out, to …"

What shocked her, made her jump away from her journal, was the sound from above of Masai crying out in his sleep. A long moaning groan of particular pain, just as the girl slipped away into the bright night, as if she had stabbed Leon in his sleep and fled—the poet sprang from the window to race up the stairs to him but stopped and forced herself to go back down and make marks in her old leather journal: "I am ready, I will be ready. Make tea. Work. Wait. All will be well."

> Masai was with Vivian in a big house, in his nightmare. Certain men were pursuing them. But the lovers eluded capture by hiding in a large empty room. They breathed. He stripped off his shirt and wiped the sweat from his glistening torso, she leaned against the faded wall and watched him. His eyes loved her, "Thank God," he said … Then footfalls and they knew that the men were coming to hunt them again!

The poet scratched at her translation to drown out Leon's groans from above. Her lips twisted, the tea lost its heat, the table lamp co-opted the moonlight. Her hands were like claws, the left trailing or shadowing the right as it crept across the wide roughcut pages.

Clytemnestra

How dare you blame me?! Your father killed your sister. His favorite, and he killed her! Ask any—No! You are not going to drive me mad.
  Why should the two of us scream at each other? Ahhh ... I'm So tired—I don't know what to say to you. You're so full of hate. But I have to try ...

She crossed out and wrote, "But I'll try, I don't know what else to do ..." Then her hand started to shake and the other one had to crawl over to hold on and rub it.

> *In Masai's nightmare the lovers escaped through a passageway between two old buildings, then walked along the sidewalk trying to melt into the Lee Street throng. Then they were in the country, on a dirt road. There was no one else. No sound, no other animal, and yet the empty hills and sky were watching the dusty road, waiting, breathing secretly and waiting.*

Downstairs the poet wrote—

Electra

Remember, mother, you're the one who said, "No more lies"!

Clytemnestra

I said it and I meant it. Fire away.

Electra

That's what you always say. Then you jump down my throat.

Clytemnestra

Just say it!—You have my word.

Leon and Vivian quit the road, walking across the yellow-stubbed-fields in the storm-filled air ... Then a thumping, thudding, thumping-thudding sound and they were running again, back into the town, or the city, through the sweatstained streets back toward Projectville.

Clytemnestra

... And when he does come home, ten years later, he walks in with that red-headed bitch on his arm and tries to put her up in my suite—my room!—and that's when I saw red!

They snuck into the abandoned warehouse. They told themselves, with their thoughtwaves, "We're safe for right now." Her shoulders sagged. He read her mind: "We can't take this much more."

Electra

... lie to me! I used to hide in the closet and watch you sitting in front of your mirrors putting paint on your face, touching up your hair with gold tint, putting rouge on your breasts, touching yourself—you whore! You whore, you, I should have cut your throat that day!

She read Leon's mind. It said, "Wait. Don't move. They're over there in another room." They both knew, then, that there were three of the hunters in another room, standing close together in a kind of circle, under a ceiling lamp that spilled shadows over their heads. So they both knew that they only had minutes left to find a way out. They read each other's mind: "We're getting a little tired."

The poet held her writing elbow with her left hand as a governor to keep the right hand from racing off the margin of the page.—

Orestes

... Saw'st thou her raiment there, Sister, there in the blood? She drew it back as she stood, she opened her bosom bare, she bent her knees to the earth, the knees that bent in my birth ... and I
... Oh, her hair, her hair ...

> Electra
>
> She stretched her hand to my cheek, and there brake from her lips a moan, "Mercy, my child, my own!" His hand clung to my cheek; clung, and my arm was weak; and the sword fell and was gone.

The poet's left hand was struggling with the right now, as if on the verge of a precipice.

> On her that I loved of yore,
> Robe upon robe I cast:
> On her that I hated sore.

Holding the wrist where it throbbed like an amputation.

> *As the nightmare closed in, Leon thought to Vivian, "We're still strong. Let's rush them and get away." Vivian thought to him, "No. I can't. We can't."*
>
> *Leon ran back to the hall. There was a window at the end of it. He ran back to get Vivian. He pointed to the window. The hunters were moving out of their shadows. Leon thought to her, "We'll jump through the window. We'll die together, we'll be together, we'll go down together!"*
>
> *Then a terrifying thing happened: Vivian said, out loud, "Leon—you go."*
>
> *It hit him. He understood. He turned toward the window, ready to sprint. He thought to her, "I'll go alone." Then he died. His last thought was, "You stay here with them."*
>
> *That thought caused him to wake up weeping.*

Kelly walked in moonlight through "THE DEAD SHALL RISE" arch looking for Ledoux. He rose up in front of her. "Oh!" He had been sitting on a marble angle at the Stewart crypt, his coat open to the windless night. "Hi. ... It feels like spring."

"Hello."

"Can you believe it's Christmas time?"

"Mr. Ledoux, I have to go."

"Sit down, Kelly, here—I was very glad to hear from you. You did the right thing."

"What?"

"Calling me."

"I had to—"

"Of course."

"Because, uh, we're almost finished with the book and, then, you know, it'll have to be, uh—we're not using a word processor, so it'll have to be retyped and edited and, then, given to the, whichever publisher, and, anyway I'm going to go back to, I'm going to 'read' political theory at the London School of Economics starting in—"

"Your father didn't—"

"My father isn't involved. The point is that I'll be over there and Mr. Howard and Ms. Battle will be here or they—anyway—you didn't have to worry, or my father, about 'saving' me from some fantasy fate worse than death. I'm fine, so leave them alone, okay?"

"Sit down a minute."

"I have to go."

"Tell me about London?"

"What about it?"

"Miss Battle—"

"What about her?"

"She has her own circle there. She might go over for a visit—to London. To visit you, there."

"So?"

"She might bring Mr. Howard with her."

"So what?"

"Then you'd be involved again."

"What're you—"

"I'm talking about terrorism."

Two people who could have been students came in through the arch, laughing, fooling—stopped—turned and walked out again, taking small quick steps, ducking their heads down. What was the matter with them? Kelly turned her back to the FBI man. She was beginning to perspire, she took off her heavy gloves, the air was sweet as if warmed by the enormous full moon.

"I'm talking about terrorism," he said, sticking out his lower lip, then pursing his mouth, "There's a Baghdad-Rome-London axis that they could play right into and you'd never know it, but you'd be involved and we couldn't, I couldn't, help because it'd be—MI-5, that's their—"

"I know."

"And they're going to—because of the Irish situation their special police go in shooting and they arrest anyone remotely involved and they go straight to trial—bang!—and no ACLU over there, and they lock you up for twenty, thirty years and no Appeals Court—throw away the key, and they hate Americans. I know."

She looked at him. Big black eyes, the moon over his shoulder. The marble was cool, a relief against her hot hands. She slapped the stone with her gloves as she stood. "Leave them alone," she said and her voice had an arc to it, like Vivian's, it sounded to her like Vivian's voice and that made her feel real, sounding like somebody else made her feel more real than just being her old stuttering self and Daddy's girl. She looked down on him. "I'm going on my own, so do not use me as an excuse to bother these people."

Better, she had never felt better. I am born again right here in this graveyard, she said to herself, on a mild Christmas night when I am not afraid. "Thank you ... Merry Christmas, Mr. Ledoux."

"Just a minute, Kelly. What about the money?" She looked down at him. She had no interest in him tonight. Tonight his nasal speech seemed ignorant and provincial, what she had taken for a wolflike elegance or efficiency of person she now saw as merely mean. "You're using her money to go to London."

"Good night, sir."

"They'll hang you with that. They'll tie you to them through the money. Listen to me, Kelly, there's going to be a 'paper trail' direct from you to her, and from her to him, and they will follow the money, don't be naïve, you take the money from her and you're compromised. Period ... London's not the answer.—Listen to me. Time's running out on them—listen—" He dug his nails into her elbow:

"They're going to make their move as soon as your book's finished and that'll be too late to help you, because they're working with the gangs and some of the Muslim splinter groups, it's a national conspiracy and you believe me when I tell you that this administration is just waiting because they need something to run against and with the commies all gone this is made to order for the next election and, like they say, if it didn't already exist, they'd have to invent it."

He followed her toward the arch, pulling out the stops on the Boston repertoire of his voice, "You could go home now, over the holidays, and you and I can meet privately up in Boston, or at your Dad's and work out a statement that's dated 1990, and then you're home free because even if they try to involve you in London or Europe—and they will do that—even so, there'll be an official '205,' a U.S. government document *proving* that you are and were cooperating as a U.S. citizen with your ..."

He stopped in the arch in the middle of a word and watched her trot away in the brilliant moonshine and disappear into the charcoal shadows of the Law School quad. He looked up into the star-filled night and took a deep breath. Masai's low-voiced baritone base hit the agent in his mid-spine:—"Let her go."

The agent turned around, knowing that Masai would be standing in front of the tall Grizzard family grave marker. "Leon Howard."

Masai was standing in front of the marker that had hidden him from Ledoux and Kelly, but not from the two students who had intended to lie down there in the darkness but had seen him crouched there in the moonlight, like a big black panther, and had changed their minds.

"Ledoux," Masai mumbled.

"You know me?"

"Yeah, man, we know you."

"... She set me up?"

"Naw, man, you set yourself up."

"... You set me up. You used her to set me up."

"... Don't do nothin' foolish now, Frenchie—let's us go over here and sit down." Masai's voice was rough, cold, prison sharp, street edged: different.

"Howard—if you're armed—I'm not alone here. If you're armed it's 'Ex-felon with a gun,' you'll go away for twenty more years."

Masai chuckled. "Sheet, man, you talkin' crazy. Why would I want a gun? You the one with a gun. You the one doin' the settin' up. You the one *been* usin' that girl—to set me up."

"... You're unarmed?"

"Mm-hm ... You wired?"

"... What do you want, Howard? ... You alone, here, or what?"

"Don't think about that gun."

"Did she set me up—you got your people here?" The agent raked the crowd of stones and slabs with his black eyes; the army of markers stared back at him, their number multiplied by the acute shadows where the steel blue moonlight struck the stones.

"That all depends," Masai stood like a stone slab.

"What?"

"That depends on whether you're here on your own."

"What'd'y mean?"

"All depends on what game you runnin'."

"... Game?"

"Set-up." Masai's peacoated bulk made him look like a massive blueblack grave slab to the agent.

"... How could I set you up? How could I know you were here? That you would come here."

"The girl."

"The girl?—she called *me*. She asked for the meet. I mean, she's yours."

"She is?"

"You set me up."

"I set you up—with your agent?"

"Who?"

"She's yours."

DONALD FREED

"Mine?"

"Right on. You're fuckin' her."

"... What did you say?" The agent's face was bluewhite, his topcoat hung like a shroud from his bony shoulders. "You think I'm fucking her?"

"That's right."

"... You're the one that's fucking her."

Masai made a low mumbling throatsound. "You sayin' we both fuckin' her?"

"... That's not what I said."

"Maybe neither one of us fuckin' her."

"I'm not fucking her."

"... That's what you say."

"That's what *I know*."

"Naw, that's what you *say*. It'll be your word against me and her."

"... Alright. Neither one of us's fucking her ... someone else is fucking her."

"Who's that?

"The one who set us both up."

"Yeah? Who's that?"

"The same one who's fucking Michael Zinzun and L'il Joe Jefferson and his gang-bang studs." The church bells from the Green began to toll the hour. A long chorus, then it was quiet again. "The same one who we *know* killed her mother and then tried to kill herself. Am I right or wrong?"

Masai opened his coat slowly, unzipped his fly and began to urinate into the pool of moonlight between the dark stones. The agent stood there looking. The water was green in the beam, arcing out near the agent's dark shoes, then back and down. Masai shook himself and zipped up. Both men knew that Ledoux had let the opportunity to shoot Masai down slip past.

"Everybody fuckin' everybody else—is that what y'all think?"

"Listen, Masai, or Leon or whatever you call yourself now, I don't—"

" 'Mr. Howard,' is what you call me now."

"Whatever. I don't care who's doing what to who with what, Mr. Howard, all we're interested in is the category of terrorism."

"Aw, man, the cheapest word in town, 'terrorism.' Sheet."

"... Mr. Howard, while you were away, a lot of things went on—a lot of funny things are going on right now, that I doubt you know anything about, but which are using your name, if you gather my meaning." Now the agent perceived his need to urinate but compensated by clenching the muscles between his legs even tighter.

"Mr. Ledoux, let me be very clear." The agent's eyes opened wider, Masai's diction was, from one phrase to the next, suddenly scrupulously standard and his syntax immaculate. "I heard, I was here, and I can deduce how she came to know you in the first place. Hoover may be dead, but you people are still up to the same old jive." He cleared his sinus and spat. "Excuse me—in the joint you had to say, 'Permission to expectorate, sir?'"

"Huh, in the Marines, too."

"Is that right?"

"Yes, sir."

"Mm—hum ... I guess they get us all, one way or another."

"Who does?"

"You tell me."

"Pardon?"

"Never mind ... just leave the girl alone. She doesn't know a thing. —There's nothing to know. Leave her alone. You got a problem, come see me." His voice switched, sinking to a ghetto growl again, "Better stay away from that young blond pussy 'fo dey puts yo' ass *under* the jail," chuckled, then shifted as smooth as a gear back into the voice and diction of the Educated Class—"You tell her father that she is not involved, that there is nothing to be involved *in*, that her research and typing work will be completed in about a month, and that she is free and white and can go when and where she pleases."

A cloudbank passed slowly across the face of the moon. The FBI man narrowed his eyes to keep the dark mass of the other man in focus.

"What about Vivian Battle?"

"What about Vivian Battle?" Masai hunched his shoulders up in the peacoat.

"... You want to talk about her?"

"... Is the Bureau still trying to get her on something?"

"Well, you know our policy, the statute never runs on a capital case. The file stays open."

"What 'capital case'?" The agent was silent. The clouds passed, making the scene brilliant again. The agent saw Masai's boots start to move toward him slowly.

"Ledoux, let me tell you something—there's no Panthers hiding in this graveyard, beause they're all murdered or in prison or insane asylums—and Huey Newton's dead." He stood close enough for the other man to touch him, but too close for Ledoux to reach for a weapon.

"And there's no black spooks in the Yale cemetery ... Malcolm X said one time, that we had a beautiful thing growing but niggers ruined it. Well—who was it ruined the niggers?—You buy my book when it comes out, if you want the answer to that. But I reckon you already know ... So leave them both alone. Let the dead bury the dead." The agent stared down at the boots, waiting for Masai's move. The boots started, then they moved off at an angle. The agent followed with his head until Masai's full figure loomed upright under the arch.

Then the agent stood there alone, squinting out through the empty arch, listening for footsteps. Nothing, then church bells. Ledoux's legs were numb, he stamped his feet twice. Then he moved behind a large headstone to relieve himself.

In the night air, his flesh was cold and shriveled in his hand.

Masai walked through the faux-Gothic of the Law School courtyard and out toward Elm, but at the last moment instead of turning left, back to the mansion, he kept walking straight until he hit Orchard Street, then turned right and walked on down into Projectville.

A few faces, first white then black, turned to look at his bulk as he passed but his face was down in the coat collar, hidden, and no one recognized him. It was darker and colder because the moon was covered by clouds and there was a wind rising.

A streetman loomed up at the approach to Projectville, signifying, "... Come up here from Birmingham to find me some work to get me a divorce—'cause I served my Uncle Sam in Korea and Vietnam, Brother, and I'm hoping that you—"

He didn't slow down so that the streetman loomed up to his shoulder and then sheared off at an angle as Masai ploughed past into Projectville, down Orchard Street with its gantlet of lampposts, like gallows, each one with a pale pool of electric light at its base as far as the eye could see. In these green spots the hookers stood waiting, and the dealers, and here and there a small circle passing a bottle of maddog back and forth except that these sharers mostly clung to the cold neon strip of illumination that filled up the entranceway to the liquor store itself.

"Say, brother, what it is?" But Masai was past the store and running the gauntlet of black iron streetlamps, his boots clicking off the distance neatly as he made his progress into Projectville. He saw them, sensed them, the streetman as well, and the people struggling into the storefront Victory Christ The King First Baptist Church, but he did not actually remark them because he was on a kind of automatic pilot, like magnetized iron moving, not a robot, not a machine or a zombie, just a man moving at a steady clip with every twenty yards another pool of light from the gallows-tree lamps splashing blue across his iron face and green across his shoulder, with the piano in the church storefront starting up his marching music.

The whores, somehow, knew better than to speak to him, and soon he was deep into the projects, where no one dared walk the streets at night, and he was alone.

A police car cruised by. Masai stopped. So did the cruiser. After a minute the police pulled away slowly, but Masai stayed still, staring.

Thinking, this is what she wants to burn down, block by block, starting here and working back block by block to the university, lamppost by lamppost—then he thought, "The Lamppost," the Panther bar and restaurant that Huey Newton had started in Oakland, and he thought of Huey dead, on a street like this, last year. Huey dead. He peered down at the cracked sidewalk, seeing, imagining again the chalk outline of a man's, Huey's, body on that Oakland sidewalk in front of the crackhouse. The waste, his face tightened, the *waste* of Huey P. Newton. He bared his gums.

He felt himself turning into iron. Burn block by block past the intervals of whores and churches and liquor stores and risen up streetmen and those who couldn't burn block by block back to the campus would have to go down in the flames—and he remembered the fire that night in San Francisco the night of the Martin King murder and the Oakland Police shot L'il Bobby Hutton down. L'il Bobby ... Masai stared straight at the nearest project building in the remnant of moonlight and in his mind's eye and his memory's eye he could already see it burning in the night.

It's cold, it's getting colder. No sirens, no sound.

He turned very slowly, like a man with moving steel joints, to stare at the dark shape of the shuttered Pioneer Market across the street. Then what? New Haven would be the "Model City" again, Vivian was right, there was enough money for bail and a tent city here, but it could not be done without the local gangs because Zinzun would have to stay in Los Angeles. He thought of Zinzun, he saw his black eyepatch and the other eye gleaming with prophecy, and he saw again that other campus at U.C.L.A. where John and Bunchy were gunned down. John and Bunchy.

Masai turned in slow motion, machinelike, counterclockwise, back toward the city and the campus. More niggers have to die, and they will, but is it worth it for the ones who have to die, because just like before for the ones who live it will be worth it and they will study at Yale and tell their grandchildren that they fought with Masai and

L'il Joe Jefferson and Vivian Battle and all the other heroes in the long incendiary march from Orchard and 23rd all the way back to the courthouse and the campus in the fall of 1992 right in the middle of the election—for those who are children now and who will later exaggerate and say that they fought with L'il Joe and them, it will be worth it for them who are too young now to realize the wild wager of "The Sign of the Fire by Night," which he knew suddenly and surely would be the anthem of their forced march as surely as "We Shall Overcome" was the marching music for Martin King and the Southern Christian nonviolent movement. Well, this would be the Northern nonviolent dialectic of that movement in time, and he saw Martin Luther King dead on the balcony in his stocking feet, shot out of his shoes by the FBI. King.

Cold.

He stood facing east toward the campus, unmoving. Only L'il Joe and the gangs could get it on after the first wave of arrests. In fact, it was mandatory that the arrests include himself and any other old Panther within a hundred miles because only then would the media be forced to see that this was not a small conspiracy of burnt-out terrorists but a new generation of flaming youth—and then they would kill L'il Joe Jefferson, but it would be too late because from the flames would rise a new generation of Panthers and that would make it worth it in retrospect to L'il Joe and the others who died—it would have to because otherwise what was the use of George Jackson dying, or Fred Hampton, or Carl Hampton, or Sam Napier, or L'il Bobby, or John and Bunchy and Big Man West and Robert X, or Long John or Blue or Geronimo, or Seco or Malik and Jamal or Red or Jones and Fastblack and D'Ruba and Kenny, all of them—Legion! —or any of their lives or deaths, if the memories of them were without purpose, if they were not only gone but had never existed.

A lanky youth swung by, giving him plenty of room. He thinks I'm a crazy man. He walks the walk. He could be L'il Joe Jefferson. Why did she say he looked like me? He could be my son. I could have passed my own father in the street in New Orleans or anywhere. Could have. Every black man's, every black woman's nightmare since slavery—could have passed your father, black or white, in the street. *Could have.*

The boy, the young man, the gangster diminished from lamppost light to lamppost light and was gone. Could be. Give him up, it doesn't matter if he's my son or not, give up my son like Abraham did Isaac. For what? Why didn't Abraham, why don't I give up my life for *him*? "The Sign of the Fire by Night." He heard the hymn in his head, heard Addie Mae pull the downbeat up from her gut, "Rolling on, just before…"

A cop car pulled parallel, saw the big man rooted, staring straight ahead down the empty street. He never looked at them. It was cold, they eased away.

I should give up my life for him, L'il Joe Jefferson, but he might call me crazy, a freak, a one million push-up freak. But what if Abraham and Isaac had combined against God. So he took a stiff step, after the youth who was gone into the night, then he stopped still again. The cold wind had swept the street clean. Ten streetlights down from where he still stood, frozen, the shadows staggered in and out of the light of the Korean liquor store and a mean laugh blew down the pavement. So, whether or not Joe Jefferson is my son or not, my words could lead the boy to his death as well as his life. "The sign of the cloud by day." He will judge either way, he will judge me, he's bound to judge me. Either way.

He started to walk. "Dead Man Walking." Heavy boots, wind rising. There's no crime left big enough for us to commit that would pay for a Revolution so I figured that justice could do it, take the place of the old crimes that the old people used to pay for their revolutions and their freedom. He passed the storefront church, shut up and silent. Dark and cold. Abraham killed Isaac, he should have killed God, but there's no God so what the man should've done was kill himself.

That stopped him in his tracks. The winos staggering around in the entrance to the liquor store must have sensed him because they wound down to slow motion, staring into the dirty darkness of the streetlamps. He saw them, the red tips of their cigarettes; the winos swayed, their cigarettes, their "Bogarts," red in the wind.

It was as if they were all waiting, would wait forever, when the little bell over the door of the Buy-Rite Liquor and Grocery Store gave a tin tinkle and the youth, the gangbanger, if that's what he was, loped out carrying a small bag with a carton of milk in it and passed with long-legged grace through the swaying circle of ancient winos who were in fact only one generation older than L'il Joe or whatever his name was, and danced with the cold wind down the street until he ran up against the big man in the peacoat and bounced back the way he would have off an iron gate, and stood looking into the red eyes; neither man nor boy blinking, with the winos watching and waiting. Standing, staring, both of them.

"Masai?"

The voice was young. Young and deep. "Masai?" That was it. That was all.

1976

MIDNIGHT

... *Orlando Letelier is dead. Dead, and my war criminal cousin is head of the CIA and I know that he knows all about it. I'm taking a Valerian root sedative and for my depression I'm taking part in various Free Chile meetings and teach-ins. I'm reading Pablo Neruda in my translation, raising some money, pointing the finger at George Bush and the old school tie.*

> *I have lived so much that someday*
> *they will have to forget me forcibly,*
> *rubbing me off the blackboard.*
> *My heart was inexhaustible.*
> *But because I ask for silence,*
> *never think I am going to die.*
> *The opposite is true.*
> *It happens I am going to live—*
> *to be, and to go on being.*
> *I will not be, however, if, inside me,*
> *the crop does not keep sprouting,*
> *the shoots first, breaking through the earth*
> *to reach the light;*
> *but the mothering earth is dark,*
> *and, deep inside me, I am dark.*
> *I am a well in the water of which*
> *the night leaves stars behind*
> *and goes on alone across the fields.*
> *It's a question of having lived so*
> *much that I wish to live that much more.*

> *I never felt my voice so clear,*
> *never have been so rich in kisses.*

I had met him, Neruda, in the '60s and been inspired by that combination of flesh and politics I've come to recognize as <u>Zoon Politikon</u>. The coup in '73 killed him. He wrote a poem for Letelier's wedding.

> *I made my contract with the truth*
> *to restore light to earth.*

> *I wished to be like bread.*
> *The struggle never found me wanting.*

> *But here I am with what I loved,*
> *with the solitude I lost.*
> *In the shadow of the stone, I do not rest.*

> *The sea is working, working in my silence.*

And, about the Kissinger coup:

> *We did not know*
> *that everything was occupied*
> *the cups, the seats,*
> *the beds, the mirrors,*
> *the sea, the wine, the sky.*

1:00 A.M.
I think I may travel after Easter. London, etc., but first I'd like to go South and try to interview your granny again. Alright? I want to write about her at different ages and stages of her fabulous life. I will catch hell, of course, for trying to write about black people. That is rubbish and I'm grateful that you do not believe that gender and race are exclusive. You don't, do you? Anyway, I intend to write about the "opposite" sex, race, age, culture, etc., and if any of these pan-African "Negritude" Cultural Nationalist dashiki niggers don't like it, they can, to paraphrase your sainted grandmother, kiss my white ass.

I love you, comrade,

V.

November 1990

DEAR MR. BAILEY,

   I AM WRITING THIS TO YOU AS A FATHER WHO BELIEVES THAT YOUR DEAR DAUGHTER IS THE VICTIM OF A HIDEOUS CRIME.

   THE TWO CONVICTED ANARCHISTS AND FREE LOVE PERVERTS ARE HOLDING YOUR PRECIOUS DAUGHTER CAPTIVE IN A DEN OF DOPE AND PERVERSION. I KNOW THAT YOU AS A REAL RED BLOODED 100% AMERICAN WILL DO SOMETHING ABOUT IT PRONTO. AND THERE ARE PLENTY OF US READY TO MARCH SHOULDER TO SHOULDER WITH YOU TO FIGHT FOR FAMILY VALUES.

                              GOD BLESS AMERICA,

                              A FATHER

DECEMBER 1990

"Vivian? ... You awake?"

"Mm."

"You alright?"

"Hot flash. Ahh ... you take the covers."

"I'm not cold. Really, Vivian."

"No, you're a hot flash yourself, 98.6°."

"Huh?"

"Women's body temperature is higher than men's."

"It is?"

"According to Yale Medical ... Girl, I'm burning up."

"What about, uh—"

"I refuse to take hormones. I'm radioactive with hormones now, always have been."

"Shall I get you a washcloth?"

"*Serviette conjugal* ..."

"Huh?"

"Never mind ... Maybe you'd better—you might be more comfortable back in your own little garret."

"Alright ... Would you be more, maybe you could sleep more comfortably."

"Nobody sleeps in this house, it's not a question of sleep, it's a question of dreaming, of, ah, 'nightmaring' in comfort. —Shh, that laugh of yours, you'll wake him."

"Does he sleep? ... Vivian?"
"I don't know ... Does he?"
"I don't sleep with him."
"No."
"... Do you? ... Vivian?"
"No."
"... Alright. Good night ... Vivian?"
"*Good night!* ... Maybe the problem is that I'm scared of the dark."
"... Vivian, I remember my mother putting on a boat lamp for me, at night. Isn't that funny what you remember?"
"You remember your mother?—Now I'm cold."
"Here.—I remember her. I loved her. I loved her, but I never really knew her ... She was a victim."
"What do you mean?"
"I don't know."
"Of whom?"
"... I don't know."
"I understand."
"She wasn't strong like your mother, like how Leonora used to be, before she—"
"My mother didn't have strength, she had power—big difference—she was weak with power, like the rest of them."
"Like your cousin George Bush?"
"Exactly."
"... My mother didn't have strength or power ... What about me, Vivian, do you think I'll ever have, uh, any ..."
"Power? Thank God, no. Strength, yes, yes indeed."
"You do?"
"Absolutely. You're a great specimen—Shh."
"Oh, Vivian, you mean I'm fat?"
"Fat? You're bones."
"I am not. Is Masai, is Leon—you said he was a great specimen, too ... His arms ..."
"Five hundred fingertip push-ups a day times twenty years."

"... His mind."
"Mm."
"He's a genius."
"I always thought so."
"Sometimes ..."
"What?"
"Well—you know, how sometimes he acts a little, uh—"
"Crazy. Hm. He is. We are. Aren't we?"
"No."
"That's your problem. Ugh! I'm burning up again—I can't even stand the sheet on—fucking Greeks, menopause in bloody Greek means that months have stopped, time stopped—fat chance—time is racing, fucking flying, no more bloody eggs and sex on the brain, in the mind and on the brain, night and day, 'Day and night you are the one, only you beneath the—' shhhhhh!"

"You are going crazy!"
"Shh!—Damn Greeks and their 'Law of the Excluded Middle.'"
"'The Law of the Excluded Middle'?"
"Mm ... That's you, isn't it, 'Kelly Girl'?"
"'Kelly Girl'—what does that mean?"
"Nothing. No aspersions on your work. A poor joke, but mine own."
"You're not saying that, uh—"
"No, I'm not saying that you're his Kelly Girl."
"Or yours?"
"Of course not.—Or your father's—anymore."
"Thank you ... You still think I should leave—go back to school?"
"... I do. For a while. Or ..."
"What?"
"No, no ..."
"No, what, Vivian, what?"
"Well—you've done so much theoretical work now on race and poverty and politics, somehow, someday, anyway, you have to actually go down into Projectville."

"... Would you go with me?"

"I could certainly introduce you to some of the outreach groups, the tutoring program."

"... Could I work with the Panthers?"

"... Panther's a Greek word, too ... What Panthers?"

"You know the, uh ..."

"The ex-Panthers?"

"Well ..."

"... Huey Newton's dead. You knew that."

"I know ... Masai never got to see him again, did he?"

"... No."

"What happened?"

"To the Panthers? ... same thing that happened to every other slave rebellion—'niggers ruined it.'"

"What?"

"That's what Malcolm X said."

"Oh, dear."

"Before they shot him. But who 'ruined' the niggers who shot Malcolm? That's what Leon used to say: 'Niggers ruined it, but who ruined the niggers?'"

"... I see."

"Think about it. The ghetto.—I could help, but you finally have to go yourself, alone ... You just have to go. And something *will* happen.—You'll run, your knees'll give out on you and you will run, or crawl, away, screaming inside. 'Fuck these niggers!' ... Then—because you're a superb specimen—you'll come out on the other side."

"I'm such a—"

"Animal courage. You have it. You need to use it. Like animal pity. We all have it.—Fear's pursuing you, gaining on you. You're cornered in the ghetto, or the barn, in the bedroom—Leon—my mother—you—me—we're cornered—"

"Oh, dear."

"Just remember—you *will* say, 'Fuck these niggers.' You will have to say that first. Before the, ah, resurrection. Will you remember that?"

"I will."

"Listen, come closer, I want to whisper something to you. Listen: Projectville is Jonestown—and there's a plan to burn it down block by block, a *political* plan, nonviolent, but it looks now like it will have to be all women who do it, otherwise it will be seen as violence against people instead of property and the State will use the occasion to liquidate the young leadership, like Joe ... that manchild looks exactly like Leon thirty years ago in the old photos from when he was in the Navy."

"He was in the Navy? Masai?" Breathing and warming each other.

"Shh, he never talks about it. Come here, listen: so it may be that only women can do this by themselves, burn the bloody 'surplus value' out of these ghetto prisons because the men are dead and gone and that leaves *us*—they forgot about us—and the children...anyway, not a word, I'm serious. Really. I'll keep you in the big picture. The code name for the operation is 'A Generation of Vipers,' get it?"

"No."

"You don't have to whisper now, just keep your voice down, but remember what I've told you."

"You mean about the, uh—"

"Just remember. The word is 'Boadicia.'"

"Who?"

"Remember!"

"I will. But I'm scared."

"Of the dark—we all are ... I'm cooling off ... Three o'clock."

"... Are you afraid of the dark, too?"

"Hm ... I'm not afraid of you in the dark. Let's cover up again. Are you afraid of me?"

"No ... I don't know what I'm afraid of."

"Well, let's see—are you afraid of being in bed with, ah, the wolf—or with Red Riding Hood?"

"Hm, both of them—all of them."

"Hm, very good, very good—you're a natural 'deconstructionist.'"

"I am?"

"A lovely wit. Like I say, you're a specimen ... There used to be an old dance song, in my mother's day, 'How could Red Riding Hood / Have been so very good / And still kept the wolf from the door?'"

"Hah. Sing it again."

"No, it's late now."

"... Vivian? ... You asleep?"

"Hah."

"Say one of your poems."

"Not tonight.—3:15."

"I can't read, my eyes are worn out from the book—what could we—could we listen to one of your mother's tapes or something?"

"Of my mother? *'Vivian!'*—shh!"

"No, her operas."

"No, it's too late."

"The *Electra*?"

"No ... You know the Greek for her name?"

"For Electra? No."

" 'The unmated one. E-lectra."

" 'The unmated one.' Beautiful.— Is that your translation? ... Have you always been, um, alone?"

"Have you always been a census taker? Shh."

"Shh—I love you."

"Mm ... I was lying there in bed, touching my breast, and there was the lump."

"Where?"

"In London."

"No. I mean ..."

"Oh ... Here. Feel."

"... Oh-oh, dear ... In London?"

"Cheers."

"So you left—America?"

" 'Temporary insanity'—not me, the country."

"I keep reading the transcripts, but there's nothing actually in the trial that adds up to—"

"You're a sociologist, you know the drill, the only justice in the Halls of Justice is in the halls—they *said* we *said* that Kissinger and Rockefeller should be executed."

"Insane!"

"Completely. I said, and I was not drunk at the time, that they should be tried, convicted, and let loose with bus fare in Harlem."

"That was your conspiracy?"

"Conspiracy. You know the Latin?"

"'Conspiracy'—breathing together."

"Champion."

"… But this was real?"

"The cancer?"

"… Poor Vivian. Tell me."

"… Lying in London, touching myself—beginning to—"

"Imagining Masai?"

"Ahh …"

"Tell me."

"You'll tell."

"*Who?* Shh. Remember when you thought I worked for the *Times*?"

"The police."

"… Tell me."

"You might tell the therapist."

"Never."

"And I know for a fact that he works for the *Times and* the police."

"Shh, no, he works for Yale and my father."

"Well … where should I start?"

"… Tell me about love."

"Love or lust?"

"Is there a difference?"

"Only in English."

"Love *and* lust. Your, you know, your fantasies."

"My fantasies … They're all in my poetry."

"No, I mean, you know, like your—"

"Like what—like men—women—white men—black men—women—young women—students—shh!"

"Shh ... Masai?"

"Who was it said that women are better than men, but you can't live with them?"

"I don't know."

"Marlene Dietrich? I forget. I think so."

"I don't know ... So, were you thinking about Masai?"

"Well, I think I was thinking about Faust and Addie Mae Gatewood."

"Faust?"

"I wanted to write a play about Dr. Faustus and Leon's grandmother, the great Addie Mae Gatewood née Howard ... A love story. I can't write it ... Was I thinking about Leon?"

"Yes. That morning in London when you found the lump, when you were t-touch-touching yourself—what were you, who were you thinking about?"

"That rainy morning?"

"Mm."

"... October 17, 1972, White's Hotel, Room 104 ... I touched my left breast—not, ah, actually thinking or imagining anything or, ah, anyone specifically ... Then, oh, my thumb, it was, grazed the, ahh ... Hmm—I thought of my mother ..."

"At that moment?"

"Mm. My mother, and her voice. The voice saying, 'Vivian, —God will punish you.'"

"... That's what you were thinking—that morning?"

"I was hearing that—her voice—the voice that people like you and me—good people—hear every morning of our lives ..."

On, they talked on, through the moonless night and into the white cold light of late December, the two voices, thin and thick, broken by sniffles and the briefest chuckles—and some silence—the libido breathing through and in the voices asking the hundred-headed question What is to be done? Until the end of the night, while their bodies raged with heat and bumped up with cold, while the church bells rang out over the Green, breaking into the alterations of heat and chill, the talk and the silence, the past and the future tense of the unremitting libido of their breathing together, their conspiracy of questions and of silence. The bells ringing out over the pitiless Green that had, like the churches and the bells, stood for the imposition of order—level, horizontal, cut, squared, measured, surveyed and laid out for the churches to sit on—so that while the Green spread law and order and reason like a carpet over the earth, the churches and their bells reached up vertically, piercing and centrifugal in a great chain of transcendent being rocketing up into the empyrean heaven toward the god of the New World, like a lightning rod of supplication and prayer, a lightning rod that, the poet promised, ran like an invisible stake down through space into the ground of the Green so that the vertical and horizontal vectors of law and order and reason smashed together to shake every house in the Village, every house *in the world*. That is why, the poet taught her, the bells must break the dark silence of the night when the Green has disappeared so that sleepers may not escape into dreams and nightmares of freedom and unreason and anarchy. The Green and the bells are not symbols of law and order, she whispered, they *are* law and order, and no cry of individual ecstasy or anguish can ever drown out those bells just as no weapon has ever been invented that could blow up the metaphysical Green. So they seized the time—panting and whispering, breathing together, conspiring—in the ticking increments between the echolalia of the complementary and overlapping warning of the bells and the eternal return of God's message down the lightning rod of history into the Green, then out radiating and radioactive into every body in the land—and, the poet breathed, "no catharsis, no epiphany, no modern ritual, no orgasm," and no solidarity yet existed that could overcome it. No psychedelic drug, no work or Faustian bargain of science, no psychoanalytic abreaction, no erection or resurrection can extricate you out of this nightmare of history—and that's why the bells toll for you, to call you back into the bound sleeper—because the waking historical day is the actual nightmare and the truncated and maimed dream the really real reality, the work of art is *the real* reality, slipped into the interstices of the official calendar printed by the government church printing press. "You understand I'm not playing with paradox here and claiming that life is death and vice versa or that the sleeper is awake and vice versa, but I do say that official, calendar, public life is a nightmare and that the living citizen is the dead dreamer, the living citizen is hanging in dreams on the back of the tiger and that tiger is the power of the state church chain of being. That's why I can't write poetry now and may never again and I'm burning up and freezing by turns and can't stabilize, can't die and can't be born or reborn, can't go and can't come."

"Oh, dear."

Finally, making finger animals on the moonlit walls, the poet told her how the wheel of history turned on that axis of dreams and waking nightmares and how no paroxysm yet existed that could interrupt this awful return from on high of the laser beam of history, or God pissing down on the earth; and how no mass, no mob, no crowd, no *communal*—much less political—abstraction, no power on earth had yet broken out of that great chain of being—neither Lucifer nor Lenin—or been capable of slowing down the unstoppable historical wheel in its grinding turn. The poet, the politician, the martyrs, the modern messiahs and their movements had all been forced, finally, to throw themselves on the wheel, to add their momentary weight to the wheel that, in turn, ground them, too, down into the grinding ground of the Green.

When the first light entered their room, the poet offered her proof: the scar, livid and white, that cut horizontally from her breastbone around and under her arm and into her back.

DECEMBER 1990

Frenchy Ledoux went down the stairs to the basement and marked a message on a piece of paper towel:

DEAR MR. LEDOUX:

I AM A BLACK MAN AND A BROTHER WHO BELIEVES IN NON-VIOLENCE. I BELIEVE IN GOD. THAT IS WHY I HAS TO WRITE YOU THIS HERE LETTER TO WARN YOU THAT THE BLACK PANTHER PARTY DONE PUT YOUR NAME ON A DEATH LIST. I KNOWS BECAUSE I HAS A NEPHEW WITH THEM AND THEY PLAN TO KILL BLACK FOLKS TOO. PLEASE, SIR, HELP US.

                WE SHALL OVERCOME.

Then he addressed a plain stamped envelope to himself, slipped out and jogged to the mailbox, and put the letter in, and banged the lid to make certain it went down.

New Year's Eve 1990–1991

Vivian said, "Merry Krishnas and a satirical rational New Year." Kelly laughed too brightly, Masai watched Vivian lay on the hot cider, the sandwiches, the cheese tray, the apple pie. "It's *King Lear* outside," Vivian said, "it's howling, Leon, I think we could build up the fire." He didn't move from the sofa, he closed his eyes.

"Tee-total New Year's Eve supper, step right up."

"Oh, yes," Kelly said, "Mm."

"Leon?" Vivian waited. "My God, you both look dead. You look black," she said to Leon, and to Kelly, "you look blue." The girl laughed helpfully and piled her plate. The bells from the Green could hardly be heard against the lashing wind. "Quiet," Vivian said in the silent room, "is that twelve? ... Yes, it is, midnight ... Well, the year of the census is over at last—drink up, and a Revolutionary New Year to us all, comrades."

She raised her cup of cider, but it was still too hot, so she gave Kelly a kiss, then bent over the sofa and touched Masai's hair with her lips. Then she went to the hearth and began to stir up the fire herself. "Nineteen-ninety-one—What is to be done?—Nineteen-ninety-one—What is to be done?—Nineteen-ninety-one—'What is to be done?'"

"Tolstoy," Kelly chimed in.

"Lenin," Masai spoke for the first time. His eyes were still closed.

Vivian straightened up, flushed, "And a cast of millions," she picked up the cider again, "A toast, brothers and sisters, to the big book!" Kelly didn't know how to react, she was frightened of the poet when she was like this. "The beeg book," Vivian called out in a fake Russian accent, "Let's burn it—and ring in the new year right.—Look, he's awake, the sleeping giant is stirring."

They watched Masai: he sat up, he stared at the fireplace, he stood up, he walked past the supper laid out to the small bookcase and fingered out a thin, dark green volume and felt it in his hand the way a blind man would. They watched him touch the book; when he spoke he looked right past them.

"If y'all're cold—a slim volume of Miss Vivian's poems might do the trick," and he took two long strides and dropped the book into the flames.

"Oh, no!" Kelly's small cry fell to earth.

Masai's empty eyes focused on the girl, "Sit down. You're not cold, are you, girl? Naw, you *hot*." They both heard the coarsening and thickening of his speech. Vivian took a step toward the girl, trying to catch her eye, but Kelly was too shocked to note the warning.

"I d-don't understand. W-we finished the first draft of the book on Christmas Day, and since then no one is speaking to each other."

"Then shut up," Masai growled, and stepped back for more slim volumes to hurl into the flames.

Vivian's laugh was a shriek—"Students of Germany, I greet this conflagration, first, with the collected works of that notorious Jewish gangster, Sigmund Freud!" She screamed it all in German straight into Kelly's face. The girl fell back.

"Stop it! What is happening here? Stop it!" and ran to catch the other volumes Masai was throwing in, "Stop it, please, is it something I've done? What've I done?"

The bookshelf was empty, the fire roared, Masai leaned forward against the shelf as if he had pulled a rib in heavy lifting, his voice was cultivated and groomed again, almost a parody of Vivian's, the girl realized for the first time:

"The, ah, noted Revolutionary Poet and critic has just given us our first review, I believe, by comparing my book to *Mein Kampf*."

"Is that what she said? I don't believe it. You misunderstood—why did you throw her poems in the fire? What's wrong, what've I done?" The girl was so frightened that her own fear was making her furious.

Vivian crossed in front of the fireplace trying to make contact with Masai. "It's a back number, your big book. It was out of date before the first word was written on the first roll of toilet paper when he lay there naked and stinking in that hole!—You burned your fingers," she said to the girl.

"What hole?" the girl was furious now, too, with pain and fear and grief, "Speak English!"

"The isolation cell that they threw his black ass into at Danbury—the soul breaker."

Masai bent over further, almost double, his voice a half groan. Then he jerked himself up violently and stumbled a step toward Vivian. Kelly's voice shook with terror—"Oh, God, please don't hit her. She's sick, she's—" Masai stood swaying over the poet. "I'm not thinking about hitting her."

"Because she's—"

"Because she is correct. The book is a record of the past, like her poems, and it does not exist."

A bell rang through from the Green and turned the fiery scene into a living picture. At a stroke all their pent-up fury and frustration drained away into something else. Masai's pitiless words and the wind-thinned church bell froze them there, in the red flickering, in their individual and combined grief. "What?" Kelly whispered.

Vivian and Masai were face to face, poet and prisoner; her voice was high New England in its diction of inflected loss.

"It's gone, he's saying it's gone, the past is gone—like my poetry and his politics, like your innocence and my breast!"

She reached out her right arm and the girl flew into its enfolding, choked with tears, against her breast,

"The past is gone, it doesn't exist, your therapist was supposed to inform you of that."

"It's not gone!" the girl sobbed.

"Yes, yes, yes—I know—yes, it is, Kelly Girl, it's gone—and we're free."

The girl pulled her head out of the poet's protecting arms. "Free?" Then she turned to look at Masai. His eyes were blank again and so large that she could see reflected twin flames burning there.

"Free," Vivian said, "remember the living dog that was better than the dead lion."

"No."

"The Bible. We're living dogs. We're free." To Masai she said, "Tell her to burn it."

The girl felt as if she were under water. "What?"

"Burn it," Masai said, "then burn the house down."

The girl tore herself out of the poet's arms and away from the fires in the prisoner's eyes; tore herself as if under water, as if in her own dream, and labored across the room to cover the four-foot-high manuscript with her body, to cling to it as she would have a child at her waist—"Please, oh please ..." Panting with the exertion as if on another planet with twice the gravity.

"Don't cry, child," Vivian called out, "they killed and buried us in newsprint twenty years ago—the Yale Cemetery down the street has that arch that reads 'The Dead Shall Rise'—you know that arch—'The Dead Shall Rise'—well, we haven't yet risen from our respective holes and isolation cells, into which each of us has been thrown by—"

"Please!"—the girl knelt with her arms around the body of the manuscript—"What can we do?"

"Rise up and leave this house!" Vivian's voice wrapped all three of them together now, "The Revolution begins when we rise up—when we leave!"

The girl panted, waiting, watching Masai for a sign. He stood still as iron. Then she turned, on her knees, looking for the poet's eyes in the shadows.

"Am I going, too?—Where're we going?" She crouched away from the pile of manuscript, back toward Vivian. The poet moved closer to the prisoner, speaking into the reflected flames,

"We're going—to take one step at a time, every day, for the rest of our lives, because—Leon, listen to me, comrade, listen, there are millions of books—they have poisoned us with their Big Lies and their Big Books—we don't lack books—we lack living *human beings!*"

The girl crept between them, "Masai, I love you, Masai," she reached out to both of them, Vivian's voice was a blackjack: "Burn it and make love to both of us. Let the dead bury the dead. *We have to rise up before we can rise up!*" The girl was in her arms again, and Vivian was laughing bitterly, "Miss Daisey's gone crazy! *We have to live, Leon*—publish the book or perish it—*we have to live!*"

Masai turned slowly in place as if he had received an interior order. He was still pitched forward at an angle as he lurched away from them, as a man will lurch out of a bar into an alley to vomit. Kelly thought to catch him if he fell, but Vivian gripped her with those thin, hard, muscled arms and all the girl could do was half fall forward herself, just as Masai stumbled to the door, swung it open and, with the door as his hinge, lifted himself through the doorway out into the storm, his weight slamming the door shut again.

The women could see him falling against the wind to stand in front of the large window, leaning against the pane staring in at them. His eyes bulged and his lips moved.

"Careful now," Vivian backed the two of them toward the hearth, away from the window. The face watching them was twisted out of focus by torment, spying and surreal through the heavy glass. The girl was more terrified than at any time in her life, only her intestines were moving, she was petrified, deadweight as the poet dragged her like a corpse away from the window and the face. "Wh-wh-wh ..."

"... Very careful ... He never left that hole ... Stand up. But Stagolee's coming out tonight—*he has to!*"

The face, the head in the window began to pound itself against the pane.

"Oh, God, he's going to kill us!" She began to urinate.

"Stand up!—you always knew this would happen—when you came here, when you stayed here—" The head thumped four times—"When you didn't turn his name in to the Census Bureau—'Every third house?' remember?—*They count us, why do you think they count us?!* Stand up, shut up—he's trying to, Jesus Christ, he's trying to talk to us ..." The lips moved against the glass, the eyes flashed open and shut like a semaphore, his voice howled with the wind.

The head fell below the level of the window out of their range of vision and the black storm was all there was. Then the handle on the heavy door began to turn. The turning handle filled up the world.

"Please—please—please don't let him in!"

"Get ready."

"Please call the police, please call Mr. Ledoux, call my father, *I want my father—*"

The door swung open with storm force.

"Oh, dear God—God—God—"

A street monster stood in the doorway where Masai had been. The girl's eyes rolled in her head: Masai had become a homeless streetman monster—body, face, and voice. The poet and the girl couldn't back up any further without setting themselves on fire, their legs were burning hot while their faces were slapped by the cold and searching wind that he had let in on them.

"Help me out, mister." The body, the voice, the outstretched hand—it was another man, some savage streetman avatar of the man they thought they had known and now realized they had never known.

Vivian gripped the sagging weight of the girl. Vivian bit her lower lip while her head shook as if she were possessed along with the stranger in the doorway except that his possession and transformation was a familiar form to her—shocking but not surprising; fated, foretold, prophesied secretly by both of them; twenty years in the gestation, two hundred years—so the monster taking shape through the magic lantern of the window glass and now before her eyes was uncannily intimate and known, and though terrific and terrifying in

285

aspect and form, she was not terrified, not even frightened in an ordinary way, because her body had taken over and her body was not appalled, only her mind—her mind saw what the girl's mind saw—a mad human scarecrow, red eyes rolling, slack-jawed, reaching for their life—only her mind registered dread, her body and soul throbbed with pity for him, a mother's ruth or radical pity for the poor monster that she has engendered.

He shuffled two steps into the room, the door swinging in the wind behind him. Vivian's legs were burning. She had to drag the girl and herself away from the flames, closer to the creature. Now she was staggered because the creature reeked of cheap wine, which was impossible because he had not drunk and there was no such wine, unless, she thought, it's her urine I'm smelling—and putting onto him, as the Thunderbird he would have drunk if he—

"Pardon me mister i'm sorry to bother you like this i'm down on my luck i wonder if i can get you to help me out i don't mean to bother you i was fourteen years in the marines i fought for my uncle sam in vietnam i want to get you to help me out me and my wife come up here from louisiana trying to get a divorce i got shot in the head in korea i'm trying to get work right now i need twenty-five cents for the bus i was in the marines fifteen years i ate dirt in the war i fought for my country in chile i got shot in the head in grenada i ate flesh i was starving to death they said what you doing i don't care my name's bob let me shake your hand mister ..."

He glared right through them, started to shuffle forward again. This galvanized the girl to jerk herself away from the poet. The man stopped, then he turned away from the poet to the girl and put his hand out toward her and she tried to crawl up her own leg.

"Help me out, mister ..."

The girl moved toward her purse, trembling as if she were a hundred years old, taking steps, inches only, her hands jerking and spastic on the canvas bag, finally throwing it at his iron feet.

The monster swayed and bent to pick up the purse, then straightened and slung it in one scythelike sweep into the fireplace. Vivian stood, rooted, her head nodding like a triphammer, watching only him. The man turned back toward the girl and stretched his arm and hand out again and took a shuffle step toward her.

"Oh, please, I don't have any more."

"Shee, Fuckyou—I aflshnkrea."

The girl sobbed in a gulp of cold air and tried to back toward the poet, but he had cut her off.

"Help! Please!—I gave you everything!"

The man's heavy wino streetshuffle was closing in on her.

"Say mofkr you jew 'ain't ya?"

"No!—I am not a Jew—get away from me!"

With all the strength of her healthy youth, she vaulted over the leather settee that blocked her way and moved behind the table. The monster shuffled slowly in a small circle to come around to face her again across the New Year's supper.

"You know wsrng wi Hitler—he din' killnufyou mafkrs—"

The girl picked up the cheese knife, and she was ready to use it, the poet could see that, too, now, as she had foreseen it before.

"Get away from me, you crazy nigger!"

She arched to stab him. Crouching, he looked up at her. She froze. Her knees gave way. She hit the table, her chest and head, sobbing, "I gave you everything ..."

The wind howled in, grabbing at the food, picking at the bound manuscript, pulling at the girl's blond head on the table. The man waited. Vivian moved. She pushed the door shut. It was cold and quiet again.

"No, you didn't give him everything." She came close to him. The wine or urine stench had been cauterized by the wind and there was only the aroma of hot cider and cinnamon sticks again. "No." The girl looked up from the table with the face of an awakened child, innocent and vulnerable, waiting for Vivian to say it.

"You didn't give him everything. But—I did."

Like a wounded animal, the streetman turned like a beast at bay on the axis of his own trapped extremities, head and torso first, iron legs and feet after, like a bear rearing in unequal struggle against the pull of gravity, like a bull in the shambles—this the poet saw as the man swam underwater toward her—stopped, swayed, and nodded his head.

The girl stood up with the knife raised again. The poet saw it all. The monster's eyes rolled red and up, his whole great frame began to tremble and heave like a beast trapped on the faultline of an earthquake. Then he froze—the poet counted four seconds—and pitched down on his face like a dead man.

"Kelly," Vivian's face was a scar of anguish, "help me ... Put the knife down.—Kelly!—Alright, against the sofa, face the fire—he's freezing—hold him steady, I'll wipe his face ..."

The poet took up a napkin to wipe his face and then wiped the girl's too. She felt his pulse, "He could die," rubbing his big hands, "He could die right here," rolling back his eyelid, "Christ—where're my poor breasts now when he needs them—Leon, wake up, Leon!—Do something, put your goddamned tit in his mouth! Leon!"

The girl pulled up her sleeveless sweater and unbuttoned her blue work shirt and did as the poet commanded.

"That's good, girl, good—alright—what's that song? 'Rolling on, just before ... I'm going to cross over into ...,' Addie's song, Leon, 'The Sign of the Fire by Night ...' Leon!" Somehow finding the approximation of a Louisiana Delta apotheosis in the New England bells of her own sound, "As they journeyed on their way..."

The prisoner opened his eyes. The women sat back on their haunches to study him. His head rested on the seat of the sofa, his eyes were completely clear, now, his gaze young and hopeful. His speech, too, was pure boy's.

"Da ich ein Kind war ..."

Vivian reached out for the girl's hand, "God—you know it?" The girl pulled her sweater down. The poet held onto her hand and whispered—

When I was a child
I was lost
Blazing by day
I searched the sky
For a heart like mine
To care

That's the first German we learned together." Masai closed his eyes. The women bent over him again. "Don't let him die," Vivian whispered. "Leon." Then Kelly called him by his Christian name for the first time—"Leon."

He opened his eyes again, they could have been the eyes of an old man or of a boy. He looked at Kelly. "Who're you?" His voice was weak and hoarse.

"Leon. This is Kelly. She's a friend. She's come to help us."

"... That's good."

"What can I do?"

"... Leon, do you want Kelly to tell you a story?"

"... Yes, ma'am."

"I don't know anything."

"Cinqué. You know the story of Cinqué."

"Oh, ya—Well ..."

He smiled, watching her mouth, starting the words himself.

"Once upon a time ..."

"Yes, ah ..." the girl breathed, and she did not stutter. "Once upon a time, there was a slave—"

"Amen," Vivian's voice was as sweet as music, all her tears were inside it.

"Yes—a man like you,"

"A nigger man?"

"Like you. And, and they put him in the stocks on the Green and—"

"The Green ..."

"Yes, in front of the Center Church."

"The church ..."

"You're telling it," Vivian said, "you're doing it."

"... Ah, so they put the man on the scaffold, in the stocks, and it was like a holiday. The women all, you know, in white, bound up in white cloth, and all the pale men in their black coats and all—"

"The children ..." Leon whispered as if he had heard his cue, and the poet saw the girl take up the cue, like a ball, with the consummate grace of an ancient storyteller. "Tell it," the poet willed, and the girl did. "The children, yes, the children all came to the Green to look at Cinqué. The children. And there were oxcarts and oyster booths, farm wagons filled with garden vegetables—"

"On the Green ..."

Vivian saw the lump rising in the girl's throat, so now she took the ball of the story,

"Yes, on the Green—you can still see it—Center Church and the Church of the Regicides where old John Brown came to speak—"

"Ossawatami John Brown," his voice had an edge of timbre in it, picking it up from the vibrant and leashed-in cadences of their mothers' cry to him. The girl shook slightly, holding her hand over her lips, head turned away, tears in her mouth.

"Old John Brown—" he leaned forward with the boy's smile on his face and the women had to hold him in their arms because his balance was gone.

"Yes, old John Brown," Vivian said, "Prop him up—"

"Yes, old John Brown," the girl repeated slipping under his arm so that he was between them now. "He's happy," the poet thought, and her voice rose again as they all faced out, "Look ... See—out beyond Quinnipiac, Fair Haven and the harbor—and the deep bells sounding from the white steeples—you can hear them!" And they did, the three, they heard and saw as one—"Hear them? And the soft grass and the smells of the farm wagons and the vegetables—"

"And the deep shadows"—The girl's voice took the story back from her, like a child's ball, and Vivian's head fell on his shoulder, but still they all saw the same vision in the dark room, "And the deep shadows all across the Green at the end of the day—"

"Sister Caroline—" he spoke and the spell was broken and now he was seeing something that they could not see and the three were separate again. Vivian pushed up on her knees.

"Sister Caroline—the mojo and the sayso." His voice was thickening again, the innocence was bleeding out of his voice and his face. The girl pulled back a little and looked over his head at Vivian. "He's signifying," the poet mouthed the words.

Now he began an excruciating effort to pull himself up. The huge strength of his shoulders and upper arms working his body in an arc, like a cripple on a wooden cart, around to the sofa so that he could pull himself to his knees. He was dripping now, his tongue out, his words like the glottal shocks of a prisoner on a chain gang—

"Hah—The grayboy's got me—Hah!"

"The white men"—Vivian translating, the two women trying to help him heave up. "Hah!"

"Mmm—but I heard the thunder—"

"He's old and wise," Vivian translating as they inched up from the floor; the three, one again.

"They give the meat-man the mad dog...mmm—"

"—Made the poor people crazy on cheap wine—"

"Hah! Got the mojo and the sayso—got me a skosh slave—"

"A little job—Ah!"

"'Cause I the stone streetmannn—"

They were half risen now, panting together, and over the storm the poet heard the gunfire from New Year's Eve in Projectville and the wail of the police sirens, then the girl heard it too, but Vivian was still translating as he said, "Uku two-cent slick—" and she, panting like a chain-gang man too, "In their millions—"

"Ukku—big bell ringinnnn—"

"Judgment day—"

"Dead Mannnn—" They were up. "Hah!"

"Dead mannn—"

"Dead Mannn—" she called out—

"Hold on," Kelly panting—

"Dead man walkinnnnng!"
"One step at a time," Vivian breathing—
"Mn-mm-mm-Uku-*got to stay cool.*"

"Stay cool," the women speaking in perfect unison, "Stay cool"—they were up and moving massively, as one—to the table, three steps, then wheel and toward the fireplace, their voices breaking out antiphonal and free over the storm and the sirens and the gunfire—

"Stay cool! Shit-storm coming!
"Streetman risinnnnng!"
"Stay cool!"
"Streetman COMINNNNNG—"
"Stay cool!"

SEPTEMBER 1991

Date: 9/5/91

To: DIRECTOR, FBI

From: SAC, NEW HAVEN

Subject: NATIONAL SECURITY, TERRORISM

Information excerpted below concerns LEON HURLEY HOWARD a.k.a. "Masai," a male Negro born 2/11/41, Baton Rouge, La. Howard is a former member of the BLACK PANTHER PARTY. VIVIAN NORTON BATTLE is a co-conspirator in the 1970 instant case: #C 371458: *United States v. The Black Panther Party.*

This report must be maintained only in headquarters offices and Seat of Government and is not to be transmitted to resident agencies.

SOURCE states that Howard and Battle have left New Haven area by auto sometime during the Labor Day holiday period. That the Battle mansion has been closed and Howard's secretary KELLY BAILEY has removed to 13 William Street, New Haven and is sharing a rented house with students MORTON KRIM and FANTASIA WORTH.

No record of Krim, a male Caucasian, appears in Bureau files. Worth, a female Negro, has a record of one arrest for Disturbing the Peace, in Pittsburgh, Pa. 4/7/88.

Bailey has reenrolled as a graduate student at Yale in the School of Sociology. Bailey has not resumed her medical appointments or contacted her father (see enclosed letter from the Boston SAC).

New Haven requests permission to continue anonymous letters concerning his daughter to Bailey's father in order to facilitate further cooperation.

New Haven requests that the SOG request Los Angeles, New York, New Haven, Chicago, and New Orleans to be on the lookout for whereabouts of Howard, Battle, and Michael ZINZUN, as well as the LEGAT, Paris Embassy, for contact with ELAINE BROWN, former Central Committee member of the B.P.P. Source states that Brown is in France writing a book about the B.P.P. that is critical of the Bureau and Mr. Hoover's Directorship.

It is believed that Brown may be hiding Howard and Battle in her home in Switzerland.

Enclosed is last undated intercepted communication from N.Y.C. between Battle and Bailey. (Intercepted 8/15/91)

BUY U.S. SAVINGS BONDS REGULARLY ON THE PAYROLL SAVINGS PLAN.

Dear Kelly,

We meet with the publisher tomorrow, then disappear for awhile. Hope you're enjoying Indian Summer, and your new living arrangements. If your seminars are too boring I hope you'll bore back from within.

Regarding your decision: I take all of your points, and I respect the thought behind your final decision. Done and done.

Leon is fine, sends regards.

Well, kid, gotta go. We'll see each other sooner or later, but anyway, as my old shrink said, "People who belong together need not be glued together." I know your opinion of Freud but his aphorisms, at least, have stood the test. He was, finally, a great poet, too.

Enough. I miss you, my Elektra. I'm blue. I'm the original blue blue-blood Red. Enough! I miss you. I. Miss. You. Period.

V.

1991

They walked down Lee Street and he showed her where Mike Mule's Arena had used to be. Even in this day and age, he told her, don't mind if people in the South, of both races, stop and look back at a middle-aged couple consisting of a brawny black man and a lean aristocratic white woman.

"That's Blackman's Laundry, she worked there off and on in the last years, after she moved back here to Alexandria."

They stood in front of the boarded building where not even a faded poster of Anglo Cistolli or Chief Little Beaver or Leroy "Jack" McGurk or any other of those battlers and grapplers of yore remained to remind a new generation that once there had been giants on this broken street.

"The wrestlers stood right here, where we're standing," she said, "then walked off arm in arm for a big steak dinner."

"Naw," he said, "they left out the back door."

"Ah-ha." It was chilly November and the people that passed them wore their ragged winter coats and sweaters pulled tight and their collars up against the fine slanting rain that would come down more or less for the next two months.

"Alexandria," she shook her head, "as in Alexander the Great—'Julius Caesar dead and turned to clay—might stop a wall to keep the wind away.'"

"Talk on, talker," he put a hand on her shoulder and turned up her collar against the stinging rain.

"I mean, you stood here with Addie, and Mike Mule stood there."

"Mm-hm."

"In Alexandria. Not the one in Egypt."

"No."

"On Lee Street, here, named after Robert E. Lee!"

"Amen."

"Robert E. Lee and Alexander the Great. And Mike Mule."

"You reckon there's a poem in it?—Let's go to the hotel."

"And you and Addie. And now me ..."

The denizens of Lee Street stole glances at them in passing while Vivian watched them in turn, thinking—"They are here. That's the beginning and the end of it. They are here." Then she sniffed and bobbed her head in her way. Leon looked at her.

"Nothing. I was just thinking—they're here, and we're here. That's all."

"That's it," he said, lowering his big voice, "the only question you got to answer is what we're going to do with 'em."

"Invite everybody as our guest to Mike Mule's Arena."

"Naw, that cracker's dead and rotten ... Now, these people, here, you either have to organize them or walk away and leave them be."

"That won't work either," she said.

"Naw."

"Let's go back to the hotel." So they went back to the old Bentley Hotel that he told her old man Bentley had built to spite an even older landmark that had refused him service in their dining room when he had insisted on dining there in his shirtsleeves. So he built it on impulse—big and much too grand for the town—in the same spirit of regional rebellion and reaction that made the Delta a latter-day scandal to the rest of a progressive nation.

They went into the bar and ordered coffee. Mirrored, clean, chilly, marble and wood; no guests and never any townspeople. Vivian took it in, "Is the air-conditioning on?"

"Three hundred and sixty-five days a year."

"Addie Mae was never in here?"

The waitress slipped up with the coffee. "Bring the pot," Masai said, smiling into the Anglo-Saxon blankness. "The only white place Addie Mae was ever in as a guest was the asylum in Pineville."

"Can we see that?"

"You going to write an epic?"

"... I should have come down here, that time, to talk to her. But would she have trusted me?"

"Well ... she didn't trust white people in general or black people, either, she'd seen too much. 'I don't take no tea for the fever,' that's what she'd say."

"What's it mean?"

"No tea for the fever, and she'd say, 'I don't bite my tongue.'"

"Ah, I see."

"Mm-hm, you don't bite your tongue much, either, do you?... Later on, she got her a pearl-handled revolver and a knife and she believed that the white race was finished."

Vivian rocked with silent laughter and tears of intimacy sprang to her eyes. Masai rubbed her hand. "But what would've shocked you, if she *had* talked to you, is that she claimed that neither her mother, her grandmother, or her *great*-grandmother was ever a slave! That's right. And she knew them all! And Miss Lilly Woods, I believe, went back to the War of 1812!"

"God, why didn't I talk to her again?"

"I believe she liked you. But you'd've found out right quick. If she'd had time, she'd 've made you some of her famous cracklin bread, that's corn bread with cracklins in it—mm!—rice pudding, chicken and dumplings, buttermilk and cornbread, egg custard, mm!"

"God! ...Who did she like? Could it be true—no slaves?"

"I don't know. She said white folks had flat asses from sitting around waiting for niggers to do something, so it didn't matter whether you were slave or free."

"But could it've been true?"

"I don't know, Vivian, because she outlived all her family. All I heard were the legends of 'ho-houses' and granny as a 'shake dancer,' moonshine and gut-bucket blues ... and I saw her old fox fur pieces ..."

"What else?"

"You sound like Kelly ... They say she caught one of her beaus with a 'red-skinned bitch' and shot her in bed in the ass. She told me, personally, that an Irishman 'was a nigger turned inside out.'"

Two salesmen walked in and up to the empty bar.

"A person who'll lie will steal, she told me, and a thief will kill. Don't lie, she told me, 'because I got no time for that tricky-time shit.'"

"No tea for the fever," Vivian said softly.

"Mm-hm. The only thing I ever knew to scare her was a little black pill. I don't know what she meant, but she had it in her mind that they were going to give her a little black pill."

"... Maybe her mother's death in the hospital?"

"Could be. When they carried her to Pineville she fought against getting that little pill. Fought like a panther."

The nightman came on and hung up his raincoat, then took up his position behind the polished wood bar. The mirrored room was empty again.

"No tea for the fever," she said again. "I'll get it," he said and took the coffee pot from her. The man behind the bar nodded politely. When Masai came back to the table, Vivian whispered, "He thinks you play for the New Orleans uh—"

"Saints. Shh. Old man Bentley turning in his grave."

"Did you know him?"

"No."

"... Leon ... let's assume that there is no tea we could take for the fever."

"... I'd put it different."

A waiter came in to get hot water for a toddy. The bartender whistled a few bars of the LSU Fight Song between his teeth. The waiter waited, looking over at the middle-aged mixed couple.

"How would you put it?—More coffee?—Is there some kind of 'tea' for fever?"

"Not tea," he said.

"What?"

"Little black pill."

"... 'Revolutionary suicide'?"

"Little black pill."

"Big black book—or both? ... Have you decided—what you're going to do?"

"Have you?"

"I'm about to," she said.

He leaned in and took her slim hand, pale against his pink palm, and held her with his eyes. She sank back. The mirrors along the walls were blank, reflecting black.

"... Leon—I want to sell the house and the Manhattan building and give you the money, and all the other money."

"... What for?"

"For whatever you decide ... I'll keep the cottage and enough to live on."

"... You going to the cottage in Maine?"

"I have to."

"To write?"

"I have to."

"Write on ... You want me to relieve you of all that money, and go organize the gangs?"

"You and Michael Zinzun and Brother Crook and the Panther remnant. What else can you do? The white race, as we've known it, *is* finished. What else can you do but act on the dictate of your own book and organize the renaissance locked in the unconscious of the dumb?"

"L'il Joe?"

"Joe."

"Yeah."

"Leon—you saw him?!"

"Shh."

"You folks want a cocktail? Happy Hour starts at five o'clock."

Their eyes blinked but did not lose their grip. "What flag you want me to fight under?" His voice was a breath for her ears only.

"The black flag."

"What black flag?"

"The black flag of anarchy."

"With your money?"

The barman drew a cold foaming glass of Regal on draft and took a sip. Vivian wouldn't look. "Why not?" she said, "to publish the book so we can hand it out free."

"Your money's no good."

"Why not? It reads 'In God We Trust' just like all the rest of it. It's as clean as they come, laundered two hundred years ago."

He looked down at her hand in his, then up again into her eyes. "No ... there isn't enough of it. Didn't we find that out twenty years ago?—There isn't enough. There'll never be enough money.—Not enough youth, either, black children. Not here. Never has, never will."

"What are you saying?"

His hand closed like a trap over hers. The pain caused her left cheek to twitch, to wink, to signify.

DECEMBER 1991

Date: 12/3/91

To: DIRECTOR, FBI

From: SAC, NEW HAVEN

Subject: NATIONAL SECURITY
TERRORISM

Information excerpted below concerns LEON HURLEY HOWARD a.k.a. "Masai," a male Negro born 2/11/41 Baton Rouge, LA. Howard is a former member of the BLACK PANTHER PARTY, and VIVIAN NORTON BATTLE a co-conspirator in the 1970 instant case: #C 371458: United States v. The Black Panther Party.

This report must be maintained only in headquarters offices and Seat of Government and is not to be transmitted to resident agencies.

SOURCE, a Deacon in the Greater Los Angeles AME Church, states that on 12/1/91 he met with Leon Hurley Howard, the Reverend James Lawson, and Michael Zinzun of Coalition Against Police Abuse (CAPA).

Source states that meeting debated how best to deal with so-called escalating minority reactions to the Los Angeles Police Department (LAPD).

Source and Reverend Lawson argued for non-violent demonstrations. Lawson was a radical aide to Martin Luther King. Lawson led sit-ins across the South in the 1960s, and he was a key organizer of the violent Memphis Sanitation Workers strike that led to assassination of King in Memphis in 1968. Lawson has spoken widely against the Bureau's involvement in the King murder.

Source states that Zinzun and Howard expressed doubt about tactics from the 1950s and 1960s having any effect in the 1990s.

Source believes that Zinzun and Howard have private and violent agenda.

The SAC LOS ANGELES has return addressed envelope from VIVIAN NORTON BATTLE to Michael Zinzun. The empty envelope is believed to have contained currency from Battle to Zinzun. Envelope is enclosed with a return address listed as "THE COTTAGE," WELLS BEACH, MAINE. This is Battle family vacation home, south of Kennebunk Beach, according to R.A., Portsmouth, ME.

BUY U.S. SAVINGS BONDS REGULARLY ON THE PAYROLL SAVINGS PLAN.

1991

December 31, 1991

Dear Leon,

Happy New Year, Comrade, and to Michael and all, including Jim Lawson—what a man!

I have to tell you that there has been a break-in here. One thing stolen: a new scene from my Faust. What a critic!

Lester and Mary Gant, the caretakers here, came back from town to find footprints in the snow, etc. What a bore! I suppose not finding any correspondence from you, they took my new final scene (the rest was at the typist) to give to their code breakers—assuming we're talking about the FBI, and if we are they must be reading this letter, so I think that you had better come up here for a New Year's visit, don't you? I will invite Kelly, if you like. I mean, I think we have to discuss whether or not to leave the country, because, of course, this break-in is an act of violence and, now that we're not together, I fear for the people I love.

As you can see, I have not taken this very well. I enclose a copy of the purloined manuscript. And I embrace you from afar.

V.

JANUARY 1992

Leon tried to write the letter to Vivian. Pasadena was blazing in Rose Bowl weather. The house was too quiet. Mrs. Zinzun was at the market, Michael was at the office on Western working on the "Gang Summit." Masai tried to compose on the computer:

Vivian,

    Don't give up. You have got a part of Addie Mae Gatewood, and you are the hippest white woman in this country. But—
    But there's some kind of surveillance or provocation going on here, out in the street, and now is not the time to get into literary criticism, but we will and (I have to wind this up) we have to meet but I can't give you a date now—-but soon.
    This letter is secure, you will not receive it through the mail. You can trust the bearer. Consider hiring the messenger for security (and she does windows).
    More soon. I have to deal with this fool.

                              Love

                                L

Masai pushed back from the word processor. Through the sparkling clean family-room window he could see the same tan '89 Chevy across Loma Place, parked in front of the "For Sale" sign. Otherwise the street was empty. Kill him now. Wait. Is it Ledoux? Wait. Masai slipped along the back hall, coming out in the dining room; from the east corner of the room he could catch the angle of the window that looked out south to where the FBI car was parked, again. If it's Frenchy Ledoux I'm going to kill him. A wasp whirred against the window. Masai could only see that the man in the unmarked vehicle had a bald spot in back, but he couldn't make out whether or not it was Ledoux without going close up to the window where, whoever it was, would be able to see him, too, in the car's rearview mirror. Wait. "OBJECTS IN MIRROR ARE CLOSER THAN THEY APPEAR," if it's Ledoux I'm going to kill him. The wasp fights silently now for its life.

The telephone rang four times in the house. The speaker had been left on: "... Please leave a message, or I can be reached at CAPA at ..." Leon was up the stairs and into Michael's closet, with his hand already reaching for the small handgun he had hidden under a box of Freedom of Information documents.

He started down, turned back up, into the bathroom—on the commode evacuating: Wait; if it's Ledoux, make him act first; hold on to a choice; Vivian!; she needs me, needs me to live; suicide by cop—not me; are you ready, nigger? He'll be gone by now—Revolutionary Suicide—Wait! Everybody's dead but me—He'll be gone now. The toilet flush is like thunder.

He approached the FBI car from the rear, up to the driver's open window. It was not Ledoux.

"Where's Frenchy?"

"Huh? Oh. What's that?"

"Where's Ledoux?"

"Beg your pardon?"

"What's your name?"

"... You showing the house today?"

Lee Kling was half Irish and most of it was on his mug. He had seen someone coming up but didn't know it was Leon Hurley

Howard. But he, Kling, had combat training and he was fast, so he swung out of the car and moved right past Masai toward the For Sale sign.

"Been waiting almost an hour. Said they'd be here at eleven. You showing it today? Hot as hell, ain't it?"

"... Let's see your I.D."

The agent's face turned a shade redder. He reached back for a handkerchief to blot his brow. Masai reached back, his right hand poised on his waist just over his right rear pocket.

"Hot as hell! If you're not the man whose showing the house, I've gotta go to work. Tell 'em Tom Hickock waited for an hour and they can call me when—"

Masai stepped up into his face. A Latino woman pushing a baby buggy moved north toward them. Kling continued to pat his red face with the white handkerchief. Kling was good, but he wasn't perfect so he knew—at that moment as the woman and carriage rolled into the space in front of the For Sale sign—Kling knew that Leon Hurley Howard a.k.a. Masai had read the initials on his wet handkerchief: LHK, not TH.

Kling was quick: Is the woman with the buggy a Panther agent, is there a weapon hidden under the doll in the bonnet lying on its face in the buggy? And he saw in his mind's eye his own wife and child and the sweat and tears ran down the sides of his nose, and he let the incriminating handkerchief drop from his hand, taking a step back and toward the curb so that he could face the suspect, Howard, and the woman with the buggy and kill them both in order to save his wife and precious child and the United States of America.

"*Como está?*" Masai's voice was a whisper.

"*Bien, gracias.*"

The woman passed, the baby made a soft sound. Across the street someone drove into the Zinzun garage.

"Give Ledoux a message: I'm going back to New Haven. In the spring. I want to see him. I don't know where I'll be staying, but it won't be at Vivian Battle's, so stay away from her. Tell him—stay away from Vivian Battle, and I will call him ... Go home, now, Larry or Luke, or whatever they call you in the Federal Building—you don't want to buy this here house. The real estate market's about to go down. Way down."

FEBRUARY 1992

Kelly came up out of the swirling snow and banged on the door with a leather-glove-covered fist. Vivian stared into the blizzard, through the ice and fur of the *faux* Russian roundhat, into the cold blue face and the blue, blinking eyes of her youngest and now oldest friend.

"Kelly, my God!"

Vivian saw the town taxi disappearing into the whiteness. She looked down at the upturned wax face, the sheer bulk of the young woman's backpack and the laundry bag she was trying to drag up the steps.

"Vivian, I didn't mean to scare you."

Vivian reached down to help her lift the dead weight of the laundry bag.

"My God!"

"You don't have a phone!"

"Let the FBI install one! Come in!"

"Ha!"

Laughing and hugging into the den and the fire. "Throw everything on that bench. Don't worry, we're all alone, you can leave that monstrosity out here. I had to let the couple who worked here go. We had a break-in and, ah—"

"I know."

"You do? Come upstairs, I'll show you the 'cottage.' Wait a minute. How did you—You've seen Leon?"

"He's in New Haven."

"Get away!"

"That's why I'm here. He's sent you a message."

"Sit down, I'll show you the place later."

"I have to use the 'facility.'"

"Are you mocking me, you little devil! I haven't used that term in years. That was Mother's word. This was Mother's house." Embracing again, Kelly's head resting on Vivian's shoulder. "Go ahead, I'll get you a hot drink. Did you have lunch? Is the 'message' in writing? No, go ahead."

Her hands trembled as she put together the pot of cocoa for the girl, the young woman, now. Kelly came in. "This is bigger than the kitchen in New Haven."

"This was the cottage in Mother's day."

"'Craftsman?' It's magnificent. The wood!"

"William Morris, the truest exemplar of that day. Wood and brass, you can disappear in the rug's designs—but it was all meant for use, for living. It was meant to be real: sanitation, hygiene, education, democracy, utilitarian beauty—Chautauqua."

"What?"

"Mother's day. Mother's words ... These beams are chestnut. No more. Blight. No more chestnut."

"It's so ... did your mother really believe in, uh, who was it?, the philosophical—"

"William Morris, Ruskin, this is all Gus Stickley original—revolutionary in its day. Yes, Mother had an inkling, she knew about Mrs. Pankhurst and women's rights. She didn't march, or go on hunger strike, or to jail, but she knew that William Morris—this house is a model of his first place, 'The Red House' in England—she knew that her class would've killed her before they'd let her vote ... But here she came and here something happened to her and here she began to go mad—while all the while that original Morris wall hanging of the serpent and the peacock looked down on her so-called childhood ..."

Kelly studied the hanging. They both did. "Your mother—even my mother—what goes, you know, what keeps going wrong?"

"They starve to death to get the vote, then, like Mother, they become monsters of the status quo. It happens to every group, including Jews, the Black Bourgeoisie, the old Labor lions: human nature. That's our struggle. A thing begins as a romantic or revolutionary vision of freedom, then by Mother's childhood it's become an aesthetic creed—beauty, use, function—and by my day it's a dead letter, moribund Art Deco counterrevolutionary kitsch ... Oh, Mrs. Pankhurst, if thou couldst see us now. Ha!"

"Do you miss your mother?"

"I miss you. And Leon. How did he contact you? He knows the FBI is all over your father."

"L'il Joe."

"Joe? What do you mean?"

"Leon's been in touch with Joe for some time."

"How?"

"I don't know. He wouldn't say."

"How did L'il Joe find you?"

"He didn't have to. I've been going down to the—they call it African-American history now."

"You have? Since when?"

"Since you both left."

"Teaching?"

"Well—it's more of a teach-in."

"It is? How many, ah, students?"

"Two."

"Two?"

"Mm. Me and, ah—"

"You and Joe?!"

"Mm."

Vivian shaking with silent laughter, stamping around the kitchen like a woman whose foot has gone so profoundly to sleep that she must dance or die. The toasted cheese is starting to spatter the oven as the two of them bounce into the breakfast room trying to catch their breath. "Wait!"

They settle in a corner of the big walnut-and-cherry-wood-walled den, at an angle to the fireplace. They blow their noses and sip their cocoa and tea, respectively. For once, Kelly takes her time and Vivian nods her approval.

"… anyway, after you left, I volunteered to go down to the Bootstrap building to try to start up the—No, look, first: Masai says—this is the message—that I should stay here with you until March, and, two, he will come up here then, in March, with, uh, L'il Joe and, uh, that, uh, then, we will, uh, make a plan."

"… That's it?"

"Yes."

"… I see. How is he?"

"Fine. He got out of Los Angeles."

"I've been numb."

"He got out. Just in time. He'll tell you about it."

"What did he say?"

"We didn't talk, except for the message, and why I should come up here. He said the police in Los Angeles knew it would come down, after the Rodney King trial, and they set the black mayor up by taking all the police off the streets, he said it was different than the 1965 uprising. He'll tell us all about it …"

"And why did he say you should come up here?"

"He said I had to 'watch your back' and, uh, do windows."

They both laugh with a momentary upsurge of their near kitchen-hysteria. "No, go on," Vivian hands out more Kleenex.

"All right, he said it wasn't a question of violence right now, in terms of the FBI, but intimidation, harassment, et cetera, and that we should keep a daily journal of anything, you know, suspicious."

311

"I do."

"Right, and uh, he says to forget about any personal correspondence or telephones. Just sit tight, he says, 'til March.'"

The poet watched the firelight's reflection break over the youth's glasses, and the rose and white of her full cheeks. "Take your time," she poured her more cocoa, and thought of Los Angeles in flames and Leon on the run to New Haven and L'il Joe Jefferson. But Leon had never, to her knowledge, even seen L'il Joe, and Kelly had met him only once, so how could the three of them ... She stared into the fire. Los Angeles. Would it all burn now—spontaneous or planned—all burn, from California to Maine? "Now," she sighed, both of them looking up from the flames, "tell me about L'il Joe?"

"Umm—well, I didn't see him again after our meeting with him, that day, until, well, actually he called me and, and, so I went down to the old Bootstrap office and ..."

"He called you?"

"Totally, you know ..."

"What did he say? What?"

Kelly doubled up.

"Are you laughing or crying?"

"Laughing! He just called to say that the White House had just informed him that he was a *direct* descendent of Thomas Jefferson!"

"No! Well, maybe he is ... So, he made you laugh. And in your case that could be fatal."

"It was."

"Can't say no."

"No."

Vivian shook her head with delight at the very essence of this budding, no longer stuttering, no longer even precocious person who had grown up before her eyes and under her hands like a child or a poem.

Then Kelly moved over to sit next to her best friend and told her how she had met L'il Joe at Bootstrap and how, when no one else appeared, they had gone on to a mixed bar called Tatums. Joe ordered a wine for her and a Coke for himself. "He's a, he says he's an alcoholic who hasn't had a drink in eleven months. He says that there needs to be a twelve-step program for the entire country. He loves you, he's absolutely brilliant and he talks much more than when you were—Is he Masai's son?"

"I don't know."

"You can tell me."

"No, I can't."

"Won't or can't?"

"Cannot. And Masai doesn't know, either, and Joe's mother is dead. Bank robbery. Black Liberation Army. Maureen."

"Did you know her?"

"No. She was part of the Cleaver gang that split away from the Panthers."

"… He says that she wasn't his mother. Maureen Cox a.k.a. some African name that I—"

"Who says? Joe?"

"He says that he believes that you're, that …"

Vivian stands and looks down at Kelly. They gaze into each others' eyes, their rate of breathing is a little quicker. Outside, the snowfall is letting up. The poet sinks down at the younger woman's feet. "Sweet baby, you and Joe—what do you think?"

Kelly smoothes the older woman's brow. Vivian's hair is flecked with gray. The poet reads her thoughts. "Salt and pepper," she smiles up.

"Silver fox"… Kelly kisses her forehead. "A part of me wants you to be Joe's mother, and a part wants you to be … my mother." Vivian lays her head in Kelly's lap. "I never had any children—and I never will." Her sobs are convulsive and silent. A half-minute's shaking, no more, the young woman holding her tight, breathing in her own tears.

They had bacon and eggs for supper. Early, five o'clock, already dark, then they toured the cottage: "Seven bedrooms, three baths, this was built in 1900, remember. There's quite a good garden. A boathouse, a pier, a dock, a barbecue, if we're still here this summer—did you want to come up here? What about your father?"

Kelly unpacked. Vivian curled on the bad, doing a leg exercise to relieve the tightness in her lower back. "All that kneeling," they laughed, "Trollope and Thackery neglect to give us the details of what must have been an epidemic of dislocated knees and sprung sacroiliacs after all that begging and proposing—"

"Ahh, Miss Vivian!" Kelly is on the bed in one leap. "I love you, more than all the world besides. Tell me you will take me—me and my thousand pounds a year!"

"No, you may not, sir. We can never be one. Must always be two!"

They roll with laughter, then lie back. The room is decorated in the style of a young woman's bedroom from before the First World War. The theme is nautical, blues and white; chests, hanging lamps, and coverlets of rough wool.

"Tell me about L'il Joe."

"Well, he says he's sick of that name. He's sick of all names, he says: Colonial Jefferson, Anglo-Saxon, African, Muslim and otherwise. He says 'X' was a good idea—in its time. But that this is a new time." She took Vivian's hand. They lay quietly. The wooden room creaked like the ship's cabin it was meant to resemble. "He has to live," Kelly murmured.

"Joe? Mm ... Does he love you?"

"I don't know ... He asked me if I would help *him*—with *his* book."

"What did you say?"

"Masai was, uh, joking with him. He'd been in touch with Masai. We didn't—I didn't know it. Sometimes I think Masai had Joe watching us—me after you left—to protect me, and that they were father and son, you know, acknowledged, and working together, because when he came back from California he stayed with Joe, upstairs in the old Bootstrap building and they had been in touch but I don't know how."

"Well, it wasn't jungle drums."

"What? No."

Laughing softly, holding hands, then looking at the quarter moon, when it materialized through the porthole, floating through the night gray sky. "No. But, I mean, couldn't we work on a second book, talking about resistance now, *today*—Joe and me and you and Leon?"

"Or vice versa. I don't know about all this writing. When Leon—when they get here—when we can find out what the hell's going on—"

"I know. Something is."

"Are you hungry?"

"Because the FBI—Mr. Ledoux—has been hanging around my father and my old doctor and my roommates—that's why I moved out."

"When was this?"

"Before Christmas."

"Where—"

"Over Bootstrap. The whole top floor. Joe and Big Man and Dougie and we, they fixed it all up into sleeping cubicles, five of them. And I—"

"That's where you and Joe and Leon've been living?"

"Well, I went to my father's for two weeks, over the holidays, then I had to come up here, so—but when Ledoux tried to talk to me I went into Boston to my—but my father's depressed, they've worn him down, and Ledoux, I think he wanted to, uh, come on to me. Can you—"

"'O, these men, these men!'"

"*Othello*."

"You remember the 'Willow Song?'"

"Sing it."

"'The poor soul sat sighing by a sycamore tree …'"

"'Sing all a green willow …'" Kelly shuddered. "It reminds me of—"

"I know. Shh …"

Then they slept. And in their dreams they were together and sometimes alone and then again with Masai or Leonora Battle or Doctor Irving, Frenchie Ledoux, all of them together—the gray ghosts of Yale and the stone skeletons from the cemetery with all their skulls and bones. Bone of their bone, flesh of their flesh—L'il Joe and the epigoni of all colors, smoldering sparks under the smoke—as if their overlapping, intertwining, interpenetrating dream actions had been shot day-for-night or filmed by the glow of the Los Angeles inferno; as if the *auteur* of the dreaming were not just the two women with their arms around each other under the ship's quilt but that it was Masai's dream, too; Joe's, and the poet's mother and even the other one's father, along with all that was once flesh and blood here in this self-same cottage. Bone of their bone and flesh of their flesh. The dreamscape was as empty as the white Maine snowfields outside that ran without a break down into the white ice of the lake and then—blink the other eye—it was the smoke and flames of Los Angeles and New Jerusalem combusting. It was all of them and everything together, flesh and bone, as the two women lay in their embrace starting and twitching—moaning, laughing, sobbing—now alone, then together, as the long winter's night accomplished.

March 1992

The Panther was the first to enter under the stone arch—"THE DEAD SHALL RISE"—and pick his way past the big Butler vault to the depths of the cemetery.

The bells from the Green and the chapel rang in counterpoint. All the marble surfaces were slick with the day's long rain, so he half sat on the hard edge with his raincoat bunched under his haunch, shifting from side to side, reading the inscription on the stone next to him as the moon swam through the rain clouds for a spell:

FREDERICK QUINCEY DANA. BORN 1848. DIED 1928. GOD WILL SHELTER THE SHORN LAMB FROM THE EAST WIND.

The enemy. Masai frowned and tried to clear his sinuses, turned to his right and was able to make out only:

ELIZABETH CAN ... LOYAL WIFE OF THO ... BORN 185 ... DIED 190 ... AN ANGEL ON ...

God. He expectorated onto the muddy path. God. The enemy and yet their lives were centered on God. God, the old Protestant God, was living here then. The moon took a dive and disappeared.

Masai listened for Ledoux's steps. Then he thought, no—what if these people were, what if some of these crypts and tombs held the bones of abolitionists or their forebears or their children? This was New Haven, Fair Haven, the City on the Hill. What if the man or woman I'm sitting on, now, fought for me and mine, for the Underground Railroad, for John Brown, for Cinqué. Elizabeth Can— (he leaned out to look) Canfield, she could have been a woman like Vivian Battle. I could have loved her. He spat into the mud and listened ... Vivian, Kelly—he saw them, he felt them—I love Vivian, I love Kelly. If we come to be buried together, not here but somewhere, that will be—what?—that will be alright. That will be right. He flicked a hot tear from his eye and stood to meet Ledoux, who was just brushing by the Butler monument and hadn't yet spotted the Panther.

Masai watched as Ledoux for some reason turned north at the Prescott vault, then circled east out of Masai's sight. ... Then he heard Ledoux's voice somewhere to his right behind the Canfield vault. The special agent's tone was a covered nasal hum. Masai failed to make out what was being said, but Ledoux had to be wired. Leon nodded, that's good, that gives me the card I need. "Ledoux. Over here."

Silence. Then the agent's rain soaked shoes squished as he took a tentative step. "Howard?"

"Who you 'spectin' to meet—the ghost of John Quincy Adams?"

"Howard. How are you? I think Adams is at Harvard."

"No, he's not, he's right here, I'm settin' on his face."

"Whatever ... *Quieti manes*, my one semester at Boston Latin. Scholarship kid."

They could see each other more clearly now. The agent had a furled umbrella in one hand and a small briefcase in the other.

"You can sit there—on Mrs. Canfield."

"Thanks."

Ledoux folded up his plastic raincoat and lowered himself on it. Then he unzipped the leather case.

"I brought a tape recorder."

Masai stared at him, at the recorder, then into his eyes. The agent didn't smile, but his eyes were the color of his raincoat and they were plain to read—he had thrown the Panther off his rhythm and now Masai's face was like a slab of black marble in the moonlight off the white piles around them.

"So did I."

"Good. We'll have a record."

But Ledoux didn't believe him and Masai knew it. "I missed you in L.A.," he said, and Ledoux shook his head.

"I wasn't in Los Angeles."

"You tellin' me that it's more than one raincoat like that?"

The moon faded away, but Masai had a clear picture of the look in the agent's eyes. The moon slipped back out and Ledoux leaned his head down over his case and pretended to adjust the compact recorder. "It's fixin' to rain some more," Masai said, thickening the accent and speech pattern.

"I'm listening."

The rain clouds slid by the moon, but the light held steady enough for the two men to watch each other without showing the strain. Masai stood and looked at the case where the tape recorder was supposed to be, then on down to Ledoux's dirty wet rubbers, then he turned his head like a searchlight as if looking for other special agents or ghosts.

"No lovebirds tonight," Masai said.

Ledoux's eyes never left Masai's hands. "No," he said, "they're inside." Masai nodded, but he was certain that Ledoux had not come alone because the agent had not moved his head to look and that meant that he knew that Masai was alone but that he, Ledoux, wasn't.

"You ready?" Masai sat down again.

"I'm listening." Ledoux moved his umbrella.

"Yeah. I know you are ... All right. First thing—I ain't got no tape recorder."

"... No?"

"That's right."

"No problem."

"No. See." Masai stood up again and held up his raincoat. Ledoux looked at him. Masai took a step closer and removed his corduroy jacket, which left his turtleneck. There wasn't a sound, the moonlight held. The Panther turned around slowly, then, "I ain't 'packin'."

"What?"

"No wire. No nothin'."

The agent put his hands on his knees. "No problem."

"Right on ... Now you go 'head and cut yours off. And we'll deal."

The agent blinked twice. The Panther was standing close enough now to see the agent's eyes. "I can't do that," Ledoux said, his brogue very Boston. No sound around them. Then a heavy door closed somewhere in the distance, in the law courtyards, but the muffled report was enough to break their staring match. The Panther took a step back and put on his jacket and raincoat again.

"Cut it off."

"No deal."

"You can take notes."

"I don't have a pad."

"Shit."

"Mr. Howard—I didn't come here to play a game."

Leon turned to hide his eyes as he sat again. Now he was sure that Ledoux had two tape recorders. "I'm not playin' no games. You not about to forget what I tell you tonight—but it's gotta be man-to-man."

The agent stood up, he was blinking again. The Panther scraped mud off his boots, using the edge of the crypt. Ledoux squinted, his face was tight. "Fuck you, Howard," he said in a half whisper, but he didn't pick up his case and umbrella and walk away.

"Man," Masai chuckled, "stay cool. I'm gonna give you what you want. You gonna be a big man. They 'bout to give you a medal and a raise. 'Cause I fixin' to tell you what you came to L.A. to find out ... Cut your tape off, man, this a one time deal. I walk outta here tonight and we ain't never gonna see each other again, 'lessin it's in another graveyard, 'cause it sure as shit ain't gonna be this one, 'cause it ain't either of us ever gonna be buried in this one."

Masai watched the agent play his hand out. Thinking: the man is good, almost perfect. Then Ledoux let out a deep breath, sat down and punched the recorder lightly with his finger. Then he squinted up at the Panther. "Okay?"

Masai smiled wide enough for the agent to see his teeth. Then Ledoux curled his top lip back and reached down and handed the miniature across to the Panther so that he could see for himself that the machine had been cut off.

Masai nodded. "You don't have a third one, do you?"

The agent snorted and shook his head. "Mr. Howard," he said, "I don't even have a second one." They both nodded in a sign of mutual respect. But the Panther had no doubt now that there was a second wire and that everyone who listened to it—and it would be everyone—would believe without exception that he, Leon Hurley Howard a.k.a. Masai, had been taken in by the laboriously planned deception that had been debated and decided with the Special Agent in Charge in Boston or even with the Director himself at the SOG, the Seat of Government in the District of Columbia. The Panther thought all this, and then he spoke in his natural voice and standard diction. That would convince them.

"Mr. Ledoux—times change, and people change. Even the Bureau."

"True." The agent leaned forward. There was an invisible drizzle now that they both ignored, and absolute silence.

"So I'm going to take a calculated risk. Going to give you confidential information. We're going to meet twice. That's all. But what I'm going to tell you is all you'll need to know."

Ledoux sat stiff and silent. This was Leon Hurley Howard and the agent knew that now was not the time for the usual CI small talk about helping "your people" or the mention in passing of a "monthly retainer." This was the Man. His skin tingled in the wet darkness as the moon floated in and out of sight. This was the Big Casino of his career, and the tricking and turning of this, the last of the great Black Panthers, would be the final and climactic chapter of his book, the procedural biography that would jump onto the best-seller list and be transformed from there into a film with Gene Hackman playing him and—the silence brought him back to the cold marble seat. "I'm listening."

"Mm-hmm. And in return you're going to give me an official commitment."

"What do you want?"

"You tell me what you want to know."

Ledoux forced himself to slow down. Every word was going live, in real time, through the wire under his right arm, directly to the SOG, to the Director's office. Eye on the ball, he repeated like a prayer, Hail Mary, this is the Man, he won't be fooled twice. He breathed in. The Panther waited. Ledoux blinked, forced his voice down. "Who was behind the Los Angeles riot?"

"No one. Next question."

"No one?"

"No one. Everyone. You don't need a history lesson. Give it up. It wasn't even an 'uprising' this time. It was a real riot, and half of it was Latino, and all of it was the cops and the trial and the white jury."

"Well ... we can come back to that."

"No, we can't. Is that all you want?"

"Michael Zinzun."

"What about him?"

"Was he involved?"

"In the riot? Don't waste my time. You know Zinzun. You have to know that he's trying to organize the young brothers to take political action. That riot cost him five years of organizing. George Bush is not Lyndon Johnson, there won't be any War on Poverty Program this time, or next time either—there'll just be a thousand new prisons."

"... Is that it?"

"You tell me."

The agent's head was starting to throb. It was dark again. He could hear Masai clearing his sinuses and spitting somewhere near him into the mud. What in Christ's name was Howard's agenda here?

Was this whole goddamn meeting a set-up to humiliate him with the SOG? Cut the crap—he could hear them breathing in Washington. He could taste the book and the film. "We know about 'Strike and Burn.'"

"What is it that you know?"

"Mr. Howard, we know everything about it. You and Vivian Battle."

"You know 'everything'? What? ... If you know all about it you don't need me."

"We know about the plan—in theory. What we need to know is the timetable."

"Mr. Ledoux, if you know the theory, then you have to understand that it's the opposite of what went down in L.A. ... Mr. Ledoux?"

"All right."

"All right ... All right. Let's cut the issue. 'Strike and Burn'—you know the plan. You want to know *when*?"

"Go ahead."

Masai stood up. He sensed that the agent could not see his face. The Panther moved in the darkness, close to the agent, stood over him, pitched his voice straight through the man, like an arrow, into the wire and all the way to where they were huddled over the transmission in Boston or Washington.

"Mr. Ledoux—I'm going to give you the timetable you want."

"... Go ahead, Mr. Howard."

"... After you give me what I want."

The chapel bells chimed 10:15. Further on, the echolalia from the Green filled up the interstices of the night.

"And what is that, sir?"

"No more 'black bag' or 'special measures' or 'COINTELPRO' or 'counterterror' operations against Ms. Vivian Battle, Ms. Kelly Bailey, and Mr. Joseph Jefferson."

"This is completely—"

"I'm not talking about phone taps, mail, snitches, CIs, and what y'all used to call 'Rabble Rouser Control' before that one became politically incorrect even for the G-men back at the SOG—that's what

I'm told by a certain attorney, who ought to know—But you hear me: I'm talking about violence—against these three people—violence of any kind—to property or person—violence, physical or psychological. Example: Ms. Battle's manuscripts and domiciles; Ms. Bailey's virginity, sexpionage—her personal relationship with her husband, Mr. Jefferson—"

"Her—"

"And finally, Mr. Jefferson. His life."

"... What about it?"

"It has to continue. Mr. Jefferson is my son. He is Ms. Bailey's husband. And he is Ms. Battle's godson and *heir*. *This* the Central Intelligence Agency is aware of through her law firm—Cromwell and Sullivan—and now you've been briefed. Here's the score: these three people, especially Mr. Jefferson—if anything happens to them—there will be a legal and political reaction at a level so high that not only will you and yours go to the wolves—and that's Priscilla, your wife, and Tom and Mary Agnes, and Priscilla's son Liam—you and yours, Mr. Ledoux, and the SOG and theirs!"

The Panther spat. Ledoux blinked. Ledoux cleared his throat ("Hail Mary") and tried to pitch his voice: "What the hell you talking about?"

"Weeding and Seeding. When and if this 'Strike and Burn' theory or something like it gets turned into action and then you decide to try this Waco counterterrorism madness in the African-American community—when the Bureau declares war again on the niggers and the nigger lovers—you put an asterisk by the names Battle, Bailey, and Jefferson! Don't say anything, just listen: You're going to let these people live because I'm going to give you advance warning before the striking and the burning begins. I'm going to tell you, tonight, what the order of battle is and then I'm going to meet you in January of 1993. And that will end our relationship ... You ready? Memorize this: Where and when the Strike and Burn Plan begins—if at all—will be decided this year, 1992. When that decision has been made you will be told ..."

The quarter hour sounded. Ledoux's head throbbed with the bells.

"*Quieti manes.* Isn't that what they taught you, Mr. Ledoux? ... You go ahead now ... You leave first. Go ahead—I'll call *you*."

The agent fumbled for his case, his feet were heavy with mud and clay. The moon stayed down, he could only sense the Panther. Thinking: Hail Mary, full of grace—I'll kill him. He knows the names of my—they're going to ask me what in Christ he meant about Kelly Bailey's "virginity"—he knows that—he knows that a harassment charge would—no, I'm not going to kill him, I'm going to get Michael Zinzun to kill him for being an informer—no, I'm the Man, now, I'm the Agent Handler of America's Che Guevara—this is history, this is film—

"Mr. Howard, I will deliver your message."

"Right on, Mr. Ledoux."

Ledoux picked up his umbrella and walked deliberately out, head down, lips moving, whispering, "... blessed is the fruit of thy womb Jesus Hail Mary full of grace pray for us now and at the hour of ..."

Leon walked up and down the ranks of tombstones and monuments. Calling the roll of the dead, his dead: Cinqué, Crispus Attacks, Nat Turner, Denmark Vesey, the slave Gabriel, John Brown—as if they were entombed there—as he walked, marched, back and forth through the entire burial ground all the way to the sunken slabs in the far corners—singing to himself, "There's a man goin' 'round takin' names."

Nat "The Prophet" Turner's words sounding inside his head. "I was intended for some great purpose, which they had always thought from certain marks on my head and breast ... And I communicated the great work laid out for me to do to four in whom I had the greatest confidence (Henry, Hark, Nelson, and Sam)..."

He stopped and stared up at the moon. Don't go crazy now. I'm not Nat. Not Nat. I am but I'm not. Henry, Hark, Nelson, and Sam. Vivian, Kelly, L'il Joe and—no. No, this is now. This the white man's graveyard. My ghosts not here. Huey—Henry, Hark, Nelson, and Sam—and all the other niggers in their many millions and millions—those boys not here. God spoke to Nat and those boys, those men, and all the others, but that was then and they're not here. I'm here. God's here, every stone's marked with a cross, but God won't speak to me—there's no God for me, not even Cinque's, not even the Abolitionist's God of Nature, or John Brown's Jehovah, not Malcolm's Allah, or Paul Robeson's God of History—nobody but me, myself, and I. Me. I'm the father, the son, and the holy ghost here. Leon Hurley Howard a.k.a. Masai. I'm not Stagerlee or the Streetman, either, not yet. I'm not crazy yet. Not yet. No. Not Nat. Not yet. Not anymore. The names and numbers on the lambent marble closed in on him: B 1851, D 1921—1860, 1902—1862, 1940—1860, 1902—1850, 1933 ...

He was stumbling in circles talking to himself: Stay cool, man, stay cool. They watching you through the infrared binoculars. Stand up. Breathe. Walk on out of this place. Act like you sane. Go get your so-called son and get up to Maine. No sign and no shade. No fire by night. Just me and my shadow. On the razzle, on the spot. Breathe. Eleven bells. Think of Addie. Walk on out like Addie.

He expectorated into the mud and started his stride toward the arch. Quick long steps like Addie Mae Gatewood on a Louisiana highway—like Addie Mae. Like a man.

March 1992

Date: 3/7/92

To: DIRECTOR, FBI

From: SAC, NEW HAVEN

Subject: COUNTERTERRORISM

It is to be noted that a conference ("What's Left of the Left?") was held in New Haven, Connecticut on March 2,3,4 at Malcolm X Community Center. Awards were given to MICHAEL ZINZUN and LEON HURLEY HOWARD, Former Black Panther leaders. This was Howard's first public appearance since his release from prison on 5/16/90.

Zinzun urged the approximately 200 attending to "prepare for struggle." Reference was also made to a new book by Howard, to be published in the fall of 1992 by Random House. Howard did not speak.

DAVID HILLIARD, former Black Panther leader, spoke to the conference on the evening of March 4. Hilliard discussed the murder of Huey P. Newton, Panther founder, in a drug deal in 1989. Hilliard called for support for a "Rebirth in Oakland of a grass-roots crusade for Justice."

For the information of the San Francisco office, David Hilliard discussed raising funds with Leon Howard, relating to Hilliard's plan to run for the Oakland City Council.

Hilliard is publishing an autobiography and is scheduled to speak at Yale University on May 5, 1992. It is the thought of the New Haven Office that this will be a good opportunity to distribute copies of a throwaway indicating that Leon "Masai" Howard is actually an informant for a governmental agency.

It is the desire of the New Haven Office to neutralize Howard by the distribution of the throwaway accusing Howard of being an informant. It is expected that Zinzun, Hilliard, and others will react by distancing themselves from Howard and his group. It is the thought of this office that the leaflets could be distributed in a surreptitious manner and also mailed nationally to selected individuals on the TERROR NETWORK listing.

Enclosed herewith for the SOG is a copy of the throwaway "Masai is a Pig." This leaflet is adapted from a COINTELPRO document used in the case of Vivian Battle in 1969.

It is requested that New Haven distribute this throwaway at the Hilliard speech, taking all steps necessary to protect the identity of the Bureau as the source of the leaflet.

New Haven will be on the alert for any information indicating the attitude of the recipients of this throwaway.

BUY U.S. SAVINGS BONDS REGULARLY ON THE PAYROLL SAVINGS PLAN.

MASAI IS A <u>PIG</u>

    we don't know just what kind of a <u>pig</u> he is, but masai howard is some kind of a <u>pig</u>, a lousy informer who deals with his fellow pigs, and betrays us all.

    in march masai spoke at the michael zinzun-david hilliard conference in new haven and that <u>pig</u> had the nerve
to accept a jive medal for his so-called heroic sacrifices. that's
b.s.!

    after the conference, the very next day, <u>pig</u> howard was
spotted in the new haven federal bldg. talking to another
You-Know-What!

        WE GOT NEWS FOR PIG HOWARD *********
        <u>PIGS</u> WILL NEVER REPLACE PANTHERS!

        OFF THE PIG
        <u>All Power to the People!</u>

(Printed in a union shop)

April 1992

Date: 4/24/92

To: DIRECTOR, FBI

From: SAC, NEW HAVEN

Subject: NATIONAL SECURITY TERRORISM

Information excerpted below concerns LEON HURLEY HOWARD a.k.a. "Masai," a male Negro born 2/11/41 Baton Rouge, LA. Howard is a former member of the BLACK PANTHER PARTY, and VIVIAN NORTON BATTLE a co-conspirator in the 1970 instant case: #C 371458 United States v. The Black Panther Party.

This report must be maintained only in headquarters offices and Seat of Government and is not to be transmitted to resident agencies.

CONFIDENTIAL SOURCE reports that Howard and JOSEPH JEFFERSON (a male Negro, born New Haven, Connecticut 4/21/69) arrived at Vivian Battle home (listed as "The Cottage"), Wells Beach, Maine.

Resident Agent, Portsmouth, Maine, surveillance confirms continuing presence KELLY BAILEY in Battle domicile.

Leon Hurley Howard is believed to be meeting with Battle, Bailey, and Jefferson regarding urban terrorism project "STRIKE AND BURN."

For the information of the Portsmouth office Howard should be considered armed and dangerous, and may approach Resident Agent with offer to become Confidential Informant. (C.I.).

Resident agent should never, repeat never, meet privately with Howard, under any circumstances.

Photo attempt should be undertaken to capture any compromising intimate involvement between Howard and Battle; Bailey and Jefferson; Battle and Bailey; Howard and Bailey; Jefferson and Battle; Howard and Jefferson.

BUY U.S. SAVINGS BONDS REGULARLY ON THE PAYROLL SAVINGS PLAN.

April 1992

"... because that's their mind-set. Conspiracy." Leon faced the others as if they were a jury. "No way in the world would they believe that if we did decide to 'Strike and Burn,' the first move we'd make would be to hold a national press conference and lay out the entire scenario."

"Like the Poor People's March in—"

"Precisely." Vivian talked over Kelly, smiling an apology. "Look, follow me, we can eat and talk, and we're not having pork chops; don't groan, listen to Leon! Come on, we're having carrot soup—Joe, it is delicious, and corn pudding—" Now the laughter was uproarious—"and, and, and—lamb chops!" They staggered, howling, into the oversized dining-living room area, to the long Irish wood table.

"You see, it's delicious, it's something new. A change." "It's good," said Joe, "I didn't think it'd be hot." "I helped to make it," Kelly whispered. "It's a lot of work." "She was a big help," the poet stroked the young woman's shoulder. Everyone was smiling, even Joe, with something more than sympathy. "The eyes of tenderness," the poet thought, watching Joe's eyes. "Anyone can at some time have in their head the eyes of tenderness, whether or not they are a mother or even a woman." This she thought as she stoked the embers in the oversized stone fireplace.

They ate: hot soup, hot bread, a salad, chops, and the delicious corn pudding with its dark brown crust. Just a few words in the late afternoon April light; tasting the food, giving credit to Vivian. The food, the quiet, the wood, the light: everything was good, they belonged together; they loved each other and themselves and being together, but yet and still, inside they could not keep from questioning—will this last, how long can this last? Is it too much for us, is America too much for us?

After they all cleared the table, Vivian set out mugs for tea or coffee. How much longer could it last? ... Masai started. "David Hilliard's going to run for the Oakland City Council. He needs seed money and volunteers, but he's got a good chance, a helluva chance. He wants to use his book and mine for a series of fundraisers. I told him go ahead. Some Hollywood people from the old days are going to do a letter, and the Oakland Brain Trust at Merritt College're cranking up."

The others listened, saying nothing. If they all left here and moved to Oakland, would they be spared from what was coming? Joe broke the silence: "If you and David Hilliard and the Panther Old Guard show up big in the *New York Times*, the first thing the FBI's going to do is trash you as a pig and Vivian as the Red Queen, who wants to use the electoral process as a front to burn down Oakland and the rest of the country."

They stared at him. Vivian's jaw dropped. Then she exhaled all her breath. "This is Big Joe Jefferson." She had to go to him and embrace his head; Kelly and Leon watching, their eyes embracing the youth. "Jane Fonda," Joe tried to laugh.

Leon watched, then he spoke quietly, "No, if they start the dirty tricks now, during a nonviolent grass-roots boot-strap election campaign, I'll go public with what Ledoux's been doing, *and* how I met him at Yale and warned him and told him that there *was* no illegal or terrorist plan."

"But the FBI'll say that—"

Leon nodded to Joe, "It will be rough." He pronounced each word slowly, "It won't be pretty. But we'll win the argument. After Kelly paints her picture of what Special Agent Ledoux tried to do to her."

All eyes turned to Kelly's red face. Her glasses steamed, but she did not stutter, because she did not speak, she simply looked back at all of them, raised her eyebrows and nodded her head.

"Big Kelly Bailey," murmured Vivian, and Leon nodded. Kelly watched Joe.

Joe said, "When it come time to burn down Oakland, will that be 'nonviolent' and 'legal?'"

"That's the issue," Vivian said. "There will be a struggle over the definition of the words, right along with the actions." "The flames burning on T.V. will bring in the 82nd Airborne," Leon's bass-baritone rumbled into the fugue. Kelly leaned toward Leon, "Masai's right, I agree with Masai, 'Strike and Burn' are two different—" Masai: "A few pundits on FM radio, but the first condemned rat-trap you torch, the National Guard will be—" Joe: "That's what I'm saying, I'm saying if *we* plan to strike *and* burn it's not cool to hold any press conferences right now." Vivian: "At least somebody's saying 'we!' Let's be clear—I'm talking about organizing for the political race in Oakland, and out of that will come the housing and new school movement, and from *that*, finally, the rent strikes, and *the* …"

They were all talking at once and then they stopped to listen to Vivian. The poet's tone was simple, unarguably honest, patient, and passionate. "We're talking about at least four years," she finished. Silence. "Tea?" she asked, "Coffee?" Kelly stared into her empty mug.

"I'll get it," Leon said, circling around behind the wooden counter to the kitchen, talking, "You're going to get people killed if you try to take over a legal political movement in Oakland—" "I'm not—" "That's what it will look like and that's what it will be—" "That's unfair—" "With your name and your money and your New Haven cadre—" "No," Joe broke in, "If I go, I'm going underground and I wouldn't get anywhere near the council election. I'd be at Merritt

College and I'd use those four years to build an underground so that when the burning and the 82nd Airborne, when their time came, we'd have an armed defense of the families living in the tents that we'd provide and in the city buildings and schools that we'd defend ... That is, if I was going ..."

Kelly was the first to speak, "It sounds so—" "It's an old dream," Leon poured four cups of tea. "Honey?" "Listen, Leon," Vivian leaned in—"It's old and it's new and Joe is a realist, it seems to me, but Kelly feels that it's suicide—just let me make a point—and we won't parse 'Revolutionary Suicide' at the moment, but may I remind you, comrade, of Denmark Vesey before you—"

"No!" Leon was up, getting honey from the kitchen. "Don't even think about Denmark Vesey. Denmark Vesey was betrayed by slaves. They couldn't keep a secret for four weeks and there's you and L'il Joe—excuse me 'Joe'—giving us a four-year plan. I'm not gainsaying the need for rent strikes, and 'urban renewal' by fire, and self-defense by any means necessary, but this is all woofin' until you go there and elect the man to the City Council and start to march for housing and schools—then whatever happens, happens; you can't sit up here in Maine and plan it."

Kelly kept nodding her head continuously even after Masai had subsided. Then she ventured, "Because, I mean, when Abraham Kardiner and, uh, after the war in the late 1940s—they did their studies, but they never, ever predicted Martin Luther King and the Southern nonviolent civil rights movement."

"That's right," said Leon.

"Can I smoke in here?" Joe asked Vivian, not looking at the young woman.

"No," Leon answered.

"Denmark Vesey," Joe growled or chuckled as he rolled the name around. "Denmark Vesey—" "We know all about Denmark Vesey," Leon started in again, but this time Joe kept talking over him. "Denmark Vesey was the Man—the man was organized; the man's plan would've wiped out the complete white population of Charleston." Now it was Joe who was facing the jury, his voice as stong as Leon's. "All right—he was a city man, Charleston was the number three city in the country. South Carolina and Charleston were heavy black, like Oakland today—you know the 1820 Census figures?" His eyes grinned at the census taker, Kelly laughed silently but her eyes stayed on Joe. "All right—he brought together the African Methodist Church and Muslims and African French-speaking slaves from Haiti—a United Front. Nine thousand strong. They were going to fight for their freedom and then go back to Africa—that's the only difference from today."

"But they—" "They were betrayed," Joe said. "The man spoke four languages—" "Everybody's interrupting me," Kelly's voice was soft, but she didn't look down. "I'm sorry," Joe looked down. Leon waited, then he said, "They were going home. They wouldn't've killed the ships' captains." "Everybody else?" Kelly asked her mentor. "Everybody else," Leon sighed. "Men, women, and children—it will always come to that."

The light was gone now, and Vivian stirred up the smoldering logs, poured more tea; Joe covered his cup with his hand. "Denmark Vesey had a simple order of battle," Vivian said, sitting down. "And so would we—organize–rent strike–burn. And our jungle drum is the twenty-four-hour-a-day media that snakes through every poverty project in this country."

"But he was sold out and hung before the word could get out," Joe said, leaning back in the shadows. "No," Vivian turned on a hand-hammered copper lamp, "No, John Brown and others, later, but we wouldn't be acting in secret, we'd be holding press conferences, Leon's quite correct, we would be legal and nonviolent—" "Except for property!" "That's quite right, Joe, except for property— at the very last phase of a very long legal and mass action campaign, and including a rainbow coalition of poor people, with some of the best lawyers in the world working with us, with—" "With Masai in the U.N.!" Kelly beamed. Then, they all laughed again, reaching out to touch her with their hands and eyes, even Joe brushed her elbow with his long fingers. "Yes! Yes, Leon on his legs in the U.N.!" Vivian sang out. They subsided. A log snapped in the huge fireplace.

"They killed Denmark Vesey," Joe said, looking at Vivian, "and they would kill us. One way or another." Silence. Leon spoke, "That's the truth." Vivian thought, their voices are so close, so close they must be father and son. "The property's all they care about," Joe added as if to himself. "And that's the truth," Leon picked up the meditation, "because anytime the rebellion comes from below you're talking about revolution, not civil war; and in a revolution property changes hands." "Right on," finished Joe in a whisper.

The poet pushed her chair back. "I am not a mother-figure for the 'Infantile Left,' gentlemen. I can see it, too: the flatlands burning, the smoke rising, the sirens wailing, lights burning all night in Sacramento, and D.C., and yes, the United Nations, with or without Leon and his young blonde aide-de-camp. And I can hear it, too: a million gates in front of a million gated communities clanging shut and George Herbert Walker William Jefferson BushslashClinton on CNN in a five-piece suit denying that there's a 'Chinese connection' and warning the white bankrupt farmers and their rural militia to stay out of it if they know what's good for them. Yes, sir, I can see New Jerusalem in flames and the rent-a-cops in their serried ranks around the gated communities ready to die in their hecatombs if for any reason the 82nd Airborne mopping up operation below, in the Cities of the Plain, should in any way be stalled ... I can see it and hear it and smell and taste it ..." She stood, she loomed over them. *"But so can they, so can they*! No poet that ever lived could compute the cash—hundreds of billions—down to the last bank-run—the way that the wizards of Wall Street will compute the apocalypse of forty American urban centers in flames and the farmers' militias' seizure of the great government parks and lands! And that is why it will never come to that—either revolution or civil war. But it could come close enough to bring about a domestic Marshall Plan that would rebuild these rotten cities and the hope of these people. And that, I do believe, would be worth dying for."

Then she stopped. The big room was filled with moving shadows. No one wanted her to stop. They needed her passion and her dream. They needed her; they needed each other.

Finally, "I'm so sleepy," Kelly rotated her neck. "Me, too," Joe stood up. "I'll let you pick your room," Vivian started; Leon stopped her, "Wait," he stood, too. "Whoever goes to Oakland, except Vivian, has to plan to get their own money—" "Not now, Leon—" "I have fifty thousand more coming on the book. I can pay Kelly—" "No, I have my—" "And I can pay Joe something if he's going to school and he can easily get a scholarship—" "I'm not going to Oakland." "Well—yet and still—Vivian's going to need every penny she's got before it's over." They laughed softly. "Follow me," said Vivian, "the Fifth International is adjourned *sine die*. Until breakfast."

They climbed the front stairs. "Kelly's in the 'Navy Room'—Joe, Kelly can tell you the story, the *provenance,* of this place."

Kelly called up, "Joe, it's called the 'Red House'!"

"The Red House? Right on!"

Vivian paused on the first landing to breathe and finish her laugh. "This is the second-floor library, all the Trollope, Dickens, and Thackery ever printed."

"Anything American?" Joe's chuckle set them all off laughing again.

"Third-floor den is Walt Whitman, Karl Marx, and all-American; come up and see me sometime, my room's up there. Joe, you're in here in the 'Rose Room,' sorry."

They all stood in the bedroom doorway, almost touching, breathing together. Joe took in the dark wallpaper and the old saw-wood floor and the window over the garden.

"Don't be afraid of that Lily Lamp," she said. "Turn it on, use the place, that's why they started it all, to get away from the nasty trash of the Industrial Revolution, to bring some use and beauty into ordinary lives."

"Teach," Leon blessed her.

"So don't be afraid of anything in this house. Stay here forever and read and write." They stood in the door. Vivian switched on the Art Nouveau Tiffany treasure. The roses on the walls sprang to life, and Henry Varnum Poor's *Pensive Woman*, on the wall, looked down at them. Joe looked back. "I'm not afraid," he said.

The poet turned slowly back to the hall, "From the Rose Room we now move to the 'Green and Green Room'—actually, that's an upper-class joke that was never funny."

They all laughed, then Joe closed his door.

Leon turned on a wall lantern in his room, shadows danced, he touched a figurine standing on a mahogany fern table. The women lingered in the doorway.

"Nothing personal," the poet purred—the sculpture was a naked nymph poised over a tulip and a frog—Kelly led the chorus, "Everything's striking me funny," she said.

"Goodnight, ladies," Leon said. There was a pause; the two women watched him.

"We'll be upstairs," Vivian said, "Good night, comrade." He stepped to them, kissed them both on the forehead. "We'll finish the 'Red House Manifesto' tomorrow," the poet said, but still they lingered.

"Good night," his voice was as soft as a parting sigh.

Up they went to the Navy Room and the poet's den. A good night embrace, the doors clicked and the Red House was a still, silent collection of shadows. Outside no moon could be seen; Joe had checked.

The first thing Joe did was peer out the window, over the garden down toward where they had said he would find a lake, but it was too dark, he couldn't find the face of the moon, and it was too quiet, except for the lake sounds that were foreign to him, alien, gave him goosebumps.

Then he toured the room: the wood, the roses on the walls, the sad woman in the painting. He paced in the silence and the lake sound, then he eased open his door and took a step into the corridor. The house made no sounds. He stared at Leon's door. No sound except an irregular ticking of a very old case clock below. He angled his head up the stairs. No. Retreated back into the isolation of the Rose Room, held onto the doorknob considering whether to sneak down the stairs and look for some wine. Stood there in a state of doubleness, then slowly closed the door, thinking, I'm not thinking about no wine. *I'm not a bum!* Seeing the mad dog wine bottle in the brown paper bag, smelling it—*I'm not a bum!* He caught the shadow of his image in a small mirror almost lost in its white quartersawn oak frame: his forehead and cheekbones and chin caught the low light—like a dead man, he thought. He moved closer, fingered his short-cut hair, pushed it up to make it look "natural," then massaged it down again. He took a deep breath; to the right of the mirror and higher up was the painting of the *Pensive Woman*, it made his throat feel sore. "Denmark Vesey's dead," the thought shot through his head, "that nigger's dead." Then he thought maybe he was coming down with a flu and that he'd better use the bathroom and brush his teeth. That corn pudding was something.

He stripped down to his shorts, hesitated, then slipped into the robe that Vivian had draped across the bed for him. It wasn't cold, but he shivered and crawled under the quilt, leaving the lamp burning. He cupped his groin and thought about Kelly. "That's trouble," he said to himself, "they're all trouble. Get me killed ... The 'Red House'—these people're crazy. Not thinking about going to Oakland. They might say that David Hilliard's my father, out in Oakland, or Huey P. Newton, or Marlon Brando, he's supposed to've slept with—that woman who raised me. They're all crazy, don't know who they are. Could try a D.N.A. test." Chuckling silently. "Crazy. Not thinking about Oakland ... Yale. Fuck Yale."

He rose silently. The carved wood floor was getting colder. He pulled on his socks so that he could pace without getting a chill. Turned off the lamp. The window still dark, no garden or lake or moon—turned on the lamp again. Paced. The robe felt clean and warm ... "Not thinking about Oakland *or* Yale—*not a bum!*"

Thinking about the man and the two women and how much he loved them, in every way that it was possible for him to love. Paced.

Kelly tiptoed out in front of her room to listen. From the third floor she could not hear the clock ticking. She could not see any light under Vivian's bedroom door. She rubbed her nose and reentered the Navy Room and lowered herself into a *faux*-bosun's hammock. She thought she would read her Thackery novel, then not, the lighting was too dim. Up to the window, one story above Joe's, can't see a thing. What's he doing?

She took a hot shower, trying to make her mind a blank. Big rough towels with anchors embossed. "Think about Oakland," she thought. She rubbed and toweled, "Think about Oakland," then a silent burst of laughter, "Think about England"—the private joke with Vivian—was Vivian asleep? Was she in Leon's room? "Think about Oakland." She took a Tranzene and jumped into bed still wrapped in the towel.

But she thought about Joe and Leon and Vivian and then Joe again. The two of them in Oakland. There could be a "there" there, she told herself. Then she thought of Vivian again, of their reading Trollope to each other—"young women are always robbed when their money is left altogether to the gentlemen ... But woman's rights are coming up." "I hate woman's rights." Then she laughed out loud, remembering Miss Thoroughbung's motto and Mr. Peter Prosper's reply. What would Joe say about Trollope? Oh, dear. She turned toward the wall. The Roycroft mirror was just above her head. The vertical motto was "Be Yourself," the horizontal was "Head Heart and Hand." She had read them a hundred times since she first came. She read them again and then she began to hate the Navy Room and the Red House.

She slept. She dreamed: She stood, alone, in a burial ground, under a star-filled night and then she began to freeze. Then forced herself to walk, one step at a time, sweating. Then she walked faster. Then stars went black. Then she ran! Then she was home safe.

Then she slept again.

The poet knelt by her fireplace and burned the pages of her manuscript. Her *Faust* play was no more. "I can never get Addie Mae Gatewood born Howard right. She lived, Leon remembers her; I've traced the third-generation carbon copy and it won't do, that's all, it won't do. A revolution is not a work of art, and this was never going to be a work of art. Write and burn …"

Then she thought, "Why not die? The cancer's coming back. Maybe. No more doctors if it does, no chemotherapy, no radiation, nothing. Just die like a dog, if I have to, and give the money to the three of them, or a political foundation, or buy a dozen city council elections. What difference does it make?"

She rose—favoring her back, rubbing her knee, dizzy, her face hot—and opened a window, to the lake sounds. She sat in the rocker, panting lightly—no more hormones, no more Tranzene tablets. "Age and Burn."

She moved to the desk and started a letter to Leon, then she threw that page into the fire too, and stood again at the window, the perspiration beading on her brow. The fire was burning down, the photographs on the mantle sinking back into darkness.

"Like my mother—tyrant, bully, *Stalinist*! Let them be, I have to let them be, they must have permission to be. Let that girl be—she's not your daughter or your slave. In ten years you'll be screaming 'Kelly!' And she'll race in to throw a Dylan oldie on the—no, no more phonographs. God in heaven! Go now, leave a clean odor after you—leave all the money to 'The Caucasian Society for the Forgiveness of the Black Race for the Sin of Slavery.'"

Her body was on fire; she pulled off the heavy knit sweater. "They will never be forgiven. No more than the Jews for the Holocaust. Joe's right. 'Slavery wasn't so bad,' that's the line for the new millennium. Even Marx wrote that it was a necessary evil without which we would never have reached the Industrial Revolution. It was 'Progressive.' No Agricultural Revolution without the world-historical defeat of women, no Industrial Revolution without the destruction of the African race—it all comes under the heading of 'Progress!' Plato and Aristotle and St. Thomas and Hegel and Marx—all my money can't buy off or change the history of Western civilization because their portraits are on the coins and the bills. Marx is too much for me. For God sakes, we couldn't even put a dent in Henry Kissinger!"

She laughed to herself. The night air was cooling her, the fire was sinking. "I will offer them the money and property, except for the Red House. I will stay here and write—something ... Except that they won't take it and we'll be right back where we started. And if I were to kill myself they would hate me. And I cannot commit suicide in Oakland—political and otherwise—and take innocent people down with me. So what does that mean? Strike and *not* Burn?"

She closed the window. She was dry and cool now, kneeling slowly in front of the fireplace to pick up the manuscript folders. Then she stood erect, her back making the small snapping sound, and looked into the photograph on the mantle of her mother as a schoolgirl standing in front of the Red House all by herself. The room was full of shadow and she had to peer into the scene: The girl in the sailor suit, the straw hat, the sash, the white socks and black buckle shoes. "Mother, I cannot help you. I cannot save you. And you—you could not and you cannot help me ... Please, God, let me, at least, do no harm. I am no political physician, but at least and at last let me first do no harm. Let me live well and then, when the time comes to die, I will know how to go without hurting anyone."

She put her face up against the cool glass of the photograph frame.

"Good-bye, mother. The acorn doesn't fall far from the tree. You're trapped inside your photograph, and I'm stuck here—you can't get out, to harm me or to help me—you're on your side of the glass and I'm on mine ... But I see you now—and your one life, your one and only life, which led to my one and only life ... We wanted each other to save each other. And we couldn't do that. We loved each other—once—and that should have been enough. That's what we have to hold on to now. I have no reason not to remember our love. It's enough for me now. It's more than enough. Mother? It's sufficient. It is."

She lay down on the bed in her clothes and knew somehow that she would go to Oakland and that there, with the life left in her body, she would work and she would labor with all her might to do no harm. Even if none of them came to Oakland to join her: Not Joe or Kelly—not Leon—no one: they would always belong together. This ran through her thoughts for the thousandth time, like a mantra and out load she just said the words: "No harm."

Masai stood still, listening. He heard Joe come out of his room, then Kelly, up above, then he heard them go back in; the lake frog sounds boomed in his eardrums like a terrific pulse. He dropped to the floor and did twenty quick fingertip push-ups, then he stood still again, breathing lightly. "I can hear them," he thought, "but they can't hear me." He dropped down for twenty more, the wood under his fingers felt alive. Then he switched on the lamp. Then he saw Addie Mae Gatewood looking at him from out of the long dark mirror.

Stood there straining to see. The illumination from the lamp was too diffuse because of its mineral shade. Moved toward the mirror, closer—saw the mahogany frame, the ebony splines and pegs—closer until he was in it. But Addie was gone ...

The Panther sat at the desk and wrote a note to himself:

1. OAKLAND
2. L.A.: BOOK WITH ZINZUN ("MESSAGE TO THE 'HOOD'"). CALL N. AT RANDOM HOUSE. ½ ORAL HISTORY FROM "GANGBANGERS." INCLUDE JOE?
3. JOE?

He leaned back in the chair; it creaked under his weight. Joe. L'il Joe Jefferson filled up his consciousness. What would Addie say? To Joe? To him, Leon? He closed his eyes, waiting to hear the melodic tension of her voice. There was nothing but Joe. Joe filled up the room and the house. Joe filled up the world. Joe was in the mirror now, looking at him, and back from the black window, and peering through the glowing hard surface of the mineral lampshade. Everywhere he turned, he saw Joe.

Leon swam toward the floor looking for something to push against. For a split second he lay there, gathering his energy, then the chalk outline of Huey P. Newton trapped him. The chalk outline drawn by the Oakland Police Department on the sidewalk in front of the crack house. The chalk outline that was constantly redrawn so that visitors and tourists and children taking the Black Panther History Tour could get off their tour bus and look down at the final chalk image of the First Panther.

The wood was cool against his cheek. I fit this chalk outline. I should run one of these tours: "Stop the bus. Last stop. Comrades, this is 1456 Center Street. This silhouette here, in chalk, is Huey P. Newton. He was shot down by a drug dealer who, at his trial, told the jury that as a child he had been fed by the Black Panther Free Breakfast program ... Next stop—28th and Union, where L'il Joe, I mean, L'il Bobby Hutton was cut down by the Oakland Police ..."

He pushed himself up, arms rigid, head hanging—like an ox, he thought, just take it like an ox. His arms were iron. A tour guide in Oakland. That's me. Why not? Just take it now. Stay up off that sidewalk. "Our first stop will be Market and 55th. A little girl was run over here, and the first act of Huey Newton and the original cadre was to agitate and demonstrate until the city installed a traffic light ..." Don't fall. Stay up. If you go down you'll never get up. He was starting to buckle. He felt like there was a hole opening up inside his chest. A black hole where Addie Mae Gatewood and God had once lived inside him. The Panther's heart missed a beat. "Last stop ..."

DONALD FREED

He pushed against the chalk trap until the breath sawed out of his lungs, then he fell flat and rolled over onto his back. He was blank now. Addie Mae and Joe were gone. He started to drift. *There was Addie with L'il Joe hurrying beside her, keeping up, across the weed-filled field, heading for Lee Street and a cool cone of colored ice. His throat was calling out for the cool colors, orange and strawberry and grape; orange, red purple.* The Panther smiled in his sleep.

He woke up on the hardwood floor deep in the night. Lay there trying to capture the dream. It was gone. But something in him had been eased. Some equation in the dream had been reconfigured. What? Joe. Something about Joe. Joe and—? Who? The lake-life throbbed in the darkness. That same pulse had pounded through the dream. Joe ... Joe—and Frenchie Ledoux!

The Panther arched up slowly to a sitting position. That was the equation: Joe = Ledoux. How? Then he sensed the change, like a wind shift: *If I let Ledoux live—then Joe will be saved.*

He would let Ledoux live. He had intended to kill the agent as part of the graveyard promise that he, the Panther, would inform Ledoux or give him a sign when and if the Strike and Burn plan was a go. The sign he had intended was Ledoux's cut throat. The code name would be "Denmark Vesey"... No. Wait. Had that been a dream, too, another nightmare? He rose up and looked into the empty mirror.

Addie. Addie had brokered the deal, in the graveyard, in the nightmare: Ledoux for L'il Joe. His throat burned and the colored snow cones came back. He swallowed. Something in the mirror caught his eye: his cell, his prison cell, his Bridgeport prison cell. He turned slowly, rotating his shoulders. Slow. So slow. Then his head. Then his eyes, cornered, staring down the room until the shape fell back into its original early American configuration, a room designed by Greene and Greene. So he believed that he was not still dreaming.

Still slow, he moved to touch wood. He ran his hand over the inlaid music stand. He heard a click. He looked. Something in the music stand, some hidden hinge or spring had clicked open. His fingers trembled toward the aperture. Felt the shape of something smooth inside the opening. Closed on the thing ... A book. Drew it out. Held it with both hands. Went for the floor to push again.

But this time he stayed on his knees, arrested, with the Bible gripped in both hands. Dreamlike, he parted the soft leather cover that had been closed these ninety years—pointed to a text at random as the old folks used to do in the days of Addie,

1. And Moses went up from the plain of Moab into the mountain of Nebo, to the top of Pisgah, that is over against Jericho. And the Lord shewed him all the land of Gilead, unto Dan.
2. And all Naphtali, and the land of Ephraim, and Manasseh, and all the land of Judah, unto the utmost sea,
3. And the south, and the plain of the valley of Jericho, the city of palm trees, unto Zoar.
4. And the Lord said unto him, This is the land which I sware unto Abraham, unto Isaac, and unto Jacob, saying, I will give it unto thy seed: I have caused thee to see it with thine eyes, but thou shalt not go over thither.
5. So Moses the servant of the Lord died there in the land of Moab, according to the word of the Lord.
6. And He buried him in a valley in the land of Moab, over against Bethpeor: but no man knoweth of his sepulchre unto this day.
7. And Moses was an hundred and twenty years old when he died: his eye was not dim, nor his natural force abated.
8. And the children of Israel wept for Moses in the plains of Moab thirty days: so the days of weeping and mourning for Moses were ended.
9. And Joshua the son of Nun was full of the spirit of wisdom; for Moses had laid his hands upon him: and the children of Israel hearkened unto him, and did as the Lord commanded Moses.
10. And there arose not a prophet since in Israel like unto Moses, whom the Lord knew face to face,
11. In all the signs and the wonders, which the Lord sent him to do in the land of Egypt to Pharaoh, and to all his servants, and to all his land,

¹² And in all that mighty hand, and in all the great terror which Moses shewed in the sight of all Israel.

On his knees, his face at rest. He lets the Bible drop. He breathes a while. Something is in the room with him. He is not afraid. He waits. Is God in the room? Is history in the room? He smiles a little, "God waits, history waits—I can wait, too."

His lips are dry when he starts to sing. He sings low, to himself—trying to recapture Addie's words—but the resonance works through the ancient yellow pine of the floor and the walls and out into and through all the woods of the Red House, so that all of them in their beds hear the old slave song as it rises out of his body

O THE SIGN OF THE FIRE BY NIGHT
AND THE SIGN OF THE CLOUD BY DAY
ROLLING ON JUST BEFORE
AS THEY JOURNEYED ON THEIR WAY ...